DARE TO KISS

The Maxwell Series - Book 1

S. B. ALEXANDER

Raven Wing Publishing

Dare to Kiss
Book one: The Maxwell Series
Copyright © 2014 by S. B. Alexander.
All rights reserved
First Edition: September 2014
E-book ISBN-13: 978-0-9887762-4-1
Print ISBN-13: 978-0-9969351-0-4

Visit: www.sbalexander.com
Editor: Red Adept Editing, www.redadeptediting.com
Editor: Terri Valentine
Cover Design by Hang Le: http://www.byhangle.com

This is a work of fiction. Names, characters, places and incidents
either are the product of the author's imagination or are used ficti-
tiously, and any resemblance to locales, events, business establishments, or actual persons-living or dead-is entirely coincidental.

Adult Content Warning: The content contained is the book includes
adult language and sexual content. This book is intended for adult
audiences 17 years of age and older.

DEDICATION

Tracy Hope, you've been with me from the moment my first book was published. Your advice keeps me sane. Your encouragement motivates me and your honesty helps me to get better as a writer. You're a great friend, and I love you. This book is dedicated to you.

DARE TO KISS PLAYLIST

- "We Don't have to Look Back" by Puddle of Mud.
- "All of me" by John Legend
- "Bound to You" by Christina Aguilera
- "Gone to Soon" by Daughtry
- "Broken Ones" by Jacquie Lee
- "Drops of Jupiter" by Train
- "Say Something" by A Great Big World
- "Not Ready to Make Nice" by The Dixie Chicks
- "Life in the Pain" by SafetySuit
- "Demons" by Imagine Dragons

CHAPTER 1

T he ball left my hand and zigzagged on its way to home plate, missing Tyler Langley's glove. I kicked the dirt in frustration as he yelled something back at me—what, I couldn't say. The buzzing in my ears masked all sound around me. I usually got this imaginary bee in my head when I was upset or angry with myself or even when I was nervous. I didn't know why it happened. My psychiatrist said it was a way for my body to protect me. It sounded like a bunch of crap, but what did I know about my brain?

Tyler came running out to the mound, waving his catcher's mitt at me. His mouth was moving, but the little bee zipping around in my head was still loud. When he reached the pitcher's mound, he tipped up my chin with his gloved hand.

Embarrassed at my performance, I looked away. I hated myself right now.

"Look at me."

I shook my head.

"It's okay, Lacey. You're just tired. You have both your fast pitch and curveball ready. The slider isn't that important for tryouts. It's only high school baseball."

My head snapped up, and I met his soft blue eyes that had helped to lessen the constant noise in my head. "Easy for you to say. This is important to me." I pushed him away.

What was I doing? I didn't mean to be such a bitch. He'd been patient with me over these past few weeks, helping me practice. He'd given up some of his summer fun in between his football practice, and here I was giving him attitude.

"I know it is, but you have two excellent pitches, and the coach is only requiring two for tryouts." He enfolded my hand with his callused one.

A small twinge of jealousy hit me. Things came easy for Tyler, it seemed. Whenever he'd thrown a few pitches to me to show me how the curveball looked, my mouth would always fall open at how perfectly he pitched. He'd played on the baseball team his first year in high school, but gave it up when the football coach asked him to concentrate on football. He'd agreed because he loved the game more than baseball, and it gave him better scholarship opportunities.

"I'm sorry. You're right. I'm just tired." I pushed the envy aside. It was stupid of me to feel it in the first place. My performance had nothing to do with Tyler's talents. I was just extremely hard on myself. I strove for perfection. I had to make the team. Everything I'd wanted was riding on this year, my senior year, and my last chance to show the scouts at Arizona State University that I was worthy of a scholarship. They'd seen me play at my old school, Crestview High in California, and were so impressed that they sat down with me to discuss a potential offer to play for their school.

They gave me two stipulations. One, I had to continue to improve my pitching skills, and two, keep up my grades. If I met these requirements I had a shot at not only a scholarship, but at being the first female to grace an all boys' college baseball team—or at least ASU's.

"It's getting late. Why don't we call it quits? You need to rest your arm." Tyler tapped my ball cap.

I nodded. I did need my arm loose if I was going to continue to practice hard up until tryouts next week. I prayed I could regain my skills. I'd gone a whole year without picking up a baseball. My hands started to shake as I thought about Mom and my sister Julie.

"Are you okay?" He wiped a tear off my cheek.

"Yeah." Not really.

Almost a year after Mom and Julie's deaths, I wasn't sure I had the confidence to face a new life in a new school and a new home. Did Dad and I make the right decision to move clear across the country? My psychiatrist, Dr. Meyers, had recommended it. The memories and the pain had been too much for my dad, my brother Rob, and me. We weren't healing. We weren't even living. I'd abandoned my friends. My dad moped around, hiding in his home office. My brother Rob turned down his dream of playing for the LA Dodgers.

Tyler flicked his head toward home plate. "Come on. Pack up."

We walked over to the dugout in silence. Once inside, I packed my bag, removed my cleats, and slipped my feet into a pair of flip-flops.

As Tyler changed into his tennis shoes, he said, "I'll get the lights and meet you at your car. We can go get a shake and fries before you head home. I know you like dunking your fries into your shake." He grinned. It was the same cocky grin that made the girls I'd seen watching us occasionally swoon over him, especially with his blond locks that had a way of curling around his ball cap, and, of course, his ocean-blue eyes.

He was sweet, trying to cheer me up. We'd met when I'd barged into Coach Dean's office right after I moved here in July. I wanted to talk to him about tryouts and the schedule. I didn't think the coach would be busy. After all, it was summertime, and baseball didn't ramp up until tryouts in the fall. Boy, how wrong I'd been. I'd walked into Coach's office without knocking, and interrupted a meeting between Tyler, Coach Dean, the football coach, and a scout for a large university. Immediately, Coach jumped out of his desk chair, yelling at me for my lack of manners, and to get out. As I slumped my shoulders, cowering like a turtle retreating into her shell, someone in the room had snorted. As I scurried out, I caught a glimpse of Tyler with a grin on his face. Since that day we'd become friends, mostly hanging out on the ball field for practices.

I wasn't sure if Coach Dean put him up to it or if Tyler just felt sorry for me because Coach humiliated me. In either case, it didn't matter. I'd made one friend, and to me an important one. He knew the game of baseball well. Maybe the fresh start was panning out.

"Okay" was all I said as Tyler grabbed his bag and ducked into the tunnel.

Then I lifted my Van Halen T-shirt and tied it into a knot to let the night air cool my sweating skin. The style wasn't the best-looking fashion statement, but I didn't care. It was approaching nine p.m. Who would see me at this time of night? Then I remembered Tyler wanted to grab a bite to eat. I shrugged. I'd make myself presentable before we got to the restaurant.

I threw my bag over my shoulder as I walked off the baseball field of Kensington High in Ashford, Massachusetts. Dad and I had chosen this school because it had a better academic program, and a better coach than the other schools we researched. I hoped for the umpteenth time that we had made the right decision.

Once at my car, I fished my keys out of my purse. I drove a beat-up Mustang, compliments of my dad. He was trying to restore it. But time was non-existent for him. He had recently opened a new nightclub in the heart of Cambridge, a city known for college kids and a vibrant music scene. He also owned a nightclub in LA managed by Rob, my twenty-two-year-old brother. He had offered to stay in LA and run the business for Dad. In addition to his nightclubs on both coasts now, Dad also owned and managed Eko Records, a well-known label that had signed many top-ten bands and pop singers. The flexibility of the business afforded him the opportunity to work from anywhere.

I took off my ball cap, running my hand over my long brown pony-tail. I threw my bag in the backseat and slid into the driver's side. Dad had said to let it idle a few minutes to get the oil circulating before taking off. I inserted the key into the ignition and turned. The *click, click, click* sound wasn't good. I tried again. Nothing.

Shit! I banged my hands against the steering wheel. *Damn car.* Dad and I needed to have a talk about better transportation.

Heaving a sigh, I got out of the Mustang, looking around. The sports complex stood slightly to my right with the ball field on its left. Aside from Tyler's SUV, the only other vehicle was a black truck, which sat under a tree in the far corner of the parking lot. I glanced out at the field, but didn't see anyone. What was taking Tyler so long? The lights to the stadium were still on, which meant he must've gotten tied up with something.

Ducking half my body back into the Mustang, I lifted my purse off the seat when a loud thump on the back of my car startled me. My heart rate kicked into overdrive.

I jerked my head up. Some guy I didn't know stood behind my car. Panic set in. Since the police hadn't found the creeps who had invaded our home and murdered my mom and sister, I'd been extremely paranoid.

I opened my glove compartment, grasped the handle of my nine-millimeter handgun, then slowly got out. The stranger seemed frozen. He stared at me as though he were contemplating his next move. I released a quiet breath, placing my free hand on the roof of my car and the other behind my back then met his gaze. All sense of where I was vanished in that moment. The copper eyes staring back at me made my whole body quiver and my brain seize.

Calm down. Calm down. Yeah, right. Between the sudden panic attacks that had become normal for me and trying hard to keep from blacking out, I was screwed.

Forget the tingles. My freaking belly had a thousand butterflies fluttering inside. I swallowed in order to get the saliva to coat my dry throat. Jeepers, I needed one of those five-gallon jugs of ice cold Gatorade that a team usually throws over the winning coach.

After a few more swallows, I decided to give my voice a shot. The last thing I wanted to do was show fear. Once I showed any sign of it, I was afraid he would grab me with those muscular arms and drag me screaming into the nearby woods, where he would kill me the way they killed my sister and mom.

"You...have a problem?" I asked. I didn't think this guy was going to hurt me, but I couldn't be sure. Regardless, I had the gun in my hand, and I was committed now.

"You need help?" the stranger asked as he stepped around the car toward me.

"I wouldn't come any farther," I warned. My fingers wound tightly around the handle of the gun. My muscles were tense enough to burst at any second.

When we moved to Massachusetts, I begged Dad to let me learn gun safety and how to shoot. Reluctantly, he'd only given in because I was going to be by myself on most nights, since he would be working at the club. So we joined the local gun club. No, I wasn't supposed to be carrying a gun. I forgot to remove it from my car after practice this morning. If Dad found out, I'd be in a load of trouble.

"What are you doing out here all by yourself?" The guy stopped at the back edge of the car and turned his head left then right in quick succession.

The parking lot lights hit his face at just the right angle to illuminate his copper eyes with lashes so long that I shivered. *Butterfly kisses.* I imagined the light touch of those lashes skimming over my face or anywhere on my body. I didn't want to take my eyes off of him, but just that thought made my gaze wander slowly down his entire muscular body. His blue—*or was it black?*—T-shirt stretched tight over his broad chest, emphasizing the word *Zeal*. I didn't know if it was just a word he liked, or if it was the band my father had signed. I continued my obvious assessment, holding the gun as steady as my trembling hand would allow while my eyes landed on his faded, worn jeans that hung low on his hips, tattered at the knees. "None of your business. What do you want?" I asked.

He took one step closer, and I whipped my hand around, aiming the gun at him.

He backed away, raising his hands to shoulder height, and as he did, his T-shirt lifted, exposing a small area just above his belt that made me suck in air.

"I'm not going to hurt you. I was just looking for my brother. He said he would be down here practicing." His voice was calm, and his relaxed shoulders told me he wasn't frightened at all.

I slanted my head to one side and a bead of sweat slid down my temple.

"I'm serious. Put the gun away. I'm not going to hurt you. I go to school here," he said in a husky tone.

"Prove it." My voice was calm and steady, which shocked me. I wasn't convinced this dude was a high school student. He looked older.

He laughed, a deep, throaty sound that caressed my skin as though his tongue were licking every inch of my body. "And how do you suggest I do that?" He still had his hands in the air, revealing his taut skin above the waist of his jeans, causing tingles to spark inside me.

The bright lights of the ball field suddenly went off, the area around us darkening. He used those seconds to make his move. He was now standing six inches in front of me while my hip was pressed against the driver's door.

I lifted my gaze to meet his, and my heart practically stopped cold. His masculine scent of cedar breezed over me as his honey-brown hair fell over his forehead. Up close he was downright gorgeous. His eyes flashed with playful intensity as though he dared me to use the gun, and that just pissed me off. Gorgeous or not, this guy wasn't taking me seriously.

"Well? You didn't answer my question," he said in a gruff tone.

I'd forgotten the question. So I said the first thing that was stuck in my brain. "And you haven't proved you go to school here," I said. I had a feeling that wasn't the answer.

His lips twitched and dimples emerged. *Uh-oh!* My biggest weakness.

Get it together, girl. I was doing a bang up job of scaring away this stranger. My self-defense instructor would clearly give me an F for this one.

He shook his head slightly as if to say I was crazy. "If you're going to use that thing in your hand, now is your best shot," he said as he pressed his chest into the gun, his hands still in the air.

Stupid move. "Are you crazy?" I didn't want to shoot him or anyone.

"Isn't that you?" he countered. His voice had a playful edge to it.

Yeah, I was. How did he know? Dr. Meyers diagnosed me with post-traumatic stress disorder, or PTSD, after I'd found Mom and Julie's bodies dead on the kitchen floor. *Exposure to a traumatic event can trigger such things as panic attacks, anxiety, nightmares, fainting or blackouts, memory loss, and others. Sometimes a person may feel as if they're going crazy*, my doctor had explained.

"Do you normally pull a gun on everyone who comes near you?" He raised an eyebrow.

"Do you normally bang on cars, freaking people out in the dark?" I retorted.

He narrowed his eyes.

I did the same. It seemed we were at an impasse.

"Well, use it or put it away. I'm not going to hurt you." A mocking grin threatened on his kissable lips.

"What's going on here?" Tyler asked as he came running out from the sports complex, panic in his voice. "Lacey." Tyler skidded to a stop, facing the stranger and me. "What the heck are you doing?"

"What took you so long?" I asked Tyler without taking my eyes off of the stranger.

"I couldn't find the key to the electrical panel for the lights. Kade, man, what did you do to her?"

What kind of name was Kade?

Kade slowly turned to Tyler, a muscle working in his strong jaw. "What did *I* do to *her*? Are you serious, man? Tell your girlfriend here to lower the weapon. I don't want any trouble. I was looking for Kelton. He said he'd be down here."

"What? Your brother is back? Since when?" Tyler's voice hitched.

Why was he shocked that some guy was back?

"Get the fucking gun off me, then I'll explain," Kade said.

Tyler lightly touched my arm. "Lacey, please. He goes to school here. He's cool."

I didn't move.

"Come on," Tyler prodded. "Put it away. Kade isn't going to hurt you."

Of course, Kade wasn't going to hurt me. If he were, he already would have. Still, I was afraid that if I lowered the weapon now I would collapse when the adrenaline rush was over, and I didn't want to look like an idiot. What the heck was I thinking? Which was more important—looking like an idiot, or my own safety?

Suddenly, in a blur Kade had the clip out of the gun and was handing both pieces back to me. *Smooth move.* It seemed he knew a thing or two about guns, and as morbid as it sounded, I was turned on even more by this sexy guy.

"Next time, don't get so paranoid," he said. "You could kill someone."

A wave of anger doused any remaining desire, and the buzzing in my head started again. Who was he to tell me not to get paranoid? Impulsively, my fist shot out and connected with his nose, and his head bobbed back as blood splattered out.

"Damn, woman. What the fuck was that for?" He grabbed his nose.

"Lacey?" Tyler stepped in between Kade and me. "What are you doing?" Horror was etched on his face.

"He's an asshole," I said as I held back the pain throbbing through my hand.

"So what? Do you hit all assholes? That's not you," Tyler said.

"What do you know about me?" Tyler didn't know everything about my life. He knew my mom and sister died, but I told him it was a car accident, as I told every friend of mine in California. Very few people knew the details. I had an extremely hard time talking about it. The cops had asked that we keep the facts close to our chests. Based on some of the evidence they found, they speculated that the home invasion was part of a bigger case, and they didn't want to compromise their efforts to catch the culprits. They kept the specifics out of the media. Still, eight months later, law enforcement wasn't any closer to finding out what happened. The thought alone compounded my anxiety.

"I'm sorry, Lacey. You're right. Let's go," Tyler said.

"I can't. My car won't start." My voice shook with fury. I had to calm down or a panic attack would take over again. As the buzzing in my head roared, I took a deep breath.

"Kade, man." The guys matched in height at about six-foot, although Kade was broader through the shoulders than Tyler. "I haven't seen Kelton tonight. If I do, I'll tell him you're looking for him."

In Kade's eyes, I saw anger, confusion, and then nothing. It was like my teacher just erased the mathematical expressions from the board, and all that was left was a blank slate. A shiver went up my spine, and not the good kind. I hated looks like that. My mom had always said, "Honey, watch out for those who show no emotion. Those are the ones that will eat you alive."

I narrowed my eyes at him in return.

"Fine. I'm sure my brother will be home soon," he said and seared me with a fierce look before he stalked off.

"Are you okay?" Tyler wrapped his arms around me.

"I'm fine. He's a bit of a jerk, isn't he?" I pushed gently against his chest. I wasn't looking for comfort. Maybe he was, though.

"Wouldn't you be if someone pulled a gun on you?" A muscle ticked in his jaw as he gave me some breathing room. "I don't know what spooked you, but what's with the gun? I didn't know you carried one."

"I know how to use one, if that's what you're worried about. I practice a lot."

Fear plagued his handsome features. "You're only seventeen, Lacey. Do you know how much trouble you'll get into if they catch you with that at school? Are you trying to screw your chances of making the baseball team?"

It was like I'd fallen into the frigid waters off the coast of Alaska. I wasn't thinking about baseball when I drew the gun. I wasn't thinking at all.

My shoulders slumped. He was right. I had to remember to take the weapon out of my car the next time. I didn't want to throw away all my hard work. God, I'd been doing so well since we moved here. I still had nightmares, but little in the way of panic or anxiety attacks until tonight. Dr. Meyers had warned me about triggers. Certain stimuli could set me off.

"Hey," he said, taking the gun and clip from me then setting them down on my front seat. "I know you're scared." He cupped my face with his large hands. "I can see the fear in your eyes. Kade wasn't going to hurt you. He can be intimidating, though." His head dipped slightly, but his blue eyes never left mine. "Okay?"

I let out a sigh and blinked. I wasn't scared. Whatever expression he saw on my face wasn't that. It was more irritation with myself for how stupid my actions were tonight.

"I'll give you a ride. We'll grab a bite another time." He raised my hand to inspect the redness across my knuckles. "You'll need to put ice on this when you get home."

I yanked it away. "I'll be fine."

"Grab your stuff and let's go." Frustration roughened his voice.

I snatched my bag from my car, threw the dismantled parts of the gun into it, locked my door then slid into Tyler's SUV.

As we drove in silence through Ashford, I gazed out the side window. Large houses dotted the tree-lined streets. An old man walked his dog at a leisurely pace, allowing the small animal to sniff every shrub and tree along the way.

Within fifteen minutes, Tyler rolled into my driveway. I lived in a modern New England-style brick home. In my neighborhood most homes were designed the same—three dormers, a deep front porch running the length of the house, two-car attached garage.

Stopping behind Dad's car, he cut the engine. He turned and placed his hand on my knee. "Lacey, are you going to be okay?"

I stared at his hand. We were friends. Did he want to be more? "I'm fine." I wasn't. *Christ, how stupid was I for grabbing my gun? What if I had panicked?* Oh, yeah—I had. *Okay. What if I'd shot Kade?* I silently berated myself for my stupidity. *Would Kade retaliate?* That wasn't something I wanted to think about. If he did, I'd probably roll over and ask him to scratch my belly.

"Thanks for tonight," I said, holding the door, ready to jump out. "I appreciate all you've done for me this summer."

"Get some rest," Tyler said softly. "Tomorrow is your first day in a new school. It should be fun."

I didn't move from the vehicle.

"What?" Tyler asked.

"Who is that Kade guy?"

"He's no one that you need to be concerned about. Now go."

"Tyler, I just pulled a gun on him. You need to tell me more."

"I will, but not tonight." He glanced at the dashboard. "It's getting late. You need a ride in the morning?"

I stared at him.

"Seriously. He's not going to come after you, if that's what you're worried about."

"I'm not worried about him," I lied. While a small part of me thought Kade would retaliate, a larger part of me worried I might fall for him. Getting involved wasn't in my plans.

The corners of his eyes crinkled. "Only girl I know who would pull a gun on a badass dude like Kade Maxwell. Now, about that ride?"

"No, I'll get my dad to take me. That way he can check my car, and he and I have an appointment with the principal anyway."

"Then I'll see you in school. Oh, and Lacey." His tone dropped, and he lost his smile. "Trust me when I tell you, stay away from Kade."

"Thanks for tonight." I climbed out of his SUV.

"Put some ice on that hand," he said.

I closed the door and waved. The engine faded as he backed out. I started for the house, examining my swollen knuckles. I grinned, thinking of how idiotic I was to punch that handsome guy, let alone pull a gun on him. Nevertheless, I had a sneaky suspicion I was going to see him again. I mean, a person didn't let things like that slide, did they?

CHAPTER 2

I tossed and turned all night. More than once I jerked awake, sweating from some dream I couldn't remember. It wasn't unusual for me to wake up soaking wet, with my hair plastered to my head and my T-shirt stuck to my body. Immediately after the funeral I'd become very depressed, and the nightmares began.

Tragedy had a way of seeping deep into my psyche, driving my thoughts and actions and how I viewed the world around me. I hadn't wanted to live. I moped around school, ignored my friends, gave up baseball, even my love of airplanes. It wasn't hard to do, especially when Dad and Rob were in the same boat. There wasn't anyone around to kick us in the ass to get out of the funk we were in. Usually the parent would help the kids through the death of a loved one, but the murders were so sudden and tragic that Dad became a zombie, too. When we were home we'd hide in our rooms, barely emerging to eat. If we did eat as a family, our conversations centered on bland details of our day. The sessions with Dr. Meyers helped, but she'd said it would take time to heal. She'd suggested that I do the things that I loved before my life changed, and for me, that was baseball.

It hadn't quite been a year, and I still had a long way to go before I overcame my PTSD, but my life was getting back on track.

The morning air had a chill to it—a sign that winter was just around the corner. Even though some of our family vacations were spent skiing at Mammoth Mountain, I wasn't a cold-weather person. Vacations and living in frigid temperatures were two vastly different things. Dad and I hadn't even thought about warmer clothes, not even a winter coat.

As we drove to school, I studied Dad. He had one hand on the wheel and was running his other hand through his newly showered brown hair. His large, muscular frame filled the driver's seat of the antique Impala he was driving. He'd been quiet since we got in the car. I knew he'd gotten in late. I couldn't sleep, so I'd heard him come in around three this morning. The nightclub he'd just opened a month ago was taking up all his time. On some days he seemed to regret that he even decided to take on a large project, but it kept him busy and focused, which I was grateful for. To see him in pain hurt even more than him not spending time with me.

"Are you okay, Dad?" I asked, sliding him a sideways glance.

"I'm just tired, Sweet Pea." He shifted his attention between the road and me. The sun beamed in through his side window, and I caught a glimpse of the dark circles under his green eyes.

Dad and I hardly talked about Mom and Julie. *God, how I missed their bright smiles.* While I had most of Dad's genes, Julie resembled Mom. They were so much alike. They both had thick light brown hair, amber eyes, and every time they smiled, one corner of their mouths turned upward more than the other. According to Dr. Meyers, people deal with tragedy in their own ways, and for Dad, it was burying himself in work. For me, I tried to think about all the good in them, although I always ended up crying.

So letting the subject drop, I rubbed my swollen knuckles, and an image of me hitting Kade skittered across my brain. I smiled. Okay, not the best move, since it was my pitching hand.

"You want to tell me what happened to your hand?" Dad asked.

I glanced out the side window.

"Lacey." His tone dropped. "You know you have a lot riding on this. Look at me."

I turned, seeing the hard angles of his jaw twitching.

He glanced at me, his nostrils flaring. "Adding one more suspension will not look good on your college application."

I swallowed. After the funeral, I had been in a very dark place, and any little slight set me off. When I'd returned to school, I'd gotten into several fights with kids. When they looked at me the wrong way or whispered when I walked by, I lashed out at them. On two occasions I'd received detention for fighting with snarky girls for their rude comments on my appearance. I'd let myself go, but I didn't need to hear it from them. After my third infraction I'd been suspended. I wasn't sure how I was going to handle myself at this new school. However, if last night was any indication, I was doomed to fail. Dad was right about keeping my record clean for college, but my more immediate concern was having a chance of making the high school baseball team.

"I know, Dad. It's just..." I'd thought I'd gotten better, but Kade somehow set me off.

"Just what?"

My stomach became a ball of knots. The Froot Loops threatened to rise. I blew out a few quiet breaths, squinting at the bright sun glaring through the windows.

"I'm nervous. It's a new school. What if the kids are just as rude as they were at Crestview?"

"We talked about this. The kids at school don't know what you've been through, and I know you don't trust easily anymore, but you have to learn to make friends again."

He was right, of course, and I wanted to, but I didn't know how to trust again. The thought of even allowing someone to get close to me made my stomach ache. It was bad enough that after the funeral my longtime boyfriend, Brad, decided to break the news to me that he'd been cheating on me with my best friend, Danny. So many issues with that one. I wasn't ready to share that story with anyone.

"I've made a friend in Tyler," I said, flexing my hand, trying to keep it loose.

"Lacey, you need to make friends with girls. All the friends you ever make are boys."

"Not true. What about Melissa? She was a girl."

He laughed as we stopped at the red light at the corner of Main Street and First. A barbershop sat on one corner and a real estate office on another. The parking spaces along the curbs were empty, except for two cars parked in front of a coffee shop up on the right. "Melissa was your sister's friend."

Okay, she was Julie's friend. But I used to hang out with them. They would drag me to the mall every chance they had. Julie was a total girl, and would love to get me to try on clothes other than jeans. "So? It still counts."

"Lacey, please, for me, make some female friends at this school. I like Tyler, and he's been great helping you with your pitching, but you need to shed some of that tomboy you have in you."

"Dad. I'm playing baseball. I'm going to be surrounded by boys."

The light turned green, and Dad gave the car gas as we rolled through Main Street. The school was on the other side of town. "I know that. And I'm not saying stop being a tomboy. That's who you are. But off the field, I would like to see my little girl wear a dress or a skirt every now and then."

I rolled my eyes. I had only worn dresses when Mom had made me. She'd been in charge of the rotary club in LA and every year they put on a benefit for some local charity. And every year I had to attend. It was always a big to-do with gowns and tuxedos. I hated playing dress-up. Worrying about what to wear was a waste of time. Give me a pair of jeans and a T-shirt and I was just as happy as any girl who loved to wear dresses.

My mother always told me that I would make any guy happy. When I'd asked her why, she'd said, "Because, dear, you don't worry about what you're going to wear. You're beautiful without make-up, and you're confident in your own skin." God, I missed her. She'd always known what to say to people. She was a calming presence.

I was deep in thought when Dad's rough knuckles scraped across my cheek. "Hey, Sweet Pea, everything okay?"

"Yeah, why?"

"You're crying. Were you thinking about..." He had a hard time saying Mom's name or even Julie's. He always stopped midsentence or changed the subject. While it irritated me more now than in the beginning, I still didn't push. I didn't like when I was forced to talk about my feelings.

"Sorry, I...yeah, I was thinking of Mom." I hadn't realized I was crying.

"Don't be sorry. I know it's still hard." He turned into the school lot. "Now, let me see what the problem is with your car. Then we can go meet with the principal."

We still had an hour before school. We both got out of his restored 1964 Chevy Impala. According to Dad, they just didn't make cars the way they used to.

I agreed with him. I'd taken the Impala out one night and got into a fender bender. Okay, it was more than a minor accident. I hadn't been paying attention to the road. I plowed into the back of the car ahead of me that had been stopped at a red light in downtown LA. The Impala didn't have a scratch on it. The other car wasn't so lucky. After that night, he decided to make sure I drove a relic—the beat-up Mustang he was sitting in now, trying to turn over the engine, which was still making the *click, click* sound.

I was leaning against my car when a black Ford 150 pickup pulled in, slowly maneuvering into a spot three car lengths from us. I was surprised to see anyone here. We were in the parking lot near the base-ball field. It was somewhat of a hike to the school.

Dad lumbered out of the Mustang, circled around, and popped the hood. My eyes were still fixed on the black truck. The windows were tinted, so I couldn't tell who the driver was, although it did look like the one I saw last night. The more I stared, waiting for the occupants to emerge, the more my heart began to beat erratically. The truck sat there with its engine running under the morning sun, looking all mysterious. I shouldn't be paranoid. Dad was here. I couldn't help it though. Since the people responsible for killing my family were still at large, I was always on edge.

Keeping my eye on the truck, I dug out my phone. Casually, I snapped a picture of it. I was being a little nuts—just a tiny bit. I examined the picture, then glanced up at the truck again. Well, if the driver were following us, it wouldn't be hard to describe the vehicle to the cops. Five red hearts were painted on the passenger door just above the handle.

Tearing my gaze away, I bent down, leaning on the Mustang. "Dad, how goes it?"

"It looks like the cable to the battery came loose."

"How?" I straightened as warning bells jangled in my mind. My pulse sped up and the sky above me seemed to grow dark. I was about to have one of my panic attacks.

Dad grabbed my shoulders, lightly but firmly. "Lacey, breathe. The cables came loose. That's all. It happens."

My vision blurred. It had to be the stress of a new school, new home, and new friends.

"Remember your exercises," Dad reminded me.

Dr. Meyers had told me, "Breathing is important. Inhale, hold it for five seconds, then let it out slowly. Do that as much as you have to." But that exercise had only worked once, when I caught the attack early. I was going to pass out cold, or worse, wake up somewhere strange with no memory, like the time Dad found me walking into the ocean behind our house in California in the dead of night.

Closing my eyes, I took a deep breath through my nose. Then I counted to five very slowly and expelled all the air through my mouth. As I did, the pounding in my chest slowed, easing the tension. I waited another two seconds before I opened my eyes. When I did, Kade popped into view, looming next to my dad.

Oh crap! He was inches from me. Sweat beaded on my forehead—so much for staying calm.

His honey-brown hair was swept to one side of his forehead, the back of it curling on his neck. He hid his copper eyes behind dark sunglasses. It was probably a good thing. If I'd had one peek into his eyes, Dad would have to take me to the hospital for bottled oxygen.

"Lacey, are you okay?" Dad asked, releasing his hold on me.

"What's wrong with her?" Kade asked in a husky voice.

Dad didn't answer as he kept his worried eyes on me. I nodded slightly to Dad, letting him know I was okay. Well, as far as the panic attack, but not all right with Kade so close now.

"Nothing," I said. "I had an asthma attack. I forgot my inhaler."

Dad gave me a puzzled look and walked to the front of the car.

"You sure?" Kade asked in a voice that made me squeeze my thighs together.

Yeah, I'm screwed. I'd never reacted to Brad this way. "Is that your truck?" I asked.

"Yep. Why are you taking pictures of it?" He cocked his head to one side, his shades still hiding his eyes.

Busted.

"Do you know this boy?" Dad asked as he closed the hood of my car, the sound making me flinch.

"Um...not really."

Kade grinned. "How's that hand this morning, Lacey?" The way Kade said my name sent warmth cascading downward.

"How's the eye, Kade?" The question rolled off my tongue with ease.

"Lacey, did you hit this boy? Is that what happened to your hand?" Dad glanced at me, then Kade. "Young man, what did you do to cause my daughter to punch you?" Dad asked as he stalked up to Kade, who held out his hands in front of him.

"Dad, he didn't do anything. He was just being a smartass. He didn't touch me." I would've loved for Kade to run his hands all over my body. Still, I couldn't let Dad use his own fists on Kade. After all, I was the one who lost the screw in my head, unleashing my wrath on him. Kade's eyebrows rose slightly above his sunglasses.

Swiveling my way, Dad said tersely, "What did we talk about, Sweet Pea?"

I cringed at my pet name. I was going to kill Dad.

Kade smirked at me before he said to Dad, "It was just a misunderstanding, sir. I promise I didn't lay a hand on her."

"That's a good thing, son." Dad walked over to his Impala and ducked his head inside.

Relief washed through me. My actions at my last school gave Dad reason to pause before lashing out at Kade. "Did you lose your brother again, or are you following me?"

Kade's head snapped back around to me. "I park in this lot for school."

"So, you must be an overachiever to be here so early then." My tone was sarcastic—it had to be with this guy. He was hitting nerves that I didn't know I had.

"Lacey, manners." Dad glared at me as he wiped his hand on a towel he'd gotten from his car.

I left my manners at the gravesite many months ago.

"So where's that thing you had last night? It wasn't a bat. What was it now?" Kade asked.

I clenched my jaw, glowering at him. I didn't know if he was looking at me through those dark shades. Still, I wanted to rip off his Raybans and sucker punch him again. "We need to go, Dad." My father couldn't know about the gun. He would kill me.

Kade shoved his hands in his jean pockets and strode over to Dad. "By the way, sir, I'm Kade Maxwell. I met your daughter last night. She's got a wicked curveball."

Oh, my God. He was watching me? A shiver crept up my spine. Why was I surprised? We usually had a lot of people observing from the stands. Most of them were girls watching Tyler, although we hadn't had any spectators last night.

"You mean a wicked hook," Dad said matter-of-factly.

"Da-a-ad." I couldn't believe my father had just said that. Okay, I needed to break up the love fest, or at the very least get Kade to leave before he said anything about the gun. "Did you fix my car, Dad?"

"I'm James Robinson, by the way. Nice to meet you, son. You go to school here, I take it?"

"Yes, sir. I love your Impala. Did you restore it? Let me guess, 1964, six-point-seven liter engine."

"Correct. You like old cars, Kade?"

"I do, sir. My dad has a 1965 Shelby GT350 Street. One of the first Mustangs made."

Dad's brows shot up. "I would love to check it out sometime."

"Anytime, sir."

I had no idea what model Mustang I was driving, or I should say not driving. The one I was resting my butt against was a piece-o-crap. Still, these two were gushing like two girls talking about shoes. I didn't know if I should be happy about it or not. If they were talking cars, at least they weren't talking about a certain gun I shouldn't have had in my car.

"I need to go. I have a meeting to get to. If there's anything I can do to help, Mr. Robinson, please let me know," Kade said, glancing my way.

"Sure thing, son."

Kade held out his hand. "Great to meet you, sir."

Dad shook his hand. "Next time my daughter hits you, please call me."

Horrified, I stalked over to Dad as Kade walked past me. Our shoulders brushed and an electrical charge zapped me. I cast him what I hoped was a snarky glare over my shoulder, but he didn't even turn around.

"Nice boy," Dad said as he fished the keys to my car out of the front pocket of his faded jeans.

I harrumphed and crossed my arms over my chest. "Really, Dad. You want him to call you if I sucker punch him again. He deserved it."

"Everyone deserves to get punched—because that's what you've been doing since the funeral. I told you already, you need to learn restraint."

I dropped my head, looking at my black flats. I hated that he was right.

"When is your appointment with Dr. Davis?"

Since we'd moved, we had to find another psychiatrist. Dr. Meyers had recommended Dr. Larry Davis, who had an office in Lancaster, which was the next town over. Good thing—I wasn't all that tickled about being seen walking into a psychiatrist's office. This was a small town. I didn't want to have my name on the lips of everyone who lived here as they talked about how crazy the new girl was.

Blowing out a breath, I lifted my head. "At the end of the week."

Dad folded his bulk into my car and started the engine. It turned over like the well-oiled machine it was. He gave it more gas, and the engine purred. "Let's let it run for a few minutes. Actually, why don't we take it around to the front of the school? I'll follow you over there," Dad suggested. He jumped into the Impala, and I got into my car.

It only took two minutes to pull into the visitor parking at the front entrance of the two-story brick building. Grabbing my book bag, I slid out of the car and threw my keys into my purse. I didn't think students were allowed to park here, but I was new, after all. I walked up to stand at the flagpole and waited for Dad. He'd parked two spaces over from me. *What was taking him so long?* I was about to go over to his car when he jumped out, flattening his lips and biting on the bottom one.

"What is it?" I asked.

"Nothing, Lacey," he said, sauntering up to me.

"Are you sure? I know you don't like to tell me things because of my..." *Geez, I didn't know what I had anymore.* I was beginning to believe I was nuts. Maybe something other than PTSD festered inside me. Whatever it was, I had to get it under control. After yesterday and this morning, I really did need help. I prayed my new psychiatrist would help me like Dr. Meyers had.

"You worry about school and baseball. After all, that's why we're here, right? Your future and to get a fresh start." I didn't like the sadness in his voice. He made it sound like it was my fault we moved three thousand miles away.

"Dad, we both agreed to this." Tears threatened. The last thing I wanted to do was be the cause of my father's unhappiness.

He threw his arm over my shoulder. "I'm sorry, Sweet Pea. The club is just a little out-of-control right now."

"Why did you even buy another club?"

"We'll discuss it later."

Cars were slowly filling the parking lot in the distance. As we made our way into the school, Dad and I talked about my classes and what was expected of me. I had to hunker down and make sure my grades were top-notch—otherwise ASU wasn't even going to consider me for a baseball scholarship. The problem was I still had to take a few junior classes that I hadn't had a chance to catch up on since we were moving, not to mention my senior subjects, too. I had a tough year ahead of me.

We were on our way to meet with the principal and guidance counselor to see if they would allow me to test out of trig and calculus. I'd always been good in math, and I needed those two subjects to graduate. I'd been teaching myself both all summer. If I passed, I would have more free time for all my other subjects and baseball.

Dad opened one side of the double glass doors of the main entrance. The building stretched out on both sides. I wasn't sure how many students attended. I knew from registering that the senior class alone had two hundred kids.

As soon as I entered, I bumped into a girl with bluish-black hair, wearing skinny black jeans, a yellow V-neck sweater that hugged her curves, and black patent leather flats.

"I'm sorry," I said.

She scrunched her perfectly manicured eyebrows at me, adjusting her backpack on her shoulder.

"Cat got your tongue?" I asked.

She stood frozen in the hall, sizing me up as if I was some idiot that dared to bump into her.

Dad had gotten stuck holding the door open for a few other students that trudged in behind us.

"You're the new girl. The one that's here to play baseball," she said.

Ooookay. How did she know that?

"Hi, I'm Becca. Becca Young." She extended her hand.

I checked on Dad, who hadn't moved, then turned back to Becca.

"Don't worry. I don't bite. I'm one of the few girls in this school that doesn't." Her pink lips stretched into a smile.

"Hi, I'm Lacey Robinson."

We shook hands. Hers were colder than mine.

"How did you know who I was?" I asked.

"I didn't. I took a wild guess, since you're wearing an LA Dodgers T-shirt. And who comes to the first day of school with their father, anyway?" She tossed a handful of hair over her shoulder.

I loved the Dodgers and had several T-shirts with their logo. "Nice guess." *God.* I hoped she wasn't going to be like the girls at my last school, berating me for my appearance.

Dad finally abandoned his post as temporary doorman.

"This is my dad, James Robinson. Dad, Becca."

"Nice to meet you," Dad said. "So, Becca, can you point us toward the principal's office?"

"Sure. I'll walk with you." Becca's shoes clicked on the tile floor as we headed to see the principal.

"I'm so glad girls are trying out for baseball again," Becca said.

Dad and I exchanged a perplexed look.

"Oh, you don't know," she said. "We haven't had a girl play since Mandy Shear was killed two years ago."

I stopped in my tracks, Dad and Becca walking ahead. *She was killed? How?* I had just freaked out over my battery cables coming loose. *Don't freak. Breathe.*

Dad turned, holding out his arm. "What happened?" he asked, waiting for me to join them.

"Hey, Becca," a boy's voice came from behind us.

"Yo, Scott. How goes it, dude?" she yelled over her shoulder.

The exchange between her and the boy allowed me to take a few deep breaths.

"We should keep walking. The halls will be crowded soon. And we're not allowed to talk about Mandy's death on school grounds," she said in a hushed tone.

"Why?" I asked, even though she'd just said the topic was all but closed. Dad placed his hand lightly on my arm.

She glanced up at the wooden sign above the frosted-paned door. "Here's your stop." She waved me off. "I'll see you around. You're a senior, right?" she asked, backing away.

"I am," I said.

"Then I'm sure we'll have a class or two together." She bounced on her feet and sauntered over to Scott, a short blond wearing black-rimmed glasses.

"Why do you think the topic of Mandy is off limits on school property?" I asked Dad as we stood in the admin office. A counter separated the room into halves. Behind the chest-high glass counter stood a metal desk. Three windows separated by thin pieces of wood were built into the gray walls that overlooked a small grassy area outside with decorative trees.

"It's probably still a sensitive subject. You should know that, Lacey." Dad sauntered up to the counter.

Even though Dad was right, I couldn't help my curiosity or my trepidation.

The red-haired lady behind the counter was busy with paperwork.

Dad cleared his throat. "Excuse me."

"Oh, I'm so sorry," she said in the softest voice. It wasn't even seven thirty in the morning and this lady looked as if she had worked an entire day already. Black circles marred the area under her blue eyes, and her pale skin had a sheen to it as though she had been sweating. "I've been working non-stop, getting things in order. I just hate the first day." Her eyes met Dad's, and I swear all stress left her face.

Dad flashed his winning smile, and the woman looked like she had one of those moments that I had when I laid eyes on Kade. Sure, my dad was ruggedly handsome. He had brown wavy hair like me. His green eyes usually sparkled when he was happy. These days, though, I hadn't seen any glimmer in them. He always kept a five-o-clock shadow on his face like he had now. My mom had loved him with "that scruffy look," as I called it.

"No problem," Dad said. "We have an appointment with Principal Sanders."

"Oh, yes. Please take a seat. She's busy at the moment. I'll let her know you're here." She scooted around a desk and the counter before opening the door to the principal's office. "Your seven thirty is here."

"Tell Mr. Robinson I'll be right with him," the principal said.

"Yes, ma'am." Then the lady turned to Dad, with a distant expression. "She'll be right with you."

"I didn't get your name," Dad said.

We were still at the counter while she made her way back to her desk. "I'm Barbara. Everyone calls me Barb, though." Her cheeks turned red to match her hair.

Oh, geez. Dad was making this lady flush.

"Everyone calls me James," Dad said, leaning forward on the counter.

It was like I wasn't even in the room. I didn't know if I was happy about that or not. True, Dad needed to move on with his life. Eventually, he needed to find someone he was interested in. Still, it might be too soon, but then again, did love ever have a timetable, or was there ever a good or bad time for romance? *Oh, shit.* What the hell was I thinking? I had my father already in love with this woman and married off before I even started my first day of school.

"This is my daughter, Lacey," he said, looking at me.

"Pleased to meet you, Barb," I said.

She nodded. "I'm sure I'll get to know you over the next year, Lacey. Anyway, Ms. Sanders will be with you shortly. I need to get back to class schedules."

Dad nodded to Barb before guiding me over to the empty chairs that lined the wall. We both sat down. Aside from Barb tapping the keys on her computer, the room was eerily silent. Dad and I were lost in our own thoughts when the door to the principal's office opened, and I couldn't believe it—Kade Maxwell stalked out, looking all badass. My heart stopped, my mouth became dry, and my hands clammy. He wasn't wearing his sunglasses, and when our eyes met, a voice in my head screamed to run. *Yep, this was going to be one hellish senior year.*

CHAPTER 3

Principal Sanders sat behind her mahogany desk, writing on a notepad, when Dad and I entered.

"I'll be right with you," she said, not looking up.

As we waited, I took in the spacious room. Beside the expensive looking desk, several bookcases lined the left wall. Just behind Principal Sanders, a bank of windows brought in bright sunlight, showing the specks of dust floating in the air. A small sink with an under-counter refrigerator abutted the bookcases, with a loveseat against the right wall. No guest chairs. Normally, there would be two in front of the desk. How odd. The principal's office at Crestview had chairs for guests. Even my dad's office at Eko Records had chairs.

Standing next to Dad, I checked my phone for messages—I didn't have any. I didn't expect to, but I was nervous all of sudden and needed to do something. Dad stood with his hands crossed in front of him like he was a bouncer at his own nightclub.

Setting her pen down, Principal Sanders rose, smoothing her skirt. Her long black hair cascaded down around her shoulders, and her gray eyes had dots of blue in them, coordinating with her gray suit. I bet they looked different when she wore different colors. Brad's greenish-blue eyes had seemed more blue when he wore a green shirt.

"I don't believe in chairs for my guests. Please take no offense.

When my guests are usually out-of-control kids, I don't want them relaxing in chairs. However, since neither of you is here to get reprimanded, please have a seat on the sofa." She revealed bright white teeth behind red lips, enhancing deep laugh lines.

Turning, I took a few steps and sat down. Dad did the same.

Ms. Sanders collected her chair, rolling it over to the sitting area.

The door creaked open, and a blond-haired lady carried in a straight-backed wooden chair.

"Thank you, Mrs. Flowers, for joining us."

Did all staff members come with their own chairs? Then something tumbled through my brain. Had Kade been in trouble? He hadn't walked out with a chair. But the first day of school hadn't started yet, so how could he be in trouble? I quickly dismissed the thought. I was here for me and not to think about Kade.

After everyone was settled, we went through the introductions.

"Okay. We have about twenty minutes before the first bell." Ms. Sanders crossed one leg over the other then flipped open a notepad.

"Very well, then." Mrs. Flowers opened a file. "Lacey, I'll be helping you throughout the school year to stay on track with your goals. Prior to this meeting, I was able to get all your former school records together." Her short bob fell forward as she scanned a piece of paper in the file. "I will say I'm impressed with your grades until...anyway, you have a tough schedule this year."

I guess she didn't want to bring up the funeral or whatever it was that she was about to say.

"So if you're set on trying out for the boys' baseball team, then you're going to have to put your nose in the books during your free time," Ms. Sanders added. "We're all about sports here at Kensington, but we're strict when it comes to academics. We want our students to be well prepared for college. We have several competitive academic clubs that have won awards every year. I understand from Mrs. Flowers you're extremely good in math. Maybe an academic team would suit you." She tucked a few strands of hair behind her ear.

An odd noise rumbled from Dad. I glanced at him to find he had a scowl on his face. "What is this, Ms. Sanders? Are you trying to steer my daughter away from something she's dreamed about all her life?" Dad's nostrils flared.

"Mr. Robinson, please. I didn't mean anything other than to say that she has gotten excellent grades in the past. I was just suggesting another alternative," Ms. Sanders responded.

"Lacey will not be competing on any academic teams. Baseball is it," he said.

"What happens if she doesn't make the team?" Mrs. Flowers asked.

I didn't want to think about that. I wanted to stay optimistic. "Regardless of baseball, I'm still going to ASU," I said. "So how can I test out of the math subjects?"

A pregnant pause filled the room. Ms. Sanders jotted something down on her notepad, and Mrs. Flowers sifted through my file. Dad and I exchanged a look. His stress level seemed to have evened out. I only knew that because the pained expression on his face had softened.

Was there something wrong? Why wasn't the answer straight-forward?

Thankfully, Dad spoke. "Is there a problem, ladies?"

Mrs. Flowers swallowed, a sound that grated on me in the quiet room. Ms. Sanders, on the other hand, stood, rolled her chair back behind her desk and dropped the pad on top. It made a snapping sound like someone had popped a balloon.

"Mr. Robinson, I'll be honest with you." She came around and leaned against the shiny piece of furniture, crossing her arms over her chest. "It's going to be hard for Lacey to meet her goals this year."

"What does that have to do with testing out of a few subjects?" I asked. Did she have other plans for me?

Dad pushed to his feet. I caught his wrist before he moved away. His grimace told me to back off, so I let go of him. I liked that he was taking control to support me rather than apologize to the principal for my bad behavior, which was what he'd done a few times at Crestview.

"Principal Sanders, I respect your position, and what you're trying to do here. But my daughter has been to hell and back this past year. I don't expect you to understand, and for certain, I don't want your pity. You assured me on the phone more than once that you would work with us to ensure Lacey worked toward her goals. So aside from telling us that she can't test out, I don't want to hear that you're not going to allow her to try out."

"Mr. Robinson, the boys on the baseball team are tough. So much so that I had to reprimand them when the last girl that was on—"

"That's not my concern," Dad said. "You don't know Lacey at all. If you did, you would know that she doesn't put up with anything, especially bullies. My daughter is probably tougher than most boys in this school. Regardless, she always sticks to her goals. If it weren't for... anyway, she can handle herself."

Way to go, Dad!

Mrs. Flowers's mouth was agape and her eyes were wide. Ms. Sanders had a completely blank expression on her face.

After several agonizing seconds, the principal broke the silence. "Please forgive me. You're right, Mr. Robinson," she said. "Mrs. Flowers, please set up a date and time for Lacey to take the tests." She smoothed out her skirt. "Mr. Robinson, I appreciate your candor. My staff will help, but Lacey, it's up to you to put in the work. I expect two things from you. One, you do not cause any trouble while a student here, and two, you maintain good grades while playing sports. Is that understood?"

I went to stand next to Dad. "Yes, ma'am. But...I'll also protect myself." Just like I had at my last school. I wanted her to know that regardless of tough boys or girls in this school, I wouldn't let anyone bully me.

She eyed me up and down for a moment. "Very well then. This meeting is over."

Mrs. Flowers didn't move.

"Thanks for your time," Dad said. We both headed for the door. I was out in the admin office when Ms. Sanders called to Dad.

He turned back toward her office and stabbed his thumb behind him at Barb's desk. "Go. I'll talk with the principal. I'll see you later this afternoon."

I shrugged then inclined my head. I had no idea what the principal was going to say to my father, and frankly, I didn't want to know. Between the night before and that morning, my life seemed to have taken a turn for the worse. Was she really trying to steer me clear of the boys' baseball team? If so, why? She said she had to reprimand the boys for the last girl on the team. Had the team had something to do with her death? I'd had a dose of naysayers at Crestview from a couple of boys on the team. They didn't think a girl helped their chances of winning games—until they saw me pitch. So whatever the boys at Kensington had to dish out, I would be ready.

The first bell rang just as I was weaving into a crowd of students in the hall. Anxiety pangs from being a new student ate at my stomach when I merged into traffic. I didn't know where I was going. I had my schedule, I had my locker number, but I had no clue where anything was.

"Lacey," a female voice called.

Scanning the hall, I saw Becca standing against a locker up ahead, waving at me.

I slipped out of the herd of students and stopped beside her.

"How did it go?" she asked.

"Fine." I wasn't about to tell her that my father almost took off Ms. Sanders's head.

"Do you know where you're going?" she asked.

"No. I have English first. Well, after homeroom. I need to find my locker, too."

Her dark eyes sized me up.

I angled my head. "You have a problem?"

"Not me. But the girls in this school will. I hear that you've been hanging out with Tyler Langley."

"Yeah, so?"

"I don't know what your last high school was like, but this one, the claws come out for anyone who pisses on their parade, if you know what I mean."

I wasn't naïve about the cliques in high school or the groups of cheerleaders who ruled the schools. Not that I'd had any problems with them at my old school. In fact, as a sophomore, my sister had cheered for Crestview. "I couldn't care less. I'm not into cliques or groups or girlie shit."

She smiled wide. "That's good. We'll get along just fine then." She pushed off the locker. "Why don't we head to English? I have class with you."

"What about homeroom?" I asked.

"Homeroom is usually in the same wing as your first period. That way students don't have to walk too far between the two since they don't give us much time."

Students congregated at their lockers and near windowsills as we made our way over to the English wing. I learned from Becca along the way that the school was sectioned off by subject. We had just turned a corner when Tyler sauntered up to us, towering over the crowd.

"Here we go," Becca muttered, scanning the hall.

"Hey, Lacey," Tyler said. "Everything okay this morning?"

The conversations in the hall stopped. An eerie silence reigned around us. If I listened hard enough I could probably hear Becca's heartbeat. Like the audience, Becca's gaze fixed on Tyler. I hoped it wasn't the fact that the good-looking football player was paying attention to the new girl.

"Yeah. Why?"

"You know, last night." His eyes softened. It was one of his looks that made the girls who'd watched us at practice melt into liquid. For some reason, I wasn't melting. Sure, he was handsome, strong, tall, and had a quiet personality. In a lot of ways, he reminded me of my brother, Rob. Maybe that was why he didn't appeal to me as boyfriend material.

One girl gasped, latching onto her friend. Even though I hated drama, I also hated when others were nosy. I decided to have some fun instead of biting their heads off for ogling.

"Oh, Tyler. You really were great last night," I crooned. It wasn't a lie—he was amazing at helping me with practice.

His mouth curled into a wolfish grin. He stepped into my little taunt without any hesitation. *Cool!* "It was great, wasn't it?" he said, slipping his arm around me, dragging me to his broad chest. His lips grazed my ear, sending a shiver down my spine.

A chorus of gasps resounded, mostly from the girls.

"You're playing with fire, Lace."

"Didn't you know my middle name is fire?" I eased out of his embrace.

He chuckled.

Camera phones flashed. I'd bet the photos would be all over the Internet. I didn't care. It wasn't like I had a boyfriend. As for Tyler, he'd mentioned he dated, but no one steady at present.

Becca's slightly open mouth closed. "How long have you two known each other?" she asked.

"Don't worry. We're not exclusive," I said teasingly.

She leaned in to me. "Make sure you know what you're doing, New Girl." A streak of envy colored her tone.

"Thanks for the warning." I knew how to handle myself.

"So what do you have for first period?" Tyler asked.

"English. And you?" The three of us had huddled near a locker, which to my surprise was actually mine. I grabbed the combination from my purse and punched in the code on the lock.

"English too," Tyler replied. "So what about tonight? Do you want to do it again?"

Becca choked.

"Baseball," he said, glaring at her. "Get your mind out of the gutter." A hint of anger threaded through the last sentence.

"Chill, Tyler. It's not like I'm still...whatever. Lacey, I'll see you in English." Then she stomped off to a classroom down the hall.

The crowd had dispersed with the exception of five girls. All of them were pretty, toned, with boobs that any guy would love, and every one of them was a brunette. What were the odds? Was that one of the prerequisites to be in that clique?

One glance their way and red sparks shot out of their eyes. *Oh, yeah. They hate me.*

"Ignore them," Tyler whispered.

I hadn't planned on giving them my undivided attention. "Who are they?"

"Cheerleaders. We call them Grace's Posse." Tyler relaxed against a locker next to mine.

"Which one is Grace?" I flicked my eyes toward them then back at Tyler.

"She's not here." He swept his blue gaze over me as he inched closer.

"What?" I stuck a couple of books that were in my backpack into my locker and shut it, the tinny sound of the metal door bouncing off the walls.

"Do you want to grab something to eat later? I still owe you a shake and fries." His blue eyes darkened.

"As friends?" I needed to be clear on the subject.

"Isn't that what we are?" He looked past me.

In my mind, yes. In his mind, I wasn't so sure. We stood there in awkward silence. The cheerleaders had vanished. A girl and a boy sucked face at a locker farther down from mine.

Finally, I said, "Do you want to go to Roy's? They have the best fries."

"Six?" he asked as the bell rang.

I'd wanted to ask him more about what had happened between him and Becca. I filed it away for now. I could ask him tonight.

Slinking into homeroom, I shook my head. It seemed I was right back in a drama-driven high school. How I fit in was still to be determined. After all, I was the new girl who had made friends with one of the hottest guys in school.

CHAPTER 4

The rest of the week flew by. After the first tense day of school, I was able to get into a routine. I knew where my locker was. I knew where all my classes were, and my car even cooperated the entire week. Tyler and I had hung out a couple of nights. We talked mostly about baseball. I did have a chance to ask him about his relationship with Becca.

"She's a good girl with a big heart. We dated a couple of years ago. When it started to get serious, I broke it off. I wasn't ready to be exclusive with anyone," he'd said.

I'd been on the lookout all week for Kade Maxwell. I hadn't seen him after the day he walked out of the principal's office. Tyler mentioned Kade had asked for a few days off. He wasn't sure what it was about, but the rumor around school was that it had something to do with family.

Dad told me his private conversation with the principal had gotten tense, but ended on a good note. When I asked him to be more specific, he'd said it was just two adults disagreeing. While I was curious, I dropped the subject. I had a lot on my plate, and Dad didn't seem concerned.

In between practicing and studying, Becca and I hung out, too. She became my cheering section when I was on the mound throwing pitches to Tyler. I liked her a lot. She was honest. She didn't beat around the bush, she didn't sugar coat anything, and best of all, she wasn't fake.

It was the end of the school week and Becca and I were sitting on the hood of my Mustang, chatting. We still had about thirty minutes to the first bell. I'd swung by the coffee shop in town and picked up a latte for me, and a hot chocolate for Becca. I sipped on my coffee, hoping the hot liquid would take away the chill that had settled in me.

"You know it's going to get much colder than this," Becca said, smiling.

"Yeah. And your point is?"

"You look like you're about to freeze to death and it's only forty-five degrees out."

"So why don't we go in and hang out before the bell?" I knew the answer, but I asked it anyway.

"The halls have ears," she said, rolling her eyes. "When are you going to get your winter clothes, anyway?"

Great question. I had no clue. Dad had been busier than he had ever been with this new club, Rumors. He'd told me that with the college semester in session, his club was packed just about every night. It was good for him, but bad as well. We had little time to talk. I'd only seen him briefly after school. When I got up in the morning he was sound asleep. Since he was going to be home this evening, I made a mental note to ask him for some cash to go shopping. I'd offered to get a job when we moved here. He'd said to concentrate on school. With Dad's businesses, lack of money wasn't an issue. He'd given Rob, Julie, and me allowances as we were growing up, provided we did our chores around the house. I didn't have any specific chores now. Dad and I had fallen into a routine of picking up after ourselves.

"Hey, maybe we could go to the mall this weekend," Becca said. "That way I can get a new outfit for Saturday night."

I'd forgotten all about Saturday night. Her dad owned a teen-only club in town. He opened it several years ago as a place where the high school crowd could go to eat, dance and sing karaoke. The only adults allowed were the ones who worked there.

"I'm not sure I want to go," I said, taking another sip of my latte. Clubs weren't my scene. I'd been in my dad's club in LA on a few occasions when I had to drop off something he'd forgotten, like his wallet. The club was like standing in a fireplace with all the hot bodies packed in, not to mention the sweaty bodies I had to plow through to get from the front door to his office.

"You're going. You need to see my dad's club. Besides, your dad will be there, too."

My father had gotten a call from Becca's dad when she found out that Dad owned Eko Records. Apparently, Mr. Young was in the market to hire a band or two to headline on the weekends. Dad had made some calls, but most of his clients were currently on the West Coast. Maybe he could book some new clients who needed exposure.

"I don't have anything to wear." It wasn't a lie. My wardrobe consisted of casual clothes—very casual clothes. Well, I still had a few dresses from the charity events I'd attended, but those were way too fancy for a teen club.

"Hence the mall, silly. I'm not taking no for an answer."

I guess I'd been told. I blew on my hands, since my latte was now cold and almost empty. I was all for finding warmer clothes, especially gloves with warmers in them.

"Lacey, if you're this pathetic now, what are you going to do in subzero temps and mile-high snow?" Becca asked.

"Fly back to LA," I joked. It wasn't a bad idea.

"You're not going anywhere," Becca said. "I just made a friend that I like."

"Okay, don't get all huffy on me. I was just kidding." I'd been curious why she didn't hang out with any of the other girls in school. It wasn't like *she* was the new girl. I'd learned her best friend had moved at the end of last year. Since then, she just kept to herself. Sure, everyone knew her and she talked to other girls in school, but there weren't any that she cared to hang out with on a daily basis. She said a lot of them were fake and just using her to get into her dad's club.

At that moment, Tyler walked up with Grace Edison tethered to his arm. Just like he'd said, the head cheerleader ruled her clique of friends. If she said jump, they would ask how high. She was in my English class, but it wasn't until chemistry that I had a chance to meet her. She was nice to me, but it was a phony nice. She'd smile, but it never reached her eyes. I wasn't certain what her deal was yet, so I kept my tongue in check.

"Hey, guys," she said in her mousy voice. Her brown hair was swept up into a high ponytail with a blue and black ribbon wrapped around it. All the cheerleaders displayed the school colors somewhere on their clothes or bodies. I'd even spied one of her minions who had a tattoo on her wrist with the school colors. I wasn't sure if it was real. I'd always wanted a baseball inked on my upper right shoulder in the back. I had to wait until I was eighteen, though.

Becca growled her annoyance.

"Hey, Ty," I said.

"Lace, how goes it this morning?" he asked.

Becca glowered at Grace's hand glued to Tyler's arm. "Is there something you need, Grace?" Becca mashed her lips into a thin line.

"No. I saw Tyler coming out of the sports complex, and I walked with him over here." Her voice had a bitter undertone.

Tyler eyed me, trying to give me a signal of some kind. It didn't matter. I wasn't going to bite her head off—not today, anyway. I couldn't say the same for Becca.

She stuck out her chin. "You're not wanted here," she said.

Wow! This was a side of Becca I hadn't seen before. Sure, she was feisty, but not this bitchy, even when she had that small altercation with Tyler at the beginning of the week. I had yet to ask her about her and Tyler. I was saving it for a time when we knew each other a little better.

"Grace, why don't you head inside? We'll talk later. Okay?" Tyler pried her fingers from his arm.

"Sure." She pinned a death look on Becca before traipsing off.

Once she was out of earshot, Becca let loose on Tyler. "What the hell, dude? You know I hate her."

"She hasn't done anything to you," he shot back.

"What's with all this animosity, Becca?" I asked. I was the newbie and still learning the hierarchy of all the cliques in this school.

"Just old history between me and Grace." Becca hadn't spoken much about Grace except the usual cliquey stuff of the "Barbies with claws," as she liked to call them. Did I want to know? *No.* Did I need to know? *Yes.* Only because she was my friend, and friends took care of each other. If she needed a shoulder to cry on or someone to back her up, I'd be there for her.

"She's been nice to me," I said.

"That's because it's just the first week and they're feeling you out," she said. Anger still laced her tone. "Trust me. It's the calm before the storm. I've heard the rumors already. The cheerleaders don't like you."

"Hey, calm down." I narrowed my eyes. "I don't care about who likes me and who doesn't. And until they give me a reason, I'll be nice to them."

Her dark brown eyes shot daggers my way. We studied each other for a second.

"I'm sorry, girl. Grace gets under my skin." She smiled.

"We don't have much time before the bell," Tyler announced. "Let's head in."

Becca frowned at Tyler.

So Becca and I had our first little spat as friends. Given that we both had strong personalities, I was certain we would have more. While she was starting to become a good friend, I wasn't going to hate Grace just because Becca did. Sure, my intuition was telling me that Grace and her posse were bad news. I just hoped for their sake that they didn't give me a reason to go toe-to-toe with them.

As soon as we were inside, I threw my coffee cup in the trash and blew on my hands as I made my way to my locker. I had to get my trig book to study during my free period. I was cramming for the test that was set up for early the next week. My calculus test was scheduled for the week after that. Whatever Dad had said to the principal seemed to help my schedule.

"I'll see you two in English," I said over my shoulder to Becca and Tyler, who both had been scooped up by some friends. When I turned back, my face collided with a hard chest.

Strong hands grasped my shoulders. "Watch where you're going, Lacey," a male voice drawled.

Oh, no! A tingle skittered up and down my spine. I slowly lifted my gaze, and Kade Maxwell was grinning as his dimples flashed, causing the butterflies in my stomach to take flight.

I glanced behind me in search of help, but Tyler and Becca had their backs to me. I eased away, landing against the door of a janitor's closet. He grinned as he tilted his head to one side. I swallowed. He scanned the hall in both directions. I followed his line of sight. Kids talked with their friends. Others disappeared down another hallway.

"You have a problem?" I asked, looking up into his copper eyes.

Without a word, he tugged me into the janitor's closet, shutting the door. It closed with a resounding thud. I flinched. My brain screamed to run. My body didn't agree. I stood frozen. Sweat beaded on my forehead. Then he switched on the light.

Holy hell. I was alone in a closet with this god-like guy. A quick glimpse of the small space showed shelves of gallons of cleaning liquids and paper towels. *Great!* There wasn't anything of value to use to protect myself. Suddenly, my throat closed, and I struggled to swallow.

He backed me into one of the shelves, positioning his hands on either side of my head. He studied me with an intense glare, as if he were trying to pluck the life out of my soul.

My breathing became shallow. *Don't panic.* I silently laughed. I was in a closet being held captive by a guy I'd held at gunpoint. To make matters worse, I wanted to reach up and lock lips with him. *How freaky is that?* I should be worried about what he was going to do to me, especially after I sucker-punched him too.

"Nice shiner," I managed to squeak out. I'd meant to tell him that the first day of school when he walked out of the principal's office. At the time, though, it hadn't been this black.

He blinked, then a muscle ticked in his jaw. *Oh yeah. I hit a nerve.*

My heart pounded in my ears. My tongue became sandpaper rough. I tried to get saliva to wet my mouth. A combination of fear and excitement had my knees weak. I locked them just in case my body decided to betray me. *What was I saying?* It was already betraying me as tingles spread way below my belly, and down through my legs.

"What do...you...want, Kade?" I asked in the same strange raspy voice as I had that first night in the parking lot.

At the sound of his name he flinched. "An apology to start." His right hand came down, and he trailed a finger along my jaw, as his gaze dropped to my lips. He stared at them as if he were trying to decide whether to kiss me or not.

He wouldn't dare.

Then he lowered his head, so our lips were a hairsbreadth apart.

I couldn't concentrate. All I wanted him to do was touch me. I wanted those lips on me. I wanted his arms around me. I wanted to wrap my legs around his waist while I buried my hands in his hair, and to learn every muscle, dip, and valley on his body.

Yeah, right—like he would let you do that. You pulled a gun on the guy and gave him a shiner. Think about it. He's messing with you right now.

"Back away." I raised my hand and placed it on his rigid, toned stomach and pushed. He wasn't going to kiss an apology out of me.

He didn't move. "Not until I—"

"Either move or I'll make you." What was up with the stare? Was that how he scared women? If I yell, would anyone hear me?

"You think so," he whispered practically against my lips. His breath smelled of minty toothpaste.

"You want to go another round like the other night?" I asked. My lips were tingling, and he wasn't even touching them.

His hand snaked around my neck, cupping the back of my head. "Where's your gun?"

"Do you value your manly parts?"

His eyes grew wide. "You wouldn't."

"You want to test me? I mean, that shiner is looking pretty good. I could have your balls match it in color."

He laughed; I struck. My knee hit him square in the balls and he dropped to his knees. Pain etched his face along with a freaking grin that spread from ear to ear. The jerk was actually smiling.

"Who the...heck...are you?" His voice was strained.

"I'm your worst nightmare and your best wet dream all wrapped into one." *Oh, God. Why did I say that last part?*

His grin grew wider.

I rolled my eyes. What guy laughs when his crotch is in severe pain? I wrenched open the door and bolted out of the closet. I had two minutes before the final bell rang. When I got to my locker, the adrenaline was still coursing through me, and a small twinge of excitement made me laugh. I shouldn't be laughing. The guy was going to have my hide on a silver platter. Once I had the books I needed, I slammed my locker and ran to homeroom.

The door to the classroom opened and I jumped.

"Problem, Ms. Robinson?" Ms. Vander, my homeroom teacher, asked.

I shook my head vigorously.

"Then get in before I mark you late." She flicked her thumb toward the open doorway.

I walked in and dropped into my seat. Closing my eyes, I sighed. As I thought about everything I'd done to Kade, Tyler's warning flashed across my mind. *Stay away from Kade.* I still wasn't sure what that meant, but after our most recent little incident, maybe it should be the other way around.

⚜

During announcements in homeroom, the principal sent out good luck wishes to the football team—they had their first home game tonight. A pep rally was scheduled after lunch. She also reminded everyone that baseball tryouts were scheduled for next Wednesday and Thursday. I had two shots to show Coach Dean my fastball, slider, and curveball. Even though I still had a few more days to practice, my stomach did a flip at the mention of tryouts.

I had just slipped into the hall when Tammy Reese, one of the cheerleader Barbies, stalked up to me. She was a beautiful girl. Her reddish brown hair was cut short to highlight her wide blue eyes and full lips. Pity she ruined her pretty features with a scowl. I flashed her one of my winning smiles.

"You think you're so much better than us, don't you?" she asked.

Becca's words suddenly resonated in my head. *They don't like you.*

As if to prove Becca's point, she grabbed my arm, hard. Biting my lip, I glanced at her hand on my arm then up at her.

Her brown eyebrows lowered. "Well, you're not," she said. "Just because Tyler's your friend doesn't protect you."

"Good to know," I shot back. "Now, get your slimy claws off me."

"Or what?" she taunted.

A crowd had formed. Surprise, surprise. A tiny voice in the back of my head warned me to keep it together. I didn't want to disappoint my dad.

"I don't want any trouble," I said in a softer tone.

"Are you afraid, bitch?" she spat out as her nails dug into my skin.

I could take name-calling, but I stopped at "bitch." Sure, the word did describe my moods sometimes. That didn't mean I had to hear it from a person who didn't even know me. Not only that, I hadn't done anything to warrant her animosity.

That buzzing sound whirred in my head. Anger bubbled to the surface so fast I shuddered. As I blinked, the hall narrowed to just her and me.

Walk away. Baseball, baseball, baseball. I had to remind myself why I was here at this new school. "Take... your... hand... off me." I clenched my teeth.

"Or what?" she scoffed. This girl was relentless and itching for a fight. Then a malevolent grin split her burgundy lips. Her cocksure smile broke my resolve. I jerked my arm out of her hold. In the process, my elbow accidentally connected with the underside of her jaw. She stumbled backwards, her backpack falling to the ground.

"Next time, think before you put your hands on someone."

The voices grew louder as the buzzing faded in my head. Several clicking sounds from camera phones echoed in the hall.

"Watch your back," she hissed, holding her jaw.

I stalked closer to her. "Newsflash—I'm not afraid of you or anyone at this school. Spread that around."

The warning bell rang.

As I turned on my heel, a camera phone flashed in my face. *Great! Now there was evidence. Whatever.* As I strutted away, a group of girls rushed to Tammy's side. I was surprised that teachers didn't storm the hall.

All of a sudden another hand grabbed me, and my fist came up before Tyler caught it. "What the heck, Lacey! It's just me."

"Oh." I kept walking to my locker, trying to shake the nerves.

"What happened?" he asked as he followed me.

When I got to my locker, I punched in my code. I stuck my head inside and took several breaths, trying to quell the adrenaline pumping through my veins. On my last breath, I turned toward Tyler.

He pulled me to him, wrapping his muscular arms around me. "Talk to me."

Becca ambled over with a frown on her face. Was she mad because Tyler was holding me?

I pushed Tyler back. "I'm fine."

He raised his hands. "Okay. I just want to make sure."

"What's going on?" Becca asked, concern in her voice. Then her phone beeped. She opened it up and gasped before laughing. "Seriously, girl. You didn't just get into a fight with Tammy Reese."

Tyler ripped the phone out of her hands.

"Hey!"

Tyler's face tightened as he studied the screen. He lifted his head, meeting my gaze, sparks of fury in blue eyes.

"What? You're not my father. Don't look at me like that," I said.

"I'm only going to say two words. Baseball tryouts."

Why was he always the one who rained on my parade? "She started it." Now I sounded like I was talking to my father. Those were always the first three words out of my mouth when Dad looked at Julie and me after one of our sister fights. I let out a sigh. Dad wasn't going to like this if he found out, even if it was an accident.

Tyler laughed. It wasn't a funny laugh but a nervous one.

"I'm not going to let anyone threaten me. Besides, it was an accident."

The tightness around his eyes loosened as he handed the phone back to Becca. The bell rang. "I'll see you ladies in English," Tyler said, shaking his head as he strode off.

I closed the door to my locker.

"Okay, I'm not going to ask right now what that was all about between you and Tyler." Becca's words dripped with resentment. "But I do want you to spill about Tammy."

"Later," I snapped.

"Pissy, aren't you?" She laughed, her eyes dancing.

Then I laughed. We both walked into English giggling. Tyler peered at me from his seat near the far window. Then he dropped his gaze to his phone. After taking our seats, Becca tapped another student's shoulder—Zane, a lineman for the football team. He was tall and built to tackle. He turned, flashing soft brown eyes at her.

"Kade Maxwell finally showed up. Where's he been all week? I also heard that some girl gave him a shiner," Becca said, gushing with excitement.

Burying my nose in my backpack, I pulled out my English book, trying to hide the heat staining my cheeks.

Zane laughed. "Yeah, right. What girl in her right mind would hit Kade Maxwell?"

"Who's this Kade guy?" I asked. I didn't want anyone other than Tyler to know it was me who'd ruined a handsome face like Kade's. I'd have all the girls after me, for sure.

"Just the hottest badass guy in school," Becca gushed. "I also heard his brothers are back."

Zane's jaw dropped. "What? Kross, Kody, *and* Kelton are all back?"

"What kind of name is Kross?" I asked.

"Who cares about names?" Zane asked. "It's party time. They always throw the best parties. This just might be the best senior year ever."

Zane had a man crush on these guys. Then it dawned on me— Tyler's voice had hitched with excitement that night in the parking lot when he'd asked Kade about his brother Kelton. Was Tyler excited about the parties, too?

Mr. Souza, a short, gray-haired man, sat at his desk, taking roll. A couple of students snuck in, sliding into their seats before their names were called. Mr. Souza had a policy—if students were not in their seats when he took roll, then he'd mark them tardy. After the third tardy, he took points off the offender's next test. "Good morning, class," he said as he closed his red-covered grade book.

Zane swiveled forward.

"The topic for today is Shirley Jackson. We'll begin with her background, then we'll talk a little about some of her stories."

I drifted off into my own world—a world of *who the hell was Kade Maxwell?* And why did he unnerve me so? I got hot flashes when I replayed the closet scene and how his mouth barely touched mine. My lips tingled. *Snap out of it, girl.* Then I replayed the scene with Tammy. I bit my lip. Why did she hate me? I hadn't done anything to her.

Becca nudged me, ending my trip down memory lane. She nodded to the door. A tall, sexy male specimen walked in. All heads followed his movements as he made his way to Mr. Souza's desk.

Whoa!

"Welcome back, Kelton," Mr. Souza said.

So this was Kelton? He had artfully messy black hair, a strong angular jaw, and a small scar on his chin. He wore a tight, fitted black T-shirt that emphasized a toned chest and arms, and his worn-out jeans fit nicely on his hips. The only resemblance to Kade was in the build. I wasn't surprised, since Julie and I had had different features.

"Take a seat behind Ms. Robinson."

"Like I'm supposed to know who that chick is?" he asked, glaring at Mr. Souza.

"Manners, Kelton. Did you lose them at your last school?" he asked.

"I never had any. You know that, Teach."

"Enough. Ms. Robinson is right there. Raise your hand, Lacey."

Okay. Now I wanted to run out of here and hide in that closet Kade had had me in. In fact, maybe being held hostage by this guy's brother was better than this.

I didn't raise my hand, but out of the corner of my eye, I caught Becca pointing at me. Great. Just what I needed—a distracting testosterone factory staring at me, thinking I didn't even know my own name.

Running a hand through his hair, he sauntered down the aisle toward me, casual, cool and confident. In the five long strides it took him to reach me, several whispers and a few squeals erupted. "You're Lacey?" he drawled with a cocky-ass grin, showing a set of white teeth.

Grace Edison, who sat in front of Zane, muttered something about me under her breath.

Kelton's blue eyes gleamed when he met my gaze. Folding his tall physique into the seat behind me, Kelton grabbed a handful of my hair in his strong hand and sniffed, loudly.

Who did that? Well, he did, of course.

"Wow, woman, you smell delicious," he said.

I whipped around. "Get your paws off me, shithead."

"Kelton? Lacey? Quiet," Mr. Souza commanded. "Okay, class. I want everyone to turn to page twenty-five, and read 'The Lottery.' I'll give you a few minutes, then we'll discuss it. There will also be a quiz tomorrow."

Gathering all my hair, I swept it forward so the animal behind me wouldn't touch it.

"Man, you're turning me on with that spunky attitude of yours, girl. I would take a punch from you any day," he whispered.

Horrified, I shot another one of my death glares at him. "Maybe you would like a hard knee to your crotch," I whispered.

"Gee, you know how to make a guy flinch, don't you?" His voice was tight.

"Just ask your brother, Kade," I muttered.

"Lacey," Mr. Souza called. "Read."

I was trying to, if it weren't for the cocky little shit behind me.

"What?" Becca asked, horrified. "You? You're the one who gave Kade a black eye?"

I shrugged one shoulder.

"Oh, my God," she mouthed.

I opened my book and skimmed through the pages. I'd read "The Lottery" before. Shirley Jackson was one of my favorite authors. I had a collection of her short stories on my shelf at home. Before long we were discussing the themes of the story.

"We talked about the randomness of persecution as a theme. What's another one?" Mr. Souza asked, setting his gaze on me. "Lacey?"

"How dangerous it can be to follow tradition," I said.

"Very good."

"She's smart too," Kelton whispered.

The bell rang. Students scurried for the door.

I stuffed my English book in my bag. I had to get out of there.

Between Kade, Kelton, and the incident with Tammy, I needed to hide for the rest of the day.

Kelton stood in front of me, looking down from his six-foot height. "My brother was right. You're freaking gorgeous." His lips curled on one side of his mouth.

I rose. "You got a problem with that, jerk face?" *Kade thought I was hot?*

Becca giggled.

Kelton leaned in, his lips at my ear. "I don't, Sexy. But if my brother didn't have eyes on you, I would make a play for you in a heartbeat."

I shivered. His brother had eyes on me? Why didn't I believe him? After what I'd done to Kade I wasn't certain of his intentions.

I pushed him. "Get away from me. Are you, like, an animal or something?"

"I would like girls to think so," he rasped. *Christ!* His deep, smooth voice sounded just like Kade's.

"Hey, man. What brings you back to school?" Tyler asked, dodging a couple of desks to stand next to me, resting his hand on my lower back.

My muscles tensed. What was he doing with his hand on me? I wasn't his possession.

"Tyler. What's shaking?" Kelton wagged his finger between Tyler and me. "You two going out or something?"

"What? Why would you ask that?" I asked. Was it because Tyler had his hand on me?

The remaining spectators, Grace and Becca, pinned their gazes on me, Grace's being especially forceful. Her eyes were burning a hole through me. I didn't know if it was because she'd heard about my run-in with one of her squad-mates, or if she was jealous of Tyler hanging out with me.

"He's being all protective of you, Lacey. My brother isn't going to like that," Kelton announced.

"And why is that?" Tyler asked, a scowl forming on his face.

"Kade doesn't share his women, dude."

What the..."I'm sorry. I'm not an animal like you, Kelton. I don't belong to anyone. I don't even know your brother." *Although I would like to.*

"That's not what I hear," Kelton said.

Grace's face twisted into all kinds of pain as she glared at me, muttering my name and Tammy's under her breath.

Was she implying Tammy and Kade? Of course he would have a girlfriend. Why wouldn't a gorgeous guy like Kade not have one? Maybe that was the reason she had lashed out at me earlier.

The room had become deadly quiet.

"What did you say?" I asked Grace.

She glowered.

"Don't you have somewhere to be, like soothing Tammy's wounds?" I slung my backpack over my shoulder.

She narrowed her eyes at me. "Watch it, Robinson," she all but growled, which was a new sound coming from of her. "The Tammy incident isn't over. But then again, I'm sure you knew that. You started a war."

"Grace," Tyler warned.

I stepped closer to her. "As I told your Barbie robot, I don't take kindly to threats."

Grace walked backwards, never taking her eyes off me. I waved, wondering what other drama was in store for me. I'd only been at this school for a week, and already I'd managed to bully a badass dude and one of the cheerleaders.

CHAPTER 5

O n our way to chemistry the next period, Becca had explained
that Kelton was one of a set of triplets. While Kody
certainly looked like Kelton with blue eyes, the same black
hair and strong features, he had a quieter personality. We talked about
the assignments he'd missed. Class was quiet, thank God. Kelton was
paired up with Grace, of all people. Her face lit up when Ms. Clare
switched out her lab partner. When Kelton sat down, Grace sent me
one of those ha-ha looks that said *I got him and you didn't*. Little did she
know I didn't want anything to do with the guy.

I was content with Tyler as a lab partner until the teacher switched
him out and told me to sit with Kelton's brother Kody. Tyler frowned.
He got stuck with a nerdy girl who glowed ten shades of red when the
hot quarterback sat down next to her. I laughed as I watched the
exchange. She kept pushing up her glasses as she ogled Tyler.

Toward the end of class, we were working on a short experiment
when Kody turned and gave me the strangest look, as though he were
trying to read my mind.

"Lacey," he said, "are you sure you want to play baseball?"

Now that had me scratching my head. Normally people ask me why
I want to play baseball. Not *are you sure*? "Absolutely. Why do you ask?"

"No reason," he replied. "Boys can be assholes, that's all."

"Oh. I can handle them," I assured him. He reminded me of my conversation with Principal Sanders, and how she had to reprimand a few of the boys on the team. "Does your question have anything to do with Mandy Shear?" I whispered.

His knuckles turned white around the pen he was holding. The bell rang. He hurriedly gathered his books and stormed out.

Later that afternoon I sat in the gym, still puzzled by Kody's reaction to my question. But when the pep rally began, I pushed the thought aside for now and focused on the event. The cheerleaders entered first, performing a cheer in the middle of the basketball court. Once they finished, Tyler and the football team ran in, decked out in their blue and black football jerseys. The crowd exploded, whistling and clapping.

Since Tyler was the captain, he stepped up to the microphone. "Are you ready to beat Northwoods' butts tonight?"

More whistles and claps and cheers.

"Good. This is the beginning of our season. And we're taking this school all the way to state this year," he said.

Stomp stomp stomp. The bleachers rattled with excitement. Then cheerleaders jumped into a routine, ending the cheer with a human pyramid.

After the rally, I went to my last class of the day. I'd found out from Kody that neither he nor Kelton had psychology. I'd thought I'd be free from the Maxwell brothers, but then Kade walked in, chin up and confident. Next to him was a guy who looked exactly like Kelton and Kody—I assumed that was Kross.

I slithered down in my seat as I buried my head in my psychology book. *Great. Just freaking great.*

"Looks like your boy is proud of his shiner," Becca whispered over her shoulder.

She was in most of my classes. I was thankful for her presence, although Tyler seemed to be shielding me from all of the Maxwell brothers, for some reason. I had to have a talk with him, especially after the little possessive act in English this morning.

"Turn around," I whispered.

"Maybe you should. Your boy has eyes on you." She waggled her eyebrows.

Becca and I sat in the first row. Kade and his brother had taken seats in the last row near the window in the very back.

My brain told me not to turn. My body didn't listen. Sneaking a peek, I froze. Kade was staring at me intently. After my heart stopped sputtering, I glared at him. *Two could play this game.*

"I told you," Becca whispered.

"Shut up," I muttered under my breath.

"I would say he wants you bad." She giggled.

What guy would like a girl who pulled a gun on him and kneed him in the balls?

The teacher, Mr. Dobson, a gentleman of fifty, walked in at that moment. When he spoke, I tuned him out. The class went by in a blur. If we had homework, I wouldn't know. My brain was so consumed with how it would feel to have Kade's lips on me. I replayed each event from the first day I met him. Then I couldn't shake what Kelton had said. "My brother was right, you're freaking gorgeous." I bristled when I remembered his other comment. "Kade doesn't share his women." Who did these guys think they were?

I didn't realize that class was over until Becca nudged me. "Are you staying here?"

Blinking, I scanned the room. Except for Becca and me, the room was deserted.

"Whoa! You look like you've seen a ghost," she said, with her hands on the straps of her backpack. "He's not going to kill you, if that's what you're worried about."

I let out a nervous laugh. "Did you see the way he looked at me?"

She snorted. "Yeah, Lacey. The guy wants to do something to you, but I don't think it has anything to do with killing."

"Ha ha. I'm sure he has lots of girls he can go out with."

"Oh, you're right. But Kade Maxwell doesn't do steady girlfriends. I don't know if the triplets do. They haven't been here since their freshman year."

I sat up straighter in my seat. "Where have they been?" I asked.

She walked to the door and closed it then sat down in the seat next to me. "You're new, and you should probably know some of the history." She made it sound like knowing whatever she was about to tell me would condemn me.

"Yeah, like Mandy Shears. Are you ever going to tell me about her?"

She flinched. "Not at school." Her gaze darted to the door then back at me.

Wow! Something bad must've happened to that girl.

"Anyway, a guy named Greg Sullivan hated Kade. Actually, they despised each other. It was an ego thing. You know how guys are. They both competed against each other for the same spots in football, basketball, and baseball. Each time, Kade won. They would always get into fights. When they both started their sophomore year, Greg thought a new year, new tryouts, and maybe this would be his year. But when Kade won again, Greg had a freaking cow. He destroyed the boys' locker room—threw a trashcan at the mirrors. Then to top it off, the triplets got positions on the varsity baseball team that year as freshmen, even over some of the returning seniors. Then Greg made it his mission to get back at the Maxwell brothers, especially Kade. They said that Greg and his buddies beat the shit out of Kody, because he was the weakest of the brothers. When Kade found out, he went nuts. The rumor—and it was never verified—was that Kade, Kross, Kelton, and some friend of Kade's, Hunter, jumped Greg and put him in the hospital."

I gasped.

"I know, right?" she said, pushing a strand of hair behind her ear. "But there's more. Kade ended up in jail. Greg's family pressed charges against him."

"So why didn't Kade go to the police when Kody was beaten?"

"I don't know. All I know is when school started up again the next year, the triplets were gone and so was Greg. The triplets went to some military academy. Now, they're back at Kensington, to graduate with Kade. They tested out of most of their junior subjects. At least that's what I heard."

And Kelton called *me* smart. "What happened to Greg?"

"No clue." She shook her head slightly.

"Why didn't Kade go with his brothers to the academy?"

"Don't know that either. Listen, Kade's hot. And as a friend, I warn you. He spits out women left and right. Not to mention that he's known for his temper."

Tempers didn't bother me. I had one. "Is Kade dating anyone? Like Tammy Reese?"

She laughed. "He dated her last year. I think it was one date. Why? You like him, don't you?"

I shrugged a shoulder, playing with my notebook. "He's hot, like you said. But if he's anything like Kelton—"

"Nobody's like Kelton." She giggled. "So, why did you punch Kade?" She studied me intently.

I hardly knew Becca, so I wasn't ready to tell her about the panic attacks I got because half my family was violently murdered—not yet, anyway. "He was being an ass. So you don't want me jumping his bones?" Laughing, I changed the subject quickly, hoping that she wouldn't probe.

"Girlfriend, I would love for you to jump his bones. But I like you a lot, Lacey, and I don't want to see you get hurt. You don't seem like the kind of girl that does one night stands."

She was so spot on. I'd only had sex once, and that had been with Brad. I thought he loved me. Boy was I wrong.

We left and talked all the way to our cars. She filled me in on how she thought the triplets would be a shoo-in for this year's baseball team. Kade was awesome, too, she said, and the last time the team had won a championship was when Kade and his brothers had played.

When we made it to our cars, the parking lot was completely empty except for our cars. I wasn't surprised, since it was Friday.

"Is Kade trying out, too?" I asked with a hand on my car door.

"No, I don't think so. He hasn't played since his sophomore year."

"Because of the Greg Sullivan thing?"

"Yeah. Since that incident, Kade hasn't played sports. It's a real shame because the four of them were a force to be reckoned with on the field."

"What position did Kade play?" Not that it mattered. I was just curious.

"Third base. He was awesome. He had a great batting average. He was always hitting homeruns. He was major-league good. Scouts would be all over him after the games." She leaned against her VW bug.

A lump lodged in my throat. My brother Rob had been scouted by the major leagues when he was playing at ASU. In fact, he was ready to sign with the Dodgers' organization when he'd found out about Mom and Julie. He had just driven back to Arizona to pack up his apartment when Dad called him after the police left our house that night. I still held out hope for Rob. Like me, he was still grieving, although he dealt with the deaths a lot like Dad did, keeping himself busy at the club in LA. I'd told him that he should pursue his dreams, but he'd said he just needed time. He was still in touch with the Dodgers. I was praying like hell that he would take their offer.

"Are you okay, Lacey?" Becca rubbed my arm. "You have tears in your eyes."

"Yeah, just thinking."

"You want to talk about it?"

"No. I have to go," I said, blinking away tears. I silently berated myself. I didn't want anyone to see the weaker side of me. I had to be tough. I had to make the team.

After Becca and I parted, I rushed to my psychiatrist appointment. This was the first time I was meeting Dr. Davis, my new shrink, and I was looking forward to it. My former psychiatrist had nothing but great things to say about him. I was also anxious to talk to someone. I would've met him sooner, but he'd been booked during the last few weeks.

I parked in the lot behind a gray two-story building in the town of Lancaster. I snatched my purse, got out, and locked my door. As I was walking around to the entrance, I caught a glimpse of a black truck stopped at the red light on the corner of Fifth and Main. I did a double take. *Please don't let it be Kade.* He was the last person who I wanted to know that I was seeing a psychiatrist. Dad had been specific when he asked Dr. Meyers to find a therapist who didn't have an office in Ashford.

I squinted to see if the truck had the hearts on the passenger door, but I couldn't tell from this distance—although this truck had tinted windows like his. What were the odds? Not wanting to look like a lost idiot, I strode right past the entrance to the building as though I was headed to one of the other shops in town. Several establishments and restaurants lined Main Street. I crossed over the side street. Up ahead, a small boutique like the ones my sister and I used to shop at in California caught my eye. Well, she shopped. I just went along with her on our way home from school occasionally. She would always say, "Lace, you need to dress like a girl." I hadn't cared much about clothes, and still didn't. But the more Dad's words rolled around in my brain—"I would like see my little girl wear a dress or a skirt every now and then"—the more I considered giving the girlie-wear a try, to bring one of those elusive smiles to his face.

I was so deep in thought I'd forgotten why I was walking this way until a couple of beeps sounded from behind me, indicating someone had unlocked their car door. I flicked a quick glance over my shoulder, and I shouldn't have. The black truck idled, waiting for a pedestrian to cross the road. I still couldn't tell if it was Kade or not. The picture I'd taken didn't show his license plate. Regardless, I put some energy in my step and practically ran into Darla's Boutique.

"Something wrong, miss?" the sales clerk asked.

"No," I said, and I swallowed.

"Can I help you with something, then?" She wore a tight red dress, tons of old-fashioned jewelry, and she smelled like a nursing home.

"I'm sorry, I was looking for the deli. I must have gone too far."

"No, you didn't. Just one more block down," she said, pointing to her right.

"Oh. Thank you." I didn't move. I had to wait a few minutes to be sure the coast was clear.

"It looks like you're running from something. Can I help?" Her thick mascara lashes stood out over her smooth, pale skin. Her soft tone made me relax a tiny bit.

"Uh...no. I was just trying to dodge a friend."

"Why don't you look around? Give the friend some time to realize you're not here."

She had a point, but I needed to get to my appointment. I checked my phone. Crap. I had two minutes to run down to Dr. Davis' office. He charged by the hour whether I was there or not. If I didn't show, Dad was going to have my hide. "Thanks. I do need to go though." I'd been in here a few minutes. The truck had to be gone by now.

She shrugged as I turned for the door.

Once outside I turned left, and my heart sputtered. The black truck was parked on the street, to my right. I could almost touch it. My pulse started to sprint. *Freaking hell.* The five hearts painted on the passenger door above the handle—*oh, it* was *Kade.* I dropped my head and sped past the vehicle. I was just about to cross the side street when someone grabbed my arm. I spun around. I was ready to swing my purse when the guy let go.

"Hey, chill, lady," the blond-haired dude said, holding up his hands.

"Buddy, if you value your life, I would back off." I was shaking inside. Alarms were blaring in my head.

He lowered his hands. "I'm just here to give you a message." His voice was deep.

I glanced past him. The black truck was still parked at the corner. "What's the message?" I asked.

Flicking his finger behind him, he said, "Kade wants to talk to you."

Quirking an eyebrow, I snorted. "What are you? His bodyguard?"

"I don't want any trouble."

"If you didn't want any trouble, then you shouldn't have grabbed me the way you did. Now, tell Kade to eff off." I had to go. Dad was going to kill me if I didn't make this appointment. I was about to cross the street when he laughed.

"He said you would tell me that."

I wasn't angry anymore. I was downright infuriated. I clenched my hands into fists. *Who the hell did he think he was to send a message through this guy?* It wasn't even a message. If he wanted to talk to me he should've just gotten out of his truck and said something. Then again, maybe he was afraid of me after this morning in the janitor's closet. I discarded that thought. He'd seemed to be enjoying himself. "Oh, and I didn't catch your name," I said.

"Hunt."

"So, Hunt. Do you go to our school?" This was the guy Becca had mentioned.

"Nah. I graduated last year."

I suspected as much. I'd only been at the school a week, but I would remember seeing this dude. He had a large scar over his left eyebrow that he tried to hide with his wavy blond bangs. Plus he was built like a bear. I'd bet he played football.

"I'll tell Kade what you said." He turned to leave.

"One more thing," I called. "Tell him when it comes to me, hunting season is closed."

Hunt grinned. I ran down one block, around Dr. Davis' office, and to my car. I was too worked up to meet Dr. Davis for the first time, and I wasn't sure if Kade was watching. I didn't want to take that chance.

By the time I pulled out of the lot, Kade's truck was gone. Waiting for the light to change, I spotted a gun shop down the street. I had to tell Dad about it. I wanted a new gun. Joe, who worked at the gun range, recommended I check out a Glock. He'd said it was lighter than the Kimber I had.

Driving back to the house, I turned up the radio. They were playing Zeal's new song. *Oh, my God. Dad didn't tell me that they'd released it.* I loved them. Their songs were alternative rock, and the lead singer had a raspy voice with a great tone. All the females loved J.J. When he sang I always felt like he was singing just to me. When he stared into the camera with his deep green eyes in his music videos, it was heart-stopping, especially when he sang his gut-wrenching ballads. The emotion he put behind each song made women want to drop their panties. I'd hung out with the band when they were in the studio recording. I knew J.J. had had a bad breakup with a pretty model, and from that he wrote killer love songs.

As I listened a tear came to my eye. I'd watched them rehearse this song, but I hadn't heard the final version. *Wow!* J.J's fans were going to weep. The chorus was amazing. However, the part of the song that sent my body into tingles was, *"Her touch was magical, her caress was soothing, and her silky voice slid along every nerve, awakening the man in me."*

Sniffling, I pulled into my driveway as the song ended. When I did, Dad came storming out of the house, grimacing. *Uh-oh.* Cutting the engine, I jumped out. Dr. Davis must have called him.

"Where have you been? You missed your appointment." His tone was deadly as he came down the brick path from the front porch to my car.

"I'm sorry, Dad. I ran into that Kade guy in front of Dr. Davis' office, and I didn't want him to know I was seeing a psychiatrist." I'd never lied to my dad, and I wasn't going to start now. Besides, fear fueled his anger. He knew I could handle myself a little better now. Still, he worried about me. I mean, he couldn't be with me every minute of the day. Dr. Meyers had told him that he needed to let me breathe and not suffocate me. The only way I was going to learn to deal with life was to get out and face my fears.

"Lacey Robinson," he said, rubbing a hand along his jaw. "I thought something happened to you." His chest rose then he let out a breath.

"I'm sorry. I should've called you."

"You're damn right." He threw his arms around my neck, hugging me. "I know I need to let you live your life, but...I can't lose you, Sweet Pea."

Forget the one tear that fell when I listened to the song—I now had a river of them coursing down my cheeks. "Dad, you're not going to lose me," I said between sniffles. "I'm so afraid of people in school finding out about my PTSD."

"It's okay. I explained to Dr. Davis about our concerns about privacy. He understands. But you can't keep missing appointments because you run into classmates." His voice was firm yet gentle.

"I know, but I panicked."

"You've got to learn to trust a few people in your life," he said as we walked into the house.

"I don't know, Dad. It's not like I'm going to be here another year, especially if I get the scholarship to ASU." I was afraid to get too close to anyone. Not because I was off to college in another year—I didn't trust myself. The whole breakup with Brad hurt, but part of me was also humiliated for not seeing the signs: he cheated on me with another guy.

Dad shrugged. "Trust your friends. I'm not saying that you have to tell them your life's story, but you do need to relax. You know that's going to help you with your PTSD."

Again, I couldn't argue. I was frightened I would snap at school, in front of everyone. I didn't want people to know I had a mental illness. The bullies would come out of the woodwork like cockroaches. *Oh, God*—what if I wasn't allowed to try out because of my PTSD? After this past week, I was beginning to think that moving to Massachusetts might not have been a good idea. "Relaxing has nothing to do with trusting people, Dad."

"Regardless, remember what Dr. Meyers told you. You need to learn to break down your walls. When you do that, then you'll begin to heal. You've made significant improvement in less than a year, Sweet Pea. And baseball is helping that, I'm sure. Now allow your friends to get to know you, that's all I'm saying."

I only had two friends—Tyler and Becca. Could I trust them? The jury was still out, although Tyler had a large part of my trust. He hadn't said anything to anyone about the gun incident with Kade—at least, not that I knew of.

Dad made a pot of chili for dinner. He had a few signature dishes—aside from chili, he made the most delicious lasagna, and he loved to make beef stew.

After dinner, I washed dishes and cleaned up while Dad went into the family room to pick out a couple of movies. I decided to ditch the football game. I sent Becca a text message letting her know I would be hanging out with my dad. She was disappointed that I would miss the game. I hated that she was upset, but it was the first time in a long time Dad didn't have to work on Friday night. He'd hired a night manager, and he wanted to see how the guy handled the situation without him for one night. If Dad had to go in, though, he would. He'd said he was tired, and the dark circles under his eyes supported that, plus he wanted to hang out with me.

Once the kitchen was cleaned, I popped two bags of popcorn in the microwave then joined Dad in the family room. Halfway through our second movie my phone beeped.

It was a text from Tyler. *Where were you? You missed my game.*

I'm sorry. My dad stayed home tonight. Hanging with him. Did you win?

Of course.

Cocky, aren't you?

Maybe. Need help practicing tomorrow?

Yep. I could always use his help.

See u at the field.

"Everything okay?" Dad stretched in the leather recliner.

"Yeah. It was just Tyler asking if I was practicing tomorrow. I have to keep the momentum up for tryouts next week."

"Jot down the dates on the calendar in the kitchen for me, please," he said.

After I put my phone on the coffee table, I curled up again on one end of the couch. We resumed watching *Miracle.* Dad loved this movie. We'd watched it at least a dozen times during the past year. He'd said the story instilled a sense of how humans could overcome adversity. I liked it because it showed me dreams could come true. As the credits rolled and Dad snored, I said a small prayer that we would both make it through this next year.

❧

PUFFY CLOUDS DRIFTED LAZILY across the sky as the sun rose on Saturday morning. I met Tyler at the school's ball field bright and early. He had everything ready for our two-hour practice instead of three. I couldn't do more than that. My arm was becoming a noodle with all the pitches I'd been throwing.

"Hey, Lacey," Tyler said in a chipper voice. "You look well rested." He wore a Kensington High sweatshirt and black sweatpants.

"I do? Or are you being sarcastic because I didn't go to the game last night?"

"Maybe." He dumped a bag of baseballs into a five-gallon bucket behind home plate.

"I told you I was sorry. Why was it so important for me to be there?"

He raked his gaze over me slowly. *Ooookay.* Under his scrutiny, a sinking feeling swirled in my stomach. Dropping the bag he'd been holding, he gently grasped my wrists.

I didn't move. What was he doing? We were friends. Moving closer, his gaze lowered to my lips. I blinked a few times, praying I didn't have to kick him in the balls like I'd done to Kade.

"Get a room, you two." Out of nowhere, a familiar voice cut through the sudden tension between Tyler and me. I was never so glad to hear Kelton's voice.

Slowly, Tyler dragged his attention from me to Kelton. "Hey, dude." He let go of me.

What the heck just happened? "What's he doing here?" I asked, trying to shake the haze from my head.

"I asked him and Kross to join us this morning. They're both vying for a position on the team. I thought they could help—you can throw pitches, they can practice their batting and fielding."

"Yeah, girl. We'd like to see what all the fuss is about. Tyler seems to think you're great. Me, I don't believe it," Kelton said.

I narrowed my eyes. *What an ass.*

"Hey, don't get your panties in a wad. I'm just saying," he rasped as he put a blue ball cap on backwards.

Images of me strangling Kelton popped into my brain. I'd been hanging out with boys my entire life. I even put up with a lot of crap from the team back in California, but Kelton was one for the books. Why he got under my skin more than anyone was beyond me. Or maybe I knew, and I didn't want to admit it. After all, he sounded just like Kade. It was clear that Kade and Kelton were related. Granted, all the Maxwell brothers were gorgeous, but looks only went so far. Kade had a quiet intensity about him. He gave me the impression he fought hard and loved harder.

"Where's Kody? Doesn't he play?" I asked.

"Not this year." Kelton tossed his bag on the ground near the backstop. "He's 'pursuing other interests.'"

Kelton's lookalike brother strode over from the dugout, tall and muscular. Side by side, I could see that he had bulkier biceps than Kelton.

"This is my brother, Kross."

I flicked my head at him. "What's up?"

"Well, now. I've heard so many things about you," Kross drawled in the same voice as Kelton. His blue eyes seemed a little darker than his brother's.

I rolled my eyes. "Did you now?" At this moment, I realized that Kody had a slightly lower pitch to his tone than these two brothers.

"When I first saw you in psychology I didn't agree with Kade. I only saw the back of your head. Up close, though, Kade was right. You are freaking hot," Kross said as he sized me up like I was some piece of meat.

A faint buzzing whirred in my head. "Is that how you two pick up girls? By looking at them as if you're starving?"

"It works," Kelton said nonchalantly, like I should know this.

"You must pick up tramps, then."

"Lacey?" Tyler snapped.

"What? I'm tired of these two morons talking to me like I'm some prize that they have to compete for. Their innuendos are disgusting."

"Lacey," Kross said, slipping his sports bag from his shoulder. "I'm sorry. I'm not a jackass like my brother Kelton here can be." Unlike Kelton's and Kade's shaggy crops, Kross's black hair was cut short and shaved on the sides.

I was thankful for the different hairstyles. Plus it also helped that Kelton was wearing black track pants, and Kross wore a pair of gray wind pants. At least I could tell these two apart. "Could've fooled me," I said.

"Hey, whose side you on, bro?" Kelton demanded.

"Shut up, man." Kross whirled on his brother. "If Dad heard the way you talk to some girls, he'd tan your hide. If Kade heard it, you know he wouldn't hesitate to go a few rounds in the ring." Turning his attention back to me, he smoothed his hand over his head. "Forgive us —or at least me. There's no excuse for his behavior."

"I accept your apology, Kross. Maybe there is hope for some of you." I glowered at Kelton.

He batted his long lashes my way. "I'm not changing who I am, so get over it," he said.

"Whatever. Just remember I can dish it out too," I countered. "I have a mean right hook. Just ask Kade."

Tyler pushed Kelton. "Get out to shortstop."

"Anytime, girl. The ring awaits." He stalked off to take his place at shortstop with his glove in his hand.

I had no idea what he meant by "ring." Given that Kross referred to something similar, I guessed he meant a boxing ring. It might be fun to box with one of these guys.

"Lacey, take the mound," Tyler said with a little irritation in his tone. "Kross, why don't you catch for now?"

Kross donned a catcher's mitt and ball cap then got a ball out of the bucket.

"Take a few warm-up pitches and loosen your arm," Tyler said as he grabbed a bat out of his bag near the backstop.

I got my glove then trotted to the mound. Loosening up, I threw the ball lightly into Kross's glove. After a few warm-up pitches, I adjusted my stance on the mound, placing both feet on the rubber. I held my glove chest high with my right hand inside, gripping the seams of the baseball. I took a small step back, preparing for my windup. In one fluid motion, I raised my left knee in a high kick, pivoted my right foot and threw the ball, hitting Kross's glove dead on with a thud.

"Holy flippin' crap," Kelton said from behind me at shortstop.

Kross whistled.

I went through the same moves again. Pitching was a unique combination of many movements, and all of them needed to be in sync to deliver the perfect pitch. If the moves were fluid and performed correctly, then I could add velocity to my fastball. My mind and body weren't quite in sync yet to throw the perfect pitch. I had to remember to relax. Pitching always reminded me of dancing.

My parents had insisted that all of us kids take ballroom dancing at an early age. They believed that learning dance moves helped to learn balance and coordination. My mom had said it instilled confidence and grace, which was what every girl needed to learn. I'd hated ballroom dancing. It interfered with baseball on Saturday mornings. But as I got better at pitching, I thanked my parents for forcing me to dance with boys. The results had helped me to gain the stamina needed for pitching.

I threw a few more fastballs and curveballs.

"Did I tell you that I love you?" Kelton teased from behind me. "So I take back what I said. Are you sure you're a girl?"

I turned. "You realize you just said you love me but doubt that I'm a girl. Is there something you'd like to share?" I asked, smiling the whole time.

He flipped me the finger. Kross and Tyler laughed.

Maybe it wasn't an apology, but it didn't matter. Kelton and I were going to have a very tense friendship. Sometimes guys showed how they felt about girls in different ways and Kelton's way, I was starting to see, was sarcasm. I could handle him. After all, I was just as feisty.

We practiced for over two hours. I pitched, and each of them took turns batting. Kross struck out. Kelton hit my fastball into the outfield. Tyler hit a homerun off my slider. I still had work to do on that pitch. Then I played shortstop and outfield. Pitching wasn't my only position. I'd learn to play just about every one, growing up. I'd even played left field for a women's softball team when I was twelve. I only settled on pitching because the ability to strike out a batter gave me a high—when the batter would swing, then realize he'd swung at nothing.

When we decided to call it quits, I looked around. Until that moment I hadn't seen the audience who had gathered. A group of boys sat in the front row of the stands along the first base line. Several girls congregated in seats behind the dugout on the third base side. I laughed as we packed up.

"What's so funny?" Kross asked.

"I'm always amazed at the number of girls you guys seem to draw. It's like they found out some hot music group was down on the field, so they dressed up and came down to get an autograph or something." I couldn't blame them for their interest in hot guys. But surely they must have other things to do on a Saturday morning.

Kross laughed, as did Kelton. Tyler, however, remained straight-faced. Maybe he was used to all the attention.

"It's flattering, but I try to ignore them." Kross handed me a Gatorade out of his bag.

"Wow, thanks." I'd brought water, but Gatorade was way better, especially since it was the orange flavor.

"I am a nice guy."

Kelton stuck his finger in his mouth as though he were forcing himself to puke.

"Shut up." Kross glared at his brother.

Kelton picked up his sports bag. "Meet you at the car, bro. I have a fan base to attend to. Lacey, nice job, girl. You're ready. Tyler, later, dude." Then he swaggered into the crowd of girls who were calling his name.

"Close your mouth, Lacey," Kross said, tapping my chin. "My brother may be an ass most of the time, but he knows when to give a compliment. And he's right. You're amazing. Tyler was right too. I've never seen a girl who can pitch like that. How fast is your fastball?"

"She throws at about seventy miles per hour," Tyler said as he tucked his catcher's mitt in his bag.

"I gotta run. Let's practice one more time before tryouts on Wednesday," Kross said. "Until then, see you around." He patted me on the shoulder, then half the girls around Kelton swarmed Kross like bees to a hive.

Silence stretched between Tyler and me. I helped him pick up the handful of baseballs sitting next to the backstop and pile them into the bucket.

"Are you going to the Cave tonight?" I asked, swinging my bag over my shoulder. Girls tittered loudly around Kelton and Kross.

"My dad and I are having dinner with a scout from Florida State." Tyler lifted the bucket by the handle. "Lace, can we talk?"

"Becca's waiting for me," I said. "I have to go." I wasn't prepared to discuss that awkward almost kiss. Besides, with the gossipy girls hanging close by, this definitely wasn't the place to talk. "Good luck with the scout." I jogged off the field.

As I ran, I thought more about the compliments Kross and Kelton had given me. They were validation, which was what I needed to stay focused and to boost my confidence. I just had to keep that swagger intact and through tryouts on Wednesday.

CHAPTER 6

Becca and I had a great time at the mall. After I'd left the guys in the crowd of girls, I'd bolted home, showered, and changed, then picked up Becca. Dad gave me five hundred dollars to buy clothes. I couldn't buy a whole wardrobe, and I didn't want to. If I was only going to be here until the end of the school year then there was no sense in investing too much money in winter clothes. I bought a winter jacket, a pair of knee high leather boots, two pairs of Buckle jeans, a couple of sweaters, and gloves—I wasn't leaving the mall without gloves. Becca tried to coax me into buying a crocheted mini skirt, but I chickened out. I wasn't that brave yet.

Dad had to work that evening at his club, Rumors, but before he headed out, he had to stop by the Cave. He'd secured the band *Two for Two* to play at the club, and Mr. Young, Becca's dad, was stoked.

"I might see you over there, Sweet Pea," he'd said as he grabbed his keys from the kitchen counter. "If not, don't stay out too late."

"I won't, Dad."

"Let me know how the band does, too. I have high hopes for them. They've only played a few venues. They're still trying to find their groove," he said, pocketing his phone. "My cell is on vibrate, so if you need me, I'll have it in my pocket."

"I know, Dad. Don't worry. I'll be fine."

He'd gotten in the habit of reiterating the same message every night he went to work. Guilt was etched on his face. He couldn't babysit me every minute of the day.

When Dad left, I went upstairs and changed. I figured I would wear my new Buckle jeans. They were straight through the legs— perfect to wear with my new boots. The style I bought was their Rock Revival, which had that worn out look with little nick marks just below the front pockets, and heavy cream colored stitching around the pockets and waistband. I decided on a short-sleeve, black cotton scoop-neck top that hung below my breasts. Underneath I wore a pink cami. I didn't know if it would get stuffy in the club or not. I checked myself in the mirror.

My phone beeped as I was walking down the stairs. Pulling it out of my back pocket, I opened the text message.

Where are you? It was from Becca.

On my way.

The band your father booked is hot.

No kidding. Most of the boy bands Dad signed were hot. Turning on a few lights, I locked the front door then got into my car.

Darkness pressed in and the breeze carried the faint scent of grease as I pulled into the parking lot, looking for a place to park. There wasn't a single spot open. Maybe it was always packed.

Abandoning the parking lot in front of the Cave, I drove into a lot across the street. More vehicles were filling up the empty spaces around me. I found one in the back, sandwiched between two large trucks, and facing an open field. I grabbed my purse and slid out. The area businesses catered to equipment rental companies and ware-houses, with a deli and a pizza place nearby. Becca had mentioned that her dad wanted a place that wouldn't complain about loud music or crowds.

The marquee blinked as I walked across the street. *Tonight: Two for Two.* I dodged cars as I made my way toward the factory-like building —two-story brick with tall thin windows and black bars across them. A lighted sign above the glass double doors read "The Cave." I could already hear the beat of the music getting louder as I approached the entrance.

A hulking bouncer stood guard outside under the portico, with his massive arms crossed in front of him. "ID, please," he said.

Flipping open my purse, I dug out my wallet and flashed my license.

He scanned it under a light on the small table he was standing next to. "Stop at the window and pay," he said.

I kept my wallet in hand and did as I was told, waiting behind a group of boys. When they scurried away, I paid the five-dollar cover charge before the goth lady at the window stamped my hand with the word *cave*. Dumping my wallet into my purse, I strode up a carpeted incline leading into the mouth of the club.

A roped-off balcony with plush couches and chairs wrapped around three sides of the room. Dad's club had a similar setup for VIP guests. I laughed, wondering who the VIP teenager guests would be. Bodies gyrated and swayed to the beat of the music. Since Dad had just signed *Two for Two,* I didn't know this song.

Trying to find Becca in this melee was going to be a monumental task. It seemed the whole school was here. Standing near an empty table, I sent her a text to let her know where I was.

Then the band stopped. "We'll take a break and be back in fifteen," Lenny, the lead singer, said. I'd only met him a couple of times in the studio in LA.

The crowd dispersed as the jukebox took over, blaring a Kenny Chesney song. I checked my phone and Becca hadn't responded. *Oh well*. Since the crowd thinned out a bit, I decided to walk around.

Then I stopped. Kade was stalking toward me. The closer he got, the more my pulse jumped. He didn't strike me as the type of guy who hung out at a teen club. Something hot and wild heated up my insides, spreading like wildfire throughout my abdomen. His eyes fixed on me with such intensity that a bead of sweat rolled down my temple. A voice in my head told me to run out of the building, but another weaker voice whispered to run to him. The inner debate was settled when my feet wouldn't move. Maybe it was the challenge in his eyes— if I did, he would chase me, and I believed that he desperately wanted to. Our recent encounters were far from over. I just wasn't prepared to deal with him right now.

His hand grazed my thigh as he passed me. Disappointment and relief whisked through me until his fingers brushed along my thigh again. I sucked in air, lots of it. Then his hand crawled up my hip, pressing lightly as though he wanted me to face him. If I hadn't been caught like a girl in heat, off-guard, and standing in a public place, I would've kicked him in the groin again.

"Walk with me," he whispered. "And don't make a scene."

What was with this guy? Was he here to settle the score for me kicking him in the balls? Or all the other things I'd done to him?

"I'm not going anywhere with you." I turned slightly and locked eyes with him.

He grinned. "Wanna bet?"

Kids walked past us, oblivious to our exchange. I moved out of the way of incoming traffic, closer to a round table against the wall. "Yeah. And you'll lose."

"How so?" One stride, and he was close to me again.

"Are you thick or something?"

His eyes darkened, and the amused look transformed into that blank expression again—the kind my mom told me to be careful of.

I didn't flinch. I didn't run. I didn't even move. Out of the corner of my eye, I caught a glimpse of Becca bouncing toward us.

He didn't say a word. He didn't even take his gaze from mine. I wanted to slap him out of his unnerving glare.

"Too much tension between you two." Becca's voice was chipper. "Lacey, let's go. Your dad is backstage with the band. Oh, my God, I can't thank him enough for what he's done." Her white sweetheart-neckline top glowed in the lights.

Kade blinked. Then he tipped his head, brows knitted.

I didn't want too many people knowing Dad owned a record label. Like Becca, I didn't want people to suck up to me to get an audition, like some of the kids had at Crestview. I waved mockingly at Kade as Becca tugged me with her.

"I think he wants to kick your ass," Becca said, plowing through standing bodies.

"Now you believe me?"

"Nah. I was just kidding. Christ, girl. The lust between you two was off the charts." Her dark eyes sparkled with delight.

"Shut up. Where's my dad?"

"Oh, change the subject. Fine. But don't say I didn't warn you."

"Whatever."

I was so confused. Kade wanted something from me, but if he had lustful intentions, then he had a funny way of showing it. I mean, why not just ask me out? Or why couldn't he just say what was on his mind? Why did he have to send Hunt to talk to me while I was in Lancaster yesterday?

Slowly, we made our way toward the back of the club. "I saw you out on the field today, Lacey," one of a group of boys said. "You were awesome."

I nodded silent thanks at them. I had no idea who they were. Then someone grasped my arm. Thinking it was Kade, I balled my hand into a fist. Tammy Reese had her dirty fingers around my arm.

"What is it with you and my arm? Do you want to date me or something?"

"Ha ha. You're so funny."

"Back off, Tammy," Becca said.

"Or what?"

"Or I'll have the bouncer throw your ass out of here. Better yet, I'll make sure you're not allowed in the club again."

"Fine." Tammy let go of my arm, and leaned toward me. "The guys are never going to let you play baseball. They're going to make your life hell, like they did the last girl." Then she disappeared back into the crowd.

"Don't worry about her. The scuttlebutt around school is that you're better than some of the guys on the team. Plus she's jealous of the attention you're getting from Kade. Come on." Becca flicked her head toward the stage.

Tammy could have the attention. I was more concerned about what they'd done to the last girl. After all, she was supposedly killed.

Strong hands landed on my waist, lifting me in the air. *What was it with the people in this club?*

Becca's eyes went wide as she smoothed her hands down her mini skirt, looking past me with puppy dog eyes.

My feet barely touched the ground as my attacker spun me around to face him as if he and I were ice dancers. "Put me down, jerk."

"Now, girl." Kelton's lips curled into a wolfish grin. "Don't get nasty. I was just going to say hi."

"Then tap me on the shoulder if you want to get my attention."

His arms were cemented on me as my feet dangled. The guys standing next to him were laughing.

"Kelton," I said in my sweetest voice. "Please set me down." Kids were staring.

"Don't make a scene. My father will cream your ass." Becca laid delicate fingers on Kelton's biceps.

His handsome face darkened into a frown. "I'm not letting you down until you apologize."

I wasn't buying his feigned pouting. "Apologize for what?" My voice hitched higher.

He lowered me until my feet touched his. "The longer I hold you, Gorgeous, the harder I'm going to get, if you catch my drift."

Every muscle in me tightened. The crowd behind Kelton parted and Kade strode up.

"Let her go, Kel," Kade said. "Her dad is coming this way. I don't want any trouble."

"I'd say you're screwed." I grinned.

"I just want an apology. She called me a jerk, and I was being nice," Kelton said.

"Poor baby." I stuck out my lower lip.

Kade shot me a glare, jaw clenched. Then his eyes softened, as though he were pleading with me to give Kelton what he wanted. It was clear to me Kade didn't want to make a scene. I didn't either, but I couldn't help myself. Kelton was a pain in the butt.

People were staring. "Fine. I'm sorry, Kelton."

"I don't like your tone, but I'll let you off the hook for now. Besides, I'll have plenty of time to get under your skin, anyway," he drawled, the muscles in his face relaxing. *Asshat.*

He relaxed his arms, and I slowly backed away into a solid wall of muscle.

"What the hell, Kelton?" Becca grabbed his arm, dragging him away.

"Hey, Sweet Pea," Dad said from behind me. "Are you okay?"

I nodded at Kade before turning to Dad. A deep line creased the spot between his eyebrows.

"I'm good. Just a little bantering with one of the ball players—you know how guys can be."

"Who's the boy?" Dad asked, gesturing at him with his chin.

"Kade's brother. Believe it or not, there are two more of him —triplets."

Dad harrumphed. "Do I have to be worried about them?"

"Da-a-ad. We're not having this conversation right now." *No way. Not in a room full of high school kids.*

"Hey, Kade," he said, looking past me. Was Kade still behind us? *Oh, God. Was he stalking me?*

"Mr. Robinson," Kade answered.

The band began their sound check, and the fans made their way to the front of the stage.

"I need to run. I'm sure you want to hang out with your friends. The band did great their first set. Why don't you say hi to Lenny?"

"Sure, Dad."

"I'll see you in the morning," he said in a low voice. He didn't like people knowing our business either, especially when I stayed home alone. My mom and sister were home by themselves when they were murdered. "Don't stay out too late."

"Sure, Dad."

He kissed me on the forehead, and then he was gone.

I was about to move when Kade whispered, "I just want to talk."

I shivered. *Oh hell.*

For a second, I thought of turning around to read him the riot act. Instead, I leaned into his chest, twisting my neck so his lips were an inch from mine. A jolt of lightning zinged through me. "Can I at least spend a few minutes with my friend? And I have to talk to the band before they go on again."

His mouth slid to my ear again, the feel of his hot breath blanketing me with goosebumps. "Why? Do you know them?"

"Yes." I was now waving at Lenny, who was watching me. *Maybe he did remember me.*

"You do?"

My body tensed. "Do you think I'm lying?"

He laughed softly. "When it comes to you, Lacey, I don't know what to think."

"If you don't believe me, why don't you come with?"

"Now that I have you, I'm not sure I should let you go," he whispered.

At any second my solid state of being would be nothing more than a bowl of red-hot liquid. "Kade, I promise I won't tell anyone I gave you the black eye." Although I'd already told Becca.

He chuckled. "I don't care if you broadcast it to the world."

Was he proud of a girl giving him a shiner?

"Let's go visit your friend."

Kade didn't let go of my hand as we weaved through the throng of people. As we did, I bumped into a group of girls accidentally. I was about to apologize when Tammy bared her teeth at me, as did Grace.

Tammy narrowed eyes heavy with mascara at Kade, then at our joined hands. "You're dating her?" she asked. "Are you kidding me?" She put her hands on her hips. "Grace told me you were, but I didn't believe her."

Anger bubbled to the surface. I hated rumors. When I'd started playing baseball at Crestview, I was supposedly sleeping with the boys on the team. I tried to pull my hand from his, but he squeezed it tighter. *Oookay.*

"Tammy," he said. "Don't make a scene."

Grace whispered something in her ear, and she huffed, disappearing between bodies. Grace shuffled behind her.

"Can I have my hand back?" I asked, looking up at him. "You're cutting off my blood supply."

He grinned. My stomach flipped a few times. Then he let go.

"Excuse me," I said to three guys who were chatting near the stage. They moved out of the way.

"Lacey," Lenny said, jumping down. Lenny was a good-looking guy in his late twenties with shoulder-length, cinnamon-colored hair, a strong jaw, and a nice smile. Unlike J.J. from Zeal, Lenny had more of a male following. His style of music was bluesy rock, and all of them in the band hailed from New Orleans. I wasn't surprised that some of the girls were infatuated with him. He'd just released a killer song, appealing to the young female audience. Dad had suggested he write a ballad or two to help increase his female fan base.

"Wow. You look amazing. The last time I saw you...well..."

The last time I'd seen Lenny, I'd been in Eko's studio in California. Occasionally I would visit Dad after school, when one of the bands was recording. He liked to use me as a gauge, especially if it was a band who played to my age group. On the day I'd met Lenny, I was in a

major funk. I couldn't remember what I wore, but most of the time I was wearing baggy clothes and a ball cap. Who dressed up after a losing two loved ones?

I pushed up onto my toes and kissed him on the cheek. "Thank you." I eased back. "It's good to see you, too. Dad tells me you guys are doing great."

"Yeah. If it weren't for your dad, we'd still be playing those dives in New Orleans." He pointed with his chin. "Are you going to introduce me?"

I glanced over my shoulder. Kade had one of his masterful blank expressions. "Oh, I'm sorry. This is Kade."

"Boyfriend?"

"God, no."

Kade tugged me to him, his fingers pressing into my hips.

Lenny's eyebrows shot up. "Mmm. I don't think he agrees with you, Lacey."

I lifted a shoulder. My back molded to Kade's chest. *Was Kade staking out his territory?* Then Kelton's words rang in my head: *Kade doesn't share his women.* A miniscule sliver of me warmed to the idea, then I quickly discarded it. I didn't belong to anyone. I itched to knee him in the balls again. I would've, if it weren't for the subtle circles he was tracing on my hips. *Didn't predators calm their prey before attacking?*

"Nice to meet you, Kade," Lenny said.

"Same here, man. I like your music." With the barest of movements, he mashed his thighs against me.

Desire rushed south. Annoyance climbed north.

Placing my hands over his, I dug my nails into his flesh, hoping the act would cause him to release me. Instead he pulled me even closer. His tall, hard body, all male, all hotness, pressed into me. My cheeks warmed, as did other places on my body.

Lenny laughed. "You sure about that, man? I'm not convinced coming from someone wearing a Zeal shirt."

Kade laughed. "What can I say? I like them too."

"Fair enough. Lacey, are you going to hang around to listen?" Lenny asked.

"That's why I'm here."

"Good. See you later then." Lenny hopped up on stage.

I didn't move. Neither did Kade. I probably should find Becca, but the lazy circles he was still drawing on my hips had me spellbound. Plus I didn't want him stop. I hadn't had this much attention from one guy since Brad. Even with Brad, he didn't make my heart race like it was doing right now.

Lenny adjusted the mike.

I turned, and looked up at Kade. He looked down at me through his eyelashes. "I'm going to find Becca."

"I thought we could talk first. I'm sure she's fine. Let's stand over by the wall." He nodded to his left.

I guessed talking couldn't hurt. After the way he'd just held me, I was curious about his intentions. We found an empty spot close to a table of two boys and two girls.

The band dove into a slow ballad called "Crazy," and couples embraced, swaying to the soulful beat. Instantly, I was taken back to the time when Brad used to hold me like that as we listened to Zeal rehearse at the Eko Records studio. Now he was probably holding my best friend, Danny, like that. I had nothing against them playing for the same team. Regardless, humiliation still clung to me like a wet blanket. Why hadn't I seen it? And why had Brad broken the news to me only two weeks after the murders? Plus there was a part of me that was mad at myself for giving him my virginity. I shook my head, hoping it would clear the past, at least for the present.

"Are you okay?" Kade asked.

"Yeah, why?"

His eyes met mine. "You're clenching your fists like you're about to punch me again." He gave me a crooked grin.

I did want to punch someone, but it wasn't him—not now, anyway. Thankful for the distraction, I smiled back.

"You should smile more, Lace."

I did smile, more so now than a few months ago. "I thought you wanted to talk."

"Too loud. On their break."

That probably wasn't for another thirty minutes or so before the band was done with this set. "Then I'm going to look for Becca," I said. If I stayed, I might ask him to hold me again and trace circles on my body. *I hardly knew him.*

"She's fine. She's with Kel," he said, watching the lead guitarist transition into a solo, while Lenny took a long drink from a water bottle. "They're on the other side of the stage."

Standing on my toes, I glanced over that way. Kelton had his arm draped around Becca's shoulders while a tall blond guy spoke into his ear. Her body moved slightly as she focused on the guitarist. No sooner had the blond guy vanished than Kelton caught Kade's eyes and angled his head toward the exit.

Kade straightened. Leaning down, he whispered in my ear. "I'll be right back. Don't leave. Regardless of what you told my friend yesterday, hunting season is definitely open when it comes to you, Lace. And I always get my prey."

I rolled my eyes and focused on the band as the guitarist wound down his solo. Then Kade nibbled on my ear. White-hot heat slid down my belly, pooling between my legs. I screamed internally at my sex hormones to go back to sleep. My damn body was a second away from rolling over and letting him have his way with me.

"Did you hear what I said?" His hand cupped my chin gently, guiding it so our eyes met.

"Whatever." I rolled my eyes again. "I may or may not be here."

One side of his mouth twitched. "Don't say I didn't warn you."

He brushed his lips over mine, lingering for a long second before he pulled away. My body quivered for him to kiss me. My brain snarled in protest. Then he strode away.

My body was in yo-yo mode. One minute I wanted to strip him naked, the next, I wanted to beat the crap out of him. Snapping out of the Kade trance, I pushed off the wall. Becca weaved through the crowd, panic painting her pretty features.

The majority of the people were heading for the exit.

"What's going on? Why is everyone leaving?" I asked.

"Oh, my God," she said. "Greg Sullivan is outside. The guy I told you about, who got into it with Kade and his brothers a couple of years ago."

"You're kidding."

She waved for me to follow her. The band finished their song. Lenny gave me a *what the heck?* look. I shrugged as I went with Becca. A few people jumped into the empty seats that were vacant now.

"Is there a fight or something?" I asked, following her.

"Not sure, but if Kelton and Kade are involved then probably," she said over her shoulder.

A voice in my head told me to go home. *Get the hell out of there before Kade returned.*

CHAPTER 7

Once outside, the night air sent a chill through me—or maybe it was the ominous scene of hungry spectators looking for a fight. A swarm of teens crowded the lot, lounging on tailgates of trucks, leaning against cars, and a few girls even sat on the shoulders of boys.

I didn't move from under the marquee. Becca stood beside me, scanning the lot.

The burly bouncer who'd checked my ID earlier raised a walkie-talkie to his mouth. "Buster, get outside. We have a situation."

In the open lane of the lot, Kelton and Kade faced Aaron Seever, the captain of the baseball team, and a short stocky dude who I hadn't seen before. I assumed it was the infamous Greg Sullivan. With their backs to me, I couldn't see Kelton's or Kade's expressions, but Aaron stared down Kelton, and Greg stared down Kade.

"Greg is here to kill Kade," someone in the crowd whispered.

"Over here." Becca tugged on my arm, leading me to a pickup truck parked directly in front of the building. We were still behind Kade. She jumped onto the bed.

I hesitated. The voice in my head shouted to skedaddle while I had the chance, especially if blood was going to be shed. I shivered at the memory of me slipping on the floor in a puddle of blood when I found Julie's body.

"It's okay. It's my dad's truck."

Go home. Baseball tryouts are next week. You can't get into any trouble.

"Lacey," she said nervously, holding out her hand.

I glanced out into the lot where my car was parked.

"Lacey!" Becca snapped.

Swallowing hard, I took her hand and hopped up. I was going to regret this. Once Becca and I found an edge of the truck to sit on, a queasy feeling skated through me. *Did Greg intend to kill Kade?*

There was clearly bad blood among the four guys. *Why Aaron?* I wasn't sure. Another wave of nausea washed over me. If he were involved in this, did that mean we were going to have trouble on the ball field? Kelton was trying out, and so was I. I didn't know Aaron that well, so he shouldn't have any ill feelings toward me. Still, tension on a team never won games.

"You're not wanted here," Kade said.

The crowd quieted. The bouncer's walkie-talkie beeped twice.

"What's wrong, Maxwell? Afraid I'm going to finish you this time?" Greg said. His greasy black hair looked as though he dumped a bottle of Wesson oil in it.

Someone snorted.

Kelton laughed. "You think you have the balls to try?"

"I'm here, aren't I?" Greg countered.

"So, Aaron, do you want to ruin your senior year? You know you just started a war bringing your cousin here," Kade informed him.

"Bringing your brothers back was a mistake, Kade," Aaron said.

"Oh, I don't think so. You see, unlike you and Shorty here, my brothers are a force to be reckoned with. Mess with any one of them, and you'll have me to deal with."

"Are you threatening us?" Greg asked.

"No threats, man. All promises," Kade drawled calmly.

"Aaron and Greg are related?" I asked more rhetorically than anything. The acid in my stomach intensified. If Greg was trouble, that meant Aaron was too. Maybe I should be worried about Tammy's comment. *The guys don't want you to play baseball.* Was she talking about Aaron in particular? I searched the crowd for my new arch-nemesis. I hadn't seen Tammy and Grace since they stormed away from Kade and me.

"I know, right?" Becca said as she watched intently.

The entrance door to the club slammed open. A hulking man

with a buzz-cut stalked out and up to the other burly bouncer. They had a few words before the man with the buzz-cut started barking orders.

"Let's get back inside before I call the cops," he said as he strode past everyone.

A few obeyed. Burly Bouncer sprang into action, helping his partner guide teens back inside.

"I didn't think it would take long before my father sent out his security team," Becca said, sounding disappointed.

"Wow, that guy is huge," I murmured.

"That's my dad's head of security."

The name Buster fit him well, reminding me of a bulldog—husky and mean looking. "Is there a problem, Kade?" Buster asked, stepping in between him and Greg.

"Just talking, man," Kade said.

"You'll have to take your discussion somewhere else," Buster announced. "We don't want any trouble on the premises."

"How's the wimpy brother of yours, Kelton?" Greg taunted.

Kelton pounced, tackling Greg to the gravel surface. Kelton delivered punch after punch anywhere he could while holding Greg down. Greg tried to push Kelton off him, but all he could do was protect his face.

"Get him, Kelton," one boy shouted.

"That's it," another yelled as Kelton drove his fist into Greg's gut.

Everyone started talking and shouting, a few betting Kelton would win.

Buster and Kade yanked Kelton up by the arms. He struggled to get free while Greg pushed himself to his feet. Blood trickled out of Greg's nose as he brushed off his jeans, as though it was just another day at the office.

Buster waved at his partner. "Take Kelton inside."

The bouncer jogged over and wrapped his fingers around Kelton's biceps.

Kelton jerked his arm away. "I can walk on my own, man." He raked a hand through his disheveled hair.

"I'm not going to say this again," Buster announced. "Either go home, or get back inside. If not, I will take names and you won't be allowed in the club anymore."

Several teens scattered back into the club. Buster's directive was my sign to go home. I started to push off the edge of the truck when Becca grabbed my arm.

"Where are you going?"

"There's nothing more to see out here," I said.

A wiry-looking boy who walked past the truck said to his friend, "It would've been cool to see Kade lose it on Sullivan."

"Nah, dude. That wouldn't have been pretty," the other boy said.

Would Kade have killed Greg?

"Yes there is," Becca told me, ignoring the boys. She released me. "Pay attention."

To what? The fight was over. Or at least I thought it was, until I shifted my gaze.

Aaron was pointing in my direction. "I hear the new girl is good. She yours?"

Kade turned his head. As though someone had control of my body, I waved. What was wrong with me? I was trying to avoid attention. *I am such an idiot.*

Anxiety curdled in my stomach. *I should've listened to my damn intuition and gone home.*

Turning back, Kade grabbed Aaron by the shirt. If anything was said, I couldn't hear it.

"Man, step off," Buster said to Kade.

Kade hesitated before letting go of Aaron.

"You two leave the premises before I call the cops," Buster said, waggling his finger between Aaron and Greg.

Without another word, Aaron sauntered over to a black BMW.

"It's good to be back. It's going to be like old times," Greg shouted as he joined Aaron.

The few remaining spectators dispersed. Car doors slammed. Engines roared to life. *Time for me to leave, too.* Buster hung around for a few minutes, making sure Aaron and Greg had left, and everyone else did as he'd said.

Becca hopped down from the truck and I wasn't far behind her. I started for my car.

"I'll call you tomorrow," I said. With the eerie feeling I'd just gotten from the Aaron-and-Kade interaction, I was ready to get on a plane to California. I didn't want anything to do with anyone else's problems. I had enough of my own.

"Wait," Becca said. "The band is still playing."

"I'm not feeling good." It wasn't a lie. "We'll talk tomorrow."

Becca frowned as she turned back to the club. I was surprised she didn't protest more. Maybe she had Kelton on the brain.

Buster and Kade were still talking behind Kade's truck. "Can you check on Kelton for me?" Kade asked. "I need to take care of something."

"Sure thing, man." He spoke as though Kade was the authority and not him.

Uh-oh. He'd told me not to leave. *Don't look.* I picked up my pace, digging for my keys in my purse. Vehicles trickled out of the pebbled lot across the street, their headlights putting me on display. Just what I needed—a beacon for Kade to find me. I scurried into the lot, walking past the last car waiting to exit.

A halo ringed the moon. The field beyond the open lot shimmered under the bright night sky. The night dew was settling in. I was no more than a foot away from my car when I caught the sound of gravel crunching under heavy footsteps.

"I told you not to leave," Kade said from behind me.

I closed my eyes and stilled. *So close to making a run for it.* I opened my eyes and was about to turn when his lips landed on my ear. He really had a thing for ears, apparently. "If you value your sex life, you'll let me go. I'm sure your girlfriends or Tammy would be disappointed."

He laughed, nibbling on my ear for the second time tonight. "There are lots of ways to please a woman," he said, low and husky.

Oh, crap on a cracker. The guy was going to make me take off my clothes right here. "I would like to go home," I said, trying to keep my voice from shaking or my body from melting into his.

"We have some unfinished business." He grasped my hips, drawing me to him, my back to his front.

I almost kicked and screamed, but decided not to. I was beginning to like our little interactions, and frankly, I loved his strong hands on me. Plus it was time to hear what he had to say. Maybe then he would leave me alone. "If you want to talk, then talk." I took in a deep breath. The fresh night air was a welcoming relief as it breezed over my heated skin.

His tongue licked my earlobe, his hot breath making me squirm against him. "I don't want to talk," he whispered.

Tingles rushed along my spine. "Kade?"

"Shhh. No talking." I could imagine a night of wild pleasures listening to his husky voice.

The guy was torturing me. If pleasure was his form of punishment, it was definitely working. So do I push him away or give in to temptation? Before my brain caught up with my body, temptation won out. I turned in his arms, and my hands snaked around to his tight butt.

He groaned. "Be careful, you might like how this ends."

"Nah, I know I would hate it," I lied.

He chuckled as he rested his forehead against mine.

"Is this your way of talking?" I asked hoarsely.

"Maybe." His hands slid around to my lower back and began tracing circles as he had earlier on my hip.

We stared at one another. If he knew my tragic past and how seriously screwed up I was, would he still try to lure me into his seductive web?

His gaze dropped to my lips. My pulse jumped. He gently eased me toward the back of my Mustang.

"I need to go home," I said in a pathetic voice.

"Do you want to run, Lace?"

He never kept a girl for very long, Becca had said, and I wasn't in the market for a one-night stand, no matter how good-looking he was. Heck, I wasn't even ready to date yet. Sure, Kade made my body react in a way that was new for me, and every fiber in me knew he wasn't gay. If I were wrong, I'd introduce him to Brad myself. Still, my focus had to be baseball and school, nothing else. Then there was Tammy. Where did she fit into Kade's life? I didn't need trouble.

"Cat got your tongue?" he asked as his hands reached up to frame my face.

My breath hitched, and heat spiraled down to settle between my legs. *Damn body*. He slowly lowered his head as his eyes darkened, desire flashing. Heat met cold along my arms, and I didn't know whether to shiver or melt. As his lips drew closer, mine prickled in anticipation.

He stopped just as my tongue darted out. A deep rumble rose from his chest. Then his lips wandered teasingly over mine, and my legs were like warm saltwater taffy. Yep, I was done, fried to a crisp, and he hadn't even kissed me.

Then he sucked my lower lip, in a slow sensuous tango.

I whimpered.

Groaning low, he eased back as though he were trying to get control of himself. His breathing was ragged, his gaze never wavering from mine. I reached up and curled my hands into his hair. *Heaven.* I ran my fingers back and forth, feeling the softness of the brown strands. I moaned softly. As if that little noise was his cue, his lips slammed into mine as he pressed his chest against me. Hard against soft. His tongue plunged into my mouth, desperately searching for something as though I had what he needed to survive. When our tongues collided, jolts of pleasure slithered down my belly, and I mashed my hips into him. He groaned again, taking, tasting, teasing as he bit and sucked. Then he gentled the kiss, with nips to my top lip then my bottom one before he grinned.

"Something funny?" I asked, breathing heavy.

"I've never tasted anything as sweet as you."

"You mean I'm still sweet after those things that I did to you?"

His hands roamed underneath my shirt, one sliding down, the other sliding up close to my bra. Then his lips found my ear, nibbling. "Those things were only foreplay, for me."

My muscles tensed; my body stiffened.

"Don't freak, Lace." His lower hand met the other that was now on the clasp of my bra. "Kiss me again." His tone was demanding yet gentle.

I grabbed hold of his face and followed his command. Not because he told me to, but because I wanted to. I didn't know what to make of his foreplay statement except that he was crazy, but so was I.

After a long, slow, wet kiss that had my insides screaming for release, I let my fingers roam over his face. The moonlight hit at just the right angle, illuminating his handsome features, even with the black eye. I loved his mile-long eyelashes, the flecks of amber in his copper eyes, his dimples that made me squeeze my thighs, the softness of his honey brown hair that I just realized had streaks of blond on one side, and I absolutely loved his lips. I wanted to kiss them all day long.

"I'm happy to see you two finally sucking face," a male voice said in the distance.

My brain had forgotten where we were. Kade pulled away. I bit back a whine.

"What do you want, Kel? I thought I told you to go home." Kade growled as he leaned against my car.

"I hung out with Becca." Kelton took long strides into the lot from the road.

"I should get home anyway," I said in a throaty tone.

Kelton shoved his hands in his jeans pockets in front of us, grinning as though he knew how Kade had affected me.

"Wipe the smirk off your face, ass-wipe," I snapped. At least this time my voice was normal.

"I love it when you talk dirty to me," Kelton said snidely.

I rolled my eyes—something that was becoming routine for me around these brothers.

"Go home, Kel," Kade barked.

"Chill, bro. I saw your truck. I just wanted to make sure you didn't need my help. But I can see you have it under control." He waggled his brows.

"I'll be right behind you," Kade said. "Now go."

"Night, girl. Don't drive my brother too crazy." He winked at me then sauntered away.

"Don't let him bug you." Kade wrapped his arms around me.

"Kelton is fine. I can handle him. I need to get home," I said, staring at his lips.

He rubbed his thumb over my cheek. "I know." Blowing out a breath, he let go of me.

I didn't want to go home. I wanted to go anywhere he was going. *Christ. What had he done to me?* Shaking the thought of Kade's lips on me, I circled around to the driver's side. The two large trucks that were parked on either side of me were gone.

He waited, not saying a word, while I opened my door. "I'll be fine, Kade," I assured him.

"I know. But I'll wait to make sure anyway."

I climbed in, inserted the key into the ignition, then turned it. *Click, click, click.*

Seriously? Again? If my father didn't fix this car for good, I was going to take out one of my panic attacks on him. I tried it one more time. Nothing. *Shit!* I jumped out, slamming the door. I wanted to kick the tires.

Kade was shaking his head. "I'm going to tell your father to let me work on that car," he said, frustrated. "Let's go. I'll take you home."

I froze. Several thoughts flitted through my brain. *Him and me alone in his truck, and after that kiss? I should call my dad. Or maybe Becca can give me a ride home.* I glanced at the Cave.

"I see your mind working, Lace. It's just a ride." He pulled his keys out of his front jeans pocket.

"Can't you check? Last time the battery cable was loose, according to my dad."

"I'm sure he was right, but sometimes the terminals can get corroded. If that's the case, we're not going to fix it tonight. Better to check it in daylight, anyway."

"You know, I'll ask Becca to take me home." I plucked my purse from the Mustang, checked for my phone, then locked the car.

Turning, I plowed in to his hard chest and stumbled. "Geez, dude! A little warning!" What was it with the Maxwell brothers and their stealthy nature? Why was I even worried about the car? I should be praying that someone would steal it. Maybe then Dad would get me a new vehicle. It wasn't like he couldn't afford it.

"Becca is probably helping her dad. You might have to wait for her. Didn't you say you needed to get home?" He cupped one of my elbows.

I did want to go home. I didn't want to wait. I threw caution to the wind. We walked the short distance to his truck. I was grabbing the handle to step up on the shiny running board when he palmed my butt.

"Do you mind?" I asked, slipping onto the leather seat.

He had that impish grin on his face again. Not saying a word, he closed the door, circled around, and jumped into the driver's seat. We didn't say much as he maneuvered out of the parking lot.

"So, I live—"

"I know where you live." He turned left onto the main road.

I gaped at him. "You do?" I didn't know what to think other than that he was stalking me.

He laughed as he ran his fingers through his hair. My fingers itched to replace his with mine.

"Of course. You didn't think I wouldn't find out about the girl who pulled a gun on me."

"Yeah, about that—I'm sorry."

"What were you doing with a gun, anyway?"

"I'd forgotten to leave it at home. My father and I joined the Ashford Gun Club."

"Why?"

I wasn't ready to tell him the real reason. I'd just met him, and while he was a fantastic kisser, I wasn't sure I could trust him. I didn't want my life to be the focus of every kid's conversation at school. I didn't want to hear the gossip, or whispers, or pity. I'd had enough of that at Crestview. "Aside from baseball, I like to fly planes and shoot guns." It was the truth. I had taken flying lessons in LA and was a few classes away from getting my pilot's license—for small planes, of course. I loved the rush, the freedom I got when I was thousands of feet in the sky. I hadn't flown since we moved.

"Mmmm. You are something else, aren't you, Lacey Robinson?"

"What does that mean?"

He shook his head as he drove through the streets of Ashford. There weren't many people out. I didn't expect to see any. After all, it was almost midnight.

"So do you think you'll make the team?" he asked.

"Maybe. What was all the fuss about in the parking lot with Aaron and Greg?"

"Old history."

An uncomfortable silence filled the truck as I waited for him to elaborate. When he didn't, I spoke up. "That's it? You don't want to give details?"

"Not tonight."

There was a lot of old history around here. First Becca and Tyler, then Becca and Grace, now Kade and Greg. Regardless, I didn't push. I had my own secrets locked up that I didn't want anyone to know.

As he drove, I leaned back and relaxed, breathing in his masculine scent. I'd been replaying the kiss between us when he pulled into my driveway, and everything around me disappeared, including Kade. Suddenly, I struggled to breathe as I stared at the dark, ominous house. There wasn't a single light on. I remembered turning on a few lights before I left. Then my breathing grew shallow, and the sides of my vision darkened as I took hold of the truck door with a shaky hand. A buzzing sound whirred in my head. I tried to get oxygen into my lungs, but it was like someone had cut off my airway. I couldn't stop the panic attack or the visions. I shook my head several times as I tried to escape my memories, but it was too late.

The large house had been dark as I got out of my car. Not one light glowed. Even the lights on the outside of the garage were off. Something was wrong. Mom's Audi was in the driveway and the garage door was open. Mom never left the garage door open, even when she was home. Julie's Volvo sat in the drive-

way, too. Why was she home? She wasn't supposed to be home from her friend Melissa's house until tomorrow. As soon as I stepped into the bay of the garage, a strong odor penetrated my nostrils, a mixture of sweat and a man's cologne. It wasn't my dad's cologne, either. He didn't even wear the smelly stuff—it irritated Mom. I covered my nose with my hand as my brain suddenly became fuzzy.

I climbed the few steps to the door leading inside the house. I turned the knob, pushed the door, and tentatively walked in. I flipped the light switch next to the door, but nothing came on. I hesitated before going any farther. I took out my phone and hit the button so the backlight on it would help guide me. As I headed down the hallway, bile rose in my throat. Unlike the smell in the garage, the scent inside had a strong metallic odor. Every hair on me stood up.

"Mom," *I called out, but I didn't get an answer.* "Mom," *I called again, but nothing. Where was she? Why wasn't she answering?*

Suddenly, someone was calling my name.

"Hey. Lacey. What's wrong?" a familiar-but-scared voice asked.

Pain seared from my right elbow up through my shoulder, and I screamed.

"Lacey? Lacey? Can you hear me?"

My vision blurred, then a flash of light blinded me before a hot wind breezed over my face. I blinked a few times. On my last long blink my vision cleared a little, my breathing still shallow. "K-K-ade?"

I was leaning against the garage door, and Kade was standing in front of me.

"Are you okay?" he asked, his hands around my face.

"How did I get out of the truck!"

He studied me with a mixture of fear, sympathy, and pain. "Shhh. You don't need to scream."

Oh, my God. This couldn't be happening to me. *Breathe.* I had to get away from him. He couldn't see me like this. He was probably thinking I was mental. I shook my head, but he wouldn't let go. I balled my hands into tight fists and swung.

Letting go of my face, he grabbed my wrists. "Stop. I don't know what's happening here. Please," he begged, his words floating like ice in a sea of fear.

Wincing, I stilled. I wasn't prepared to tell him. *Of all the people to witness one of my episodes, it had to be him. This guy must think I was a freak show.*

My vision darkened, and a warm feeling blanketed me. *Oh no, please don't shut down on me. I can't pass out. Not now.*

"You need to tell me what to do here, Lace. I'm at a loss." His left hand moved to my lower back, and the other moved to the nape of my neck.

"Kade?" His face became fuzzy as dizziness set in. "I'm probably going to…" My knees gave out, and he caught me.

"Pass out," he finished for me.

"Sorry I—"

Then the world around me went dark.

☙❧

My brain awakened to voices around me, familiar voices. Then a hand brushed my hair. Goosebumps covered my body.

"Does she always have these attacks?" Kade's voice registered above me.

"It depends. Something had to trigger it," Dad said from a distance.

Dad? Where was I? I remembered the flashback, Kade asking me what was wrong, and then nothing. If I wasn't mistaken, my head was in Kade's lap, and we were sitting on my couch in the family room. The smell of leather furniture surrounded me. My heart fell into the pit of my stomach. Why had Kade had to witness one of my freak shows?

I kept my eyelids shut for the moment. I wanted to see how far this conversation was going to go. I had to know what Dad was going to tell him. I was already embarrassed. Now I had to find out if I should move back to California tomorrow.

"Tell me what happened when you drove up," Dad said.

Every instinct in me told me to run to my room and lock the door, but I was enjoying Kade's hands on me. He was tracing the outline of the shell of my ear, and the sensation was soothing.

"We drove in, and she got out of the truck then walked up to the garage door and threw her elbow into it several times. I tried to get her to stop, but she seemed like she was in a trance, her eyes were wide open as though she just saw something horrible. When she snapped out of it she passed out. I found her keys in her purse, then I brought her in the house and called you. Why does she have attacks?"

"I'm not prepared to discuss that with you, son."

"Mr. Robinson, I might be out of line on this, but have you considered a doctor? I mean therapy."

"We have. She missed her appointment on Friday."

I was going to kill Dad. *Please don't say any more.*

"I see. I know you don't want to tell me, and frankly, I don't blame you. It isn't any of my business. But I can tell she's been through some type of trauma. If it helps, my dad is a psychiatrist for the military. He counsels a lot of the veterans coming back from battle and other intense situations. He's on assignment for a few weeks. And it's just something to think about, but when he returns you may want to talk with him."

"I'll consider it. I should get her to bed." Dad sounded defeated.

I could understand. I hadn't had an attack in six months. The last one hadn't really been an attack—more of a nightmare. Dad had found me walking into the ocean. I'd never sleepwalked before, but PTSD had different effects on people.

"I can carry her. Where's her room?"

Oh no, Kade wasn't going into my room. If he ever had the chance to set foot in it, it would have to be under better circumstances. I pressed my head into Kade's stomach and slowly opened my eyelids.

His hand stilled on my ear. "Hey there," he said softly.

"Sweet Pea." Dad rose from his chair.

I sat up. "What are you doing home?" I asked. I didn't want them to know I had been listening—at least, not yet.

"Are you okay?" Dad sat on the couch next to me.

"Yeah. My arm hurts like crazy, though."

"Should we get it X-rayed?" Dad knitted his brows.

"Oh, crap. I have tryouts coming up." I held my arm.

"You should put ice on it," Kade said.

I was afraid to look at him—actually, I *couldn't* look at him. I felt so humiliated. He'd probably never want to see me again, which was probably for the best. I had to concentrate on baseball anyway. I ran out of the room, down the hall and into the guest bathroom, closing the door. Immediately, I dipped my head in the sink and splashed cold water on my face. Taking a towel off the rack, I dropped down on the bench in front of the vanity and patted my skin dry.

The TV wasn't on, so their voices resonated clearly.

"Is she going to be okay?" Kade asked.

"She'll be fine," Dad said. "It's late. You should get going." His voice sounded tired.

"I'll have the car towed to my house tomorrow," Kade said.

Hmm. It sounded like they'd already talked about my car. *What else had they discussed? Did Kade bring up the gun incident? Did Dad share anything else about me?*

"You don't have to do that, son. I can get it tomorrow."

"I insist. Please, let me work on it. I've been dying to get my hands on one of those cars and play a little. My dad doesn't let me touch his cars all that much."

"Sure. I guess it wouldn't hurt."

Great! Now what was I going to do for a vehicle? If he had my car that would mean I would have to see him again soon. Their voices trailed off, and the front door shut. I slunk out of the bathroom and went back to the family room. Pulling a blanket out of the wicker basket, I unfolded it and curled up on the couch. Aside from the humiliation and my arm throbbing, I was tired. Panic attacks always wore me out. My eyes drifted shut.

"Do you want to talk about it, Lacey?" Dad asked.

The cushion dipped near my feet.

"Is Kade gone?" I asked.

"He is," Dad said. "Now what happened?"

I sighed heavily. "The house was dark, Dad—completely dark when we drove up. Just like that night. I freaked. I know I left the outside lights on and a few inside too. Why were all the lights off?" My eyes slid open as I willed the buzzing in my head to go away.

"I don't know. I checked the house thoroughly earlier. But I'll check it out in the morning." He ran his hands through his hair. His skin appeared ashen, and he had a few more wrinkles around his sad green eyes.

My heart hurt. "You didn't have to rush home."

"Yes, I did. I'm sorry I wasn't here, Sweet Pea."

"Dad, you can't be with me every minute of the day."

"No, but someone should be here with you at night. I've called Mary. She'll be flying in tomorrow."

"What? I'm a big girl. I don't need a babysitter, Dad."

Mary Mills had been our housekeeper back in LA and had become family. I adored her. Still, I was going to be eighteen in a week. I didn't need anyone to hold my hand.

"Lacey, Mary is not coming out here to babysit you. It would be nice to have her around. Don't you think? We do need more home-cooked meals, and she can keep you company at night while I work. And she knows your issues and knows what to do."

The more I thought about it, the more I liked the idea of having someone here at night. After Mom passed, Mary and I had become close. She listened to me and gave me advice when I needed it, especially when Brad broke up with me.

"How's your arm?" he asked.

"Sore. But I think I'll be fine for tryouts." The fires of hell could burn me, but I'd pitch through the pain.

CHAPTER 8

I spent Sunday studying for my trig exam. Dad and I decided to forgo our ritual at the gun club. He had some work to do in his home office and needed to pick up Mary from the airport. He'd also found out that there'd been a power outage at about the time I came home on Saturday night. I was relieved it was nothing more than that.

Becca and I chatted. I apologized for leaving abruptly. She'd said I looked pale, and she wanted to check on Kelton. Once we had that out of the way, she proceeded to tell me all about her and Kelton. It was good to hear how giddy she was about the guy. I just listened. After Brad's coming-out-of-the-closet news, and the way he'd broken up with me, I wasn't in any position to give advice on boys. Kelton, though, seemed like a player to me, more so than Kade. I'd tried to erase Kade from my thoughts. Yet every time I touched my lips, an image of his tongue on mine or his hands on me left me daydreaming instead of studying. I had to mentally kick myself in the butt a few times.

Dad and Mary arrived back at the house late in the afternoon. When she walked in, my jaw dropped. Her petite frame had gone from plump to slim in three months. She'd cut her brown hair in a layered bob, which seemed to shave a few years off her thirty-something age.

We showed Mary the house. She loved to cook, so she was anxious to see if our kitchen was anything like the one in our house in California. It was roomy, but not as expansive as our old house.

After she unpacked, we ordered Chinese food. Dad wanted Mary to relax on her first day here. She'd argued with him that she would cook, but we needed to go grocery shopping first anyway. We hung out in the sunken family room off the kitchen, eating and chatting. She told us she'd been cleaning Rob's apartment once a week. She seemed to think he was doing well. At least, to her he didn't look so pale or withdrawn anymore. Throughout the week, he was eating meals she prepared for him. Tears stung my eyes as I listened. I missed him. I made a mental note to call him. With the time difference, it was hard to connect.

On Monday morning, I sauntered into the kitchen, moving my arm around. Stiffness had set in overnight, and today my arm hurt more than it had on Sunday morning. I was trying to keep it loose—tryouts were two days away. The hand I'd punched Kade with fared better than my arm at the moment.

"Good morning, Lacey," Mary said, flipping her famous blueberry pancakes on the griddle. "Hungry?" Her brown eyes appeared tired.

"What are you doing up so early?" I hopped onto a stool at the kitchen island.

"I couldn't sleep. So, pancakes?"

"I could always eat your pancakes. You know that."

She'd never been married. When I'd asked her why, she'd responded, "I haven't found the right man." The man she did find was going to be one lucky dude. The woman knew how to cook.

"So, who's the boy, and why didn't you tell me about him?" She handed me a glass of orange juice.

"Excuse me?" It was a good thing I didn't have juice or food in my mouth—otherwise she'd be wearing it right now.

"Some sweet boy, Kade, called here this morning. He wanted to know if you needed a ride."

My mouth was hanging open. After my panic attack on Saturday night, I didn't think he would want anything to do with me. Butterflies fluttered inside me. "He's just a..." I didn't know what he was. I'd only just met him. "He's in one of my classes, and he's supposed to be fixing my car."

"You mean your father is still trying to push that clunker on you?"

"Yep. He loves that Mustang for some reason."

"Good Lord," she said, wiping her hands on a paper towel.

"So what did you tell Kade?" I took a sip of OJ, looking at the pulp in the glass.

"That a boy shouldn't be calling a girl's home so early in the morning. And that if you wanted a ride you would call him."

Why was I surprised? Mary always read Brad the riot-act if he was out of line with his manners when it came to women. The first time she unleashed her wrath had been the night Brad was my date for one of Mom's charity events. Mary had stayed late that night to help with my hair. When she escorted us to the car, Brad jumped in before me. Her eyes narrowed to slits. Red-faced, she'd directed him to get out and open my door.

"Is he cute?" she asked, looking at me intently.

Cute wasn't the word to describe Kade. "Well, he's not gay." I had to get the elephant out of the room. Mary had been at the house the afternoon Brad came over to breakup. I had a meltdown, throwing anything in my room I could get my hands on. She'd been there to comfort me. "And, yes, he's hot."

"I guess I'll have to meet him," she said, turning toward the griddle, flipping the pancakes. The warm, delicious scent of sugary bread permeated the kitchen.

"That's not going to happen."

"And why is that?" She set down a plate of pancakes on the island in front of me.

"I'm not here to get involved with anyone. I'm on a mission this year. And heaven help me, I need to get my PTSD under control." After Saturday, I wasn't so sure I could. But I would die trying.

"I'm here to help, Lacey. And I know you want that scholarship. My advice, though...have fun. You deserve it." Leaning forward, she reached over from the other side of the island and rested her cold hand on top of mine.

I wanted to have fun. I wanted to have friends. But after what happened on Saturday night, I was even more frightened now. I couldn't let anyone see me like that again. I would die from humiliation. It was bad enough that Kade had. Or what if I got angry and hurt them for ridiculing me? One of my symptoms of PTSD was anger. Suddenly, I wasn't hungry.

I did swallow a few mouthfuls of pancakes, even though the nervous butterflies in my stomach were having a field day. I didn't want to disappoint Mary after she had gone through all the trouble of making breakfast.

The ride to school was uneventful. Dad and I hardly talked, probably because I was thinking about Kade. My stomach was still swirling with nervous energy, especially as we got closer to school. Part of me was dying to see him. The other part, well, not so much. I needed to thank him for helping me, but that would lead to him asking me questions. What would I say to him? Was I ready to spill all the details?

By the time Dad dropped me in front of the school, I was already twenty minutes late. The grounds were deserted. I walked briskly toward the doors.

"Lacey," a male voice called from behind me.

Turning, I adjusted my backpack and my eyebrows shot up. Greg Sullivan sauntered toward me, his short legs covering a great distance. I assumed he knew my name from Aaron, since he'd pointed me out in the crowd at the Cave.

"You're Lacey, right?" He swaggered as if he owned the world. His thin lips stretched into a sleazy grin. *Yuk!* His greasy black hair was as bad as I remembered.

"Who wants to know?"

"You're Kade's girl?" he said.

"You have the wrong person, buddy." I pivoted on my heel. If I didn't get my butt inside, I was going to be late.

"No, I don't think so. Tall, curvy, attractive girl with long brown wavy hair, deep green eyes—"

I spun around. "Buddy, I don't know who you are, or what you're trying to accomplish here, but a lot of girls in this school have brown hair and green eyes." Out of the corner of my eye, I glimpsed Kade's truck pulling in.

Removing his phone from his back pocket, he inched closer. "No. I have it right." He pushed a button on his phone and then shoved it in my face. "This is you, right?"

Stars danced in my vision as I glanced at a picture of Kade and me kissing. A chill crept up my spine. Without another thought, I slapped the phone out of his hand. It fell to the ground with a resounding crack.

I wasn't having a panic attack or an anxiety attack—not yet anyway. Pure, raw anger coursed through me. The same angry feeling I had when kids at my last school were being jerks, although this guy wasn't just being a jerk. He was something worse.

"Are you some sort of pervert that you get your rocks off taking pictures of people kissing?"

He rubbed his pimpled jaw, his eyes narrowing, nostrils flaring. Then a sinister smile etched his face. "I like a feisty woman. I see we're going to have fun."

I whipped off my backpack and was clenching my fists when Kade jogged up.

"What's going on here?" Kade said, inserting his muscular body between Greg and me.

"I'll kick your ass if you come near me again," I bit out, clenching my teeth.

"Maxwell, you have a spunky one here," Greg said.

"Sullivan, get the fuck out of here or I'll let her beat you. Then once she's done, I'll take my turn," Kade said. "And we both know you don't want my fist in your mouth."

"The time is coming, Maxwell. Just remember that."

As Greg stormed off, disappearing into the vast lot of cars, Kade said, "Breathe, Lace. Just breathe."

I took his advice, inhaling the morning air. My pulse slowed.

"So, what was all that about?" Kade asked, concerned.

"He's a creep. And he had a picture of you and me kissing against my car on Saturday. I don't remember any camera flashes." My veins filled with ice.

He raked a hand through his soft hair. "With digital cameras, it's possible. My dad has one. He's taken pictures in very low light."

I knew nothing about photography, but the thought of Greg hiding somewhere around the Cave watching us gave me more than the chills. A stabbing pain pricked my skin as though someone was sticking a thousand needles into it. My buzzing friend started quietly, humming in the back of my head. I squeezed my eyes shut. I inhaled a long breath. *Hold. Count to five. Release.*

"Lace, you okay?" Kade's voice fluttered to my ears, soft and smooth.

I didn't want to tell him I was dizzy. I didn't want him to see me have another panic attack. But if I didn't tell him, I was afraid my body and the concrete were going to become friends.

"Can you take me home?" I said, slowly opening my eyes. When I did, the world tilted slightly. I swayed. I wasn't going to pass out. Sweat coated the nape of my neck.

Kade wrapped an arm around me. "Maybe you should see the nurse."

I lifted my brows. "No. Take me home. If you don't want to, I'll call my dad." I was not walking into that school with a panic attack festering. *No way, no how.*

He snagged my backpack, slinging it over his shoulder. "Can you walk? My truck isn't far." His worried eyes searched my face.

I nodded. "Just stay close."

He interlocked his fingers with mine. *Okay.* I liked his big hand and warm touch. I also liked the tone of his voice. Maybe it would help to take my mind off of me.

"So since you're carrying my bag, does that mean we're going steady?" Yep, that was my first thought.

He laughed, a great sound to help soothe my nerves. "Do you want to go steady?"

"Hell no." *Yes. I also want you and me naked.*

"Liar," he said, squeezing my hand.

The sun dipped behind the dark clouds that were rolling in. The weatherman had predicted rain today. A gust of cold wind blew. I shivered, wrapping the thin sweater I wore around me with my free hand.

As we approached the truck the buzzing slowed, the pricking-skin sensation was gone, but I still felt lightheaded. "I thought you normally parked near the ball field."

"I do, but I was running late this morning, so I parked in front." He pressed the key fob, and the locks clicked. He let go of my hand as he opened the door. I wobbled.

"Lace." He moved so I was between his body and the inside of the door. "Step up slowly."

"You're not going to grab my butt?" I lifted one brow, anchoring myself with the inside handle.

"Who, me?" he asked, his eyes looking so innocent. "Lace, why would I touch you? You just told me in so many words that you wanted nothing to do with me."

"So? That didn't stop you on Saturday at the club." I smiled.

"Get in, Lace. I'm not going to feel you up...yet."

BEFORE KADE DROPPED me off at home, I called Dad to let him know I was on my way. I didn't want him to flip out when I walked in the door. I didn't tell him about my almost-panic attack. I didn't want him to worry, especially after Saturday night, so I used my sore arm as an excuse. He'd wanted to take me to the doctor, but I convinced him to give me one more day. We agreed if my arm wasn't any better by tomorrow, I would go see a doctor. Mary made me a cup of tea, gave me two Advil, and sent me to my room. I spent the morning sleeping, until my phone woke me up around eleven a.m.

"Hello." I cleared my throat.

"Lacey, are you okay?" Becca asked.

I stretched my good arm over my head. "Yeah. Just a little cold. I'll be fine." Considering I wasn't quite awake, I didn't want to get into the specifics of why I was home or my run in with Greg. If I did then that would lead to more questions I wasn't prepared to answer yet.

"Good. By the way, Kade was asking about you. He seems sad over something."

"How do you know? What did he ask?" I sat up. *Oh, God. Did he tell Becca about my panic attacks?*

"He wanted your cell number. So I gave it to him. I hope you don't mind. I know you like him." She giggled.

"Becca, what else?" I bit my lip.

"Okay, chill. He had a sad look about him when he punched your number into his phone."

I flopped back onto my pillow. "He didn't ask or say anything else?"

"No. Listen, I gotta run. Class is starting. I'll take notes." Then she hung up.

I didn't know whether to be relieved Kade hadn't said anything about my attacks or concerned he might be feeling sorry for me. I was all for a little consoling when needed, but people who took pity on others acted differently around them. Or they didn't know how to act. I couldn't handle someone taking pity on me. All it did was bring me down, and according to Dr. Meyers I had to be around those who supported me.

No sooner had I swung my legs off the bed than my phone chirped again. "Hello."

"Hey. Are you feeling better?" Warmth slid down to pool between my legs at the sound of Kade's voice.

"I am. Aren't you supposed to be in class?"

"I signed out. I thought I would finish working on your car. You want to come with?"

I did, but not to work on my car. "I'm not sure my dad will let me since I stayed home from school." I got up and crossed my carpeted floor to the window. Trees lined our property along the back. The wind blew, shaking the dead leaves from the branches. They fluttered to the grassy yard below.

"Tell him you'll be in school, learning how to fix your car."

I did need my car. I had an appointment this afternoon with Dr. Davis. Dad was going to take me, but if he didn't have to he could go in to work early like he wanted to. Mary didn't have a car yet, so she couldn't help. "I'll ask."

"Good. I'll be there in fifteen minutes." Then the phone went dead.

To my surprise, Dad thought it was a good idea for me to help Kade as long as I was feeling better. I'd asked why.

"It would be good for you to learn," he'd said. "Plus you do need your car. And I can get into the club early like I planned."

After Dad gave me the nod to hang with Kade, I freshened up. I'd fallen asleep in my clothes. My jeans were fine, but my blouse was wrinkled. I opted for a long-sleeved, V-neck cotton T-shirt. With the cloud cover and the cool fall temps, I wanted to be warm. Kade was prompt, showing up within fifteen minutes like he'd said. I grabbed a jacket, my phone, and my purse, then we were on our way.

He navigated through town, and in no time at all, we were traveling on a country road. Two-story colonial homes dotted the road's edge as we passed.

"How far out of town do you live?" I asked, keeping my gaze out the side window.

"We're almost there."

"Did you grow up here?"

He turned right, off the two-lane country road and onto another. Tall trees rose majestically along both sides, the tips of the branches gracefully arching over the road, creating a tunnel effect.

"No. My dad was in the military, so we've moved around a lot. This is the first place we've lived for more than four years."

Before I had a chance to ask any more questions, Kade was turning onto a paved driveway.

My jaw dropped. "You live here?" A massive two-story brick home sat with tall oak trees in the background and a lake behind it. A large wraparound porch skirted the house, and the front yard was land-scaped with manicured shaped trees, green grass, flowers and bushes. His family must be wealthy. He did say his dad was a psychiatrist.

At the end of the long driveway, he drove past the house, and braked in front of a six-car detached garage. Killing the engine, he jumped out. I had my hand on the handle when my phone buzzed.

Sliding the bar on the screen, I answered it. "Hello."

"Lacey? This is Coach Dean." His voice was low-pitched.

"Oh, hi." *Why was the coach of the baseball team calling me?*

Kade stood in front of the truck with his head cocked to one side, watching me.

I shrugged a shoulder.

"I understand you're not in school today. Are you feeling okay?"

"A little better now. Is there something wrong, Coach?" I twirled a strand of my hair around my finger. *Wow! I couldn't recall the last time I had played with my hair.* It used to be a nervous habit of mine. I let go.

"I was hoping to discuss a few things with you today before tryouts Wednesday."

"Like what?" I asked. A knot formed in my stomach. *What could he possibly want to talk about?*

"Why don't you stop by my office after school tomorrow? I'll see you then," Coach said. Then he hung up.

Kade opened the truck door, his face tight with worry.

"Who was that?" Kade asked.

"Coach Dean." Pocketing my phone, I hopped out of the truck. "He wants to see me tomorrow."

Kade let out a breath as though he was relieved for some reason. "For what?" he asked.

"He didn't say." I racked my brain, trying to think. *Was I in trouble? Was he going to tell me I couldn't try out?*

Kade enfolded my hand in his, and when he did, worry about Coach Dean and why he wanted to see me slowly dissipated. I swore the guy had magic in those large hands of his.

He led me into the garage through a side door. My car sat in the second bay with its hood open. All the other bays were empty, except the last one had a boxing ring set up in it. I yanked my hand away and went over to the ring. So this must've been what Kross and Kelton were referring to the other day.

"Kross likes to box," Kade said, walking up to me.

"Is he any good?" I asked, picking up a glove from the padded floor of the ring.

"Yep. Do you like boxing?"

"Maybe." I glanced up at him and shouldn't have. His lips curled into a sly smile as his gaze skimmed over me. I knew that look. It was the same one he'd had on Saturday night, right before he kissed me.

I didn't have time to run. The glove fell from my hand when he backed me against the boxing ring. My legs hit the padded base while my head connected with the bottom rope.

My chest rose and fell in rapid succession.

"Do you want to go a round in the ring?" he rasped, grabbing the ropes on each side of my head.

Oh yeah. I would love to go a round—just not in the ring. "You know I would kick your ass," I said.

One of his hands got lost in my hair. "I hope so," he said, his eyes darkening. "But right now"—he leaned down, his lips so close to mine — "I would like to kiss you."

The cocoons of butterflies in my stomach burst free in a happy frenzy.

Sliding his hand from my hair to the nape of my neck, his lids half closed. "I've been dying to taste you again." His voice was hypnotic, caressing, and if he didn't kiss me I just might have to punch him again.

"Kade?"

Grinning, his lips brushed the corner of my mouth, then he kissed his way to my ear, where he sucked and nibbled. I arched into him, our body heat igniting an inferno between us.

"What is it with you and ears?" Every hard inch of him molded to me.

"I love the way your body responds," he breathed.

"Is that one of your lines to get girls to do what you want?"

"Only you, Lace."

I didn't have time to squeak out a comeback. His other hand wrenched me to him, and the fire grew in my belly, sending sparks of pleasure lower. Reaching around him, I slid my hands into his jeans at the small of his back—warm, hard, and smooth.

He sucked in a breath and a low groan followed. Snaking his tongue through my lips, he felt his way around slowly, teasing my tongue with his, coaxing me to engage. Pressing in closer, I sucked on his tongue.

Growling, he dove deeper into a punishing kiss as though he couldn't get enough. He tasted all male, all sin. Desire blasted in me, making my brain foggy.

I didn't hear the footsteps echoing across the floor until Kade broke the kiss.

"Get out, Kelton," Kade barked, trying hard to control his breathing while he held me tightly to him.

Thank God he was, or else I would've collapsed right there. This kiss had been even more intense than the first, and I wasn't sure I had control of my limbs. As my brain cleared and I tried to get my own breathing under control, Kelton's laugh doused the flames inside me.

"Bro, you know you have a bedroom up at the house," Kelton drawled.

If Kade didn't kill Kelton, I just might. I kept my head buried against Kade's deliciously scented black T-shirt. He rested his chin on my head, his back to his brother.

"Kelton," he warned. "I will kick your ass if you don't get the fuck out of here. And what are you doing home from school?"

"I could ask you the same thing."

"Don't move," Kade whispered to me. "I'll be right back." He let me go and stalked over to Kelton, who was leaning against my car, ankles crossed, with one of his cocky grins on his face.

I eased down onto the edge of the padded ring floor.

"I swear, Kel," Kade said through clenched teeth.

Kelton grinned, raising his hands chest high. "Calm down, man. I have a dental appointment. Remember? I had a few minutes to kill. I came home to brush my teeth since the dentist is just down the road."

"Then go."

"Chill." Kelton started for the door. "Oh, and I thought you would like to know Sullivan is working for Pitt."

Kade ran a hand through his hair. "Who told you that?"

"I heard it at school. You should probably get Hunt to confirm it with his brother."

I jumped to my feet. *What was going on? Did this have anything to do with the confrontation at the club the other night?* I joined Kade and Kelton at my car. "Who's Pitt?"

"Jeremy Pitt runs an organization out of Boston that would put the mafia to shame," Kelton said matter-of-factly.

A muscle ticked in Kade's jaw as he looked at his brother.

Kelton glanced at his black-banded diver's watch. "I gotta run. Have fun, you two." He walked out.

Kade stared absently at the pristine, painted, gray concrete floor.

I moved to stand in front of him. "What happened between you and Greg?"

"I told you," he said in a hardened tone. "Old history."

"Not good enough, Kade." I placed a hand on his soft cotton T-shirt. "Have you forgotten I'm involved now?"

"Lace, the guy wants revenge for me beating his ass into the ground a couple of years ago. I'm afraid if he's working for a gang, he has more firepower to retaliate." He pulled out his phone from his front pocket. He tapped out a text as he paced over to the boxing ring. When he finished, he came over to me. "Come on." He held out his hand.

"That's it? You're not going to share anything else about Sullivan?" With the anger coursing through me, I dug my nails into my palm, then I shook my head. I wasn't going to get upset. I didn't want to go into freak mode for the second time today. *Let it go for now. Concentrate on relaxing. Tryouts are in two days.*

"Lace, there's not much to tell. He and I got into fights. As far as the gang he's supposedly with, that's his business unless he decides to make it mine. I'll address it then. I'll explain more when I know more. Right now, I would like to show you something." His expression was soft, yet impenetrable.

I relaxed enough to finally let my breath out, and I unclenched my fists. "I'm not going into your bedroom." *Although I would like to.*

One side of his mouth turned up. "You're not. Not today, anyway."

I almost pouted. "What about my car?"

"We'll work on your car later. I promise this won't take long." His arm was still stretched out. Curious as to what he wanted to show me, I took hold of his warm hand. His touch was electric, sending little prickles of pleasure dancing along my skin. We left the garage through the same door we came in. Instead of going up toward the house, we went left toward the lake.

CHAPTER 9

The breeze carried with it the scent of damp earth as we made our way down toward the lake. A panoramic view made a picture-perfect scene. Myriad beginnings of fall colors hung from the trees surrounding the water that was smooth as black glass. A tangled mass of sticks and leaves covered the ground as the landscape dipped down to a boathouse that skirted the water's edge.

"What did you want to show me?" I asked. I'd seen lakes before. While this one was nice, it didn't compare to the ocean-blue water of Lake Tahoe. My family had vacationed there in the summertime. Dad would rent a house for a week. Mom, Julie, and I would hang out and sunbathe by the lake, while Dad and Rob played golf. At night we'd play board games and have a cookout. I blinked a few times to stave off the tears pooling in my eyes.

"You'll see," he said as he padded up the wood steps to a small deck that led to a door on the boathouse.

"You want to show me a boat?" I climbed up after him.

He pushed open the door and waited until I went in first. *If Mary could see Kade now, she'd probably kiss him.*

Looking around, I realized this wasn't a boathouse but a man-cave, of sorts. A pool table was the focal point in the middle of the room. A poker table stood in the right corner adjacent to the door, with a refrigerator and a tall two-door cabinet in the far corner. A couch sat in front of the window that overlooked the lake, comfortable fabric chairs at each end.

After shutting the door, Kade crossed to the fridge. "Water?"

"Sure," I said as I circled around the pool table to check out a large photograph that had caught my eye. The triplets stood behind Kade, who was on one knee, all of them clad in fatigues. The brothers all looked to be in their early teens. Lying on the ground in front of them was a large, dead buck. I smiled. I didn't like to hunt, but Kade clearly did. *Why was I even surprised? He'd handled my gun that first night like a pro.*

"I love that picture. We caught two more bucks that day," he said, suddenly behind me.

"You guys look so happy." I thought of Julie and Mom again. Aside from summers in Tahoe, we'd spent winters skiing at Mammoth Mountain. Rob and I used to race each other downhill. He'd always beat me, but I always loved giving him a run for his money.

"How come your dad isn't in this picture? Does he hunt?"

"He took the picture. We do have one with him in it somewhere in the house. He liked this one so much he wanted to hang it up in here."

"What is this place? I assumed it was a boathouse."

He guided me over to the sofa, handing me a bottle of water. I twisted off the cap and took a long drink.

"It was. But my dad didn't want all our friends trashing the house, so he remodeled this place for us." He sat down with his water bottle in hand.

I did the same, but couldn't understand why I felt awkward. "Should we work on the car?" I did have my appointment late this afternoon with Dr. Davis. I absolutely could not miss it, or Dad would have my hide for sure.

"We will. Do you have somewhere to be?" He sat back, angling his body so his left arm rested on the back of the couch.

Oh crap. My throat became dry. Thankful for the bottle of water, I took another sip.

"Well?" His languid copper gaze moved over me.

"I do. At four thirty." I couldn't lie. If I did, I might miss my session.

"Okay. So how's your arm?"

That was it? He wasn't going to pry? Or ask what my appointment was for? I sighed and sat back, mimicking his position.

"It's not as sore." The Advil I took this morning had helped. I needed to remember to take two more pills before practice.

"Can we talk about what happened on Saturday night?"

Was he asking about the kiss? Or was he remembering what I did to hurt my arm? "Which part?" I was pretty sure what he was asking, but I had to be certain.

"At your house." He rested the water bottle against his stomach.

My hands became clammy. *If he heard the story, would he look at me differently? Would he run?*

"I haven't had the chance to thank you for helping me."

He moved his water bottle from the couch to the floor beside him before sliding closer to me. Every hormone in me sparked to life. He took my water bottle and put it next to his. Then, slowly and seductively, he threaded long, sure fingers through my hair. He gently coaxed me forward as his hand settled on the back of my head. Without thinking, I swung my left leg over his lap. His hands slid down to grasp my hips, and he lifted me. I was now straddling him.

With his hands on my butt, he drew me closer to him. A paper-thin space separated our chests. "Now this is a position that I really like," he whispered.

I buried my hands in his soft, thick hair.

"Are you taking advantage of me, Lace? Or are you avoiding talking to me?"

"Does it matter?"

He searched my face for a split second before his hands got lost under my shirt. His callused palms scraped along my back, soothing and prickly. Desire flashed in his eyes as he feathered his lips over mine. Gripping the sides of my waist, he lifted me before laying me down on the couch. All of a sudden, I was on my back and he was on top of me.

"Um...Kade?" Every hard inch of him pressed into me, but I did need to breathe.

Rolling off to the side so his back leaned against the couch, he propped his head on his hand then shifted a throw pillow under my head. He slid his leg between mine. His gaze roamed over the length of my body, slowing down in certain areas before making the climb back up to meet my eyes.

"See something you like?" A smile formed on my lips.

He nodded, his tongue wetting his bottom lip. Then he reached under my shirt and lightly stroked the area around my navel. The feeling was tranquilizing and erotic at the same time, and I had a strong desire to guide his hand farther south or farther north. I mentally shook off the fantasy—for now, anyway. I wasn't ready to take the next step. After all, we were practically strangers.

"So tell me about what happened to you." Leaning down, he licked circles around my bellybutton.

I gasped. *How was I supposed to concentrate with him making me squirm?*

"Tell me more about your rivalry with Greg," I said hoarsely. I didn't want to talk about Greg *or* me. I just wanted him to keep his hands and tongue in motion.

"You're avoiding me," he said seductively.

"Is this how you get females to talk? By luring them into your den and having your way with them?"

"Only you," he drawled.

"I have to go," I said weakly.

"Has anyone ever told you that you have amazing abs?" he said, ignoring my statement. He drew circles around my navel. "I've been dreaming about them since I met you in the parking lot that first night. How you had your T-shirt tied into a knot. Your skin glistened." He peppered kisses up and down my stomach.

"You were checking me out, even with a gun in my hand?" My mouth was slightly open.

"Oh, yeah. Now, I'll save the gun incident for another time. I want to hear about your attacks. Your dad wouldn't explain."

"Kade, I can't. I'm not ready. And I don't want people to know." I was so angry with myself. I had been getting better. I hadn't had an attack since we moved here, but that one had been one of the worst ones in a long time.

He scooted up, placing a hand on my cheek, staring directly into my eyes. "Lace, I'm not one to gossip."

"You told your brothers I punched you."

"I had to when I walked in the house with blood coming out my nose. You're avoiding me." He smoothed his fingers over my lips. "I need to know."

"Why? It's not like we're..."

"I want to get to know you."

"What about Tammy?" After the interaction between them at the

Cave, I got the impression he wasn't into her. Still, *never assume*, my brother always told me.

He laughed. "I was curious why you hadn't asked about her at the Cave. I'm not dating her. We went out one time last year. Since then she's been trying to get me to go out with her again. And I'm not interested in her, Lacey."

Silence hung between us as we stared at each other. The light poured in from the window, showcasing the honesty in his copper eyes, and something more. What, though, I couldn't quite figure out. I really hoped he wasn't trying to save me from my inner demons. Only I had the ability to cure myself from the nightmares and panic attacks.

Aside from all that was the million-dollar question: *was I ready to allow anyone into my world?* I'd only known him for a week at most, and during that time I had done nothing but physically abuse him. All of a sudden, Dad's words blared in my head. *You need to learn to trust. You need to relax.* I didn't know if I could trust Kade. I didn't know anything about him.

Reaching up, I traced the outline of his mouth with the pad of my finger, and his eyes drifted shut. "Kade, tell me one thing about yourself."

Opening his eyes, he leaned over and kissed me. "I like you."

My body warmed at his touch. "Of course, you do. I'm a girl and you're a player." My fingers glided along his strong jaw.

He groaned softly. "A player? Where did you hear that?"

"Rumor around school."

"And you believe rumors." He bit my lower lip.

"Hey. I need that lip."

He chuckled. "Lace, I've never had a steady girlfriend. If that makes me a player, then it does. Nothing I can do about that."

"Why no girlfriend?" My hands were on the move, feeling hard, sleek muscle through the soft fabric of his T-shirt.

"Most girls are too serious. They want love and all that."

"And the player, Kade Maxwell, doesn't do love, right?"

"Does Lacey Robinson do love?" he asked.

"Hell no. I don't have time for mushy stuff like that. I'm here to make the team, so I can get my scholarship to ASU, and nothing more." I wouldn't be opposed to dating. I just didn't want it to distract me from my goals.

"Wait." His tone was serious and surprised all of sudden. "You're not just trying out to prove a point, like most other girls?"

Typical of men. I pursed my lips, and shook my head. "Why would I? Arizona State was scouting me for their college team until..."

"Until what, Lace?"

I turned my head. *Don't cry. Don't show weakness.*

"Look at me, Lace." His thumb smoothed over my eyebrow. "Please?"

Blinking, I turned, meeting his gaze.

"It's okay if you don't want to talk," he whispered. "I'm here when you do. But can I ask you one question?"

I nodded, willing the lump in my throat to go away.

"If you do have an attack, what can I do? The other night, I had no idea how to get you out of your trance."

"What makes you think you're going to be with me when I have an attack?" I was surprised my voice didn't fail me.

"I'm not letting you out of my sight if I can help it."

"Why? Because of my attacks?" My muscles tensed, overpowering the ache in my chest. "I don't need anyone's help, and I'm certainly not anyone's charity case." I punctuated the last two words by trying to lift up on my elbows, but he held me down.

"Hey, chill," he said softly. "It has nothing to do with your attacks and everything to do with that first kiss the other night."

"English, please?" I asked.

He slipped his tongue inside my mouth, and my core went liquid. *Damn.* He was good.

"I haven't been able to get that kiss out of my brain," he whispered against my lips. "It's imprinted on it. I want to kiss you all day long."

One side of my brain said, *keep your goals in front of you.* The other side was Mary's voice. *You need to have fun.* Maybe I could do both. "Kade, I—"

He gently placed his finger on my lips as though he knew what I was struggling with. "Hey, no commitments," he said. "Just two people getting to know each other. And the last thing I want to do is get in the way of your dream."

"So you're not asking me to go steady, Kade Maxwell?"

"To quote a beautiful brunette who has lick-worthy abs, 'Hell no.'"

We both laughed.

"You forgot ears," I added.

"That too. So will you allow me to kiss you until the end of the school year?"

Was he prepared to know the real me? Was I prepared to open up to him? Or did I want to get to know him? He was rumored to be a player. Would he break my heart? What if I fell in love with him? I was leaving at the end of the school year. Dad and Mary's words resonated —*learn to trust, have fun.*

"I have one request."

"I don't bargain," he said, grinning.

"Maybe not, but you'll like this one."

He quirked an eyebrow.

"That you give my abs as much attention as you've given my ears."

"I'll give *any* part of your body all the attention in the world," he said before kissing me with such intensity and emotion that the wall around my heart cracked open.

His phone vibrated on my leg. He broke the kiss, plucking it out of his pocket. "Yeah. We'll meet you in the garage." He tapped the screen. "My friend Hunt is here."

We both sat up. I smoothed out my shirt. He combed his fingers through his hair.

"So is Hunt here to help you fix my car?"

"Not really. I sent him a text before we came down here. His brother Wes works for Jeremy Pitt. I wanted him to see if he can confirm if Sullivan is working for Pitt."

The name Sullivan jarred my brain. I didn't want any part of that rivalry. Greg gave me the creeps. "You know, Kade, maybe we should get to know each other after you've resolved your feud with Sullivan."

His hands latched onto my waist, and he yanked me onto his lap. "Sullivan is not going to do anything stupid. If he does, then he'll do it to me."

"Then why did he tell me that he and I were going to have fun? What did he mean?"

"He's trying to provoke me through you. If I lay a hand on him again I'll probably go to jail." His hands tightened on my hips. "We need to go."

I hopped off his lap. "Like you did last time?"

He pushed to his feet. "Did Tyler tell you?" Annoyance colored his tone.

I hadn't seen Tyler since Saturday morning. Was he jealous of the quarterback? "Becca told me."

"Look, I have a past, just like you do." His tone mellowed. "As we get to know each other you'll learn more about my life, just as I will about yours."

I suddenly had the desire to flee. Not because of Kade's past but because of mine.

"Are you okay? You look pale."

"I'm not sure I can do this, Kade." I waved my hand between us.

"I promise Sullivan isn't going to be a problem. Though something tells me you've seen a different ghost."

"Isn't Hunt waiting?" I looked at the pool table.

"He can wait." He placed two fingers under my chin. "Look at me."

Get it together, girl. Take a chance. Face your fears. You're going to have to let people in if you want to get on with your life. I dragged my gaze upward to meet his.

"Are we cool?" He brushed the backs of his fingers over my face.

"We are."

"Are you sure?"

"Yeah." *Not really.* Nausea swirled in my stomach at the thought of him knowing more about me.

He twined his fingers with mine as he pressed soft and tender kisses on my lips. "Thank you."

I shuddered. Kade Maxwell thrilled me and terrified me. His kisses tortured me. His touch electrified me, and his husky voice turned me into mush, and I wasn't the mushy type. Even with Brad, I wasn't the lovey-dovey girl. Maybe because Brad taught me that you didn't have to touch someone all the time. I mean, we barely held hands. Regardless, Brad had never kissed me the way Kade had—Kade's kisses were soft, tender, sensual. Brad's were hard quick pecks with little tongue. My body never reacted the way it did when I was with Kade. One look from him and my pulse jumped, my panties dampened, and my stomach somersaulted. The only time I'd gotten butterflies over something that was near and dear to me was when I was on the pitching mound. Suddenly, that desire to flee intensified. Only now, I wanted to run from myself.

"Hey, Lace. Are you in there?" Kade's hand swept across my cheek.

Stop analyzing the situation and have fun. "Yeah." For now, I would try to loosen up.

CHAPTER 10

Hunt had both his hands on the front of the Mustang, his six-foot frame hunched over, examining the engine.

"Hey, man," Kade said as we strode into the garage.

"What's up?" Hunt straightened. "Oh, hey, Lacey. Nice to see you again." His brown eyes regarded me as he rubbed his hands down his tattered jeans.

I gave one nod as my stomach growled.

Both guys looked at me. "Sorry, I haven't eaten lunch." How embarrassing.

"This won't take long. Then we'll get something to eat," Kade said.

"Then my car?" I snatched my phone from my back pocket to check the time. I still had a couple of hours before Dr. Davis.

"What's wrong with her car, man?" Hunt asked.

"Battery for one. The spark plugs need to be checked. And I want to change the oil."

"Do I need a new battery?" I asked.

"I already replaced it." Kade tucked his hands in his jean pockets. "So, Hunt, what did you find out about Sullivan?"

Did my dad give him money? If not, I needed to make sure he did.

Hunt looked at me then at Kade.

"She's cool," he said to Hunt.

"Wes said Sullivan is not working for Pitt. But he is friends with a couple of Pitt's men." He hooked his thumbs on the pockets of his jeans.

"Would they do anything stupid like support Sullivan in a plan to get revenge?" Kade asked.

"Nah, dude. Their bread and butter comes from Pitt, not that weasel."

"What does your brother do for Pitt?" I twirled a section of my hair.

"Pitt is a Harvard grad," Hunt said. "Smart as a whip, knows his way around a courtroom, and makes his living running several businesses in Boston. My brother manages one of his companies, the Guardian. They farm out bodyguards and bouncers."

"So what did Kelton mean when he said this Pitt guy would put the mafia to shame?" My hair was going to be knotted by the time we were finished with this conversation.

Kade reached over and gently circled my wrists with his fingers, tugging my hand from my hair. *Really?* I could've been snarky, but I chose not to be and lowered my hand. Something told me he was trying to keep me calm, which I appreciated. I didn't want to morph into crazy-girl in front of Hunt.

Hunt glanced at Kade. Kade cocked his head slightly as he looked at me.

"What? I'm fine. I'm wearing my big girl panties." I had to show them I was cool, even though I didn't like the sound of mafia, or Pitt, or Sullivan.

Hunt roared with laughter. Kade just smirked. I even laughed.

"Come on, let's get something to eat. Hunt, are you hungry?"

Ooookay. We were done talking. Which was fine with me for now. Hunger pangs kept poking at my stomach.

"Go ahead, man. I'll check the sparks on the Mustang."

Kade and I left Hunt in the garage. A mist of rain had started to fall when we stepped out. I shivered. The temperature had dropped too. Wrapping his arm around me, Kade drew me to him as we headed the short distance to the house.

Every stainless appliance in Kade's kitchen sparkled under the recessed lights. Even the black granite countertops shone. It reminded me of our kitchen back in LA. Mary would die if she saw this place.

"What will it be?" Kade asked with his hand on the open fridge door.

"Um...don't laugh. But if you have peanut butter and jelly, I would settle for that."

His head whipped around. "Why? We have lunch meat." He said it as though PB&J violated the rules of American cuisine.

"So? I like PB&J."

Closing the fridge, he opened up a cabinet and pulled out the peanut butter. "You're in luck. Kody likes it too."

"Let me guess. The rest of you are meat lovers."

"We're growing men," he said matter-of-factly. *Wasn't that the truth?* All of them were at least six foot or more, muscular, and handsome. He'd talked a little about his father, but he had yet to mention anything about his mother. I couldn't wait to meet his parents to see what they looked like.

"Does your mom only eat meat too?"

"Nah, she likes the PB&J."

After he had all the ingredients on the long granite island, he made his sandwich of salami and cheese. I made my own sandwich, making myself at home. Then he disappeared into a pantry on the other side of the fridge before emerging with a bag of chips and two plates.

He studied me for a second then said, "Let me guess. You want milk with that sandwich."

I sat down on one of the bar stools. "Duh." I bit into my sandwich. *Heaven.*

He poured me some milk and then sat on a stool next to me.

I chased my next bite with a mouthful of milk. He at his sandwich in four bites.

"So does your mom work?" I asked.

"Our mom doesn't live with us."

"Are your mom and dad divorced?" *Careful, girl. If you ask questions, he'll ask you questions.*

"No." He slid off the stool suddenly, as though I'd asked the wrong question. He dumped his plate into the sink then returned the chips to the pantry.

"You don't want to talk about it?"

"No. Not now."

I was cool with that. I finished my PB&J, downed the last of the milk, and then set the glass in the sink. I'd just filled it with water when Kade's body pressed into my back, his hand sweeping my hair to one side. Tilting my neck, I shuddered.

His lips skimmed the sensitive spot behind my ear. I turned in his arms, his darkened gaze meeting mine. Angling his head slightly, he lowered it until his lips skated across mine, his tongue tracing a pattern along my lower lip. "So soft," he whispered.

A soft sound escaped me. I loved when he spoke to me in that husky voice. The deep timbre of it slid along my skin like pure silk.

"Baby, don't make sounds like that." Flames shone in his eyes. "Unless you want to go to my bedroom."

I wanted a lot of things, but nothing more than him right at this moment.

Someone cleared his throat. "Kade," Hunt said. "The car needs new plugs. We should run to the store."

"Can you give us a minute?" Kade asked, not moving.

"I'll be out in the garage." Hunt's footsteps clattered against the wood floor as he retreated.

The microwave clock to my left read three p.m. If he went to the store would he be back in time for me to make my appointment? "Will I be able to use my car today?" The nervous-butterflies perked up inside me.

He, too, glanced at the clock. "If the spark plugs are bad, then the car could stall. I'd prefer if you didn't use it until we can get new ones. I can take you to your appointment." He placed his hands on the sink at my sides.

I glanced at my distorted reflection in the stainless appliances. He already knew I had missed an appointment with my shrink. Maybe this was a way to see how he reacted, and if I could trust him. I curled my fingers in the waist of his jeans.

"Careful. My room isn't far." No grin, no smile, just a serious expression on his beautiful face.

Yeah, so. "Um." I chewed on my bottom lip.

He framed my face in his hands. "Baby, you're shaking."

"I'm cold, that's all," I lied. A low buzzing began in my head. "I can still drive my car, though?" *Should I take a chance with my car?*

"I would feel like an ass if your car broke down. And I'd hate to face the wrath of your dad. I practically begged him to let me fix it. He put his trust in me." He placed his forehead against mine. "Please, Lace. I'd worry."

Wow, he sure knew how to make a good argument. Closing my eyes, I inhaled. When I did, the tang of mustard and salami accosted me. I giggled.

"What's so funny?"

"Your breath smells like meat."

His tongue snaked out, trying to push through my lips.

"Yuck."

"Hey, yours isn't any better, Peanut-Butter Breath." He grinned. "So, what's your answer?"

Did I have a choice? What if it did break down? Dad would be furious at me for not seeing Dr. Davis again. Then he would turn his rage on Kade for not fixing it properly.

"Okay. I have a doctor's appointment in Lancaster."

"Was that so bad?"

"Yeah, Kade, it was." My tone was even. "This is hard for me, and I've been nothing but bitchy to you."

"What did we talk about earlier? Getting to know each other, right?"

"I honestly thought you only wanted me for my body," I teased. I had to make light of the conversation to shake off the little bee in my head.

"Oh, you don't know how much," he drawled in a pained voice.

I had a good idea. But right now, I needed to be sure I could trust him.

He grabbed my butt, pulling me to him, hips to hips.

I gasped. *Yeah, he was definitely ready to take me to his room.*

⚜

KADE DROPPED me off at Dr. Davis's office while he went to the auto parts store. Hunt stayed behind to continue the tune-up on my car. Kross had come home as we were leaving, and Kade asked him if he could help Hunt. He agreed, only if Hunt would spar with him.

"You'll have to ask him," Kade had said. "The last time he sparred with you, he got stitches over his eye."

I'd been curious about how Hunt got that scar. I wouldn't have minded having a go in the ring myself, especially with Kelton. The idea of punching the cocky grin off of his face thrilled me. But I couldn't do anything to screw up my arm. Not with tryouts in two days.

I climbed the stairs to the second floor, thinking about what questions Dr. Davis might ask me. Since this was my first meeting with him, would he make me go through the details of that night? My stomach knotted at that thought.

I had just turned to go up the second set of stairs when heavy footsteps sounded above me. Looking up, I practically did a double take. One of the Maxwell triplets came down the stairs, fiddling with his keys. His shaggy hair hung over his ears. He wore a white T-shirt underneath a blue buttoned-up shirt opened in the front over black jeans. If it weren't for Kross's short hair and bulging biceps or the scar on Kelton's chin, I wouldn't have known this was Kody.

"Hey, Lacey," he said in a placid tone, as though he wasn't surprised to see me.

"Um...hi." My tone was full of *what the heck was he doing here?* Was he coming from Dr. Davis's office? If so, why hadn't Kade mentioned Kody went to the same doctor?

We were both standing on the landing. He studied me with deep-blue eyes that held so much sadness, and I didn't know what to say.

"You weren't in chemistry today. Is everything okay?" he asked.

No. "I didn't feel well this morning."

"Well, we have a quiz tomorrow on properties of matter," he said. "Make sure you know boiling point, melting point, and all that."

"Thanks. I better go." I started to climb the stairs. While I wanted to know why he was here, I couldn't ask without telling him why I was, and that wasn't going to happen.

"Lacey?"

I grabbed hold of the railing and turned.

"I did come from Dr. Davis's office. We all have issues." He played with his keys.

"What does that mean?" Did he know I was going to see Dr. Davis? I gripped the rail tighter.

"Look, the only office on the second floor is Dr. Davis's."

Okay, but why was he coming out this way? Dr. Meyers always had a private way out for her patients, so they didn't run into the ones coming in for their appointment. Or she timed it where patients didn't run into each other. Maybe Dr. Davis's office wasn't set up that way.

"I have to go. I have a guitar lesson. Is Kade coming back for you?"

Drawing my eyebrows together, I almost slipped off the step. "Yeah. How did you know he brought me here?" *Kade told him about me?*

He cocked his head to one side. "Lace, we're brothers. We do talk."

Oh, God. Did Kody know about my panic attack on Saturday?

"You knew I would be here?" My nails dug into wood railing.

"Kade sent me a text a few minutes ago."

"Why?" Suddenly, I wished the stair rail were Kade's eyes. Several things were going through my mind. One, I was going to kill Kade. Two, why hadn't he told me about Kody being here? Three, now Kody knew about me seeing a shrink. Who else knew? A large bumblebee zipped around in my head.

Noticing something was wrong, Kody said, "Hey, it's okay. Seeing each other here doesn't go past these four walls."

"Past these walls and your brothers," I all but snapped. *God, I was so stupid to trust Kade.* Tears stung my eyes.

"Lacey, we talk. We don't gossip. Besides, do you think I want people at school knowing I see a shrink?" He grinned crookedly, and it reminded me of Kelton and Kade—disarming and warm.

I guess he had a point.

"I'm sorry," he said. "I promise—on my end, no one will hear it from me. Okay?" He shoved one hand into the front pocket of his jeans.

"Yeah. I promise too. I gotta go." I ran up the stairs on shaky legs and into the reception area of Dr. Davis's office.

"I was just going to call you," said a handsome man with perfectly coiffed salt-and-pepper hair with a goatee to match. I assumed it was Dr. Davis.

"I'm sorry." I was numb walking into his office. Two people now knew that I was seeing a shrink. Before long, the whole school was going to know. My breathing became shallow as I eased down onto a leather couch, trying to calm the whirring in my head.

"Are you okay?" Dr. Davis asked.

I squeezed my eyes shut. *Get it together.*

"Lacey?" His voice was calm as he sat down next to me.

My eyelids slid open, and a tear escaped.

"What's wrong?" He stretched to grab a box of tissues from the end table, slanting it toward me.

Pulling out a tissue, I patted my eyes. "It's just...ever since I started school, things haven't been going well."

"Like what?" He rose, walked over to his desk, and snagged a notepad. Then he settled into a chair opposite me.

Staring out the window, I gathered my thoughts. The clouds finally opened up and a steady rain fell. I hugged myself as I turned my atten-tion to Dr. Davis. He kept his gaze focused on me with his hands clasped in his lap, one leg crossed over the other. His gray eyes were soft but concerned.

I swallowed. "I'm sorry I missed my appointment the other day."

"No problem."

Silence dangled as he wrote on his notepad. What was he writing? I hadn't given him any details yet.

Subtle tans, reds, and oranges colored the walls while a soft glow from the table lamp next to me enhanced the coziness of the room. "So, do you like Ashford?" he asked in a soothing voice.

I wiped my nose with the wadded up tissue, and nodded.

"What's one thing you like about it?"

"The trees and the fall colors," I said quietly. Fall was one of the seasons I was excited about. I'd only seen pictures of how beautiful this area was when the leaves changed. In California, we had some trees that changed colors, but we didn't have the dense wooded land-scape like New England.

"The fall is pretty. This is only the beginning, too. The colors don't peak until October."

"I'm scared," I whispered, tears forming again.

"About?" His voice softened.

Even though I'd just met him, I wanted to spill my guts to him. Maybe it was his nurturing tone, or the gentleness in his dark eyes. "Life. Living on edge. Not getting the images of my mother and my sister out of my head. Always waking up in a cold sweat from nightmares."

"Did something happen recently, Lacey?"

A tear dropped on my jeans. I curled my legs underneath me. "I had one of my panic attacks the other night and Kody's brother, Kade, was with me when it happened. Now he wants to know why I have panic attacks. I'm afraid to tell him. Heck, I'm afraid of anyone knowing that I'm broken. Now Kody knows that I see a shrink."

"Why are you afraid of telling Kade?"

A tinge of anger surfaced. "Would you want people to know that you're crazy?"

"Having PTSD doesn't mean you're crazy." Compassion laced his words. "After a traumatic event, the mind and body are in shock."

"You didn't see the look on Kade's face when I came out of the flashback. He was frightened. I don't want him to be afraid of me." I didn't want to see his eyes bulge like that again.

"I think he might be afraid *for* you. He probably didn't know how to help. Take me through what happened the other night."

I explained what I remembered from when Kade and I drove up to the house.

"So the trigger was the dark house?" he asked.

I nodded. "So how could Kade have helped?"

He scribbled on his notepad. "For one, he would need to know the triggers. During the next session I would like to explore some of the details of the trauma. That way we can determine what other things generate an episode. We'll take it slowly and gradually. Fair enough?"

"Yes." I only knew of the lights trigger for sure. However, a few other things were scorched into my memory of that night—all the blood I'd slipped in on the kitchen floor, and the scent of it—the insect-repellent smell of the cologne in the garage, and the worst part —Mom and Julie's bodies. For as long as I lived, that memory would haunt my dreams. "Dr. Davis, will I ever get better?"

He crossed one leg over the other. "I can't say you will ever forget what you went through. Trauma is hard on anyone, and everyone processes it differently. But with some hard work, there is the possibility you can get to a point where you're not having attacks or flashbacks."

"I know I will never get that night out of my head, but I don't want to be afraid anymore." I wrapped my arms around myself.

"Let's shift topics for a moment. In the file I received from Dr. Meyers, it says you like to play baseball. What position do you play?"

"Pitcher." His question had nothing to do with what happened to me, yet it had everything to do with my life. I knew this was one of his ways to learn more about me. When I first met Dr. Meyers we'd talked about the weather and so many other topics before she even asked me about that night.

After forty-five minutes of talking about baseball and the move from California, I got up and moved over to the window. Main Street in Lancaster bustled with late-day traffic. Cars waited in line to get through the red light. The torrential rain had slowed to a drizzle.

"Between now and the next time we meet, I would like for you to try an exercise."

Exercise? Turning, I raised an eyebrow. He got to his feet, walked over to stand behind his cherry-wood desk, and set down his notepad. He had one hand in his pants pocket, and the other smoothing out his goatee. "Don't worry. This won't hurt a bit. I want you to play a game with a friend. It's an icebreaker game." He circled around his desk. "You tell your friend one thing that they don't know about you, then you have them tell you one thing you don't know about them. When we meet again, I want to hear how it went." He met me at the window, both his hands in his pockets now.

"Wait. I don't want anyone to know—"

"It doesn't have to be about what happened to you. It can be anything. For example, I'll tell you something about me. Then I want you to reciprocate. Fair enough?"

"Sure." My brain worked to find something about me to share.

"I love to dip my bacon in maple syrup."

"Really?" I'd have to try that. It did sound tasty.

"Yes. Now it's your turn."

"I like Kade Maxwell." I slapped my hand over my mouth. *Did I just say that?*

"Was I not supposed to know that?" He angled his head to one side.

I let out a nervous laugh. "Um...I guess...I don't know. It's the first time I've said it out loud to anyone."

"So he doesn't know?" His expression was impassive, although there was a smile in his eyes.

I shook my head. "We've kissed, but I never told him that I like him." He definitely knew I wanted him, but that was a different story.

My cheeks were scorching hot from embarrassment. I was having a conversation about a boy with my psychiatrist. I'd never spoken to Dad about boys. That topic was always reserved for my mom or my sister. I wished they were here so I could talk to them about Kade in particular, especially Mom. She always had the answers. When I debated whether to date Brad, she'd told me to make sure the boy you build a relationship with supports your dreams, and you support his. Brad had told me he supported me playing baseball, but on several occasions he always had an excuse for not showing. Yet I'd cheered him on at every one of his soccer games.

"I see. Then maybe you've already picked your friend for the assignment." He walked me to the door.

"Oh, I don't think so," I said. "If I play that game with him, he'll be asking me more questions."

"Lacey, you have to dip your toe in the water. You can't be afraid or else healing will be difficult. Do you understand?"

I nodded. I could always play it with Becca.

"Good. I'll see you next week." He held the door open for me.

The waiting room was empty when I walked out. I didn't know if Kade was outside or not, but as I made way downstairs, I thought about the game that Dr. Davis wanted me to play. In part, Kade and I had played it already. He'd told me that he liked me. I hadn't reciprocated, though. There was so much to learn about one another. Could this game be the key to unlocking both our worlds?

Kade's tall, sexy body came into view through the glass doors. I hesitated for a second before exiting the building. I wasn't even near him and butterflies took flight inside me. He was leaning against his truck, looking all hot and hunky. His eyes skimmed the length of my body as I drew closer. He smiled when we locked gazes.

I wiped every expression off my face, steeling my shoulders, breathing evenly. *Hell.* Who was I kidding? I was a complete wreck—inside and out. My feelings always showed on my face.

I pushed through the glass doors. The drizzle had turned into a mist. I crossed my arms over my chest as I walked over to him. The ball of knots in my stomach tightened as though someone were wringing out a wet towel. I stopped a few feet from him. I couldn't get too close. I didn't trust myself. Still, I couldn't decide if I should punch him, kiss him, or just walk away.

Getting to know people used to be fun. I'd been the girl at Crestview who mentored incoming freshmen. I volunteered for the position. I was assigned two students at a time. My role was to show them around campus, answer any questions they had and check in with them periodically to see how they were doing. In the process, I made a friend or two. But now here I was, debating whether I wanted to spend my energy on Kade.

"What's wrong?" he asked in that sexy voice of his.

"Oh, I don't know. You want to tell me?" I'd put money on the table that Kody alerted him to our conversation in the waiting room.

His fingers got lost in his unruly hair. "Shit. You ran into Kody, didn't you?"

"*Why*, Kade? Why didn't you tell me? And why did you have to tell

Kody?" I swallowed hard, trying not to lose it. I wouldn't be so freaking mad if Kody had walked out of the office and been surprised to see me. At least with that scenario it would've built a little trust between Kade and me.

"If I had, you would've bolted." He straightened his posture. "Your dad said you missed an appointment last week. I didn't want that to happen again. And I told my brother because he would've gone ballistic seeing someone from school here." He crossed one arm over his chest to hold his other.

"You're not my father. You don't get to decide if I miss an appointment or not. And what makes you think I would've run?"

"You ran last week when you were here. You didn't go in because of me. Right? Tell me I'm wrong."

I dropped my gaze.

He closed the distance between us. "I'm sorry, Lace," he said as his hand reached out to grab my arm.

I backed away even though I wanted to leap into his arms. I had to make him understand he couldn't make my decisions for me, and trust was important to me. He hardly knew me. How could he know what was right for me?

Well, if you open up to the man, he might...

Shut up, I shouted at the stupid voice in my head. *God.* I was losing it. "If you want to get to know me, Kade, acting like you know what's good for me isn't the way to do it. Do you know how hard it was for me to ask you to bring me here? Huh?"

"I was just trying to help." He shoved his hands into the pockets of his faded jeans.

"Why do you care? You don't know me. And I've done nothing but—"

"Stop, Lace." He raised his voice. "I screwed up." Regret flickered in his gaze. "I care because" —he gentled his voice— "I like you."

"I'm not sure I like *you* right now." *Okay, that was a big fat lie.*

With a deadpan expression he retrieved his keys from his pocket. "Get in. I'll take you home," he said.

Yeah, I had either pissed him off or hurt his feelings. I couldn't tell. I wasn't going to take it back just to make him feel better. "I'll find my own way home," I said, digging my phone out of my purse.

"No," he snapped. "Get in the truck."

Now he was showing a little attitude. Becca had said Kade had a temper. At least I got some emotion out of him. I hated the blank looks or not knowing what he was thinking.

"No," I blurted out. Who did he think he was talking to? I was getting tired of him ordering me around like he did at the Cave the other night.

"You're not going to like it if I have to put you in the truck myself." His tone had an edge to it.

I laughed.

He didn't. The imposing ass-hat stalked toward me. He was an arm's length from me when Dr. Davis emerged from the building, his briefcase in hand.

"Lacey. Kade," Dr. Davis said. "Is everything all right?"

"Yes, sir," Kade responded.

"You know Kade?" I asked, my jaw practically coming unhinged.

"Yes," he said. "Now, is everything okay?"

No. I was seeing a doctor that knew Kade. *Was that the reason he was in town when I was here last week?*

"Do you see a shrink too?" I asked, glaring at Kade.

If I'd asked Dr. Davis he wouldn't have told me. Doctor-patient confidentiality bound him.

"I should after today," Kade mocked.

He was now holding my hand. *When did he glue his hand to mine? God, I needed to pay attention around him.*

"We're fine, Doc," Kade said. "We were just leaving."

Dr. Davis nodded, then headed to his car.

"Let's go, and don't make a scene," Kade whispered.

"Or what?"

"I'll take you back to my house and lock you in my room." His eyes narrowed to slits, soft lashes belying the anger in his eyes.

"You and whose army?"

"Lacey," he warned.

Large raindrops fell from the sky. I yanked my hand from his. "Fine. Take me home." I only agreed because the clouds were about to open up again. I got into his truck, slamming the door. When he slid into the driver's seat, he mumbled a string of curse words. After he turned the ignition, his glance shot daggers my way.

Whatever. I relaxed against the seat, pinning my gaze out the side window. An uncomfortable silence filled the truck as we headed to my house. I itched to get home, to lock myself in my room and bury my head under a pillow. I wasn't even going to try and make sense of anything that happened today. All I knew was that my focus had to be sharp for tryouts on Wednesday. So I shoved my emotions in a box and taped it shut. Then prayed like hell I would make it through the rest of the week without seeing Kade Maxwell.

CHAPTER 11

K ade consumed my world the previous day, leaving me little time to think about my meeting with Coach Dean in the afternoon. My thoughts since I'd gotten home had focused on Kade. One minute he was tender and sweet, and the next he was betraying my trust. I tried studying for the chemistry quiz, to no avail. The words blurred across the page. I gave up and studied trig. After the first problem, I found myself transposing numbers. So I resorted to sleep. The minute I closed my eyes images of Kade licking my abs popped into my brain. Needless to say, I didn't sleep well. The only good thing about my mind wandering was that I didn't have nightmares.

Since I didn't have a car, I'd called Becca to see if she could pick me up. No answer. I texted her. Still no response. I would've asked Dad, but he arrived home late last night. Reluctantly, I called Tyler. I wasn't sure I was ready to see him, given our awkward moment on the ball field Saturday morning.

I inhaled, taking in the fresh morning scent of grass and wet leaves as I sat on the porch waiting for Tyler. Our front lawn wasn't as nicely landscaped as the Maxwells'. We didn't have perfectly manicured shrubs or a clean carpet of grass. Leaves littered our lawn. Dad and I had yet to pay much attention to the yard. We'd always had a landscaper take care of our property in LA.

I'd been staring off into space, rubbing my lips when my phone chirped in my hand. I looked at the screen then hit the ignore button. I didn't want to deal with Kade this morning. With my luck, when I heard his voice I'd probably cave. I had no idea how I was going to act when I saw him at school. I'd worry about it later. Right now, I had to ride to school with Tyler.

The sound of an engine cleared my head as an SUV drove up. "You ready?" Tyler asked through the open passenger window, his blond hair, so unlike Kade's, ruffled from the wind.

"Yeah." I gathered my backpack then followed the brick path down to the driveway. I still didn't know what I was going to say to Tyler. Would he want to talk about our almost-kiss?

The heat blasted me as I climbed into the SUV, a welcome change from the chilly morning temperatures. I set my phone in my lap and waved my hands in front of the vents.

"What happened to you yesterday?" Tyler asked, backing out of the driveway. "I almost called you, but I got tied up with football practice."

"I didn't feel good. So I have a meeting with Coach today. Do you know what it's about?" Tyler was well connected with the sports staff at the school.

"No clue." He shifted the SUV into drive.

"You don't think he's going to tell me I can't try out, do you?" I didn't know why I kept thinking that.

"Why would he?" Tyler asked.

My phone rang. I hit the ignore button again.

"Avoiding someone?" he asked, leaning an elbow on his console.

"Are you still helping me practice after school?" Kross, Kelton, Tyler, and I had agreed to practice one more time before tryouts.

"Okay, now you're avoiding me." His gaze darted to me then back out the windshield. "What's going on, Lace? You ran off Saturday after practice. You weren't in school yesterday. Now you're ignoring calls and questions. What are you hiding from?"

My life. "I'm worried about tryouts." I rubbed my arm as I said it. I'd taken Advil at breakfast. My elbow had more of a dull ache than my shoulder. I could work with a sore elbow.

"Tryouts wouldn't have you ignoring a phone call. Who is it—Kade?"

My head jerked toward him so fast I might have to worry about whiplash. A pregnant pause stretched through the stoplight. "Why would you automatically think it was Kade?"

A muscle ticked in his jaw as he regarded me cautiously from the corner of his eye. "Lacey, I told you to stay away from him."

"Why does everyone keep telling me that? First you, then Becca. I'm a big girl. I can take care of myself."

He laughed. "I know that," he said in a mirthless tone.

"What is your problem, Tyler? Are you jealous or something?"

"Don't flatter yourself, Lacey." His brazenness set me off, especially when he gave me the vibe that he liked me as more than a friend.

"Then what is it?" I bit out. I wasn't letting him off the hook now.

"I'm sorry. Let's just drop it." He sighed. "It's none of my business. I was just trying to make sure you don't get hurt."

Why was everyone worried about me getting involved with Kade? Was there something about him that I was missing? Sure, I witnessed a sliver of his temper. But he wasn't a monster.

My phone dinged. *Speak of the devil.*

I'm sorry. A sad-faced emoticon followed the two words.

Tyler pulled into the school's lot. I put my phone in sleep mode. I'd deal with Kade later, if at all.

"Forgive me?" Tyler asked, throwing the SUV into park.

I sighed heavily. "Ty, I like you as a friend, and nothing more." *There. I said it.*

"I get it, Lace." His pensive look as he focused on the red truck in front of us didn't match his words. "As your friend, I don't want to see you get hurt."

"While I appreciate your protective nature, I don't need a big brother. I have one. I appreciate your concern, but the guy is not what you or anyone else may think. I've heard about his rivalry with Greg Sullivan. And, if you must know, I now have my own rivalry with that creep."

I had my hand on the door when his fingers latched around my arm.

"Explain that last part, please?" He regarded me, lines creasing his forehead.

"I had words with Greg yesterday morning."

"Where? I thought you were sick. And why?" He dropped his hand from my arm.

"He was being a jerk."

"You mean he took a picture of you and Kade kissing," he said.

There it was. The thing that was bothering Tyler.

"And you know that how?" The hairs on my neck rose.

"It went viral yesterday."

Whatever. I hopped out of the SUV, slipping my phone into my pocket. I wasn't hanging around to hear any more of Tyler's wisdom about why I shouldn't be seeing Kade. I had my own reasons I shouldn't be seeing the sexy hunk.

"Lace?" Tyler called after me.

I waved my hand in the air as I jogged toward school. Kids strolled in, chatting to one another or on their phones. I sailed past them, through the doors and right into Aaron Seever.

"Hey, watch where you're going." He grasped my shoulders, glaring down at me.

"Sorry," I said, shrugging out of his hold.

I'd only seen Aaron from a distance at the Cave, and he wasn't in any of my classes. The guy was taller than I'd realized.

"I don't think we've had a chance to meet yet," he said. "I'm Aaron." Students roamed the hall, appearing to be in their own worlds.

"Lacey," I said, extending my hand.

We both knew who the other was. Still, I went through the motions. *Be nice.*

He closed his hand over mine. "Nice to meet you. Now that we have that out of the way." He clamped down on my hand as though his were a vise. Leaning in, he said in a low voice, "I don't know why you want to be on this team. Frankly, with a hot body like yours, you'd look better in a swimsuit than a baseball uniform. I hear the swim team has an opening."

"Is that so?" My eyes were locked with his. "What's wrong, Aaron? Are you afraid I'm better than you?"

We stared daggers at each other until a group of girls walking by giggled. He blinked. I swung my gaze to my left. Tyler and Kade strode toward the doors. *Great!* They were absorbed in some conversation. Aaron followed my line of sight.

Immediately, he let go of my hand. "Watch your back, Lacey. And for your sake, I hope you don't make the team."

I turned my attention back to Aaron. His green eyes narrowed.

In the softest voice possible, I said, "Bring it, asshole." Not waiting for his response, and mainly to avoid Kade and Tyler, I ducked into the crowd. What was it with male egos? I'd had my share of ribbing from the boys at Crestview, but nothing as tense as what Aaron was dishing out. Suddenly, the principal's concerns tumbled through my brain. *I had to reprimand the boys for the last girl that was on the team.*

Maybe times were changing. Maybe she would be reprimanding me instead of the boys on the team. I certainly wasn't going to let him or any other guy scare me away. I had too much at stake.

When I got to my locker, I found Becca chatting with Kelton in the hall next to her homeroom class. Was he the reason she hadn't answered her phone this morning? I debated whether to interrupt what looked like an intimate moment then shelved the idea. With my mood, I'd probably bite her head off. She didn't deserve it. Plus I certainly wasn't in the mood for whatever cocksure attitude Kelton had in store today. Instead, I unloaded a couple of books from my backpack then quietly slipped into my homeroom class. We had English next, so I'd be able to catch up with her then.

After homeroom, the day dragged. In English, Becca told me her phone had died last night, and she had been charging it this morning. She hadn't turned it on until she'd gotten to school.

Kelton was his old asshat self. The first thing he said to me when he sat down in English was, "What did you do to my brother? He bit my head off when I asked him why you weren't in school yesterday."

I failed to answer him. Thankfully, Mr. Souza started class. Becca even tried to find out what had happened between Kade and me. I waved her off. I wasn't in the mood to dish out details. Besides, I reminded her the school had ears. That was one of the reasons she never wanted to hang out inside the building before school started. Tyler and I avoided each other. I had no idea what he and Kade were chatting about when I'd seen them walking into school. I was dying to know, though.

Kade had sent me several texts throughout the day telling me he was sorry. Since the only class I had with him was psychology, which was the last class of the day, I was able to avoid him. If I saw him in the halls, I went the other way.

Now, my pulse sped up as I plucked out my psychology book from my locker. There was no way to hide from him in class. I could skip, but there were too many negative consequences for me to skip a class for no reason. I'd just closed my locker when out of the corner of my eye I spotted Kade walking toward me. I started to blend in with student traffic, but my feet got tangled with a boy who had big feet. He caught me before I fell. By the time I tried to merge again, Kade had me caged against the lockers.

"You're avoiding me," he said in my ear.

I laughed. He sounded like Tyler. I guess that was my theme today. "What gave you your first clue?" His scent of cedar washed over me, and I bit my lip to keep from whimpering.

"I'm sorry about yesterday," he whispered.

"So you *texted* and called a million times."

Voices grew louder then faded as students passed. If they were watching us I couldn't tell. Kade had me trapped in his remorseful gaze. We stared at each other—him through lowered lashes; me, well, I wasn't sure. Before my brain caught up to my body, I brushed his bangs to one side. His eyelids slid shut. When he opened them, relief shone through as though he'd been waiting a thousand years for my touch.

"I promise I will not make decisions for you. I will not betray the trust between us. I will not tell my brothers what we share. If you want them to know, then it's up to you to tell them. Please forgive me."

The warning bell rang. I was sort of relieved for the distraction. I wasn't ready to forgive him yet. I wasn't sure if I ever would be. "We need to get to class," I said.

He searched my face before he erased the despair from his and walked away. If it weren't for the final bell, I would've slumped to the floor. *Was I being too harsh? No.* Trust was important to me. People grow by learning from their mistakes, Mom had always said. Everyone deserves a second chance, Dad would say. I didn't have time to analyze it. I headed to psychology. Mr. Dobson was closing the door when I ran up. He gave me an exasperated look as I slunk by him.

As soon as I sat down, Becca twisted in her seat. "Do you want to hang out after school?" She glanced past me and waved.

Who was she waving to—Kross, Kade, or both? "I can't. I have a meeting with Coach Dean. Then I have practice."

Mr. Dobson wrote on the board.

I shot a quick look behind me. A girl with light brown hair and amber eyes stared my way. I swallowed hard, mentally shaking off the cold and eerie feeling. The girl looked just like my sister Julie. My hands began to shake, so I sat on them. *Calm down. She's not Julie.*

"Who's the girl?" I hadn't seen her before today. Then again, the last time I was in psychology, Kade had dominated my thoughts. I still couldn't remember what the lecture was about.

"Renee Spellman," Becca said.

"Let's begin," Mr. Dobson announced.

Becca faced forward. I slouched in my chair, taking in quiet breaths to ease my racing heart.

"Today's topic is Elisabeth Kubler-Ross. Who's heard of her?" Mr. Dobson asked.

I hadn't. Apparently a few kids in class knew the name, one of them being Renee.

"Isn't she the woman who came up with the five stages of grief?" Renee asked.

Dr. Meyers had explained them to me. Anger and depression were the two that plagued me. Denial, bargaining, and acceptance hadn't surfaced yet, and according to Dr. Meyers, they might never. Not everyone experienced all five stages. I hoped one day I could accept what had happened to them. Maybe if I knew who killed them I might be able to.

So as Mr. Dobson talked, I tuned him out. The last thing I wanted to do was think about death or anything depressing that might trigger a panic attack. It was bad enough Renee could pass as my sister. The resemblance was uncanny. Even the way one side of her mouth curled higher than the other when she smiled. *Think of something else.* I began doodling in my notebook. The simple act of drawing circles and squares usually helped to clear my mind. After most of the page was covered in geometric shapes, I drew a broken arrow through a cracked heart with the letter L inside the heart. This was one picture that wasn't worth a thousand words, but a million emotions—anger, sorrow, grief, fear, pain. Could my heart ever be repaired? Would my life ever be normal? I propped my right elbow on my desk, resting my head in my hand. As I did, I glanced around the classroom and locked eyes with Kade.

A smile formed on his face, causing goosebumps to cover my arms. What was it with him that made my body react the way it did and my mind forget what I was just thinking? *It isn't him. You're just messed up.*

"Your homework for tonight," Mr. Dobson said. "Write a short essay on one of the five stages we discussed."

Tearing my gaze away from Kade, I shifted my attention to the board. As soon as Mr. Dobson finished writing the bell signaled the end of class. I said a quick good-bye to Becca and bolted out. I wanted to get to practice. The ball field was a place for me to lose myself and forget my problems. But first I had a meeting with Coach Dean.

⚜

STOPPING OUTSIDE COACH'S DOOR, I steeled my shoulders before rapping my knuckles against it.

"Enter," his voice boomed from the other side.

I twisted the doorknob and stepped in. A blast of hot air hit me along with a stale smell. For the briefest of seconds the scent reminded me of that ill-fated night, and I repressed a shiver. A coach's sweaty office was the norm. Wasn't it?

"Sit, Lacey," Coach said as he banged on his keyboard.

Blowing out a few puffs of air from my nose to get rid of the smell, I did as I was told. The fierceness in his brown eyes and the way he seemed to look through me intimidated me. It was just like when I'd interrupted his meeting that first time we met. He'd risen from his chair, bushy eyebrows pinched together, a scowl on his face, and marched toward me like he was going to stomp on a cockroach. I wished I'd been a roach that day. It would've been better than him humiliating me in front of Tyler and the football coach.

Today, however, he didn't have a scowl. Still, I regarded him with caution. Something was up. He was rubbing his chin, deep in thought as he studied his computer screen.

Swallowing, I gave his office a once-over. I'd only been in here a couple of times and never had the chance to check out the cool photos he had hanging on the wall. There were four large framed pictures of major league ballplayers that he'd coached when they were in high school.

His computer beeped, then he grunted.

I'd just started admiring his trophy cabinet when he cleared his throat. I shifted my attention to him as he swiveled the monitor toward me. A screenshot of my elbow meeting Tammy Reese's face was displayed on the screen.

Holy cow! I just knew it would come back to bite me in the ass.

"Do you want to tell me what this was all about?"

Why did he care? Scratch that. I knew why. Before Dad and I decided on this school, Dad had a long conversation with Coach Dean on what it would take to be a member of the ball team. One of his requirements was that all players had to respect others on and off the field, which meant no fighting. More importantly, the selection process involved many factors from how well I played to my attitude, stamina, and interaction with others.

Sitting up straighter in my seat, I blew out a breath, examining the picture. Tammy's eyes were wide. Her face was a thousand shades of red.

"It was an accident, Coach," I said.

"Accident?" His tone deepened as he scrubbed a hand over his balding head.

The hackles on my neck went up. I was close to becoming that cockroach. "With all due respect, Coach, why am I here? I haven't made the team yet."

He chewed on the side of his cheek. "Lacey, do you know how good you are?" He gentled his voice somewhat.

"How do you know?"

"I've seen the video footage that Crestview sent me."

"Those are old tapes. I'm not quite back to my old self yet." I fidgeted as I said the last sentence. I desperately wanted to go back in time.

Coach knew I'd had to take time off for family reasons. Dad hadn't told him much about our background. Coach didn't want to know, anyway. He'd told Dad that our personal business was our own—that was one of the reasons I respected Coach.

"If you're as good as you are in those tapes, then you better get your crap in order. I don't want to see you in any trouble."

"Yes, sir."

"Very well, you're dismissed."

Was that it? *Get out of here before he thinks of something else, Stupidhead.*

Listening to my crazy inner voice, I grabbed the arm of the chair then stopped. Maybe this was the person to ask about Mandy Shear. No one would tell me about her, and if anyone knew her it was Coach. After all, she played for him. "Um...Coach?"

He looked up from the computer screen.

"What happened to Mandy Shear?"

He leaned back in his chair, scrutinizing me with his brown eyes. "I've been waiting for that question."

My eyes widened.

"We don't like to talk about Mandy around school." He glanced at a photo of him and a ballplayer holding up a trophy before looking back at me. "Mandy was good. She played right field two years ago. The girl had a hell of an arm. She threw the ball from deep right to home plate without any effort. With her and the Maxwell brothers, the team was unstoppable." He let out a breath. "We won state that year. Then"—he paused, his fingers resting on his chin— "two weeks later, Mandy died in a motorcycle accident."

"An accident? So why won't anyone talk about it?"

"Ah," he said, propping his elbows on his desk. "Some speculate it wasn't an accident. There were some tense rivalries between a few of the ballplayers. Anyway, the police never found evidence to support it being anything other than an accident."

"Principal Sanders told me the boys on the team treated Mandy badly. Is that true?" Given my run-in with Aaron this morning, I had an inkling that he was one of the boys.

"She had to have a few words with a couple of boys on the team, but Mandy was protected by the Maxwell brothers."

"What do you mean?" I knitted my brows.

"Lacey, it's in the past." He turned his monitor to face him.

I got that. But they protected her how? Suddenly Aaron's threats dominated my thoughts. Did Aaron have anything to do with tormenting Mandy? Then another question popped up. "So why after two years is the school allowing girls to try out, much less play again?"

"Why all the questions?" He picked up a pen.

"If you were in my shoes, would you want to know?"

He studied me for a second. "Since you put it that way... There are no secrets here. After Mandy's death, no girls signed up to try out. They were spooked by the rumors and strongly discouraged by their parents and the school board. We were under a lot of scrutiny by the media when rumors started that a couple of the ball players were responsible for her death. Of course, that wasn't the case. The whole incident put us under a microscope."

"Are there any other girls trying out?" I'd been so busy practicing I didn't even think to ask.

"One other girl, Renee Spellman." He clicked the pen a few times.

She's not Julie. She's not Julie. "What position does she play?" My stomach churned with nerves. At least Julie hadn't played baseball.

Okay, I somehow had to get over the fact that this girl reminded me of Julie. But how? Maybe God was trying to test me. Or maybe this was God's way of helping me to heal. *You loved Julie. Think of all the good times you had. Don't think of how you found her covered in blood.*

Ha! How was I going to do that?

He set down the pen. "She's a left fielder."

At this point, I wasn't concerned so much about who was competing for a pitching position. I had to get my PTSD under control or else I wouldn't be pitching, period.

I stood. "Um...one more question?"

"What is it?"

"Why was Mandy protected by the Maxwell brothers?"

"I know they've been practicing with you. Maybe you should ask them that question."

CHAPTER 12

After I left Coach's office, I stopped at the girls' locker room and quickly changed. Then with my bag over my shoulder and my glove in hand, I headed out to the ball field through the tunnel that led out to right field. Once I stepped onto the dirt track, the scent of grass penetrated my nostrils, clearing my mind and the rough edges of my nerves. Kross and Tyler were talking at home plate. I jogged up to the dugout, set down my bag then joined the boys who were deep in conversation.

Tyler had his back to me. "Make sure she works on her slider," he said to Kross.

Kross ran his hand through his short black hair, and his blue eyes sparkled as he blinked.

"Are you guys talking about me?" I asked.

Tyler turned, smiling as though we hadn't fought this morning. "Yeah. Sorry, Lacey. I have a football meeting. I should've told you earlier."

"It's okay." I might be mad at him for trying to play big brother, but I certainly wasn't going to be mad because he couldn't help me practice. Football was important to him, and it should come first. Of all people, I knew that, since I was standing on the field of my passion.

"I'll be back to take you home." Tyler started to walk away.

"Actually," Kross piped in, bending down to retrieve his glove and ball cap from his bag. "Kade wanted me to tell you that your car is ready. If you want to pick it up you can ride home with me. If not, I can drop you off at your house."

Tyler lost the smile on his face as though the mention of Kade's name was a knife stabbing him. *What was it with him?* I told him I wanted be friends. *Was he ever going to accept that?*

"I'll get a ride home with Kross."

Tyler pivoted on his heel and stalked off the field.

"I thought Kelton was supposed to be here." I rolled my right shoulder back a few times. The soreness was still there.

"He had to get new cleats before tryouts tomorrow. Let's see what you got, Lacey Robinson," he said as he covered his head with his ball cap, the bill facing backwards.

I trotted out to the mound, taking a deep breath, then released it along with all thoughts of Tyler and everything else in my life. My sole focus right now was to perfect my pitches.

When I turned, Kross was crouched down into a catcher's position, ready to go.

I stepped up to the rubber and threw a few balls to loosen up. After a handful of easy throws, I started with my fastball that thudded into Kross's mitt.

"Not fast enough, Lace. Relax," he said, throwing the ball back.

I bent my neck to the left then to the right, walked around the mound.

"Find your zone," my brother had always told me. "Tune everything out and your zone will emerge."

I hadn't been in my zone since the last game in my sophomore year. I desperately needed to find it if I was going to make the team. Stepping up on the rubber again, I closed my eyes and focused on my breathing. In and out. In and out. Each time, I visualized every move from my wind-up to my delivery. I opened my eyes, looked down at Kross, glanced over my shoulder at first base like I had a runner on, wound up, and threw a curveball.

"Good," Kross shot back. "Again."

I threw several more pitches, each one getting better. I practiced my fastball, curveball, and even my slider. After about thirty minutes, Kross retrieved a bat from his bag near the backstop, then planted his feet into the batter's box.

"Let me hit a few before we call it quits," he said, throwing me a ball.

I pitched. He hit or he missed. In all, the ball connected with the bat seven out of twenty pitches. I did a mental jig. It would've been nice to gloat about it if it were Kelton. But Kross was nothing like Kelton. No sarcasm. No sexual innuendo. Not even a word about Kade. Which, by the way, I appreciated. I didn't want any distractions.

Once we had all the balls back in the five-gallon bucket, Kross and I scooped up our bags and headed for his car. The sun dipped lower in the sky. We still had a few hours before night fell.

"So, do you want to go home, or my house to get your car?" he asked, his six-foot frame making long strides.

I did need my car. I had no desire to call Tyler to pick me up tomorrow. I couldn't rely on Becca unless I called her tonight to give her ample notice. I didn't want to bug my dad. Mary still had no car. If she needed to go out, she used Dad's for errands.

"It's not that hard a question, Lacey."

Yeah, it was. Would Kade be there?

"Kade isn't going to bite," Kross added as we arrived at his red Jeep Wrangler.

I might, though.

He grinned. I noticed he had one dimple on his right cheek.

Wow, did I say that out loud? "My car."

"That wasn't so hard." He set down the bucket of balls in the trunk area.

It kind of was. We both changed out of our cleats. He donned a pair of Nikes. I slipped on my flats. We threw our bags in the back and hopped in.

"Do you mind if I make a quick stop?" He inserted the key into the ignition. "I have to drop off a gun at the club to get it serviced." He turned the key, and the engine started.

"As in the Ashford Gun Club?"

He nodded as he shifted into gear.

"Are you a member?"

The Jeep jerked every time he shifted gears. "Yeah, we all are. My dad and my brothers."

How come Kade hadn't told me? I'd mentioned to him that Dad and I were members. "How come I haven't seen you guys at the club?" I would've noticed these boys for sure.

"You belong?" Stubble dotted his angular jaw.

"You mean Kade hasn't told you? Don't answer that." Not that my membership at the gun club was a secret. But I had one secret I didn't want anyone to know, and I still didn't know if Kade had told them about my panic attacks.

The passing landscape whizzed by even through the side streets of Ashford. Kross drove aggressively. My body jerked several times when he went around corners, and an uneasy feeling settled within me.

"So, Kross—why were you guys protecting Mandy Shear?" I figured this would be a great time to ask one of the sources since we weren't on school grounds.

He slowed behind a car that was turning into a driveway. "Who told you that?" His head jerked toward me as he gave the Jeep some gas.

"Coach Dean. What did he mean?"

"She was dating Kody." He shifted, his biceps flexing. "We're protective of our friends, Lacey, especially ones who are more than friends."

"Oh." I hugged myself as tears stung my eyes. Kody had lost his girlfriend. *Was her death the reason why he was seeing Dr. Davis?*

"You all right?" Kross asked, his voice sounding faraway.

"Yep." *Nope.* I felt for Kody as I tried to keep the tears from spilling over. Death of a loved one sucked.

I didn't have too long to mourn before Kross slammed on the brakes as he pulled up in front of the weathered, one-story wood building. The Ashford Rod and Gun Club had a high A-frame pitched roof. The place reminded me of the Los Angeles Country Club that we'd belonged to in LA—both offered space for weddings and other events, and had a members' lounge and a restaurant.

Several cars were parked in the lot. I wasn't surprised. The place was always busy as it had a youth program, several gun and archery leagues, and both an indoor and an outdoor shooting range. A group of men were gathering their gun cases and supplies from a trunk while a young lady scurried past them, tying her apron behind her. She was probably late for her shift.

Kross turned off the engine. "I should only be a couple of minutes."

"I'll grab a drink in the restaurant." Or maybe try to find my stomach, which I'd left on the road somewhere.

We climbed out. Kross retrieved a small metal box from his trunk.

"What kind of gun?" I asked as we headed for the entrance.

"Glock. It hasn't been serviced in a long time. We have a competition coming up in another month." He held the door open for me.

"You're in a league here?" I asked over my shoulder as I walked in.

"Yeah, Kody, Kelton and Kade too," he said like I was supposed to know this. "You should join a league."

Dad and I had checked into a league, but I was still learning. Maybe after tryouts I would consider it.

I banked left into the restaurant as Kross continued down the hall to the shooting range. A heavy dose of grease permeated the air. My stomach growled.

"Hey, darlin'," Jackie said as she came up to the hostess's podium. "Are you here all by yourself?" Her reddish-blond hair was pulled back in a low ponytail. She worked on Sundays too, when Dad and I came in for breakfast before hitting the range.

"No. I'm waiting for a friend. He had to drop off his gun at the range. Can I get a Coke?"

"Come on. Sit at the bar."

The restaurant was set up with booths along the left and back wall of windows, square tables and chairs over the middle of the room, and a mahogany bar at an angle on the right as I walked in. Aside from a couple of men sitting in the corner booth, the place was empty. It wasn't quite dinnertime yet.

I followed Jackie over and sat in a bar chair.

"Pete, can you get Lacey a Coke?" Pete was a tall man, dark haired with streaks of gray throughout. "So who's the 'he' you're here with?"

"Kross Maxwell."

"Ah, one of the triplets." She sighed. "If only I were younger." I'd guess Jackie was in her thirties. Her bronze eyes flickered with excitement.

Pete placed a glass of soda in front of me.

"You know the Maxwells?" I asked, taking a swig of soda.

"Lacey, when you work here as long as I do, you know everyone." She picked up a knife and started cutting lemons and limes on a small wooden cutting board.

"How well do you know them?" I felt like a detective today, after asking Coach and Kross questions. It wasn't exactly the get-to-know-you game Dr. Davis wanted me to play.

She laughed. "Which one do you like?"

I shook my head. "None of them."

"Lacey, are you telling me you don't like *any* of them?" She stopped cutting the fruit, a disbelieving look on her face.

Heat pinched my cheeks. *Was I that obvious?* "I might like Kade," I said, my voice low.

"The mature one." Her bronze eyes lit up as if I said the right answer. "Also the one who carries the weight of the world on his shoulders."

"What do you mean?" I tore apart a napkin.

"There's a ton of anger and sadness brewing in him. I can see it in his eyes."

"Why the sadness?" I agreed Kade carried some anger, which probably stemmed from Greg Sullivan. He also had regret written over his face today when he apologized to me.

"According to his dad, Kade closed himself off after the accident."

"Huh?" I sat back in my chair. Was she talking about Mandy? But Mandy had been Kody's girlfriend. If anyone carried the weight of the world on his shoulders, that would be Kody.

"Not my story to tell, darlin'."

Out of the corner of my eye, I spied Kross talking to an old, bald-headed man. "I should go. How much do I owe for the soda?" I'd forgotten my purse in the car.

"It's on the house," Jackie said.

I thanked her then went out to meet Kross. The old man he'd been talking to patted him on the back before disappearing into the club. We walked in silence to his Jeep. I wanted to ask Kross about what Jackie had mentioned, but I didn't know how without sounding like a nosy person. I didn't like when people pried into *my* life.

"Is something bothering you?" Kross asked as we got in the Jeep.

Lots of things. "No."

Anything I had on my mind quickly vanished as Kross drove like a maniac to his house. By the time we parked in front of his garage, I wanted to puke. "Drive much?" My stomach fell out the window somewhere between the club and there.

His lone dimple emerged as he grinned. *Asshat.*

I clicked off my seatbelt as Kross hightailed it out of the Jeep. I thought he took off until he opened my door. "Sorry, Lacey. I didn't mean to scare you." He held out his hand.

I laughed. "I'm not sure I can walk."

"Do I have to carry you?"

God, no. I took his offered hand and slowly put two feet on the ground. When I did, the world tilted. "Can I use your bathroom?" I needed to collect myself before I got back on the road.

I held onto Kross as we made our way toward the deck. As the world around me righted itself, I glanced back. The only car in the driveway was his. *Kade's truck could be parked in the garage.* It didn't matter. I desperately needed to use the bathroom, and I had a feeling I wasn't getting my car without seeing Kade. Letting go of Kross, I climbed the steps to the deck. He slid the glass door to the left and a sweet smell of chocolate floated out. Was their mother home? Intrigue drew me into the kitchen. The room was empty save for a cookie sheet on the stove.

Kross followed me in, closing the door. "Kody likes to bake," he said, answering the question I had been about to ask. *What was it with Kross answering my thoughts?* "Take a left out of the kitchen and the guest bathroom is down the hall on the right."

Skirting the kitchen island, I went down the hall, following Kross's instructions, and locked the bathroom door behind me. I stood there for a moment, glancing at myself in the large oval mirror that hung over the sink and almost gasped. My skin was ashen, thanks to Kross's driving. Strands of hair stuck out from my ponytail, and a sheen of sweat coated my neck—not to mention that I looked like a ragamuffin with my T-shirt dirty from me wiping my hands on it at the ball field. I splashed water on my face and patted it dry with a small brown hand towel, then I pulled out my ponytail and combed my fingers through my hair.

"Okay, now get out of here, and go home," I said to myself in the mirror. Following my own instructions, I unlocked the door and went back the way I came.

I'd only taken three steps when Kade's familiar, thigh-squeezing voice said, from behind me, "Lace?"

I froze. "Thanks for fixing my car."

I lifted a leaden foot when his voice glided over me like butter. "Can we talk?" he asked. I eased my foot down as his shoes scuffed on the wood floor.

The last time he'd said he wanted to talk, he kissed me. "I should go. Do you have my keys?" The funny thing was, my legs wouldn't move.

His arms came around to settle on my stomach. He pressed his nose against the side of my neck. "Please."

"I'm only here for my car." My muscles tensed. I looked like shit. I probably smelled worse since I'd been sweating during practice.

Heavy footsteps scuffled in the kitchen before a shadow crawled up the floor in the hall. "Goddamn, these cookies are good," one of the triplets said. A glass clinked on what sounded like the granite top.

"You're a pig, Kelton," Kross said. Or at least I thought it was Kross, since I'd left him in the kitchen.

I smiled. I wouldn't mind trying one myself. But I was tethered to a very muscled body while my mind and body waged a war on the theme of "Should I stay and listen, or get my keys and go?" How do I learn to trust? *Give him a chance. That's the only way.* "Where are my keys?"

His breath fanned my ear, light and feathery, causing a spark to ignite within me. "I have them."

My body was so close to molding to his. "Are you bribing me, Kade?"

"If that gets you to stay, then yes."

Well played. "Just talk."

"Not here," he whispered. "Let's go to my room."

"Yeah. No." His room spelled all kinds of disaster—at least for me. I wouldn't be able to concentrate or listen to what he had to say.

"Do you want to hear Kelton's mouth? If he doesn't know you're here, he won't bug me."

"Can't we go outside?"

"Not without passing by or through the kitchen."

"Fine." I didn't want to deal with Kelton, and I wanted my keys.

"This way," he said as he tugged on my hand.

I turned and followed like a good little pup. After we turned a corner, an open doorway came into view. A happy, nervous pitter-patter beat against my ribs at the thought of us alone in his room—a more intimate setting.

He went in. I stayed out. The scent of cedar drifted into the hall, and I shuddered.

"Come in," Kade said. "We'll talk, then I'll take you out to your car."

I stepped over the threshold onto a beige carpet. Neutral tans colored the walls. Two wooden nightstands flanked his bed along the right-hand wall. Over his bed hung a large poster of Zeal's cover album, and aside from books strewn over his desk, the rest of his room, including a dresser and a chair, was immaculate.

He closed the door before propping his shoulder against it and scanning my face. I crossed my arms over my chest. Silence expanded in the room like a balloon slowly being filled with air.

"So talk," I said, popping the balloon.

"I screwed up. But you have to understand that my brothers and I are tight. We look out for one another."

I tightened my arms around me. "If you want to get to know me, Kade, trust is the one thing I value most. I told you how hard it was for me to tell you I was seeing a shrink. I'm not getting into another relationship with anyone unless he has my complete trust."

"Would you give me another chance?"

Sometimes in life, people needed second chances. Dad's words came to mind. I knew *I* needed one to show ASU I could make the effort to get back on my feet. Without their consideration, I wasn't sure where I'd be with my PTSD.

"One," I said, pinning him with my gaze. Maybe I wanted to give myself the second chance with him.

Pushing off from the door, Kade closed the distance between us. He stared down at me as though he didn't know what to do next.

I flattened my hand on his chest. Slowly, I traced a path from one side to the other, feeling hard muscle under the soft cotton of his T-shirt. He groaned, drawing my attention upward to meet his gaze. Desire sparked in his eyes, causing my stomach to flip-flop several times in a matter of seconds.

Gently, he grasped my shoulders as he walked me backward, slowly and surely until the backs of my legs hit his bed. If I'd wanted to run, I didn't have a chance. His entire body held me prisoner. Even just his sultry gaze locked me in. All I could do was drop down onto the soft mattress.

He took hold of my right leg, keeping me mesmerized. Lifting my foot, he removed my shoe, dropping it to the floor with a soft thud. Without missing a beat, he slid his hands down my left leg until his callused palm met bare skin at my ankle. He rubbed his thumb over the top of my foot, back and forth, sending a string of tingles up my leg. Then he flipped off my other shoe. "Scoot back," he said in a raspy voice.

I did, as the blood thrummed through me at sprinter speed. He kicked off his shoes then crawled up, straddling me with his hands on each side of my head. His hair fell forward, and I tangled my fingers in the soft strands.

A deep sound rumbled from him. He leaned down and traced the seam of my lips with his tongue. Then he nipped, demanding access. I whimpered, parting my lips, and his tongue slithered in. At first, he explored as though he were trying to memorize every taste bud. When I whimpered again, he shifted and yanked me closer. He was hard and ready, and I squirmed against him.

"I want you naked," he breathed.

I froze, his bottom lip between my teeth. Was I ready for naked? My body was. I wanted all of Kade right here, right now. So why was I hesitating?

As though he knew my thoughts, he whispered, "I know you're not ready for that."

I was, and I wasn't. The guy made the woman in me stretch to life —every single part of my anatomy, right down to my core. But my brain kept telling me to get to know him more. *I had to see if I could trust him. I'd only given him a second chance a few minutes ago.*

He rolled onto his side. Lifting up on his elbow, he slid his leg between mine.

He moved a strand of hair from my forehead. "I want to strip every piece of clothing off you, slowly, then explore every inch of your exquisite body."

I rubbed my foot along his leg. "The feeling is mutual, Kade, but—"

"I know. Trust. But the way your body responds to me...shit," he bit out. "And to hear you say you want me"—he slid his hand over my hip—"God. Your voice. Your words." His hand coasted down my leg then around to my butt before drawing me closer. "It's all I can do not to—"

"I thought the hunter always got his prey."

"Baby, until I have you under the sheets..."

"Hey, is that all you want me for?" I asked with a smile.

"If that's all I wanted, you would've been naked a long time ago."

"Then what do you want, Kade Maxwell?" We both had said we didn't do love and mush.

He slipped his hand between our bodies, trailing his fingers up between my legs.

I let out a whimper as my core screamed for his touch. "Are you trying to...tell me...you want..." My breathing grew shallow.

His hand glided north over the waist of my yoga pants. The heat of his palm seared my skin, even through my clothes—or maybe it was the inferno blazing inside me.

"All of you," he whispered as his lips found my ear, and his hand glided under my shirt.

My whole body stiffened, bringing me back to reality. What did he mean? Like, date exclusively?

"Don't freak," he whispered, tickling my navel. "I told you I want to get to know you. But I know it's a two-way street."

A few of my muscles loosened. "Tell me something about yourself, other than you like me." My voice was raspy. This probably wasn't what Dr. Davis had in mind, but maybe he was onto something with the getting-to-know-you game.

He searched my face. "I have a high IQ."

My eyes widened. "Really?" I teased.

"You don't believe me?" His hand inched to my side.

I shrugged. He squeezed. I squealed.

"So you're ticklish?"

"Kade," I said in a strained voice. "Please."

"No. Not until..."

I writhed under him, giggling. "Okay. I...believe...you," I said in a high-pitched voice.

He raised an eyebrow. "I don't think you do."

"I do," I said, taking a few breaths. "What's 'high?'"

"Like one hundred fifty-five." He squeezed my waist lightly.

"You mean I've been kissing a genius all this time?" I giggled again.

His hand traveled up, covering my breast where he rubbed his palm around my nipple. "You want me more now, don't you?"

Yeah, I did, but it didn't have anything to do with his IQ. I shifted my glance between my breasts and his fiery copper eyes. The sensation on my breast had me arching slightly.

"Do your brothers have high IQs too?" I asked, hoping to distract both of us—at least me. It was hard to concentrate and listen to him.

His fingers coasted down my stomach, leaving goosebumps in their wake.

"Yep." His voice was low. "That's why they tested out of their junior year at the academy. They could've tested out earlier, but my dad wanted them to mature a little bit more."

"Why didn't you go to the academy with them?"

He laced his fingers with mine before bringing them up to his warm lips. "When we first moved here"—he set our joined hands on the bed between us—"my mom was living with us. We thought she was getting better. We were all on the mend. We were becoming a family again. My dad had just signed his retirement papers from the Army. He'd decided to open up his psychiatric practice to continue to help people coming out of the military. We'd settled on this area. It's close to my mom's family and it's also close to..." His watery gaze drifted past me.

After several long seconds, I snuggled into him, placing a kiss on his neck. I had no idea what he was struggling with. The sadness in his eyes spoke volumes. I had to do something so my own tears wouldn't surface. Just hearing about his mom sparked images of my own and, if I thought about her, I was afraid of a flashback or panic attack.

"Kade," I said softly. "Can you kiss me?" His kisses always took me to a peaceful place—one where I was free of my demons. Maybe I could do the same for him.

In a blur, he was on top of me, planting those magical lips on mine. This time, I controlled the kiss. My tongue explored him, tasting and sucking. I loved the way he tasted—a little hint of sugar and whole lot of spice. He purred, and I almost peeled off my clothes. Then I thought better of it. If I was going to give myself to Kade, I wanted to know more of him. I'd made the mistake of not knowing Brad that well, and look where that got me.

"You taste like sunshine," he breathed as he lifted his body off mine. He grabbed a pillow and propped it under our heads before lying on his side.

"I'm sorry I distracted you." I rubbed along the scruff of his rough jaw. "You were distant for a minute."

"Lace, you can distract me anytime."

"So you were telling me about the academy and...your...mom." I slipped my foot between his feet. For two seconds, I considered whether I wanted to hear more about his mother. But he'd already started the conversation, and I had to take the chance. If I freaked out thinking about my own mother, at least he was here. It wasn't like he hadn't seen one of my episodes. I had to dip my toe in the water, as Dr. Davis had said.

He chewed the inside of his cheek. "I almost went to the academy. A month before I was scheduled to leave with my brothers, my mom got sick. My dad needed help, and I couldn't leave him. So I stayed."

"So where is your mom now?" I asked in a shaky breath, tears threatening.

His gaze skimmed over my face. "She's in a...mental health facility three hours from here."

Okay, I wasn't ready for that. Suddenly, my body trembled. *Why the crazy reaction?* I wasn't sure.

"Hey, you don't have to cry," he whispered.

A tear tumbled down my cheek. He wiped it away.

"Talk to me, Lace."

"Why...is she...?"

"She blames herself for my sister's death," he said in a somber tone.

I gasped as the dam opened and I lost it. My breathing grew erratic. Darkness crept in. A picture of my mom on the kitchen floor with her eyes open, not moving, flashed before me. *Oh, my God.* I squeezed my eyes shut. I couldn't go there.

"Lace," Kade said gently. "Baby, talk to me."

I wanted to, but anxiety, grief, sorrow, paranoia surged through me.

"Look at me," he pleaded. "Something tells me this isn't about my mom or my sister." He feathered a kiss over my mouth.

Losing myself in his lips, I slowly opened my eyes and met his. I expected to see sorrow. Instead, I saw resignation, as though he'd come to terms with his mom and sister. For a second I thought about telling him about Mom and Julie, but I couldn't without falling into a panic attack.

"There's those beautiful green eyes. Do you want to go for a walk down to the lake?"

I shuddered then nodded. The cool air would be a welcome relief. Maybe it would clear the last of the darkness lingering in my head.

⚜

AS WE NEARED THE LAKE, the water gleamed in the last rays of the setting sun. Cold air licked my face. I was grateful for the sweatshirt Kade lent me. I was wrapped in warmth and his scent. I covered my head with the hood then buried my hands in the pockets. We walked in silence until we skirted the edge of the water. At first, I'd thought he was going to coax me into the boathouse—or the funhouse, as I dubbed it. He didn't. Instead, he grabbed my hand, and we followed the edge of the lake until we were on a trail. The lake had to be two miles around.

Trees towered over us with shades of red and orange hanging from their branches. Birds chirped and a squirrel darted up a trunk in front of us. About half a mile in, we came to an area with a flat rock that sat between two large tree trunks with the initials KM carved into it.

"Let's sit for a minute." He motioned to the large stone.

"Your initials?" I asked.

"Yes and no. You know each of our first names begin with a K. So did my sister's. Her name was Karen."

"And the hearts?" Like the five hearts stenciled on his truck, there were five etched into the rock.

"My sister loved hearts. She had them embroidered on her jeans, her shirts, even her jackets. She'd told me, 'Kade, a beating heart is the mystery behind a person. When people hurt, their hearts hurt. When they love, their hearts love, and when they cry, their hearts cry, too. The heart knows everything.' She was twelve." He played with a few strands of my hair. "So there are five hearts engraved on this rock representing us five siblings, and I had five painted on my truck. I have her journal tucked away, and every now and then I'll read it to remember her."

I swallowed, trying not to lose my composure again. But the meaning behind the hearts was enough to make my own heart cry. We both sat down on the rock. I brought my knees to my chest while Kade draped his arm over my shoulder. The sun glinted off the water, its rays sparkling like diamonds.

"How did she die?" I asked softly. I had to know. My reasoning probably didn't make much sense. It felt like learning the way she died might help me heal a little. I didn't know how. Maybe hearing someone else's tragedy might help to mend my broken heart.

"She was accidentally shot," he said into the breeze.

I gasped for the second time within an hour. Tears dropped again.

He kissed my head. "My dad, since I can remember, has always had guns. He was in Special Forces. He knew how to handle weapons. He got us boys acclimated to guns early on. But he didn't want his little girl anywhere near them. He would tell her that girls shouldn't be handling guns. He wanted Karen to stay innocent. Anyway, every time she asked if she could go shooting with him, he'd say no. Then somehow, she got the combination to my dad's gun cabinet. I don't know the exact course of events, but my mom found Karen and a friend in the garage. The gun cabinet was open, and my sister's friend had a gun in her hands. We don't know if the girl was startled by my mom's voice, but it went off, and my sister..."

I thought of the loss of my own sister, and the tears continued to flow. I unfolded my knees and rested my head against his chest.

"It's taken me a while to shed some of the pain. I'm not there yet. I have my bad days."

I wiped tears from my eyes.

He turned my chin to face him. "Lace, I've never told another living soul any of this."

"Why me?"

"Honestly, I don't know." Closing the inch between us, he planted a soft kiss on my nose.

"Were you living here when it happened?"

"No. We were living in Texas."

The sound of leaves crumbling under someone's feet echoed around us.

"If that's Kelton..." Kade growled.

"Chill, bro," a voice said from our right.

"Kross, what do you want?" Kade asked.

Clad in jeans and a gray T-shirt with "Jab, Jab, Hook" on the front in black letters, Kross strode toward us, powerful and self-assured. "Dad has been trying to call you. Where's your phone?" Kross asked, standing in front of us with his thumbs hooked in his jean pockets.

"I left it in my room."

"He needs you to call him right away," he said with a poker face.

"What does he want?" Kade asked.

"How should I know? You're the one in charge when he's gone. Are you okay, Lacey?" Kross asked, his blue gaze skating over me.

"Yeah, why?" I replied, sitting up straighter. My eyes and face must be splotchy and red. He glanced at Kade, who was glaring at Kross.

"What?" Kade asked.

"Did you make her upset?" Kross eyed Kade.

"No, man."

"He didn't," I added. It was nice at how Kross seemed to be concerned about me.

"Then why were you crying?" Kross asked.

"Drop it, bro," Kade snapped.

"It's getting late. I should get home." I rose. Twilight was descending, coloring the sky in light and dark blues.

"I swear I'm going to beat the crap out of you and Kelton. I can't get a moment of peace without one of you interrupting me," Kade said as he stood.

"Hey, I'm only delivering a message," Kross said.

The three of us walked back to the house.

"You did well today, Lacey," Kross said. "I enjoyed our practice."

"Even when you missed my pitches," I teased. I was still tickled about that.

"Hey, I was practicing." He grinned, showing that one dimple.

A light spilled out of the open side door of the garage as we approached. I was actually excited to see my Mustang. Kade had said he put in a new battery, and Hunt and Kross tuned it up as well. The bay door in front of the car was opened when we walked in. Kelton and Kody were leaning against my car. Was something going on?

"Great," Kade muttered. "The welcoming committee. Dad didn't call, did he?" Kade pushed Kross.

"No, man. We just wanted to get you two out here."

"For what?" I asked with a little trepidation.

"I will flatten each of you if you're about to pull a prank." Kade sounded nervous.

I was a bit leery, too, until Kelton's cocky grin curved his lips, and he winked at me. Kross went to stand next to his brothers. *Wow! What a picture.* Their blue eyes blazed against their stark black hair. Five o'clock shadows covered their square jaws, and their biceps bunched as they crossed their arms over well-toned chests. Still, they didn't make my thighs squeeze or my heart beat faster. Nope. Kade was the only one who energized me. I loved his honey-brown hair and how it curled at the ends. How his impossibly long lashes fanned out to frame his copper eyes. How when he grinned, his dimples softened the ruggedness of his looks. Most of all, Kade had a powerful yet quiet intensity that made my pulse race and my skin break out in goosebumps.

"Lacey, Kross tells us you did well today. I'm sorry I wasn't there,"

Kelton said. "And we want you to know we'll be rooting for you tomorrow."

I swallowed, trying to keep my emotions in check. I didn't want to cry any more today, but these boys were making it quite difficult.

"And," Kody spoke up, "when you get on the mound, find your zone. Actually, before school tomorrow, get into your zone. Tune out everything around you. Don't let anything bother you."

When Kade tangled his fingers in mine, I couldn't stave off the emotions. Tears spilled over my lashes. I hadn't had any friends who cared this much since before my life fell apart in California. "Thank you," I said in between sniffles. "Why all the encouragement? Not that I'm complaining. But I hardly know you guys."

"Because, Lacey Robinson," Kelton drawled with his signature smile, "we want to win state this year, and we know we can do it with you."

My eyes popped out of my head. They had more confidence in me than I had in myself. I had done well that day at practice. I knew I was good enough to make the team if I did my absolute best at tryouts. But winning state?

Kade drew me into a warm hug. "Okay, guys. I think you freaked her out a little too much. We should let her get home."

I eased away from Kade. "Sorry for all the tears. They're happy tears, though."

"We know," Kody said. "See you tomorrow, Lacey."

"Yeah, get some rest, girl," Kross added. "Oh, and I threw your bag in your car."

"Remember the zone," Kelton said.

The triplets left the garage.

"Are you okay?" Kade asked.

"Do they normally do this with your—"

"Girlfriends?" Kade finished for me.

"I'm not your girlfriend," I teased.

"Yes, you are." He smiled. "You're a girl and a friend."

"The genius is becoming literal on me now?"

He laughed. "I'll see you at school tomorrow." Letting go of me, he opened my car door. "Your chariot awaits."

"Thanks for fixing this clunker for me."

"It shouldn't break down anymore," he said bravely.

"Mmm." I slid into the driver's seat. It wasn't that I didn't trust his confidence. My dad was good at fixing cars, and even he had never lived up to its needs.

Adjusting the mirrors, I turned the ignition and the engine purred. I glanced at Kade, who had a smug grin on his face. I waved as I gave the car some gas, slowly maneuvering out of the garage. Once I was on the road, I pressed my foot down and headed home. The day had been a rollercoaster of emotions. I hadn't been this emotional since the funeral. I just prayed the only feeling I displayed tomorrow on the field was confidence.

CHAPTER 13

T he next day, my sole focus was tryouts. As soon as I got out of bed I started to go through my pitches in my head, and how to grip each one. *Index finger to aim my curveball at my target. Space between the ball and my palm on the fastball. Hold the ball slightly off center on the slider, cock my wrist, but don't lock it.* My shoulder was still tender, but I was going to push through the pain.

After I got ready for school, I grabbed my sports bag and backpack then headed downstairs. I'd just stepped off the last stair when Dad's voice sounded from his office. *What was he doing up so early? He normally slept in.*

I swung around the bannister and walked down the hall. His voice deepened. *Whoa! Who was he arguing with?* I normally didn't eavesdrop, but the rage in his tone kept me planted outside his open door.

"I don't give a fuck what you guys think. I know what I'm doing."

I'd never heard my father say the F word before. I stifled a gasp as a knot formed in my stomach. He grumbled before a sudden series of crashes, clangs, and dings filled the room. I dropped my bags and ran in. His glass-topped desk was clear. Everything from on it was strewn all over the tan carpet, including his laptop.

"What's wrong?" I asked, stopping.

He looked up. The grimace on his face waned. "Oh. I thought you left for school already," he said. Anger lingered in his tone—I imagined at the caller he'd been talking to.

"I was just leaving. Is everything okay, Dad?" I asked.

"Yeah. Just a disagreement with Eric and the board at the record label." Dodging the files, pens, binders, laptop, and CDs, he circled around and hugged me. "Don't worry, Sweet Pea." His tone mellowed.

"Are you sure?" I asked, returning the hug. I'd never known Dad to argue with Eric. I wasn't so much worried about his argument as I was about him, though. Maybe he was in the anger stage of his grief.

He let go. "I'm fine. Now, I'll see you at tryouts this afternoon." He kissed me on the forehead. "You're going to be late."

I left, not convinced he was okay. Something was going on. I couldn't help but think back to the first day of school and how he'd taken a long time to get out of the car. When he did he had his lips pressed together like someone had pissed him off. Had that been Eric, too?

As I drove to school, I tabled my worry over Dad, for now. I was relieved that I didn't have to rely on anyone to take me to school. I turned up the radio. "We Don't Have to Look Back Now" by Puddle of Mudd blasted from the speakers. Taking Kody's advice to get into my zone before school, I sang along. Losing myself in a song cleared my mind.

I sang three songs between home and school. By the time I parked in the school's lot, my thoughts were of Kade and his brothers—mostly the triplets. It had felt good to hear them say they needed me to make the team so we could win at state this year. Their words were going to be my mantra today.

The brisk wind battered my face when I got out of my car. At least the sun was out and not a cloud was in the sky. Tryouts would be cold but dry. With my sports bag cross-wise over my body and my backpack on my right shoulder, I made my way into school. Several kids hurried across campus while others talked and walked like they didn't have to be anywhere anytime soon.

I'd just stepped up onto the sidewalk in front of the main entrance when I spotted Kade coming toward me from my left. I smiled, my gaze roaming over him inch by inch. As usual, his jeans rode low on his hips. His blue henley accentuated every muscle of his upper body. But the one thing that had my insides sizzling was the way he looked at me with love and hunger in his eyes.

Wait. Rewind. Love? I laughed. *I think I took too many Advil this morning. It's messing with my head.*

"What's so funny?" he asked, stopping inches from me.

"Nothing." My voice hitched.

He studied me, seemingly oblivious to the kids walking by us. Then he whipped his backpack off his shoulder, unzipped the top, and pulled out a single yellow rose. "Good luck today," he said, handing it to me.

It was my turn to study him. I looked at the rose then up at him. *Was he for real?*

"Go ahead. Take it," he said.

"Yeah, girl. Take it," Becca's voice cut through my daze.

I didn't even see her walk up. She had her black hair in a side ponytail so it spilled down the front of her jeans jacket. Underneath she wore a scoop-necked orange blouse over a black miniskirt with black tights and black knee-high boots. My sister would've loved Becca and her taste in fashion.

I glanced back at Kade. Taking the flower, I lifted onto my tiptoes and kissed him.

"So sweet," Becca cooed.

No sooner had I broken the kiss than he said, "You're not getting away that easy. I've been waiting all night to kiss you again."

"I'm out of here," Becca said. "Lacey, I'll see you in English." She glanced at her phone as she wandered into school.

"We're going to be late."

"Just a taste." Before I had time to protest, he leaned down, snaked his tongue through my lips, and kissed me soft and slow.

Just as I was enjoying the taste of mint he pulled away. "The bell is about to ring."

I rolled my eyes. *Didn't I say that a moment ago?* He grinned, and I teasingly pushed him. He didn't move—he laughed.

Whatever.

We headed in just as the bell rang. The halls were thinning out. Kade gave me a chaste kiss on the lips, then he turned right while I went left. I made it to my homeroom one minute before the final bell. I didn't have time to offload my bags or my rose. I sniffed it as I sat down.

A petite girl with bright blue streaks in her black hair smiled at me. "Someone is either making up or is in love with you," she said.

"Just good luck wishes. That's all," I replied. At least, that was what

I assumed. Then again, maybe the rose was Kade's way of saying he was sorry for the umpteenth time. He couldn't be in love with me. We'd only known each other a very short time. On the other hand, *love doesn't have a timetable*, Mom always said. She'd told Julie and me how she fell in love with Dad almost instantly at a college sorority party.

After homeroom, I managed to stuff my sports bag in my locker until I had more time to move it to the girls' locker room. I used the rose as a bookmark so it wouldn't get mangled. I wasn't sure if it would last the entire day. It didn't matter. The sentiment meant more to me than the flower. Kade was racking up the thank-yous I had to deliver.

Tyler strolled into English with Grace tied to his arm. Becca muttered something I couldn't make out. Grace tossed her brown hair over her shoulder as she sashayed down the aisle to her desk two seats in front of Becca. I was glad Zane separated the two. I didn't want to see my friend hurt or in trouble.

Taking long strides to his seat against the window, Tyler tipped his chin at me. The tension between us lingered. At least, from my point of view. He'd left the field in a huff yesterday. I shouldn't have snapped at him. But I wasn't sure what else I could do to clear the air.

Kelton strode in, interrupting my thoughts. "What's up?" he asked, running his palm over my head.

"Do you mind? I'm not your family pet." My tone was light.

"No, but you're my brother's girl. So I get to pet you." He sat down behind me.

What happened to the sweet Kelton I'd talked to last night? Ignore him. Find your zone. We want to win state this year. We know we can do it with you.

Mr. Souza walked in a couple of minutes after the final bell, dropped his briefcase on the floor near his desk, then dove into a discussion on the elements of social criticism in the novel *Jane Eyre* by Charlotte Bronte. He didn't even take roll. Forty minutes later as I walked out of class I couldn't help but think how society would've viewed a woman playing baseball back when George III ruled England.

Tyler strode out and passed me without saying a word. *Was he mad at me? Well, chemistry should be fun.* Tyler wasn't talking to me. Hopefully, Becca wasn't in a bad mood from seeing Tyler with Grace. The only person I could count on to be normal was Kelton.

Whatever mood they were in, I stayed in my zone. I even silently repeated "Humpty Dumpty," one of my favorite nursery rhymes that Dad used to read to me before bed when I was a little girl.

As soon as chemistry ended, I bolted to my locker, snatched my sports bag, then hotfooted it to the sports complex. On my way I passed Aaron, who had Tammy caged against a wall and was whispering in her ear. Crimson crept up her neck to her cheeks. She curled her fingers in his blond waves. Luckily, students crowded the hall, so I was able to walk by them unnoticed. Not that I was worried, but I didn't want any temptation to get into trouble before tryouts.

Once I stuffed my bag in my locker in the sports complex, I met Becca at our usual place in the courtyard during our free period. Round tables and chairs dotted the area outside the cafeteria. A few students sat studying and talking. Becca was typing on her phone.

"Who are you texting?" I asked as I eased down into a cold metal chair. The wind blew a paper cup off a table.

"My mom. She wants me to pick up Chinese for dinner tonight." She set her phone down on the table.

"So, do you want to spill about Tyler?"

She sat back in her chair. "There's nothing to tell. We dated two years ago. He dumped me and that's it." Tears filled her eyes and she looked away.

I scooted my chair closer. "Does he know you're in love with him?"

She let out a strangled laugh. "The only thing Tyler knows is girls other than me. I see the way he looks at you."

"Becca?" I leaned forward with my elbows on my knees. It broke my heart to see her cry.

She blinked a few times.

"I'm not interested in Tyler. I like Kade."

"I know. I'm not mad at you. Although on the first day of school I had my doubts. I thought you did like him, until I saw the way you looked at Kade." She wiped a lone tear off her rosy cheek.

I wanted to probe more, but this conversation wasn't about me.

"I hate Grace's paws on him. She's been trying to get Tyler to go out with her for two years. She thinks he's her ticket out of town. You know, when he gets that football scholarship." She crossed one leg over the other.

"What about Kelton?" I'd seen Becca and him talking, but not like Aaron and Tammy had been "talking."

"There's nothing with Kelton. He just wants a fling. I'm not into that. I pity any girl who wants a serious relationship with him. He's going to be a tough guy to tie down."

"Yeah, tying him down literally won't be that hard, but a long-term relationship would be like trying to chase a fast-moving train for any girl." I snickered.

She smiled. We dropped the subject of Tyler and Kelton. Instead we made plans to hang out on the weekend at the Cave—just us girls.

The rest of the day zipped by. Before I knew it, Kade was walking with me to the sports complex. "Are you ready?" he asked.

"As I'll ever be." Despite my friends' bad moods irritating me earlier, I was calm. The mantras had helped to keep me from getting too nervous.

When we reached the locker room, he lowered his head and kissed me softly. "You're going to do great."

"I better go," I said.

He walked backwards, never taking his eyes off me. I lingered for just a second, skimming my gaze over his muscular frame before I disappeared inside. Several girls filed out of the locker room. Two sat on benches rubbing lotion on their legs. Another girl applied makeup in a mirror attached to the inside of her locker. As I skirted benches, heavy scents of sweet, fruity, and spicy perfumes assailed me. The cool thing about the girls' side of the sports complex was it always smelled like the perfume counter at Macy's. While I didn't care for the mixture of scents, it was better than a room that smelled like sweaty feet.

When I rounded a bank of lockers I came face to face with Renee Spellman. Suddenly, my nerves went from two on the Richter scale to eight. The blood roared through me. She was sitting on a bench in between lockers putting on her cleats.

"Hey, we haven't officially met," she said, looking up at me. "I'm Renee."

I'd avoided looking at her in psychology. I mostly doodled in my notebook in between taking notes. I blinked several times to clear my vision. *She's not Julie.* My hands became clammy. White noise slowly ramped up in my head. I knew she wasn't my sister. Yet my brain dialed back to last January.

She stood and touched me on the arm. "You're pale. Maybe you should sit."

"No. I need to get changed."

"I'll see you out on the field then." She swept her brown hair up into a ponytail. "Are you sure you're okay?" She grabbed her glove off the bench.

Hell, no. "Yeah. I'll see you out there." My legs trembled.

She dashed out, her cleats beating on the floor. I inhaled so deeply that all the fragrant smells in the room made me choke. The whirring sound in my head quieted as I hurried to my locker. But my somewhat-calm state vanished when I found my locker ajar.

Why was it open? Did I close it before when I dropped off my bag? I'd been in a hurry. I thought I punched in the code to lock it. All the lockers in school were designed with a four-digit number to unlock it and the same code to lock it.

With a shaky hand, I pulled it open. All the blood rushed out of me. My body became numb. It was empty. *What? How? Why?* Tears burned my eyes.

Suddenly, the volume in my head shot off the charts. It sounded like angry wasps fighting. *What was I going to do without my cleats or my glove?* Maybe I had the wrong locker. After all, the sight of Renee did blur my vision for a second. My body shook as I closed the door to check the number. Yep. 444 was painted on the door. This was my locker. As I grabbed the handle, I noticed a dent in the edge of the door around the latch. Suddenly, Aaron's words "Watch your back" screamed over the buzzing. Would he really be that devious?

I flopped down on the bench, and dropped my face into my hands. Tears cascaded down. *What was I going to do?* In the middle of the chaos floating in my head, anger roared through me. If I didn't try out, I would lose my chance at my dream. I couldn't let that happen. *Put on your big girl panties. Show whoever is responsible that they can't get to you that easily,* my inner voice coached. But I didn't have my gear. *So find a glove. That's all you need.* But that wasn't enough—I had to have my cleats. In my flats, I'd slide off the mound like an amateur ice skater. Plus I was wearing jeans—I wouldn't be able to lift my knee high enough in my wind-up.

I couldn't walk out onto the field. I'd be the laughingstock of the school. The headline would read, "New Girl Tanks When the Pressure Heats Up." I screamed into my hands. *What would my brother do?* I looked up to him. He'd pushed through a hurricane to get something he wanted. *Well, girl, this is your hurricane. Plow through the storm.* I stood, straightened my shoulders, wiped the tears from my face, and walked out.

As I made my way to the field, I ran through what I was going to say to Coach Dean. *Tell him the truth.* Would he believe me if I told him someone stole my gear? Would he even let me try out without it?

The sun blinded me when I looked out onto the field from the tunnel. Those vying for positions were working through drills. Infielders and outfielders were throwing the balls. Aaron stood on third base and threw a ball to the boy on first, who threw the ball to Kelton at shortstop. In the bullpen behind right field, one potential pitcher warmed up, throwing the ball to a catcher. I spotted Coach Dean near the right field dugout, talking with Coach Lee, the pitching coach.

Making my way over, I kept close to the edge of the field along the stands like a mouse scurrying along the perimeter. I tucked my hands in my pockets so no one would see me trembling. I didn't want to look in the stands. If I saw my dad, I would lose it. We were in this town because of me. I couldn't handle any disappointment on his face. I wanted to stay focused to speak with Coach. I thought about tryouts back at Crestview. Baseball wasn't even on the agenda this time of year —not until February. Dad and I had found it unusual for a high school to schedule tryouts in the fall, but Coach Dean's philosophy was to choose his team months before the season began. This gave him ample time to mold us into fighting shape. Whoever made the team would be practicing all winter at an indoor sports complex. And that might not include me.

As I got closer to Coach Dean, the snap of the ball into gloves cut through the angry wasps in my head. A gust of wind blew my hair over my face. Out of habit, I tipped my head to the right as I brushed the strands away from my face. When I did, Kelton was staring at me with a what-the-heck look. I swallowed hard, not acknowledging him. I'd lose it if I kept looking at him, too. The triplets were counting on me.

Coach Dean glanced up. He, too, had a what-in-the-world expression. He patted Coach Lee on the shoulder before stalking up to me. Coach Lee trotted out to the bullpen.

"What's going on, Lacey?" Coach Dean's voice was firm. "Why are you in jeans?"

I swallowed again. "I don't have my gear."

"Where is it?" he asked. His bushy eyebrows came together to create a unibrow.

Tell the truth. "I don't know. I put my bag in my locker, and now it's not there."

He flipped off his cap, ran a palm over his head, then put the cap back on.

"I can still try out if I can borrow a glove," I said.

"I can't let you try out without cleats."

"Please, Coach." Tears surfaced. *Don't you dare cry on this ball field.* This was the one place I found peace. Right now, though, the only thing I found was hell. "I need this."

He scrubbed his face with his hand. "You're sure your bag isn't in your locker? You checked the right locker?"

"Yes, sir." *I wasn't crazy.*

He scratched his neck. "Goddammit," he muttered. He turned and glanced up in the stands.

I followed his line of sight. My gaze landed on Kade. He stood with his arms crossed over his chest, confusion written all over his face. He leaned down and said something to Kody. Then he climbed over the rows of bleachers, making his way down to the field.

Coach waved a hand to someone behind me. I turned to find Coach Lee jogging toward us. What the heck was happening? Was Coach going to have me escorted off the field so I couldn't try out? When I turned back around Kade was on the field, heading my way. I couldn't look at Kelton or anyone else. I was afraid to search the stands for my dad, either. *I just wanted to play baseball.*

"What is it, Dean?" Coach Lee asked. His bulbous nose shone.

"Can you go with Lacey and check out her locker to see if there was any suspicious behavior?"

"What's going on?" Kade asked.

"My bag is missing." I started for the locker room behind Coach Lee.

"Okay, everyone in," Coach Dean yelled as I walked away.

"You mean your clothes?" Kade strode alongside me.

I still had my hands in my pockets, and they shook more now, like I had a permanent nervous tick. "You don't have to come with me."

He didn't say anything. His face was blank.

Keeping my head down, I traipsed through the tunnel, thinking of what Dad was going to say. My emotions waffled between anger and fear. In one breath I would kill the person who took my stuff, but in the next I dreaded Dad's wrath.

Coach Lee's voice brought me out of my stupor. "Anyone in here?" he said, holding the locker room door open.

No one answered. I went in first. Coach Lee and Kade trailed behind me. When we reached my locker the door was cracked open.

Coach Lee examined the door before he touched it. I sat down on the bench, chewing on a nail. Kade ran his fingers through his hair as he watched Coach Lee.

"Looks like it's been pried open," Coach Lee said. As if in slow motion, he grasped the bottom edge of the door and opened it.

The blood drained from me. *My effing bag was in my locker.* Coach Lee turned to me with his shiny nose and wide eyes. Kade stared at me like I was some loony chick. If I could look at myself in the mirror right then, I'd bet I had the same expression as they did.

"Lacey," Coach Lee's voice was dry. "Are you certain your bag wasn't in the locker all this time?"

I glared at the coach. I was not insane. I jumped to my feet. "I'm very certain." I took two strides before reaching in to grab my bag.

Coach swung his gaze from me to Kade then back to me. "Get dressed. We have an hour left." He stalked out.

I unzipped the bag. All my stuff was in it. I yanked out my yoga pants, T-shirt, socks and cleats. If Kade wanted to stay and watch, fine. I was getting my ass out on that field. I wasn't going to analyze what had happened—not now, anyway. "You can leave," I said in a rough tone. The buzzing and nerves still tormented me.

"Hey." He closed the distance between us, wrapping his arms around me.

I planted my hands on his chest and pushed. "I don't want to be coddled. I have to get out there."

He didn't move.

"Kade, not now. Please?" I was on the verge of tears. *I did want his strong arms around me. I did want to lose myself in him.* But right now, baseball was my goal.

"I'm sorry," he whispered in my hair. "I'll see you afterwards." He let go of me and left.

I almost collapsed. Who the heck had done this? Aaron was outside. Someone was trying to make me look crazy. I changed as fast as I could then carried my bag out to the field with me.

I set it down in the right field dugout. I tucked my glove underneath my arm and met Coach Dean near home plate. I had my back to the stands as I waited for him to finish reading the paper on his clipboard. I didn't have the courage to look up in the stands yet.

The recruits were running from first then sliding into second. Coach Lee took notes as each one hit the bag. Aaron, tall and lithe, ran up to Coach Dean. "Hi, Lacey. How are you?" he asked in a sugary tone as he narrowed his green eyes at me.

"What is it, Aaron?" Coach asked.

"Lacey needs to warm up and I thought I could catch for her while she does." A sinister grin etched his smooth features. "Mark Wayland is still working through his running drills. And I know we don't have that much time left."

I glared at the cagey captain of the baseball team, keeping my breathing even. *Tryouts first. Worry about who sabotaged your day later.* If I did well in the short time we had left, then I might get to chalk up this tryout as a win. I was getting ahead of myself, but all I wanted to do was rip off Aaron's head, and I didn't even know for sure if he was the culprit.

"We'll take batting practice. Lacey will pitch to batters. Everyone in." Coach Dean's voice boomed.

Everyone trotted in. I moved to stand near a few boys. I was now facing Coach and the spectators. I made the mistake of looking out. Tammy Reese sat with Greg Sullivan. Both had smug smiles on their faces as Greg waved to me. I ignored the oily-haired creep, and looked for Dad in the stands. He wasn't there. I searched again. I found Kade in the same spot as I'd seen him earlier. He was leaning forward with his elbows on his knees. Kody sat next to him in the same position. They appeared to be in a heated discussion. Becca and Tyler sat next to Kody. They had their feet propped up on the bleachers in front of them, watching. Becca chewed on a nail. Tyler had his arms crossed over his chest. One more time I scanned the crowd as Kelton and Kross took up positions near me. *No Dad.* Worry and anger began to churn, but I quickly banked the emotions for now.

"Lacey, take the mound and warm up," Coach Lee said. "Wayland, suit up. You're catching."

"What happened?" Kelton asked in my ear.

"Not now," I replied as I headed to the mound.

Kross caught my arm. "You okay?"

I regarded both triplets, who had concerned expressions beneath the bills of their caps. All I did was nod as I continued to the mound.

Wayland, a stocky guy with red hair and freckles, jogged over to the right field dugout and wrapped shin guards around his legs, slipped on his chest protector, and grabbed his mask and glove before meeting me at the mound.

"Kross, center field," Coach announced. "Kelton, take short. Aaron, third base. Finn, first base. Tim, second base. James, you're in right field. And Taylor, take left. The rest of you in the dugout. Lacey, warm up," Coach ordered. "Let's go, people."

Everyone scattered to their positions.

"Coach Lee is going to umpire," Coach Dean went on. "Lacey, you'll face two batters. Then we'll rotate to the next pitcher."

"I'm Mark Wayland. What pitches do you have?" he asked, holding his mask under his arm.

"Curveball, fastball, and slider."

"I'll call the pitches. To keep it simple, one finger for curveball, two fingers for fastball, and three for slider." His gray eyes dulled in the fading sunlight. He patted me on the back with his mitt then handed me the ball.

Stepping on the mound, I dug at the dirt with my cleat to ensure the rubber was level with the dirt. I didn't like divots in front of the mound like some pitchers did.

"Focus. Find your zone, and remember—in and tight," Kelton advised as he walked past me.

The girls in the crowd shouted his name.

I inhaled, taking in the fresh scent of grass. The white noise in my head lowered. I didn't think it would leave me now until I got through tryouts. I was fine with the humming sound. It might help me get in my zone.

"Seriously, are you okay?"

I liked this side of Kelton. Not that I wanted him to worry about me, but he was even more handsome when he was sincere.

More girls screamed his name.

What?" he asked innocently. "All girls want me." He gave me one of those Maxwell grins.

I rolled my eyes. His sweetness was good while it lasted—all of two seconds. "What you need is a clear dose of reality," I said in a serious tone.

"Those girls screaming my name is reality, Lacey. Now, let's concentrate on what we're here for."

I didn't argue. The lighthearted banter helped to calm me somewhat.

"Lacey, warm up," Mark called from home plate.

I threw several pitches, loosening my arm. I rolled my shoulders after each pitch. The soreness wasn't there. Maybe the adrenaline would keep the pain at bay.

"Let's get the show started, folks," Coach Dean called.

I can do this. I know this game. Find your zone. We want to win state. We need you on the team.

Renee Spellman made her way to the batter's box, swinging the bat first in one hand, then the other.

The hum in my head turned into a loud roar. My hands began to perspire. I picked up the chalk bag with my pitching hand, massaging the white powder into my palm to dry the sweat. After a few swipes on my leg, I moved into position. Gripping the ball inside my glove, I felt around for the seams.

Coach Lee gave me a nod as Renee crouched into her batting stance. I sent up a prayer before looking down at Mark. He flashed one finger. *Curveball.* Nodding, I checked that the players on the field were ready. Satisfied, I wound up, going through my movements and snapped my wrist down. The ball left my hand with less velocity than that of a fastball. When thrown correctly, the spin of a curveball with a good follow through would hit the strike zone. This pitch was nowhere near the plate. *Slow, follow through, and concentrate.*

"Ball," Coach Lee called out.

Mark shook his head, tamping down his palm, telling me to relax. Renee stepped out, taking a few more practice swings.

I got into position. *I can do this.*

When she set her stance, bat in hand, arms back, head turned toward me, she smiled with one corner of her mouth turned upward.

Suddenly, Julie's face flashed before me. My pulse raced. I shook my head once, twice. *She doesn't look like Julie.* I blew out a few puffs of air. *She doesn't look like Julie.* Releasing one last breath, I glanced at Mark for his signal. Two fingers flashed. A fastball. I wound up. As my arm stretched out in the follow-through, I wavered. The ball soared over Coach Lee and Mark, hitting the backstop with a resounding thwack.

"Holy hell, girl," Kelton ran up to me. "What's wrong?"

Mark trotted out. "It's okay. Nerves are normal. Find your zone." He handed me the ball then resumed his position at home plate.

My zone. Where was it? I turned my neck left then right. Relaxing my shoulders, I set my stance, and looked to Mark for the pitch signal.

When I looked back, Renee's face morphed into Julie's again. My brain tilted, and suddenly, darkness crept into my peripheral vision.

My phone lit my way through the house.

"Julie! Mom!"

Sweat began to bead on my forehead. A lamp in the living room was on the floor, the shade askew. Red splattered the white doorframe leading into the dining room. The only sound was the banging of my heart in my ears. As I skirted the dining table, something rolled under my foot. I wobbled. My hand shot out, searching for an anchor. Nothing. My feet flew out in front of me before I landed on my butt. I angled my phone light toward the floor. Lipstick and other items were strewn all over. Tears stung my eyes.

I rose on trembling legs, shuffling. "Mom! Julie!" I shouted again in a shaky voice.

As I neared the kitchen, a sweaty, metallic scent burned my nostrils. I walked through the arched doorway. A bloodcurdling scream tore from me. I dropped to my knees. The blood in my veins turned to ice. I couldn't move. I couldn't breathe. The phone fell from my hand. Dizziness clouded my brain. Nausea rose. Then darkness extinguished my consciousness.

CHAPTER 14

My brain registered voices in the distance as I slowly cracked open my eyelids. Wincing at the pain in my head, I pressed my fingers to my temple. An alarm blared and I jolted upright. "Make it stop!" I yelled, covering my ears.

Kade was sitting on my bed beside me. "Lace," he said. "It's okay." His hands circled my wrists. "Hey, baby. It's just the alarm on the medical monitor." He turned. "Kel, get the nurse."

"Turn it off," I cried. The high-pitched sound drilled into me as though someone were hammering nails into my head.

"Kross," Kade called. "Shut it off, now."

The alarm died. Quiet reigned. I took comfort in the fact that my head didn't have the constant drone of wasps. I slumped forward into Kade, my soft cheek against a hard-as-steel chest, and he wrapped his arms around me.

"What happened?" I asked as I stared at Kross, who was standing by the medical monitor. I looked down at my left hand. A white clothespin-like device was clipped onto my forefinger. "Why am I in the hospital?" I asked.

Kross dropped his gaze to his cleats. *Oh, no. I didn't have a panic attack on the field? No. No. No. Please don't let it be true. Not in front of the school, Coach Dean, Becca, Tyler...and Kade, again. I'll never be able to play now. The one place I loved was now officially my hell. How could I face anyone?*

They would look at me like I was crazy, and take pity on me. I had to get out of here. Run. Hide. My breathing was shallow. Tears dropped one after the other.

I pulled away from Kade. The weight of the world rested on his shoulders. I finally knew what Jackie from the gun club meant—he didn't have the usual spark in his copper eyes that I was used to seeing. He had pity, sadness, despair, and sorrow. *Please don't feel sorry for me.* It only served to worsen my own sorrow. I had to heal. That was one of the reasons I didn't want people to know. I could barely deal with my own feelings.

"I need to get out of here. I need to find my dad." I swung my legs off the side of the bed away from Kade.

"You can't leave. You hit your head. You might have a concussion," Kade said, his fingers lightly touching my forearm. "Your dad is on his way. And so is your...mom?"

I dropped my head and more tears fell onto my yoga pants. I stared at the dirt on my legs. He had to be talking about Mary. No one had met her yet.

"Please, Lace." His tone was heavy with desperation.

"No. I can't let anyone see me like this."

He let go of my arm. The bed shifted. His boots thudded on the tile floor, and then Kade crouched down in front of me. He placed his hands on my thighs, looking up at me. "I'm not going anywhere. You can call hospital security and I still won't leave." He grinned. "You look beautiful covered in dirt."

I reached out and touched his face. His eyes closed for a brief second. Why would he want anything to do with me? I was a complete mess. I threw my arms around his neck and cried. After a few minutes, he moved to sit next to me. I pulled away, mopping the tears soaking my face.

"Can I have some water?" My throat was parched.

"Kross?" Kade nodded at his brother, who was still standing near the medical monitor. Kross filled a cup with water on the side table then handed it to me.

"Thanks." I sipped the water through a straw, letting the coolness of the liquid sit on my tongue for a few seconds before swallowing.

"You had one of your attacks, didn't you?" Kade brushed back my hair.

"Yeah," I said in a small voice.

A nurse came in with Kelton on her heels, the lights capturing the red streaks through her blond hair. Her nametag said "Lisa." "Boys, please. Give her some breathing room. And what happened to the machine?" the petite lady in blue scrubs demanded.

"Sorry, the noise was bothering her," Kade responded.

Going over to the monitor, she turned it on. "Okay, young man, out," she said, patting Kross on the arm. "And you"—she pointed at Kade—"go with your brother. I'll let you know when you can come back in."

Kade kissed me on the forehead. "I'll be outside."

"I don't want you to leave." He gave me a sense of security that I needed at the moment.

Kade eyed the nurse and flashed one of his famous grins.

"All right. I'm a sucker for two people in love," she said, batting her brown eyes our way.

Kade's smile widened. I choked. My brain pounded against my skull, and not from my head injury. *She thought we were in love?* Yet the sexy half-smile on his face was trying to tell me something.

"Um...we're not..." I couldn't say the word.

Kade raised my hand to his mouth and planted his warm lips on my palm. Immediately, the pounding in my head lessened. *Oh good grief! Did he agree with her? Or was he putting on a show so she would allow him to stay?*

"You keep telling yourself that," Lisa said as she pressed a few buttons on the monitor. "Anyway, he can stay. Everyone else has to leave." She shot a glare at Kelton and Kross.

Both were standing in the doorway. Kross had a wide-eyed expression while Kelton had one of his sinful smirks.

A beeping noise filled the room as the machine came back online. The sound was a quiet hum now.

"Do not touch the monitor again." Lisa narrowed her eyes at Kade while adjusting the clothespin device on my finger. "Leave this oximeter on, too." She eyed me. "The doctor will be in shortly." She headed to the door, pointing at Kelton and Kross. "You two—out."

The door closed behind her, leaving Kade and me alone. We stared at each other.

"Tell me what happened," I said, clasping my hands together.

"You were standing on the mound, staring down at home plate like you were frozen. Just like that night at your house." He rubbed my hand with his thumb. "Then you fell forward. Your head hit the ground, hard. I bolted out of my seat. By the time I got down onto the field, Coach Dean was checking your vitals. I had a feeling you had one of your attacks. Anyway, Coach called the paramedics." He pried my hands apart then held my right hand. "I called your house and your mom answered. I told her what happened. She said she would call your dad. He was in Boston. She didn't have a car. So I asked Kody to go and get her."

I lowered my gaze to my dirty pants again. I didn't know how to process this screwed-up day. When I went back to school, kids would look at me differently. I would now be the brunt of all jokes, especially after the incident where my bag went missing. *Oh, my God. People were going to think I was crazy for sure.* I had to shove that aside for now. Kade deserved to know about my mom and Julie. He'd seen me in my worst state. I couldn't keep having attacks around Kade and not tell him why. Dr. Davis had said that if Kade knew the triggers, he might be able to help. But what could he have done today? He didn't know that when I looked at Renee, I saw my sister. Plus he'd been in the stands and nowhere near me to help, not like he had been at the house when he first saw one of my panic attacks.

He curled his fingers under my chin. "Look at me, baby. Talk to me. Please." The anguish in his voice brought tears to my eyes.

Slowly, I lifted my eyes to his. "I'm broken, Kade." A tear rolled down my cheek.

"Hey, we're all broken." He was still caressing my palm.

"Not like me," I whispered.

"Whatever it is, Lace, I'm here for you." The warmth in his tone wrapped me in a blanket of tingles.

"Why? I've been terrible to you."

He searched my face, placing my hand on his heart. "I've fallen in love with you, Lacey Robinson," he said, sure and strong.

The breath halted in my lungs. My head pounded. Or was it the blood roaring through my ears? Did he just say what I think he said? How? Why?

Breathe. Breathe.

"From the first night you pulled the gun on me, to kicking me square in the groin, to our first kiss."

My eyes grew wide at his admission. The world around me closed in. Amazement. Shock. Joy. Fear. They all mixed together in a blur of confused emotions. "Kade—"

"Shhh." He kissed me lightly on the lips. "Do you feel my heart beating like a damn freight train barreling down the tracks?"

I barely nodded. His heart was beating like a bucking bronco.

He trailed the backs of his fingers along my face. "The heart knows, Lace. My sister was right. Don't ask me to explain it," he breathed. "All I know is I've never felt this way about anyone. When you walk into a room, my skin heats up, and all I want to do is sweep you up in my arms and not let go."

I began trembling. The guy made my nightmares disappear. He made my body react in ways it never had. So, why did my flight instinct kick into gear?

"Please don't be scared," he whispered, gliding his lips over mine.

"I'm...not...I can't..." He deserved someone better than me— someone who didn't have mental baggage.

"I don't expect you to feel the same. But I had to tell you. After my sister died, I hated life. Then when my mom started to have problems, I wanted to vanish. Move up to the Arctic and live with the polar bears."

I scrunched up my nose, smiling inside.

He lifted a muscular shoulder. "I've always loved polar bears. Ever since I saw them at a zoo when I was a kid. They're beautiful and fearless creatures. They represent purity, intelligence, strength. Whenever I would need something to pick me up, I'd watch videos of polar bears playing. Sounds crazy, I know. But, Lace, I've been in a bad place for a long time, until you. You're my polar bear."

I laughed then cried then laughed again. "You're comparing me to a bear?" I sniffled.

"I'm saying you're beautiful, strong, pure, intelligent, and I know there's a playfulness in you."

I pulled my hand away. I couldn't concentrate when I was feeling the beat of his heart. I breathed in, hoping my head would clear so I could sew words together to form a complete sentence. "What if I'm... not all those...things you just said?" I managed to say.

"You are. You just have to open up and let me show you."

I dashed tears away from my face. "My past has ruined me."

"If you allow it to, it will. But whatever is causing your attacks, you've been fighting it."

"How do you...know that?" Panic attacks weren't a sign of fighting anything.

"Because you're seeing Dr. Davis. If you didn't want to heal, Lace, then you wouldn't acknowledge that you needed help. And you're working hard at your dream. People who don't want to change or heal don't work hard to realize their dreams. They just give up."

"So says the genius." He had a point. I longed for my dream to come true. I ached to rid myself of the illness.

"It has nothing to do with my IQ, and has everything to do with my experience. I've been through a lot, Lace. My whole family has."

"But what if I don't feel the same way...about you?" I peered at him through lowered lashes. Who was I kidding? I had feelings for him, but I wasn't sure if they were as strong as the ones he had for me. Maybe because I was frightened, and I had to keep a lock on my heart. I didn't want to get hurt. The minute I'd told Brad I loved him, he broke up with me.

Kade touched my cheek. "I didn't tell you how I felt just so you would say it back. We have a lot to learn about each other. I get that. But I'm not going to deny what's in my heart. And when I want something I go after it. No games. I know there's something in here." He placed his hand on my heart.

"It may take a bomb to open mine," I said weakly.

"I'll be sure to bring explosives the next time we're together." He flashed me his signature grin.

"Kade, the lady Kody went to get isn't my mom. My mom——"

The door to the room burst open, and Dad barreled in, a large cut on his cheekbone. A smaller cut bled slowly above his eyebrow, and his lip was split as though someone threw a hard right hook.

"Oh, my God, Dad. What happened?" I pushed myself off the bed. Dizziness washed over me. I stumbled.

Kade bolted upright, and I fell into his arms, the clothespin thing flying off me.

Kelton and Kross ran in.

Blood seeped out of the wound on Dad's cheek. "Are you okay, Sweet Pea?"

"Am *I* okay? Look at *you*," I barked at Dad.

Kade guided me over to the bed. "Sit, Lacey." His tone was dominant and commanding.

"Who did this to you?" I asked, pushing to my feet then falling into Kade's arms again. *Damn dizziness.*

"Lace," Kade said in a deep tone as though he were trying to scare me. "You need to sit."

Kelton strode over, helping me onto the bed. I sat on the edge. Kross didn't move from his position at the door.

"Does she have a concussion?" Dad asked, glancing at Kade.

"Don't know, Mr. Robinson. We're waiting for the doc," Kade replied, the mattress dipping beside me.

Dad grabbed a chair, dragging it over to the bed. "I'm fine, Sweet Pea," he said as he sat down.

"Mr. Robinson, you might need stitches," Kade said.

"I know," he said.

"Kel, get the nurse," Kade ordered.

Kelton snapped to attention and disappeared.

"Who did this to you?" I asked.

Dad's face looked like someone had a good time with their fists and a sharp object. "I had to break up a fight at the club between two of my employees. But when Mary called, I jumped in my car. I didn't have time to clean up."

"You were supposed to be at tryouts," I reminded him.

"I had to take care of a pay issue. I thought I would be back in time. I'm sorry. That bump on your head looks like it hurts," Dad said.

"I have a headache, and some dizziness."

Lisa scurried in, pretty eyes wide. Kelton was right on her heels again. She glanced at my dad and pressed a button on the intercom behind the bed.

"Yes," a male voice came through the small speaker.

"Lou, can you come to room five fifteen? I need your help."

"Sure thing. I'll be right there," Lou said.

"Mr. Robinson, I take it?" Lisa asked. "You do need stitches," she said after she examined the wound.

A short man in a white uniform came in. He looked everyone over then landed his gaze on Lisa.

"Please go with Lou," she ordered, touching Dad on the arm.

"I'll be back, Lacey." Dad left, followed by Lou.

"Didn't I tell you two to leave?" Lisa glared at Kelton and Kross.

"Go find out what's taking Kody so long," Kade ordered his brothers.

They both did as their big brother commanded and hurried out.

"I'll check to see where the doctor is," Lisa said as she left.

"Okay, baby," Kade whispered. "Now, back in bed." He rose before lifting my legs.

Pressing my hands into the mattress, I swung my legs up onto the bed. No sooner had I got comfortable than Mary walked in, her big brown eyes filled with concern. She looked up at Kade, then back at me.

"Lacey, are you okay?" Mary asked as she hurried over to me.

"I'm fine. Maybe a little dizzy. More from all the people in and out of this room." Not to mention the news Kade had shared with me. How could I not be woozy? He'd admitted he had feelings for me—strong feelings, no less.

"That's a nasty lump on your head," she said, taking up Dad's previous spot in the chair.

"Hi, I'm Kade. I was the one who called you."

She smiled. "I'm Mary. Nice to meet you in person. And thank you for calling."

"Lace, I'll be back in a few minutes," Kade said. "Nice to meet you, ma'am." He strode out of the room.

"What happened, Lacey?" Mary asked.

I explained my entire disaster, from my sports bag going missing to how Renee looked like Julie. "I'm worried I'm not going to get better. It seems I'm having more panic attacks now. Plus I'm afraid of going back to school. I'm sure I'll be the topic of all their gossip. Then I'll act out again like I did at Crestview when kids looked at me the wrong way. I'm also frightened Coach Dean won't consider me for a spot on the team now."

"Is baseball worth your health? You've been pushing yourself so hard. Even before you left California, you were practicing non-stop."

We'd had a spot in our backyard with a net set up for me to practice my pitching. She was right. I was out there every chance I had. Regardless, baseball was my love, my dream. "I have to do this."

"Are you sure you're not hiding behind a mask like your dad is? He uses work as his outlet to forget. Is that what you're doing with baseball?" Lines dented her smooth forehead.

Was I? I'd never thought I was hiding. I'd thought I was trying to do something I loved.

The only sound in the room was the soft beep of the medical monitor.

"So Kade calls you Lace." Mary adjusted the cranberry silk scarf around her neck. "The only one I've known to call you Lace was Brad."

Yeah, but when Kade calls me Lace my insides dance with delight. When Brad used to call me Lace, his tone did nothing to convey any fluttering feelings.

"I noticed he seems protective of you," she said.

"He told me he loves me." The words tumbled off my tongue.

Her full lips stretched into a smile. "And how do you feel about him?" Mary asked.

I twisted the edges of my wrinkled Dodgers T-shirt like I was wringing water from it. "I like him a lot, but I'm scared."

"You can't compare Brad with him." She scooted her chair closer to the bed. "Have you told him about your PTSD?"

"I was about to tell him about my mom when Dad came in."

"Your father is here?" Her voice rose.

I stopped toying with my shirt. "He's getting stiches. He had to break up a fight at the club."

She mashed her burgundy-colored lips together. "That man. I swear."

"Is he okay, Mary? I know my dad is hurting. But I heard him swearing on the phone this morning. He never swears."

"It was a misunderstanding with Eric at Eko Records over a contract with a potential client. Don't worry about your dad. I want you to worry about Lacey." Mary leaned over the bed, resting her hand on my thigh. "You have to allow people in." Her tone lowered. "Allow yourself some freedom to just have fun, to feel again."

"What if Kade breaks my heart or runs when I tell him about my PTSD?" I worried my bottom lip.

"First, if the boy is in this hospital with you, not knowing why you keep having panic attacks, I can assure you he isn't going to run." She sat back in her chair. "He would've already. Two, you have to take a chance, otherwise you may never have an opportunity at love again. And love is the most beautiful thing in the world when two people open their souls to one another."

Dad came back in. He had a thin piece of tape over his left eye and right cheek. His bottom lip was swollen, but the blood was gone.

"James, are you okay?" Mary's voice was distraught.

"Fine, Mary. Just a little misunderstanding at the club," he said as he sat on the edge of the bed. "I'm sorry I wasn't there today, Sweet Pea. Please forgive me." Regret shone from his green eyes.

Part of me was relieved he hadn't been there at the beginning. He would've had a cow if he'd thought I couldn't try out. But I'd wanted him there to watch me, to support me like he had at Crestview. He always showed up for my games. "I wanted you there. You promised. We're in this together, remember?"

He leaned over and hugged me. "I love you," he said. "I'll be there next time."

Would there be a next time? "Tryouts continue tomorrow."

He pulled away, wrenching a hand through his hair. "Lacey, if you have a concussion, even a mild one, I'm not sure you'll be capable of any physical exertion."

"I have to, Dad. I can't miss tryouts."

CHAPTER 15

I threw back my down comforter, letting the cool air of my bedroom dry the sweat coating my body. I turned to my right and grabbed my phone off the wicker nightstand. It was almost lunch time. I rolled back onto my pillow and raised my knees as I tapped on the screen for my text messages. I had one from Becca, one from Tyler, and one from Kade.

Kade had returned to the hospital room shortly after Dad, but we didn't get a chance to talk any more—the doctor came in. After several tests on my vision, hearing, and reflexes, he'd determined I had a mild concussion. He ordered rest for at least a day. If I felt better after today, I could go back to school. Mary had woken me twice in the middle of the night to make sure I was okay—another order from the doctor.

A knock sounded on my door before it opened. Dad walked in. "Hey, how are you feeling?" His left eye was beginning to bruise.

"Good." A small amount of dizziness still lingered, but no headache, although the lump on my forehead hurt. "I want to go to school, Dad. The second round of tryouts is this afternoon."

He eased down onto the bed. "I talked to Coach Dean this morning. What happened with your gear? He said someone broke into your locker, but then it reappeared." He studied my face.

I scooted back against my brass headboard. "I don't know.

Someone played a prank. I'd like to know who." Or maybe I shouldn't know—if I got my hands on the person I might be expelled from school. "What else did Coach say?" Could I make up a tryout? I had to show Coach I could play. I'd only thrown one or two pitches, and they were bad pitches, before I became good friends with the ground.

"He's postponing the second round until he looks into the locker incident. He wants to question a few students who might've been in the locker room at the time."

Luck seemed to be on my side. I let out a breath. Deep relief eclipsed the panic that had been brewing.

"I've got to run a few errands," he said, standing up. "Get some rest." Leaning down, he kissed me on the top of my head. Then he crossed the room to the door.

"Dad?"

He turned.

"I'm glad you're okay."

"I'll see you later." He closed the door behind him.

I buried my head in my pillow and screamed for joy. Luck was my friend today. Maybe Coach would uncover who took my gear, too. I didn't think Aaron had since he'd been on the field at the time. Besides, how would a guy get into the girls' locker room in the middle of the day, with girls coming and going? *Unless he had a partner in crime.* I briefly thought of Tammy. I did see her and Aaron in the hall yesterday morning. I hardly knew her, but she didn't like me. Well, I wasn't going to solve the case in my bedroom.

I answered my text messages. I let Becca know she could come by after school. I told Tyler I was fine, and how much I appreciated his concern. Then I replied to Kade's text. *I would love to see you later this afternoon. Can you come by around five? Maybe you can stay for dinner.*

As soon as I sent out the texts, my phone beeped.

Becca's text read, *I'll see you at three thirty.*

Kade responded, *I can't wait,* with six heart emoticons.

I typed *Me too,* with a smiley that had hearts for eyes. I was excited to see him. He deserved to hear my story, too. Although I wasn't so excited about that part. What if I had a panic attack when I told him? I moved that thought to the back of mind. If we were building a relationship, it was more important than ever to play that get-to-know-you game.

I slowly got out of bed, making sure I didn't wobble from the dizziness. Once I was on two feet, the room didn't shift or whirl or tilt. All good signs. I grabbed a pair of jeans, clean underwear, and an ASU sweatshirt before heading into the bathroom. I took a quick shower, dressed, twisted my long wavy brown hair and secured it on the back of my head with a clip. Then I went in search of food. Mary was sitting on the sofa in our sunken family room, watching Emeril Lagasse on the food channel. He was explaining how to make some type of paste for pork chops. She had her pen in one hand and her notebook in the other.

"Are we having chops tonight?" I asked.

"Yep. And if I have all these ingredients, I might be able to spice it up." She didn't look up.

"Can Kade stay for dinner?"

"Sure, sure." She waved a hand in the air, shooing me off.

I stepped up into the kitchen. The design of the house had a wall of windows that ran the length of both rooms, overlooking the tree-covered yard in the back. Bright daylight filtered in.

I went to the fridge and peered in. The leftover pizza was sitting on the top shelf with my name on it. I grabbed a piece and a Coke and closed the door. I devoured the pizza then popped the top of the Coke can and took a swig.

A commercial came on. Mary turned, her dark eyes regarding me. "I didn't mean to ignore you. You feeling okay?"

With my Coke in hand, I padded into the family room, my bare toes sinking into the soft carpeting.

"I'm good. Becca is coming over later. I'll be up in my room studying." I had my trig and calculus tests coming up—plus I had homework.

Emeril's voice came back on the TV—my cue to head up to my room. I left Mary to resume her class with Emeril.

The rest of the afternoon I spent doing my English and chemistry homework. Then I started on calculus problems when a soft knock broke my concentration on integrals.

"It's unlocked," I said from my bed. I had a desk, but I liked to spread out my books and lie on my stomach when I was doing homework.

The door opened and Becca bounced in. "I met Mary. Nice lady. She showed me where your room was." She glanced around, checking out my hideaway. "I know, Lacey, we've only known each other short time, but can I ask where's your mom?"

I sat up. It wouldn't hurt to tell her part of the truth. I just didn't want to share the whole truth. Not yet. "She passed away."

She diverted her attention from a framed poem on my wall adjacent to the door and regarded me with sorrow in her eyes. "I'm sorry."

"Do you like the poem?" I asked. The poem was by Sri Chinmoy.

Hope knows no fear. Hope dares to blossom, even inside the abysmal abyss. Hope secretly feeds and strengthens promise.

"Do you write poems?" She plopped down on my bed. My calculus book jumped a tad.

"No. I saw it in a store in LA, and I had to have it. My mom used to tell me that without hope, your dreams won't come true."

"And your dream is baseball," Becca said, looking up and past me.

Two posters of my favorite Major League ballplayers were tacked to the wall above my bed. I loved Jacoby Ellsbury, even though he didn't play for the LA Dodgers. I also had a poster of Clayton Kershaw, a pitcher for the LA Dodgers.

"You're such a boy sometimes," she teased.

"Hey, I have frilly pink curtains on my window."

She rolled her big brown eyes. "Good thing. Or I might have to stage an intervention and decorate the room myself."

I threw a small throw pillow at her.

She snickered. "So, are you good?"

"I am. Except the knot. How was school?" I sat cross-legged, touching my forehead.

"Did you not eat before tryouts? That's what Kade had said today when everyone was asking about you."

Kade lied for me? Another notch loosened in my heart. "I didn't. Then I panicked when someone broke into my locker."

"Coach Dean has been questioning girls who had gym yesterday." She reclined on the bottom of the bed, propping her head in her hand.

"Do you know if Aaron bullied Mandy?" I tossed my calculus book on my pillow.

She traced the outline of the stitching on my comforter. "I don't know the whole story, but Kody does, since he was dating her. I wasn't friends with Mandy. And I didn't hang out with the Maxwells either. But rumors around school were that Aaron didn't like the attention she brought to the team. Well, to her. The local media would come out to watch her. They did a few news articles on her. Aaron thought it should be about him. Anyway, little things would happen to her before a game. Like one time she found her glove cut up before a game."

"Was it Aaron?"

"No one could prove it was." Looking up at me, she stopped tracing the comforter. "I've been dying to tell you about Kade." Her energy transformed from dour to cheery. "OMG. When you fell, Kade jumped out of the stands." Her free hand was flying around as fast as the words spilled from her mouth. "I swear if he could fly... Actually, I think maybe he did fly." She flipped hair over her shoulder. "Anyway, when he got down on the field, he wouldn't let anyone near you except Coach Dean. It was like you were Snow White, and he was your prince. Like he was afraid that if anyone kissed you, you would fall in love with them instead of him." She giggled.

"A tiny bit dramatic. Don't you think?" I made a pinching gesture with my forefinger and thumb.

"Let me talk," Becca said. "So the ambulance came, and Kade wouldn't even let the medics around you. Somehow they convinced Kade they knew what they were doing. The girls in the stands were about to pass out. They've never seen Kade Maxwell run to a girl's rescue. He does have it bad for you, girl."

"Mmm." She was right about that.

"What?" Becca asked.

"He told me he loved me." The words came out easily.

"I knew it. When he gave you that flower yesterday. I'm so happy for you. Do you love him?" Her dark eyes were laser-focused on me.

"I like him a lot. But, I'm cautious." I folded the edge of a piece of paper. "My last boyfriend dumped me after I told him I loved him." There was more to Brad that I didn't care to share at the moment.

"Lacey. I know I warned you in the beginning about Kade, but he seems different. I don't know, more mature. Plus he is so hot, sexy, and sooooo...male." Her cheeks reddened.

We both laughed.

"I need to go." She rubbed her hands on her jeans as she rose.

I debated whether to ask her stay for dinner. I wanted to be able to talk with Kade alone.

"Do you want to stay for dinner?" I asked anyway. I wanted to bond more with her. It was nice having a girl as a friend. Dad would be pleased.

"Nah, I can't. My mom is taking me out to Wiley's Bar and Grill.

It's our mother-and-daughter night. My dad is balancing the books at the Cave. I'll see you in school tomorrow."

A pang of hurt hit me square in the chest. I'd never have a mother-and-daughter night again. I hopped off the bed. "I'll walk you out. Kade is coming for dinner."

When we opened the door, a citrusy smell drifted in.

"Whatever Mary is cooking, I'm sad I can't stay. It smells delicious," Becca said.

"I think it's pork chops," I added as we climbed down the stairs.

When we reached the front door, we hugged and said our good-byes. It was only four thirty, so I figured I'd check in with Mary and see if Dad came home. I found him sitting at the kitchen island, eating a sandwich, and Mary preparing a salad.

"I guess you're not staying for dinner?" I asked Dad, kissing him on the cheek.

"I need to get an early start at the club." His brown hair was wet, and he wore black pants and a blue button-front, long-sleeved shirt rolled up to his forearms.

"Please stay. Kade is having dinner with us." I sat down next to him.

"Maybe next time, Sweet Pea." He pushed off the granite top with his hands as he stood, grabbing his glass of water. "I promise. I gotta run." He downed the water as he went over and set the glass in the sink. "I'll see you ladies tomorrow." He snatched his wallet and keys from the counter near the door to the laundry room and disappeared.

I would have protested if it weren't for the doorbell chiming. "Kade is early." I jumped down from the stool, darting for the front door.

Mary laughed behind me.

I slowed. *A girl should be calm and proper when meeting a man.* My mom's words, not mine. I pulled out the clip in my hair then combed my fingers through it. I glanced down. I should've changed out of the sweatshirt. At least, I had jeans on and not yoga pants, for once. As my hand covered the doorknob, the bell dinged again.

I opened the heavy wooden door. The sexy beast stood on the porch, hair windblown-messy, white henley, sleeves pushed up to his elbows, black jeans, black boots, and a Maxwell grin on his gorgeous face. Maybe it was good I had a sweatshirt and a bra on since my nipples were hard.

"Hey, baby," he rasped.

Cold air followed him in. No sooner had I shut the door than he planted a soft kiss on my lips. "You look better," he said. "I missed you."

I planted my hands on his firm abs. "What did you miss about me?"

"Your beautiful green eyes," he said, staring into them.

"That's it?" I stuck out my bottom lip, snaking my hands around to his lower back.

He leaned down, threading his fingers into my hair. "I can't tell you everything at once. I have to keep you wondering," he said close to my ear.

"Just remember two can play this game."

Footsteps echoed in the hall. "Dinner is ready," Mary announced.

We separated. My bare feet slapped against the wood floor. Kade's boots thumped.

Mary had the glass dining table in front of the window in the nook area set with plates and utensils. "Sit, you two," she said, pointing at the table.

Kade sat in the chair facing the window. I sat on the end to his left. Mary served us salad, pork chops, and jasmine rice. Then she joined us. I took my first bite of the pork chop and my taste buds did a happy dance.

"Is this Emeril's recipe?" I asked.

"Not exactly—I didn't have all the ingredients, so I used mangoes for the paste."

"It's very good," Kade said, between bites.

"What are we doing for your birthday this weekend?" Mary asked as she poured dressing on her salad.

Kade's head snapped my way. "It's your birthday?" His voice was a little too excited.

I glared at Mary. She knew I didn't like anyone to make a fuss over my birthday.

As though she heard my thinking, she said, "But it's the big one-eight."

"When is it?" Kade asked.

"Saturday," Mary answered.

Kade and Mary exchanged devious looks.

"Oh, no. You two are not going to plan anything."

"Eat your dinner," Kade said. "And stop freaking out so much."

I stilled, the fork halfway to my mouth. His words cut deep. *Was he calling me a freak?* The last time he said something similar I'd punched him in the nose. Without saying a word, I set down my fork and stormed out of the kitchen before I did hit him again.

"Lacey," he called. "Lace."

His voice waned through the house as I found the one spot I went to whenever I was feeling blue, mad, or sorry for myself. I settled into an oversized chair in the sunroom, overlooking our backyard. The glass-enclosed room was cold and warm all at the same time. I imagined in the winter it would be freezing in here even though it was heated. Dad and I had seen pictures of this room on the Internet when we were house hunting. The snow had covered the glass rooftop and the trees outside were blanketed with it. I hugged a pillow and stared out at the sunny day. I loved the sense of safety and freedom the room gave me. I felt like I was part of the world, yet sheltered from all the harshness of it. I loved the beautiful scenery as the trees were turning the deeper colors of fall. It seemed that every day, green turned into oranges, reds, and yellows. If only my mom and Julie were here to see the beautiful palette.

Footsteps clomped on the hardwood floor. A fragrant hint of cedar wafted in before my guest did. Kade could smell like trash, and I'd still want him all over me. *Maybe that idea was a little over the top. You're supposed to be mad at him.* Regardless, I inhaled, letting the aroma fill my lungs.

"I'm sorry," he rasped from behind me. "I was just using an expression without thinking. I wasn't saying anything about you."

I squeezed the pillow a little harder, suppressing a shudder at the sound of his voice. I wanted to be mad at him, but his presence overpowered any resolve I had.

"Can I be that pillow?" he asked with a smile in his voice.

"Depends."

A smidgeon of his manly frame reflected in the glass in front of me. He had his shoulder propped up against the doorframe. His toned chest strained against the white henley he wore. "On?" he prompted.

"How much of an asshat you're going to be tonight."

His reflection in the window blurred, and then he was sitting in front of me on the ottoman. "Now who's being the asshat?" he asked.

"Go away, Kade. I'm sure the school will have a field day with me when I go back tomorrow."

"Let them. Why do you even care? The girl I met that first night in the parking lot could not give a shit."

That was what I wanted everyone to believe. I sometimes convinced myself, even. I was an emotional freak, thanks to my PTSD. Since my first day at Kensington, it seemed I was propelled back in time to nine months ago. Right after the funeral, I'd became a temperamental nut case. One minute I would cry, then the next I would lash out at anyone and everyone. *What happened to the girl who just wanted to play baseball, hang out with family and friends, and fly planes?* My brooding was shattered when he lifted me in the air and set me on his lap. I adjusted my legs so I was straddling him, my soft chest to his hard one. "How do you keep doing that?" I asked.

"Doing what?" He cupped my face with his callused hands.

"Kade—"

"Shut up, Lace, and kiss me."

The guy was possessive and demanding as hell, but I didn't run. I kissed him like my life depended on it. Our tongues tangled, merging into a warm and wet cavern of heated bliss. He tasted like mangoes and Italian dressing, sweet and tangy.

Kade's hands snaked under my shirt, around my back, gliding up to my bra.

"Hey, you're not getting what you want." I grabbed his shoulder and pushed.

"And what do you think I want?" He held me tighter.

"A polar bear," I blurted out.

"You are my polar bear, Lace. I meant everything I said to you yesterday," he said with certainty.

"We should get back to dinner." I changed the subject. I was still trying to wrap my mind around his declaration. Not to mention my own feelings.

He tipped his head. "Mary said she would keep the food warm. While we have some quiet time, I would like to know why you have panic attacks."

I pushed away again. He drew me closer.

I'd planned on telling him. *So why all of a sudden did I have cold feet?* I'd told Becca my mom passed away. There were no details though.

"I hate to beg. It's not in my nature. But for you, I'd do anything. I think I deserve to know, Lace." His voice was soft, less demanding. "If I know more, maybe I can help."

Dip your toe in the water, Dr. Davis's words roared. Kade had shared his painful story of how his sister died. Taking a deep breath, I climbed off him and he let me go easily. I made myself comfortable in the chair, even though this conversation was going to be far from comfortable. If I were going to tell this story, I needed my space. He leaned forward, elbows on his knees.

"Doctors have diagnosed me with PTSD," I said in a low voice, eyes downcast. I didn't want to see any emotion on his face—at least, not right now. "I get flashbacks of that night." An image of Mom's beautiful, brown, lifeless eyes surfaced. A tear rolled down, and I shivered. *I couldn't do this.*

He dragged the ottoman closer so our knees were touching. "Baby, I'm right here. I'm not going to run." His voice was warm and soft, helping to ease some of my anxiety.

He might not run, but I wanted to. "I found my mom and sister." I sucked in a ragged breath. "They weren't breathing. They were covered in blood. Someone broke into our home and killed them. Now certain things can trigger a panic attack."

"Like the dark house," he said softly.

I nodded. "And Renee was a trigger yesterday. She looks like my sister with the color of her hair and eyes, but when she smiles the resemblance between her and Julie is uncanny."

"Are there any others, baby?"

"I'm not sure I could handle seeing a lot of blood, not after that night." I could've gone into more detail about what their bodies looked like, how I slipped in the blood and fell on top of Julie. But just picturing the scene caused the small buzzing sound to surface in my head. I didn't want to risk a panic attack.

He lifted me onto his lap again, and a tidal wave of emotions poured out—sadness, anger, pain, grief. I buried my head in the crook of his neck and cried.

"Don't leave me," I whispered between sobs. It was the first time I said all that out loud to someone other than a doctor and the police. I hadn't told my dad or my brother what I saw that night. They knew it was hard for me, and they didn't want to hear the details. By the time Dad had gotten to the scene, the police had already covered the bodies.

He rubbed my back. "I'm not going anywhere," he breathed with conviction.

I held him tightly, crying harder than I ever had in front of someone else. Sure, I'd broken down at the funeral, but not like this. Maybe it was the strength in his arms, in his words. No matter what, I didn't want to let go of him.

⚜

I SAT in homeroom daydreaming of Kade and the time we'd spent together. After I sobbed until my nose was raw and shared my triggers, I told him what I'd been like after the funeral. The conversation was quite cathartic for me. He'd been wonderful as he listened and held me. Throughout that evening, I started to get a glimpse of just how serious he was about me. Love blazed in his eyes. His tender kisses and gentle caresses warmed my soul.

The speaker in homeroom crackled, severing my trip down memory lane. "Ms. Vander, please send Lacey Robinson to Coach Dean's office," the lady's voice blared.

What did Coach want? He'd talked to Dad. Maybe he wanted to ask me questions about my locker since I didn't get a chance to talk to him after tryouts. Or maybe he found the responsible party. Or maybe Principal Sanders and Coach decided not to let girls try out since they'd had problems with the baseball team bullying Mandy. My stomach churned as my throat went dry.

Ms. Vander peered over her reading glasses. "Ms. Robinson, you may be excused." She wrote something on a slip of paper and stuck out her hand.

I guess that was my cue to get out of my seat.

The noise picked up in the cold classroom as students talked and whispered. I'd been getting weird looks from kids since I walked into school this morning. I wasn't surprised—it was typical of my high school experience.

On my way to her desk, I accidentally bumped into a boy in the first row.

"Watch out, freak," he barked.

I froze, standing next to him. A buzzing sound filled my ears. *Keep walking. He's not worth your time.* I released my breath, and the blood cooled. Reluctantly, I continued to Ms. Vander's outstretched hand when all I itched to do was to beat the boy senseless. I quickly snatched the note from her and stormed out.

Once in the hall, I imagined me banging my head against a locker a few times. *Freak was simply a word. Right?*

So why did the term seep into my psyche, making me go ballistic?

Stuffing my ire into my back pocket, I trudged through the school and over to the sports complex. A few boys lingered outside Coach Dean's office. When they glanced up from their conversation and saw me, they scattered. I laughed, my voice bouncing off the walls. Were they afraid of me? At least they ran rather than calling me a nut case.

All my speculation on why he wanted to see me went out the window as I knocked on Coach Dean's open door. I was suddenly embarrassed. He'd told me I was a good pitcher. My performance yesterday was anything but good.

"Ah, Lacey. Come in," he said in a sweet fatherly voice. "Have a seat."

What was up with the tender tone? Cautious of his intentions, I slouched in.

"Please, sit." He waved a hand to one of the chairs.

"I'll stand, Coach."

"Lacey, I'm not going to read you the riot act."

I dragged my gaze over his face. He'd trimmed his bushy eyebrows. Or maybe the bill of the ball cap he was wearing shadowed his features.

"I'd rather not have to look up," he said, removing his hat, smoothing a hand over his head.

Shrugging out of my backpack, I set the heavy bag on the floor and dropped into a chair. The last thing I wanted was to get on his bad side. He'd told Dad the second round of tryouts was postponed. The doctor said I should be fine to resume physical activity in a couple of days.

"How are you feeling?" he asked.

"I'm better."

"Do you want to tell me what happened at tryouts?"

"Coach, I'm sorry. When I found that my bag was missing, I panicked. Then on the field I was nervous." My gaze flickered past him to the diploma on the wall. Coach had graduated from University of North Carolina at Charlotte, with a degree in athletic training.

"Let's talk about your nervousness, first. I've been doing this a long time. I know when someone is nervous. And something else is going on with you. Now, if you don't want to talk about it, I can accept that.

But I need to know you're healthy, and you won't put yourself or anyone else at risk out on the field."

"Did I hurt anyone?" I asked, sitting up taller. *Oh, God. Did I hit Renee with my pitch?*

"No," he said. "But the risk is there."

I lowered my shoulders. "Aside from my mild concussion, I'm healthy, Coach. I hadn't eaten a whole lot that day." I couldn't tell him the real reason. I was frightened he wouldn't consider me for the team, especially now after my blackout.

He studied me for a second. "Very well. I expect a better performance during the second round, which I've postponed until next Friday. As far as your locker incident, it's clear someone broke into it. I'm still questioning people. Has anyone confronted you about not trying out for the team?" He leaned forward on his desk.

My jaw dropped slightly. I closed it quickly, hoping he didn't read the truth on my face. I wanted to put Aaron in his place, but ratting him out wasn't the answer. He would only increase his tormenting. Besides, I wanted solid proof before I hanged him, and it had to be more than "he said, she said." I needed a witness. "Only Principal Sanders. Why?" I bounced my knee up and down.

"Trying to cover all the angles on your locker incident," he said.

"May I be excused?" The longer I stood here the more he would figure out I was lying.

"I want you to rest this weekend. No pitching, running, or practicing. Complete rest. Is that understood?" He pushed to his feet, the chair behind him rolling backwards.

"No problem. The doctor said the same, anyway."

He escorted me to the door. "I'm here if you ever need to talk."

"Thank you, Coach." I hurried out of his office before I did spill my guts to him. At the moment, his expression reminded me of Mary's. Anytime she wanted to draw something out of me all she had to do was look at me with her soft brown eyes and her head tilted slightly. It was as though she'd cast a tell-me-what's-bothering-you spell.

A lawn mower whirred as I crossed the area between the sports complex and the main building. The scent of freshly cut grass filled the air. Closing my eyes for a second, I inhaled, loving the smell. When I opened them, Tammy Reese was walking toward me with Grace Edison on her arm, giggling. *Great!* Behind them Aaron Seevers and

Mark Wayland, the catcher, were deep in conversation. *Maybe I could get by without them noticing me, and maybe cockroaches would come out of my butt.*

Grace lifted her gaze then hit Tammy on the arm. Both stopped in their tracks a few feet from me. Aaron and Mark plowed into them. Grace's purse fell to the ground. Tammy took a few extra steps, trying not to fall. Both girls were saved when Aaron latched onto Tammy and Mark caught Grace.

I laughed. *No one had ever tripped over the sight of me.* Okay, I was being a little sarcastic. But it was funny. I moseyed past them while Grace struggled to untangle herself from Mark. Tammy, well, she wasn't in any hurry to leave the strong arms of Aaron. After seeing them in the hall the other day, it didn't shock me. I'd just made it to the door of the school when someone clapped. *Don't turn around. Ignore it.* I glanced behind me. So much for listening to my inner voice.

"Are you going to pass out again next week?" Aaron asked in a snide tone.

I swept my gaze over each of them. Tammy had a smirk on her face as though she was the happiest girl alive. I couldn't tell if Aaron was the reason since he had his arm around her waist. Or maybe she was stoked that I'd screwed up. Either way, my fist twitched with the need to punch her, and I stepped in her direction.

"Oooh, please do, skank. I would love to see you fall again."

"Come on, man," Mark said to Aaron. "Let's go. We're late to meet Coach." Mark gave me an I'm-sorry look.

Grace played with her ponytail as she stood there not saying a word. I glared at her, and she dropped her chocolate-brown gaze. Odd. Usually, she wasn't easily intimidated. At least, not since I'd met her.

I pivoted on my heel.

"Where are you going?" Tammy sing-songed in a snarky tone. "You don't like our company? Oh, I know, you prefer your shrink's instead."

Ice flooded my veins as I clutched the metal door handle so hard that pain radiated up my arm. Daylight turned to nighttime as though a black cloud covered the sun. A hissing sound exploded in my head. I couldn't tell if the lawn mower had gotten closer, or my brain was erupting.

Tammy's laughter broke through the haze. I sprang into the air like a lion about to catch her prey. My backpack dropped from my shoulder as I tackled Tammy to the ground. We rolled around as she kicked violently until I pinned her in place.

Grace screamed.

"Lacey, stop," Mark said as he yanked at my jacket.

She squirmed under me until her body broke free and she pushed. I fell off her, my head bouncing on the edge of the grass. *Oh, no. My concussion. What the heck was I thinking?* Her arm shot out. A large hand grasped her by the wrist.

"What's going on here?" Coach Dean asked. He must've run up from the sports complex. His lips flattened. His eyes narrowed.

All the blood drained from me—relief and fear mingling together.

"Aaron. Mark. Get your butts back to class," Coach Dean ordered. "We'll talk later. Grace, you too. Get back to class."

The three of them hesitated for a split second before scurrying into the school.

Coach extended his hand. I took it, holding my head in one hand as he helped me up. I winced. My head suddenly hurt, even though the whirring noise was gone. *Stupid. Stupid.* Completely dumb of me to have lashed out at Tammy with a concussion.

"Now, let's go see Principal Sanders," he said in a tone that permitted no argument. "Or do you need to see the nurse first, Lacey?" He gentled his voice.

"What?" Tammy all but shrieked. "You're being nice to *her*? Maybe *I* need to see the nurse. She did punch me." She ran a hand through her messy hair.

"Ms. Reese, clam it. You've caused enough trouble in your time here," Coach snapped. "When any new girl comes into this school, you feel it's your duty to belittle them."

"I'm good, Coach," I said as I brushed the dirt off my jeans before retrieving my backpack. All I needed was to get the hell out of here. *You're regressing. Continual anger will not move you toward your goal of baseball.*

"Let's go then," Coach said.

Tammy and I walked into the school as the bell rang. Doors swung open, students spilled from classrooms and voices filled the halls.

"Keep walking," Coach commanded.

Stares and glares were pinned on us as kids stopped in their tracks to let us by. Maybe since Tammy had grass in her hair and a scowl on her face. Plus Coach walked between us like he was our bodyguard. It was as though the red carpet had been rolled out for us at a Hollywood premier. Rounding a corner, we came face to face with Kade.

"What's going on?" he asked, swinging his gaze from me to Coach.

"Nothing." This wasn't the time to explain the situation to him.

Kids were leaning against their lockers, ogling.

"Bullshit. You beat the crap out of me," Tammy whined. "Why are you dating her? She sees a shrink."

I stifled a gasp. *How did she know?*

Kade narrowed his eyes, glaring daggers at Tammy as a muscle ticked along his jaw. "What are you talking about?" he asked, furious.

"Haven't you heard the good news?" she taunted. "Your girlfriend is cuckoo." She twirled her forefinger around her temple.

Whispers zipped through hall. I cringed, digging my nails into my palms. My worst nightmare, come true. Adrenaline powered through my body as I pressed my fists into my legs. *Don't show them it's true. The more you show something bothers you, the more bullies will pounce.* I rolled my shoulders back, unclenching my fists.

"Yeah. Who told you that?" His voice dropped as anger flared off him.

"Kade, you need to get to class," Coach said.

"Answer the question, Tammy." Kade ignored Coach and stepped closer to her.

Yesterday, I'd doubted Kade until I'd learned he lied for me when people asked how I was doing. Plus by the time he left my house last night, any distrust I had about him was gone. *So how did Tammy find out?* Kody was the only other person who knew I saw a shrink.

"Kade, please. You can't like her," she whined.

"That's enough, Kade. Girls, move," Coach ordered.

Students darted into classrooms. The warning bell rang.

"Can I have a word with Lacey?" Kade asked Coach.

"No," he said emphatically. "You can talk to her later."

"Go," I urged Kade. "I'll meet you at lunch." There was no need for him to get into trouble.

Snatching his phone from his back pocket, he stalked off. We walked into the admin office, bypassing Barb, who was sitting behind the counter engrossed in her computer screen.

Coach stuck his head into Ms. Sander's office. "Got a minute?" he asked.

"Sure, Coach," she said.

"In, both of you." He nodded to Tammy and me.

We shuffled over the threshold as though we'd both lost our motor skills. Maybe it was the onset of a headache causing me to slow my pace.

"What's this all about?" Principal Sanders rose from her chair, surprise etched on her pretty face.

"Go." Coach urged, lightly touching my back.

I moved closer to the polished desk. Reluctantly, Tammy followed.

Coach proceeded to explain how he'd found us fighting outside. Tammy and I didn't say a word. When Coach finished, the principal circled her desk, heels clicking on the tile floor. Crossing her arms over her chest, she took our measure with her silvery eyes.

"So, Ms. Reese," she said. "How many times are you going to be in my office this year?" One manicured eyebrow arched up.

Tammy stared straight ahead, mouth not moving.

"I gave you one too many strikes last year." The other eyebrow lifted. "But I'm not going to be as gracious this time. This is strike one for you, Ms. Reese. Two more and you'll be expelled. I am not tolerating any of this I-own-this-school attitude from you, young lady. Are we clear?"

"Yes, ma'am," Tammy said evenly, not meeting her gaze.

"Good. Get back to class," the principal ordered.

Tammy made haste, sneering at me as she left the room.

"Now, Ms. Robinson." She dropped her arms, palms on her desk. "We had this conversation only two weeks ago about behaving. Did we not?"

"Yes, ma'am," I said as my eyes met hers.

"I know firsthand that a death of a loved one can be hard, but you can't walk into this school rebelling, the way you did at your last."

My eyes widened. *How did she know? Did Dad tell her during their conversation on the first day?*

"Yes, young lady. I've spoken to the principal of Crestview."

Why was she checking up on me? Did schools do that for all new kids? Did the whole school know about my past? What else did she know?

"I'll give you a first warning. Three strikes. That's it. Oh, and if you make the team, I will leave your punishment for Coach Dean. Understood?"

Did all schools have the three-strike rule? Back at Crestview I'd been given three chances, too, only I'd used all my strikes for the same reason I was standing in her office now. "Yes, ma'am." *Was her threat supposed to scare me? If so, it worked.* I wasn't excited about the possibility of Coach doling out punishments—primarily because he would be instrumental in talking to the scouts of ASU if I made the team.

"Lacey, we'll talk next week," Coach added. "Remember what I told you earlier. Rest and relax this weekend."

"Yes, sir."

"You're dismissed," the principal said.

Turning, I hotfooted it out of her office. I'd already missed English, and I was late for chemistry. I stopped at the counter. Barb, the admin assistant, had her red hair twisted up on her head with a pencil through it.

She looked up from her computer screen. "Do you need a pass?"

"Yes, ma'am. I'm late for Chemistry."

She tore off a piece of paper from a small notepad much like the prescription pads doctors use. She scribbled on it, stood, circled around her desk, and handed it to me.

I left the admin office for the quiet halls to the science wing. The walls above the lockers had good luck signs for the football game tonight. One read, *Beat Lancaster Christian tonight.* Before I walked into chemistry, I peeked through the window. Ms. Clare, tall and athletic, wrote on the whiteboard while the class wrote in their notebooks. I thought of all the reasons why I didn't want to go in. Grace was one reason. I didn't want to deal with her. I also wasn't looking forward to any glares or whispers from the rest of the class, not to mention that I didn't trust myself not to let my anger get to me. *I had one strike with Principal Sanders.*

As I kept reasoning with myself, I spotted Kody inside. His hair toppled over his forehead. As he ran his hand through it, he looked up and at me. Then he angled his head. *Was he the one who tattled my secret?* I refused to believe it. *Why would he?* He was seeing Dr. Davis, too. A body blocked my view of Kody. I blinked, refocusing to find Ms. Clare at the door. I rolled my shoulders back, opened the door, and handed her the note. I fixed on Kody, who was also my lab partner, and strode to my desk like I owned the world. As soon as I sat down, Ms. Clare resumed writing on the whiteboard.

Kody leaned in. "What's wrong?" he asked in a hushed whisper.

"Later." I took out my notebook and pen from my backpack.

Ms. Clare was charting the differences between chemical and physical properties. My attention didn't waver from my notebook or the board the entire class. I would've searched out Becca for a lifeline, but she had a doctor's appointment this morning. Aside from her or Kade, I felt unprotected, even with Kody next to me, and Tyler and Kelton behind me.

Thirty minutes later, the bell rang. I packed my things. I was about to dart out when Kody stretched out his hand in front of me, his bicep showing under the short-sleeved gray T-shirt he wore with a guitar on the front.

"Wait. Is something wrong?" he asked.

Out of the corner of my eye, I glimpsed Kelton heading over from the back of the room.

"I'd rather not talk about it right now." I slung my backpack over my shoulder.

"Talk about what?" Kelton asked, blue eyes appraising me.

I grabbed my hair in both hands, gathered it together and swept it to the front so my hair fell over my shoulders. "I'll talk to you guys later. I'm going to be late." I skirted around the benches.

"Kody, is she okay?" Kelton asked.

I didn't wait to hear what Kody said. I merged into student traffic. This was my free period. Since Becca wasn't here, I decided to forgo the courtyard for the library. I found a quiet spot at a table in the very back next to the history section. A few students milled around, searching shelves, while others had their noses buried in books. I slipped into a chair, folding my arms on the table. I was about to drop my head when Kade loped over, oozing confidence as though he could battle the world—a stark difference from when he'd sat on my hospital bed looking defeated. He could probably fight anyone and always rise the victor.

"How did you find me?" I asked in a library voice—soft and low.

"I have ways," he drawled. He folded his six-foot frame into a chair.

I rolled my tired eyes, and the room tilted. Yeah, that little head bounce on the ground didn't help with my mild concussion, or my stupidity for even fighting with Tammy.

"You okay?" He lugged his chair closer, his hands sliding along my thighs.

"Yeah, just a headache."

"So, what happened?" Kade whispered.

"Tammy was being a jerk, and so was Aaron. He asked if I was going to pass out again during the second round. I ignored him. Then as I turned to leave, Tammy piped in and asked if I preferred to hang out with my shrink instead of them. I attacked. How do you think she found out that I was seeing Dr. Davis? Only you and Kody know."

"Not sure, baby. I know my brother wouldn't spread news around like that. I'd put my life on it. But I'm going to find out."

"Does it really matter now? The cat is out of the bag."

"If it bothers you, then yes."

"It does bother me. But what would you do if you found that person? You couldn't get them to retract their statement. How do you take back a rumor, even if the rumor is true? It was inevitable." My goal now was to ensure that I didn't have another flashback on the field, in school, or anywhere. "Do you think Tammy stole my gear?"

He lifted a shoulder. "It could be anyone. Let Coach get to the bottom of it."

The more I thought about Tammy and Aaron, the more I became convinced they both had the spite to do it. *But how could I prove it? I might never be able to.* No, but I could take precautions to make sure no one got hold of my gear.

"Thank you, Kade." I laid my hand on top of his.

"For what?"

"For worrying about me." I leaned in and gave him a quick kiss.

But quick turned into long, slow, and wet when he took control of my mouth. I didn't bother pushing him away even though we were in school. When our mouths parted, my body trembled with the need for more of him.

A cheerleader gawked as she sat down at the empty table next to us.

"Do you want to get out of here?"

"Yes, but I can't. I just got my butt handed to me by the principal, with a warning. I need to toe the line, especially with tryouts still looming." I had to be a good girl. I had to learn restraint. Otherwise I wasn't going to make it through my senior year or baseball, let alone my potential scholarship with ASU.

"Do you want to go to the football game tonight?" he asked.

"Are you asking me out on a date?" I whispered.

"Dates with me lead to guilty pleasures. So if you want it to be a date then..." He brushed his lips along my jaw while his hands dipped between my legs.

I squirmed as a frisson of heat crawled up my legs. "Be careful. You might like it," I said, throwing back his own words he'd said to me a week ago.

"Oh, no doubt." His eyes darkened. "And maybe before the weekend is over, I just might have you where I've wanted you from the moment I saw you," he rasped.

"In your dreams," I said sarcastically in spite of the fact that I shuddered.

"You are what my dreams are made of, Lace."

A bevy of emotions—optimism, hope, joy—ran through me. In that moment, he snagged another piece of my heart.

CHAPTER 16

My last few classes crawled until the pep rally. The rah-rah festivities had been scheduled for after school, this time—which was good because I didn't care to sit through an hour of watching Grace and her cheerleaders jump around in the gym, nor everyone gawking at me. It was hard not to lash out at someone when they looked at me the wrong way. My self-control had been tested many times today. I wouldn't say I was proud of myself since I'd lost my cool with Tammy. However, one incident out of many was a vast improvement at this school over what it had been at Crestview.

"How's your head?" Kade asked as he wheeled his truck out of the school's lot.

Mary had taken me to school this morning. Dad thought it would be best if I didn't drive for another day. I told her I'd find a ride home with Kade or Becca.

"Better," I muttered, fiddling with the truck's heater, angling the vents to blow on me. I still had a weak headache. As soon as I got home, I was going to pop some Advil.

"We don't have to go if you don't want to." He turned onto Main Street. "We could hang at my house."

I sat back now, relishing the warm air on me, thawing my hands. I didn't know where my friendship with Tyler stood yet. We really hadn't talked since he brought me to school the other morning. I wanted to show him I was a good friend. He'd done a lot to help me with my pitching. "Nah. I know Tyler would like for me to see at least one of his games."

"Should I be worried about Tyler?" He sounded disappointed.

I snickered. "Are you jealous, Kade?"

"Maybe," he said, a muscle ticking in his jaw.

Reaching over the console, I placed my hand on his leg. A dimple popped out on his cheek, showing how content he was with my touch, I imagined. We listened to Daughtry belt out "Waiting on Superman," while Kade maneuvered through the streets of Ashford on the way to my house.

"I'll pick you up around six thirty." He pulled into my driveway, parking behind my Mustang.

"Okay." I had my hand on the door, but he stopped me. "What?"

"You're not getting out of this truck until after my lips have touched yours." His long lashes fell then rose.

I rolled my eyes in a fake attempt at showing him I didn't care.

"Get your lips over here," he said playfully.

"What if I don't?"

"Do you want to find out?" His grin was feral yet charmed.

Without thinking, I opened the door then dashed out of the truck and ran. No sooner had I made it to the porch than Kade's muscled arm stretched out, grabbed me firmly by the arm, and spun me around. I giggled, falling into him.

"You can run, hide, disappear, whatever. I will always catch you, Lace."

"I hope—"

His warm lips met mine until the front door opened.

"You kids finished yet?" Mary asked.

Kade lifted his head, and I almost growled in annoyance.

"I'll pick you up later," he said, relinquishing his hold on me. "Hi, Mary." He waved as he strode back to his truck.

"Is my dad home?" I asked, ignoring her lopsided smile as I fought for balance after Kade's kiss. I wanted to tell Dad about my fight with Tammy before he found out from Principal Sanders or Coach Dean. I didn't know if they called parents after a fight or not.

"He's in his study. He wants to talk to you."

I moved past her and into the house.

"A warning," she said, closing the door behind her. "The principal called your dad today."

I hesitated midstride. I turned, certain the horror on my face was evident.

"You're on your own. You know I don't get involved with stuff like this," she stated matter-of-factly. "Dinner is in an hour." She darted off into the kitchen.

Several swear words slipped from my tongue. Dad was going to freak. The yelling and shouting I could deal with. The disappointment in his eyes over my screw-up, though, pained me. He'd been warning me repeatedly not to get into any fights at school. I shed my jacket and my backpack, setting both at the bottom of the stairs. I circled around the bannister and padded down the hall to Dad's study.

"I'll check on it tomorrow. Yes, I'll be at the club tonight. Good," Dad's voice trickled out.

I waited, leaning against the open doorjamb. Fabric furnishings, tan walls, and thick brown carpeting gave the room a restful feeling. However, the mood bouncing off him was anything but tranquil. His face was drawn, almost hollow, as though he'd lost fifty pounds overnight. His stitches were no longer bandaged, and he had a red ring circling the fresh wound of his left eye. Black marred the area beneath it. My pulse stilled for a moment. His green eyes looked blank. Or, I hated to think, dead.

"Sweet Pea." A hint of hardness edged his tone as he set his cell phone on his desk.

Pushing off the doorframe, I worried my lower lip. Before I took two steps, his cell phone rang. Ignoring it, he sauntered around his desk and met me in front of it.

"Are you okay, Dad?"

He combed his fingers through his hair before rubbing his neck. Not a good sign. Whenever he was struggling with something, he scrubbed his hand over the nape of his neck. Maybe he wasn't mad at me. Maybe his anger had something to do with his work. A daughter could hope.

"I'm fine. How's your head?"

"Um...good," I muttered as I glanced up at his battered face.

"Lacey, you know I haven't grounded you in a long time, and I don't want to start. But..." A slow scowl formed on his face.

A long pregnant pause ensued. He seemed to be searching for the right words. I had no idea what Principal Sanders had told him. My stomach clenched into tiny fists.

"Cut the crap at school." His voice boomed with sudden anger. "Understood?"

"You're not going to ask me what happened?" Not that it mattered. Anytime I'd been in any principal's office, it wasn't for good reasons.

"Why? So you can tell me it wasn't your fault?" The rage in his tone increased. "Or tell me someone said something to piss you off? Neither of those excuses are enough to attack someone. Now, I'm tired of the bullshit you're dishing out. You promised me that you would learn to control yourself."

"And you promised me you would relax when we moved here. We're supposed to spend more time together. I'm not the only one who needs healing, Dad. It's clear—" I pointed to his face— "you aren't any calmer than I am."

The frown lines around his mouth deepened.

I didn't care. He needed just as much help. I wanted my old Dad back, the one who smiled frequently. The dad who didn't forget I had a baseball game. The dad who spent time with his daughter. While I wished I could help him, I had my own struggles. The deaths of Mom and Julie were still very raw, and probably would be for a long time. I pivoted on my heel and made it to the door when he cleared his throat.

"You're right," he said sadly.

I believed Dad had been hung up in two of the stages of grief— depression and denial. However, the last couple of months he seemed to have slid into the anger phase. Taking a breath, I turned. "You need to get help, Dad. I'm not the only one who needs a psychiatrist, or someone to talk to."

"I know. I thought immersing myself in something new or with work would keep them out of my memories." His eyes were downcast.

"Say their names, Dad." It infuriated me he wouldn't. It hurt, too. He loved them as much as he loved Rob and me. He hadn't talked about them. When I did, he turned inward and checked out of the conversation.

He lifted his watery eyes to mine. "I can't. I'm...not ready to. I'm sorry."

I didn't believe acceptance would ever come for either him or me. Neither was I certain if knowing who killed them would help us heal. But we had to move on with our lives. If not, we would suffer, or worse, live dying. I couldn't walk around dead inside anymore. I couldn't hurt other people for no reason. I wanted to feel again. Trust again. Since telling Kade what happened to Mom and Julie, a small sense of acceptance had settled within me. Sure, I was far from healed, and even though I grieved for them every day, still struggling with PTSD and my emotions, I could take a few baby steps. Tonight I was going to let go and relax. If someone provoked me, I was determined not to retaliate.

I went over to Dad and gave him a hug. "I'll do better at controlling myself. I promise." Maybe if I showed improvement, he would seek the help he needed.

He squeezed me. "I love you, Sweet Pea."

"Ditto, Dad."

"We should go eat," he said.

I eased out of his arms. "Sounds good. But then I'm going to the football game tonight with Kade. Okay?"

He nodded, smiling as we walked out of his study. We didn't solve anything, but he did admit he needed help, and that was a start. On the way to the kitchen we talked about the football game. Lancaster Christian, or LC as they were called, were one of Kensington's main rivals. They'd won state last year, and they were picked to win state again this year. Tyler was on a mission to make sure LC didn't get past the playoffs.

Mary talked a mile a minute during dinner, about the farmer's market she had been to earlier in the day. I didn't know there were that many different fruits and vegetables. Dad even laughed a few times, which warmed my heart. It had been eons since I'd heard his laugh.

As we were cleaning up, my phone buzzed. When I plucked it out of my jeans pocket, the screen displayed a text.

I'll be there in a few minutes.

"He's early," I mumbled to myself.

"Go," Mary said. "I'll finish up."

"Thank you." I gave her a quick peck on the cheek.

I ran out of the kitchen, up the stairs and hurriedly changed my blouse for a form-fitting scoop-neck sweater. Warmth was key for tonight. Then I scooted into the bathroom and brushed my teeth. Given Kade's relentless mission to kiss me, I had to make sure I had clean breath.

"Lacey," Mary called up the stairs. "Kade's here."

One last swish, then I spit out the pasty wintergreen liquid. "I'll be right down," I shouted as I crossed the hall to my room.

I flipped up the tops of my leather boots so they covered my knees. I checked in the full-length mirror—I could wear the boots either above the knee or lower, and I had yet to wear them thigh-high. The style screamed *sexy*. Satisfied, I ran my fingers through my hair, letting the long strands spill around my shoulders, grabbed my gloves, jacket, and phone, and headed downstairs.

Laughter floated out of the living room. Dad's laugh. For the second time this evening, contentment spread through me. Nothing pleased me more than to hear my dad express an emotion other than sadness or anger. On the heels of Dad's voice was Kade's. Warmth slid down my belly at his deep laugh.

"What's funny?" I asked, standing in the doorway.

This room had been intended as a formal living room, but Dad and I didn't do formal anymore. Rob had taken most of our old furniture for his place in California. Dad hated any reminders of Mom. Where our home in California boasted elaborate floral drapes and expensive furnishings from Beverly Hills, this home had shutters on the windows and furniture from IKEA.

Like gentlemen, Dad and Kade rose immediately upon seeing me, programmed to acknowledge that a lady had entered the room. Mary sat in the lone chair adjacent to the tan sofa Kade and Dad had been lounging on.

"It was nothing, Sweet Pea."

Kade dragged his gaze from the top of my head all the way to my toes, then back up. When our eyes met, something hot flashed in his, something primal. A delectable shiver climbed up my legs.

"We should go," Kade said.

Yeah, we should, before I melt in a puddle of water.

"Mr. Robinson, it's nice to see that you're feeling better." Kade crossed the room, long jeans-covered legs eating up the space, muscles bunching under his fitted grey V-neck sweater with a white T-shirt underneath. "Hey, there. Ready?" he asked, his voice a whisper—a very lust-ridden whisper.

I nodded, afraid to speak. Afraid that my father would hear the lust in *my* voice then ground me for the night. Or worse, for my entire senior year.

Dad and Mary followed us to the door.

"Don't be late," Dad said. "I'll be at the club tonight, so I'll see you in the morning."

"Have a good time," Mary added.

Lifting up on my tiptoes, I kissed Dad on his un-injured cheek. Then I waved to Mary.

Once we were in the truck, I relaxed. I wasn't sure why. As soon as I inhaled Kade's intoxicating scent, a sense of belonging wrapped around me. He made me feel safe, warm, happy, lusty, loved and respected. I wanted all of him, and wanted to give him all of me.

⚜

DARKNESS HAD FALLEN by the time we arrived at the football stadium. The lights illuminated the grassy field, casting a shadow outward to the rubber track. A cold, sharp breeze blew, stinging my face. Kade and I stood at the bottom of the bleachers on Kensington's side of the field, searching for Becca and his brothers.

"Do you see them?" Kade asked over his shoulder.

"Not yet." People were pouring into the stands. I couldn't see much past the ocean of bodies.

"Over here, Lacey," Becca shouted.

Kade and I both scanned the rows of people until we found Becca. Her arms flailed above the heads like she needed emergency help.

"I guess we found your brothers." Kody, Kelton and Kross lounged against the railing at the top row of the bleachers with their hands tucked into their Kensington blue-and-black jackets. We climbed up the side stairs. Cautiously, we shuffled around knees and feet before we made it to Kade's brothers and Becca.

"Tell me about Tammy," Becca asked excitedly, sitting down in front of Kross.

"How come you didn't show up to school today?" I mashed my body next to hers. I'd thought she'd return to school after her ob-gyn appointment.

"Yeah, Becca. Why did you play hooky?" Kelton asked, leaning over so his head was between Becca and me.

"Personal space, Kelton. Ever heard of it?" I gave him a sideways glare.

"Girls love when I invade their personal space," he drawled.

Becca giggled.

Kade smacked his brother on the back of the head. "Back off, Kel."

"Now, Big Bro. You know your kin wouldn't dare move in on your girl." He winked at me.

Here we go. I would be rolling my eyes all night.

"Shut up, man," Kross said, flicking Kelton in the head, too.

"So, Tammy? I heard you were in the principal's office." Becca asked again as Kelton sat back. Then she leaned into me. "Rumor is you're seeing a shrink," she whispered. "Is that because of your mom?"

To lie or not to lie? "Can we talk about that later? Lots of people around, Becca." I'd promised myself I would have a good time and not get upset with anyone tonight.

She squeezed my thigh.

"Are you cold?" Kade asked as he nudged closer to me, wrapping an arm around my waist.

"Freezing." It didn't matter that the cold from the metal bench penetrated through my jeans. As long as my body was pressed against his, I was more than warm.

"You look fucking hot in those boots," he whispered in my ear. "You're giving me all kinds of fantasies." He nibbled on my earlobe.

A shiver ran through me, and not from the cold bench or the brisk wind blowing. I turned, his cheek sliding against mine until our lips connected. He kissed me slow and soft.

"Get a room, Bro," Kody said teasingly

Wow! Kody was in a playful mood tonight.

"They say that to you a lot, I'm finding." I eased away.

"You're lucky we're here. Or you would be in my room," he threatened.

A threat I would welcome.

Finally, Kensington's band marched out onto the field. With the exception of two drummers, the band retreated to their seats in a special section of the stands. The two band members marched to the sideline behind the Kensington cheerleaders.

Lancaster Christian's team ran out first, plowing through their paper barrier. Red and white uniforms flooded the field as their fans screamed in support. Then the stadium quieted. A soft beat splintered the silence as the cheerleaders and the two drummers marched out to the end zone on the far left of the field. The sound grew louder and heavier the closer they got to the spot where Kensington's football team would emerge. Once they arrived, two cheerleaders opened the

Kensington banner while the rest of the girls and the two band members formed two lines parallel to each other behind the banner. All of this reminded me of the football games at Crestview. I loved the energy of school spirit and the rivalry between teams. Watching baseball games wasn't as much fun as watching guys tackle each other. However, playing baseball was the bomb.

"Ladies and gentlemen, please give a loud Bulldog shout for your Kensington High football team," a deep baritone voice blared through the speakers.

The drummers keyed the crowd with a drumroll before the fans barked like dogs, voices echoing in the stadium. I'd bet every house around the school could hear us.

In the distance, Tyler ripped through the banner first, and the barks and shouts turned into squeals and screams from the Kensington girls. The energy around us soared to incredible heights. I hadn't been to a high school football game since my sophomore year. I missed the excitement.

"Tyler is so good," Becca cooed.

After several deafening minutes, people settled into their seats. The cheerleaders made their way to the sideline, center stage on the track in front of the stands. The drummers joined their bandmates.

The captains of each team met on the field for the coin toss. The band played an unfamiliar song, and my gaze drifted to nowhere as I listened, but my mind narrowed in on a something that had been lingering.

Slipping my hand over Kade's thigh, I angled my head slightly.

He caught my gaze. "Your hand is awful close to—"

"Why don't you play baseball anymore?"

He covered my hand with his. "After my brothers went to the Academy, it wasn't fun anymore. I'd rather work on cars or spend time at the gun club. And by the way, I have a bone to pick with you about your gun."

"I thought we were past that." The first day we met seemed so long ago. I had the sense he didn't think I knew how to handle a weapon. Maybe he'd seen the gun shaking in my hands.

He flashed the famous grin I so loved, and then when the noise level rose, Kade and I turned our attention to the field. The game had begun, and our number twenty-two was running down the field toward the goal line. LC's players were right on his tail. He made it to the twenty-yard line when he was tackled by three of LC's players. While the teams huddled, my hand meandered between Kade's legs.

"Lace." He leaned in. "Careful." His tone held a husky warning.

"My fingers are cold," I said, sticking out my bottom lip.

The crowd screamed. Tyler threw a pass to number fifty-seven, who just happened to be one yard from the end zone. An LC player tried to intercept it, but number fifty-seven caught it in midair as he jumped over for a touchdown. We sat for another hour, clapping, screaming, and whistling as Kensington scored two more touchdowns and LC scored one. By halftime, my butt had iced up, my hands were numb, and clear liquid ran out of my nose.

"Do you want to go someplace where I can warm you up?" Kade murmured.

"Sure." He didn't have to ask me twice. My freaking body was like one of those ice sculptures. His warmth only lasted so long.

Kade hopped to the row behind and talked with his brothers.

"What's going on?" Becca asked as she blew into her bare hands.

"Kade and I are leaving."

"Call me tomorrow," she said.

It would be our girls' night at the Cave tomorrow. Tonight I was all Kade's. I had no idea where we were going. From the way he phrased the question, I doubted he was dropping me off at home.

CHAPTER 17

When we reached his house, Kade drove around his six-car garage toward the dark landscape in the direction of the lake.

"Are you dumping me in the woods or throwing me in the lake?" I asked.

"What's your pleasure?"

"Traipsing through the woods at night has been on my list of things to do in life."

"Your wish will come true then."

Okay. My pulse picked up a beat. Before my imagination conjured up all kinds of freaky scenes, moonlight shone down over the smooth, glassy water of the lake.

"Is this the Maxwells' make-out point?"

He let out a laugh, deep, warm, and rich. "My brothers will get a kick out of that one. And we don't need to make out in our trucks."

The headlights beamed, lighting the dense brush in the distance. An animal scurried into the trees.

He stopped the truck twenty feet from the funhouse. *Of course he didn't need the truck when he had a den on the lake. Stupid me.*

He killed the engine, reached around my back seat and plucked up a flashlight.

"What's that for?" My pulse galloped. The funhouse was right there.

His lips formed into a half smile. "You said you wanted to go for a walk in the woods."

I was relieved I hadn't told him I wanted to go for a swim in the lake. "Ha-ha. Seriously. Why do you need a flashlight?"

"Let's go," he said, jumping out without answering me.

I hesitated. *Was he crazy? The temperatures had dropped since leaving the football field, and we were going for a stroll in the forest. The dark forest.* I didn't see anything romantic about it. I loved animals. That wasn't my problem. I just didn't like the kind who wanted to eat me for dinner.

My door opened. "Trust me." He held out his hand.

I angled my head. The muted light of the car interior played off his face, highlighting the gold flecks in his copper eyes. Eyes that sucked me into his world, telling me I was his, and he wouldn't let anything happen to me. I relinquished my forest phobia and allowed him to fold his hand over mine. His warm touch sedated me. *Or maybe it was my hormones acting up from the way he looked at me like he wanted to strip me right here.*

As I climbed out, he switched on the flashlight. It helped that the moon provided a glow over the lake. We walked the twenty feet to the steps of the funhouse.

"See, I'm not a big bad wolf," he said. "Just a nice one who wants to taste you."

I didn't have a chance with a retort when he opened the door and a blast of hot air hit me. *Warmth. Finally.* I sailed in, squealing in delight. Kade laughed as he flicked a switch. A lamp came to life on the end table near the couch. A soft glow lit up the room.

"Do you always keep the heat on in this place?" I blew into my hands. I'd forgotten my gloves in the truck before we went into the stadium. Since then, my hands hadn't thawed completely.

"Nope." He shrugged out of his jacket and hung it on a peg adjacent to the door.

"Did you do this for me?"

"Yep."

"What happened to your vocabulary?" I removed my coat and followed his lead, hanging mine up.

"Tonight, Lace, talking will be minimal." The deep timbre of his voice unleashed a frisson of heat. "But first." He turned me around to face the table.

Images of him and me, our bodies braided together, halted as my jaw came unhinged. A cupcake with a candle in it, and a small box wrapped in dark blue paper with a large white bow sat on the wood table.

"Are you proposing?" I asked kiddingly. *Okay, maybe I wasn't. Other items came in small boxes, not only rings. Right?*

"Oh, hell, no," he said, his hot breath fanning my ear.

My skin pebbled with goosebumps.

"It's just a birthday gift, Lacey. No need to be concerned." His hands molded to my waist.

I wanted to laugh. We'd only known each other for a couple of weeks, and he'd already professed his love for me. So to see a small box sitting on the table, it was my first thought.

"If you don't want to open it, that's okay, Lace." He swept my hair to one side as he kissed my neck. "I know I've been aggressive in telling you how I feel. And—"

Turning, I placed my finger on his lips. "Hush. I'm sorry. I just never had so much attention before." It wasn't a lie. Brad had never treated me like I was the only one in his life.

His hands glided from my waist to my lower back. "Then whoever you dated was an idiot," he drawled. "But I'm glad—now you're all mine," he said.

My body tensed until he started drawing lazy circles, just as he had that night at the Cave. The sensation was both calming and endearing.

"I know you have a lot going on in that pretty head of yours, about you and me. It's okay. I'm a patient guy. Now, would you like to open your gift?"

I'd rather stay here forever while he continued to lull me into a trance. My curiosity won out, though. Every Christmas, I was the one who had to peek at one of my gifts. Mom would get so mad.

He led me over to the couch, bringing the present along. I sat first, then he placed it on my lap before joining me.

I examined the beautiful wrapping, sliding a sidelong glance his way. His expression was impassive as though the wheels in his head were turning, too. I leaned in and gave him a quick kiss, hoping to reassure him that I was excited, and I truly was.

A corner of his mouth turned upward.

I ripped into the gift, finding a red velvet box beneath the paper. My heart beat like a timpani. The jitters commingled with excitement. I envisioned him getting down on one knee, then shook off the wild notion. *I was officially losing it*. I met his watchful eyes.

"Go ahead," he urged.

Slowly, I opened the box. Inside was a silver chain with a charm on the end. "Is this a bear?" My voice hitched.

"Yep. Do you like it?" he asked, hesitation in his tone.

"I love it." I really did, even though I didn't wear jewelry, not even earrings. When I played baseball, trinkets on my body got in the way. I removed the necklace, and was about to put it on when Kade took it from me.

"Let me," he said.

I gathered my hair with both hands, twisting it up. I turned so my back was to him. He undid the clasp before securing it around my neck.

"Happy birthday." He kissed along the nape of my neck.

I let go of my hair, examining the little silver creature that rested above my cleavage. "But my birthday isn't until tomorrow."

"I know. I wanted to spend time alone with you tonight." He pulled me onto his lap. "I thought Mary and your dad would want you tomorrow night."

I wasn't so sure about my dad. Saturdays were busy for him at the club. Plus he hadn't mentioned anything about my birthday. It wasn't unusual, though. Mom was the one who always remembered our birthdays. Adjusting my position, I straddled Kade, bracing my hands on his shoulders.

He yanked me to him.

"Thank you, Kade. I really do love it," I said, soft and smooth.

"You are my polar bear, Lace," he breathed, his eyes darkening. His words, the conviction in his voice, unraveled my heartstrings. He grinned with his infamous Maxwell smirk as he cupped my face.

I had barely caught my breath when his mouth was on me. I opened to him as his tongue dipped inside, twining with mine. He tasted like forever. I wiggled against his hardness, and he moaned. Abandoning my mouth, he trailed his lips along my jaw, my ear, and my neck. He licked over my racing pulse while the heat from his hands was scorching my back. His torment was too much, yet not enough.

My clothes grew constrictive. I wanted to feel his bare skin against mine.

As if he sensed my need, he lifted my sweater over my head, throwing it to the floor. His eyes were seas of shimmering copper. The backs of his fingers ghosted up and over my abs to land on the clasp of my bra. For perhaps one second he hesitated before unsnapping it. When he did, I sucked in a breath, my nipples hardening. He removed one strap then the other before it fell behind me.

"Beautiful," he breathed, as he traced the outline of my breasts, teasing, but never touching the sensitive peaks that ached for his magical fingers or even his mouth.

I pressed my hips into him, feeling his arousal. Desire swirled down my belly in a slow, sinuous slide.

He groaned, deep and sensual. "Baby, tell me what you want."

My body tingled. My brain went blank. "You." All I wanted to do right now was feel him and everything he had to offer.

His eyes widened with a savage intensity that frightened me, yet calmed me. He pressed a kiss to my breast, gliding his warm mouth over my nipple before sucking on it. I arched into him, rubbing against him. He moaned, giving my other breast the same attention.

I fisted my hands in his sweater, tugging it up. He eased back, raising his arms. I lifted his sweater and T-shirt over his head before tossing it aside. My gaze wandered over him, drinking in every muscled inch of him from the line of light brown hair that disappeared into his jeans, to the six-pack abs that sculpted his midsection, to the tattoos on his chest. Pushing his fingers through my hair, he brushed his lips over mine.

"Are you sure, Lace?" His voice was barely audible.

"Very," I whispered.

In an instant, my back was pressed into the soft fabric of the couch, goosebumps popping up all over me. He unbuttoned my jeans, his gaze melding with mine.

Zeal's song, "She was Beautiful" filled the room. Ignoring his ring-tone, he continued his quest to get me completely naked. The song stopped. He unzipped my jeans, and the phone rang again.

"Fuck," he muttered as he stood, removing the phone from his jeans pocket. He touched the screen. "This better be fucking good," he said to the caller.

I sat up, covering my breasts with my arms, feeling cold from the loss of his warmth, but also self-conscious. It was weird to sit bare-chested, completely exposed when the mood was ruined.

"Is he okay?" His voice dropped, his nostrils flaring. "When?" Then the skin around his eyes tightened. "I'll kill him this time. Yeah. We're on our way." He shoved the phone into his pocket, hard. "Fuck."

"What's going on?" I grabbed my bra and sweater and dressed quickly. The word *kill* sprang my nerves to life.

"That was Kelton. Kody and Tyler are on their way to the emergency room." He strode over to the couch and snatched his sweater off the cushion, mumbling to himself.

I gasped. "Are they alright?"

"Kody's banged up, and Tyler has a dislocated shoulder," he bit out.

"What happened?"

"A fight broke out immediately after the football game between my brothers, Tyler, and Greg and some of his buddies." He jammed his arms then his head into his T-shirt then sweater, yanking the garments down over him.

"What about Greg?" Not that I cared. I just hoped like hell that Greg was just as battered.

"I don't give a fuck. The guy's lights are about to go out."

"Hey," I whispered, carefully stepping closer to him. Somehow I needed him to calm down. "Take a deep breath." It wouldn't be good for anyone if he was a madman. Rage led to violence. I didn't want to think of the end result. I had to stop him from doing something brainless, so no one would get hurt, including him.

He grabbed my hair, pulled back my head and destroyed my lips in a turbulent kiss. I reached around his waist, slid my hands under his shirt and traced lazy circles on his lower back, hoping to tame the beast inside him. His touch always helped to ease my tension. A groan erupted from him, low and dark. I should've been frightened, but his dominance only sparked a burning desire that inched up my legs and down my belly—a desire on a collision course to erupt in the exact spot that was pulsing out of control. It was weird how my body reacted to him, even in his state of rage. I let him take as much of me as he needed in the kiss and prayed we could both walk out of there.

❧

THE RIDE to the hospital was intensely quiet. I rubbed Kade's hand as he drove, trying to quell his nerves, or maybe I had to soothe mine.

The light ahead flashed red, and the car in front of us crawled to a stop. I checked the speedometer. Forty miles per hour. *Oh crap. Did we have enough distance between us and the Nissan to brake safely?* "Um...Kade?"

Nothing. His trance-like state sent me into freak mode.

"Kade!" I slapped him on the arm. "Stop!"

"I am," he barked. His knuckles were white as he gripped the steering wheel, his face a mixture of pain and anger.

"When? After we crash?" I was going to kill him if he killed me.

He slammed on the brakes, the tires screeching to a halt mere inches from the red taillights. My breath lodged in my throat, and my heart either stopped or fell out of my chest.

"You need to calm down," I all but screamed. "I would like to see my eighteenth birthday." The hospital wasn't far now. Maybe I should get out and walk the rest of the way.

His phone rang as the light turned green. Giving the car gas, Kade jabbed a button on the steering wheel. "Yeah." His voice was as calm as the ocean on a windless day.

"What's your ETA?" His brother's voice filled the truck.

I still struggled to figure out which triplet was speaking over the phone. The caller had to be either Kross or Kelton.

"I'll be there in five," Kade responded. "How is he, Kel?"

"Kody has a broken rib and nose. He'll be fine, Bro."

"Where is that fucker, Sullivan?" A violent undertone wove through the steadiness in Kade's voice.

"Not sure. Just get here. Then we can talk."

"What about Tyler?" I asked softly.

"Hey, Lacey," Kelton said. "Tyler has a dislocated shoulder. Coach Preston is furious." Mr. Preston was the football coach, and according to Tyler, meaner than Coach Dean.

"Where's Kross? Are you two okay?" Kade turned into the visitor's lot.

"We're good, Bro. You know no one can touch Kross." Considering Kross was into boxing, I didn't doubt it.

"We're here." Kade pushed a button, hanging up on Kelton.

I flew out of the truck, not waiting for Kade to kill the engine. Once the cool air hit my face, I took a deep breath, trying to cleanse my system of the freaking nervous butterflies still in my stomach. As I breathed out, Kade's arms closed around me.

"Don't touch me." I pushed him. Either he didn't expect the force behind my strength or he let me push him. He shuffled backward. "Did you want to kill us or something?"

"I'm sorry." He tried for me again.

I backed away. *Ha!* I was quicker than he was, this time.

"Lace, my brothers are my life."

"Oh, so it's okay to put mine in danger?" My voice edged with fury. *Calm down, girl. They're his family. How would you react?*

"I didn't mean—"

"Look, I get that you love your brothers." My tone was less frantic. "But you love me too, don't you?" Doubt broke through my voice as I said the last two words.

In a blur he had me pinned against his truck. One hand in my hair, the other on my hip. "I do love you. I love the crap out of you." He tugged on my hair as he lowered his head. "I had flashbacks to two years ago. Greg put Kody in the hospital then. I saw stars when Kelton called me tonight." His eyes softened. His voice gentled. His hand skated up my waist to cup my cheek.

"I'm sorry. I'm a little freaked out and scared, Kade. I don't want to see you get hurt or anyone else. I couldn't handle it. Not after my mom and Julie." I choked back tears. I didn't want to imagine any images of him like the ones burned into my memory of my family.

He rested his forehead against mine. "I'm not going to do anything stupid. I promise, baby."

I locked my arms around his neck and held on for dear life. I wanted to believe him. My intuition wouldn't let me. Kade and Greg had a longtime hatred of one another.

He kissed my bottom lip, which was sticking out. "Let's go see Kody." Easing away, he held out his hand.

When my palm touched his, warm and strong, another notch in my heart opened.

We started our journey through the large, packed lot full of cars.

"Kade, what did Greg do to Kody two years ago?" I asked.

He glanced at me then out across the dimly lit parking lot. "Sullivan and a few of his buddies ganged up on Kody. They beat him until he couldn't breathe."

"Why? Aren't you the one Greg hates?" I barely missed the side mirror of a white van we passed.

"Sullivan hates all of us. Our rivalry began when he and I were freshmen. We tried out for the same sports, same spots on the team. He never got selected. Things didn't heat up until our sophomore year, when he didn't get picked for football or baseball. My brothers did, though, as freshmen." His voice was even, with a hint of anger leaking through.

We stopped to let a car back out of a spot, the taillights glowing red.

"Then there were four Maxwell brothers who had beat Sullivan out for spots on the team." He looked down at me. "He went off the deep end. After school, I'd find my tires slashed or deep scratches in my truck."

"Was it Greg?"

"Don't know. The only thing we did know was that he beat Kody."

We followed behind the car as the driver took off. "Did you report him or call the police?"

"We did. But his father's a big-time lawyer in Boston. Got him off with a warning."

The lights of the emergency room brightened the area as we approached. A car skidded to a stop in front of the portico leading into the ER. A man leapt out and slid over the hood as though he were in some action movie. Grabbing the door handle, he wrenched it open. "Come on, sweetie," he said frantically, offering his hand to the passenger.

"Get your paw out of the way. I can walk, you moron," the lady snarled. She pushed off the seat, and her pregnant belly lifted into view. She trembled as she clutched the doorframe.

Kade ran to her. "Here, ma'am." He offered his hand. "Why don't you park the car," he said to her companion. "Lace, can you get a wheelchair?"

The man obeyed Kade, flying into the vehicle before peeling out.

"You're so kind, young man," the woman cooed.

Kade guided the pregnant lady under the portico toward the glass doors as she held her stomach. "Lace. Wheelchair," Kade said again.

My feet wouldn't move. Kade directed traffic like he had extensive experience in commanding an army. At this moment, I wanted to tackle him to the ground and kiss him until we both couldn't breathe.

"Lace!" Kade's voice stung me. His eyes were wide.

I ran in through automatic double doors. I found a wheelchair. "There's a pregnant lady outside. I think she's in labor," I said to a male orderly in blue scrubs who was helping an old man to a chair in the waiting room.

The woman clutched Kade's bicep as they shuffled in. Just as she moaned, the male orderly walked up and took the wheelchair from me.

"Her husband is parking the car," Kade said to the man in blue scrubs.

Sitting, the lady blew out a few breaths. Then the orderly wheeled her away. "Thanks again, young man," she said in between breaths.

"No problem," he replied.

"You're so sweet." Now I was the one purring.

One side of his mouth curled.

"There you two are," a familiar male voice boomed from behind me.

I turned to find Kelton coming our way, composed and self-assured.

Kade grabbed my hand. "Where is he?" Kade's mood darkened suddenly.

"This way," Kelton said, nodding to his right.

The three of us walked in silence down a hallway lined with empty stretchers. At an intersection we turned left. We passed the restrooms and a nurse's station before reaching a wide wooden door with a number two painted in red on it. I didn't recognize this part of the hospital from other day.

"Are we allowed to be here?" I asked. I didn't know a whole lot about emergency rooms. The one I'd been in three years ago when Julie broke her ankle from cheering wouldn't allow more than two family members to go in with her. Then again, I was just here two days ago, and they let Kade, Kelton and Kross in my room, although the nurse did tell them to leave.

"I cleared it with the nurse," Kelton said. Then he looked at Kade. "Before you go in there," Kelton warned, "I called Buster." His gaze was fixed on Kade.

"Why?" Kade's eyes narrowed.

"Did you want me to call Dad?" Kelton shoved his unruly hair from his forehead. "The cops showed up. I managed to talk Tanner out of taking any of us down to the station. The only way I could do that was to call Buster."

"Buster? The bouncer at the Cave?" I asked incredulously. Was Buster family?

"Yeah." Kelton grabbed Kade by the arm. "Look, man. We need to be careful this time. I'm not going back to the academy. I'm sure you don't want to go to jail again, either."

All of a sudden, my mind rioted with thoughts of Kade in jail. *Kade lying in a hospital bed. Kade covered in blood.* The images flashed like a screen saver sliding through picture after picture, over and over. I was definitely losing my mind. I shuffled over to lean against the wall next to the water fountain. I took in a breath, inhaling the sterility of the hospital. Maybe the scent of bleach would white out the images. I glanced at Kade. His eyes swirled with despair and anxiety. At this moment, I wanted to do whatever I could to protect him, to take away every ounce of his pain and conflict. *Maybe by helping him, I could help myself.*

He angled his head. *Did he know what I was thinking?*

"Kel, give Lacey and me a minute. We'll be in in a sec," Kade said, shifting back to Kelton.

Obeying his brother, Kelton pushed in the door to Kody's room, leaving us in the hall.

A phone rang in the distance. A tall male orderly pushed a wheelchair with an old man in it toward us.

"Lace, you're seeing that ghost again. Aren't you?" he asked as he stood in front of me. "I see it in your eyes."

Whatever he was seeing in my eyes, it wasn't the pain of a flashback like he saw in the funhouse the other afternoon. This time, I was feeling his pain.

The orderly dipped his head, and the old man smiled as they strolled by.

"I'm good." I touched his cheek with my fingers. "The word 'jail' kind of freaks me out, that's all."

"I'm not going to jail. If anyone is, it will be Sullivan this time." His shoulders relaxed as though the weight of the world was lifted from him.

"Go see Kody. I'm just going to get a drink of water," I said. I needed something to cool the sandpaper feeling coating my throat.

He brushed his hand along my stomach before ducking into the room.

Bending over the water fountain, I pushed in the bar and took a much-needed long drink of refreshingly cold water. I'd barely swallowed when Becca stormed out of the room.

"There you are. Kade said you were out here." Her voice sounded hoarse.

"What are you doing here?" I wiped my mouth with the back of my hand.

"I drove Tyler."

"How are they?" I propped my hip against the wall.

"They're overdosed on adrenaline. They're talking like they won the war." She shook her head, her ponytail wagging. "I don't like fighting. I hate to see people get hurt." Her eyes were downcast. "I can't stand blood either. It makes me woozy."

We had something in common. I knew why I hated the sight of blood. *But why did she?*

"Tyler and Kody are waiting to see you," she said. Her delicate hand circled my wrist.

"Wait. Why is Tyler involved?"

She let go of me and rubbed a finger over her chapped lips. "He came out of the sports complex when Kody and Greg were about to go head to head. He tried to help Kross prevent a brawl. Greg had a couple of friends with him."

Tyler reminded me so much of my brother. Rob always went out of his way to help people. He was the guy among his friends who had the level head. He thought with his mind and not his emotions.

"Come on. I'm sure you'll hear all about it in there," Becca said.

Voices inside ceased as Becca pushed open the massive door, leading the way in. Kody stretched out on the bed to my left with what looked to be tampons packed in his nose. To my right, Tyler sat restlessly on the edge of his bed, bouncing a knee, his arm in a sling. I hadn't talked to him in a while. His blue eyes regarded me with pain and sorrow. He and I needed to clear the air about our friendship at some point.

Kross lounged in a chair near Kody's bed. Kelton sat at the bottom of it with his feet planted firmly on the floor. Kade rested against the wall next to Kelton, grimacing. Even with a scowl, he took my breath away.

Becca went to sit with Tyler. I went to stand near Kade. "Is that what I think it is inside your nose?" I asked Kody with my brows slightly arched.

"Kind of gross," Kelton piped in. "Who would've thought tampons could be used for something other than plugging vaginas?" His tone was serious, to match his expression.

The room fell silent until Becca and I burst out laughing.

"What? I'm only stating a fact. Don't get all weird because I said the word."

"Kel," Kade warned.

"Manners, shithead," Kross added.

Kody and Tyler shook their heads.

"So, can you guys leave?" I asked. They didn't appear to have injuries that would keep them in the hospital overnight.

"We have to wait for the paperwork," Tyler said.

"Does Greg look worse?" I asked.

"Yeah," Kelton said, sure and strong.

"What's that supposed to mean?" I pinned my gaze on Kelton. "Is he in the hospital too?"

The door opened. A petite nurse with blond hair bounced in. She was the same one who was on duty the day I was in the hospital. I checked her nametag. Yep—Lisa.

She smiled and shook her head when she looked my way. "Can't get enough of this place, Lacey," she said.

I was surprised she remembered my name. "I guess not." I hoped this was my last visit to the ER.

"Which one of you is Tyler?" she asked, her brown eyes assessing Kody then Tyler.

Tyler stood. "That's me, ma'am."

"Okay. Come with me. Your paperwork is ready." She turned her attention to Kody. "Yours should be ready shortly." She opened the door, waiting on Tyler.

Becca hopped up. "I'm his ride. Lacey, I'll talk to you tomorrow."

Tyler gave a slight nod of his head as he left the room with Becca in tow.

When the door closed, Kade started in. "What happened?" He focused all his attention on Kody.

"After the game, we were headed out to get something to eat," Kelton said.

"I'm not asking you, Kel. I want to hear it from Kody." His tone permitted no argument.

"The asshole deserves to be put in jail," Kody piped up, a nasally sound to his voice. "I hit him. Okay? He said he hoped your girl didn't end up like Mandy. I lost it, bro. I fucking lost it." He clenched his hands around the sheets at his sides as his blue eyes narrowed to slits.

Up to this point, I knew very little about what happened to Mandy. A chill skittered up my spine. *Did Greg have something to do with her death?*

Kade pushed off the wall, scratching the back of his neck as he stalked over to sit on Tyler's bed.

"Would someone like to tell me what Greg meant?" I pressed my hands into the wall to anchor myself.

Silence crawled through the room. Kade leaned forward, elbows on his knees. The triplets stared at their brother.

"Is anyone going to talk?" I understood about death and not wanting to talk about it. But if my name was mentioned in the same sentence as Mandy, I deserved to know.

"Lace." Kade's tone was more lethal than mine.

I crossed the shiny floor to sit with Kade. "I know I said I was scared. But I told you once before—don't presume to know what's good for me," I said in a soft, firm tone. "Look, here's what I know. Coach Dean said Mandy died in a motorcycle accident. He also mentioned how you guys protected her from a few of the ball players. But when I asked Kross, he says you guys protect those close to you, since Mandy and Kody were dating. Okay, I can buy that. But then the principal advises me not to try out for baseball. Aaron threatens me. Probably stole my gear, too, to make me look like I'm insane. Then Greg takes a shot at me for being your girl." I took a breath. "I deserve to know. I'm not going to have an attack. I think if I was going to have one, it would've been when you almost killed us on the way here," I said with a weak smile as I laid a hand on his back.

Something told me he thought I was too fragile. *I would think that, too, if the tables were turned.*

"Lacey," Kody said in a nasally tone.

"Kody, you don't have to. It's my responsibility," Kade said, straightening.

"Shut up, Kade. Let us shoulder some of the big brother responsibilities," Kody said. "We need to talk about this. Lacey is right. She needs to know." He adjusted the tampons in his nose.

Kelton stood, shoved his hands in his jeans pockets, then rested against a small cabinet between the beds.

"So, you know, Aaron and Greg are cousins," Kelton said. "Aaron wants attention. Greg has a vendetta with us. Aaron doesn't want anyone to show him up on the ball field. Greg wants to make our lives a living hell. The one thing they have in common is that they're good at getting into your head and messing with you."

"Like what happened to my gear," I added. "How would Aaron get into the girls' locker room with girls coming and going?"

"Does Coach have evidence Aaron did it?" Kross chipped in, scrubbing his knuckles over the stubble along his jaw. "No one has ever been able to prove Aaron was responsible for all the pranks played on Mandy."

Aaron was a concern, but right now I wanted to hear what Greg meant by his comment. "So what about Greg?"

"Mandy had gone for a ride one Sunday," Kody said. "It was spring. The weather was warm. It was the first time since fall that she could take her bike out for a spin. We were going to meet up for dinner that night. Anyway, she was on the back roads in Lancaster, where she could open up and ride. She loved the freedom and adrenaline rush." He trailed off for a second before blinking. "Anyway, she pulled off at a gas station to get a drink and called me. Told me she might be late. When we were talking, Sullivan pulled into the same gas station. I told her to ignore him and get on the road. That was the last time I talked to her." His voice broke as he pressed the heels of his palms into his eyes.

Pain crawled up my chest. *Breathe in. Breathe out.*

Kade angled his body so he was facing me. "The cops ruled Mandy's death an accident. Skid marks showed she was going fast. The fact that she saw Sullivan at the same gas station that day, to us, is suspicious." He placed a hand on my thigh.

"Bottom line." Kross stood, sauntered up next to Kelton. "Baseball is Aaron's life, and he'll do anything to make sure no one takes the spotlight away. He hated when Mandy got all the attention from the kids at school and the local newspaper. Greg, even though he goes to another school now, wants revenge. And he won't stop until he gets what he wants."

"And what does he want?" I swung my gaze to Kade. "You in jail? Someone dies? Or they beat Kody again?" I worried my bottom lip.

Kody harrumphed.

"You told me why Greg hates all of you," I said to Kade. "I understand jealousy and competing, but to beat Kody like he did... Is there another reason?" I used to get envious of the girls I'd compete against for a spot on the local softball team I'd tried out for in the summertime. But my envy only drove me to work harder, not hate someone so much I'd hurt them.

"Tell her, Kade," Kelton said. "She already knows about Mom."

Kade ran a hand through his hair. "Our mom was grocery shopping one day and had one of her episodes. She was grabbing jars of food off the shelves and throwing them on the floor. A lady who was in the same aisle that day tried to help her."

"Greg's mom," I guessed.

"That's right. When Greg found out, he began spreading rumors about how crazy our family was. I couldn't tolerate the rumors. Not about my mom. So I walked into his last period class one day, yanked him out of his seat, and threw him against the wall. Before the teacher pulled me off him, I'd broken his arm." His jaw clenched.

"Is that when you went to jail?" I took hold of his hand.

"No. I got suspended from school for that incident. The first time I landed in jail was when Sullivan and his buddies beat Kody. His father pressed charges when I broke his other arm."

Oh, my God. How many times had Kade been arrested? I wasn't one to judge. I certainly had my own demons that got me suspended. Still, jail was different—permanent, depending on the infraction or the state. California had the three-strike rule. After the third crime, the penalties were more severe. "Becca made it sound like Greg had been on his deathbed."

"He was, but not from a broken arm. After Mandy's funeral, we confronted Greg. Since he was at the gas station we wanted to find out if he saw anything." Kade glanced around. "He'd said he wasn't anywhere near the gas station that day."

"I put him in a coma," Kody stated proudly.

I should've gasped or screamed or run. But I couldn't—my own family had been murdered, and I couldn't say I wouldn't hurt the creeps responsible if I had the chance. Still, I couldn't tell if they were trying to tell me my life was in danger from Greg. Nothing they told me confirmed Greg had had anything to do with Mandy's death. The only thing he was guilty of, with me, was taking a picture of Kade and me kissing, then shoving it in my face. The cops had even confirmed Mandy was going fast. Kody did say she loved to ride the back roads. There were tons of possible scenarios to cause her to crash.

"Are you okay?" Kade squeezed my hand.

"How many times have you been arrested?" I skimmed my gaze over his face.

"Twice. The second time was when Sullivan landed in a coma." His voice lacked remorse, yet regret shone in his eyes.

"I thought Kody did that to him."

"I would do anything to protect my brothers. I took—"

"Kade wasn't there," Kross said.

Kade mumbled something under his breath as my head jerked to Kross.

"Kody and I beat the crap out of Sullivan." He lifted a muscular shoulder. "Sorry, bro. We're not lying to your girl."

"Why did you let him take the blame?" My voice squeaked.

"We didn't get a choice. Sullivan told the cops it was Kade," Kelton said, arching his brows.

My mind reeled from all this information. Kade didn't beat Greg into a coma. Kade took the rap for his brothers. Kade protected those he loved. Kade had inner demons like me. Kade loved me even with mine. "Promise me again you won't go after Greg. If something happened to you...I..." His kiss gave me hope. His touch gave me strength. My heart beat faster when he walked into a room, when I thought of him, when I inhaled his scent. I wouldn't know what I'd do without him.

"What are you saying, baby?" His eyes searched mine.

I knew I didn't want to see anyone hurt, especially him. "Promise," I said again.

"Lace, I'm not going to hunt him down. But if he does anything to you or them, I won't sit idle."

I gave him a long blink of my lashes. I couldn't get excited. I'd only stopped the forward motion of revenge for now. Oh, Greg and Kade would meet in battle eventually. Maybe not in the next day, or the next week, or even the next month. How did I know? The hatred in his eyes whenever he mentioned Greg's name. "Take me home, please," I said to Kade. I was exhausted and just wanted to sleep.

Kade stood. "Kross, Kel, why don't you guys get on the road? I'll check on the paperwork."

As I was learning, when Kade spoke, people listened, particularly his brothers. Kelton and Kross said their goodbyes, and Kade, Kross and Kelton left.

I traded one bed for the other. "I'm sorry about Mandy," I said as I sat down on Kody's bed, tucking one leg under me while the other hung off the edge.

"I did love her." His voice was despondent. "She was my world."

Two beats of silence pounded between us.

"My brother is head over heels for you. You know that?" Kody said.

"I do." And I was slowly realizing my heart and all of me belonged to Kade.

"I love my brother, Lacey. He deserves the best. I don't know what's going on between you two, but please make sure you're honest with him. He's been through hell, taking care of my mom and us. And he hasn't let himself feel since my sister died, until you."

I knew the pain associated with death all too well. Maybe on some cosmic level, our pain drew us together. Maybe fate's plan was for both Kade and me to feed off each other so we would both heal.

CHAPTER 18

Storm clouds floated above us, dark and ominous. The smell of dirt, grass, and rain hung in the air. Kade and I sat behind second base, staring at each other. No words were exchanged. We weren't even touching. Suddenly, the sky opened up and large quarter-size drops of rain pelted down. Thunder boomed and lightning cracked. Still, we didn't move. Each jagged strike came threateningly close to us. When I reached out to touch Kade, a thousand bolts of electricity hit my hand. Sharp, prickly pain radiated up my arm. Now I was kneeling on the kitchen floor, brushing the black hair of a young girl who I'd never seen before.

The creak of the stairs grew louder as the unknown girl slowly faded.

"Lacey." Mary's voice drifted around me. "Are you awake?"

I stretched my arms then rubbed my eyes before opening them. Coupled with the dream and what I'd learned last night at the hospital, a foggy feeling hung over me like a black veil.

"Happy Birthday." Mary bounced in bright-eyed and all excited with flowers in her hand.

Sitting up, I removed the scrunchie that was snarling my hair. "Are those for me?"

"Of course." She set them down on my bed before opening the shutters. The sunlight spilled in. "They were just delivered from the florist."

Snatching the envelope from the bow, I removed the card.

The dark red rose is for your unconscious beauty. The lavender rose signifies how you enchant me. The coral rose is a testament of my desire for all of you. Happy Birthday. See you tonight. XO Kade.

"Well?" Mary asked. "Are they from Kade?" She sat on the edge of the bed. "They're beautiful. Is there a meaning behind the different colors?"

I shared a lot with Mary, but not this time. The message was too intimate. "I guess I'm going out with him tonight. I thought me, you and Dad would do dinner," I said. Then I remembered Becca and I planned on hanging out, just us girls. I'd forgotten all about my birthday.

"Well, Kade called this morning to ask if he could steal you. So, instead, your Dad and I would like to take you to lunch."

"Oh." I was a little suspicious. Kade and I had spent time together the previous night at his funhouse, where he'd given me the polar bear for my birthday. He'd even thought Dad and Mary would want to spend time with me on my birthday. Was Kade up to something? Or was Mary up to something? "You know I don't like people to make a fuss over my birthday."

"Don't let one birthday and one person ruin all your birthdays. Brad was a jerk."

On my sixteenth birthday, Mom had planned a big surprise bash at the country club we'd belonged to. Brad was scheduled to pick me up that night. We were going to go to dinner. Then he was supposed to take me to the country club. Only, he never showed. I called and called him. He never answered. I was in tears. Mom had been furious with Brad. I ended up driving myself over to the club. But it was the worst night. While everyone was having a good time, I was angry, sad, and completely humiliated.

"It's almost eleven. We'll leave in an hour."

"It is?" I didn't have a clock in my room. I used my phone for time and alarms. *Why was I surprised?* After four worrisome hours of processing information, I'd finally fallen asleep around four a.m. "Where's Dad?"

"In the garage, tinkering with his car. Why don't you get dressed?" She left me to get ready.

I crawled out of bed and into the bathroom. I stood in front of the mirror, examining myself. Red blended with the green of my eyes. My long brown hair seemed to have grown since we moved here—it now fell down over my breasts, and my hair looked darker. Maybe from the lack of the California sunshine. Now that I was eighteen, I'd thought I would look different. But I didn't. With the exception of the lump on my forehead, which was barely visible now, my skin didn't have any wrinkles. I smiled, thinking about my mom. On her birthday Dad would say the same thing to her every time.

"Honey," he'd said, "your beauty will always keep you young."

God, I missed her. She would always pamper Julie and me on our birthdays, by taking us to the spa at the country club. I chuckled as I pinned up my hair. Dad and I traded a country club for a gun club. Well, I wouldn't be lying on a table with a masseuse kneading my muscles today. However, a bubble bath sounded enticing. I had time. So, I filled the tub, and squirted some kiwi bubble bath into the water. Swiping a towel from the wicker shelf adjacent to the tub, I placed the folded towel on the tiled edge surrounding it. While I waited, I brushed my teeth. After rinsing out my mouth, I shed my pajamas, then sent Kade a text message.

OMG! Beautiful Roses. Thank you.

I placed my phone next to the towel then climbed in. Turning off the faucet, I eased down into the warm bubbles. This wasn't the spa, but the prickly heat of the water and the fruity aroma massaged my body and my senses.

Call Me Maybe blared from my phone. I wiped my hands on the towel, picked up the phone then tapped the screen.

"Hello."

"Happy Birthday, baby," Kade's sexy voice tickled my ear, sending a warm feeling down through my belly.

"Thank you. The roses are beautiful, and are you some sort of poet?"

"You bring out a different side of me." Keys jangled in the background.

"Where are you?" I asked.

"I'm just leaving the house. I'm meeting Hunt for lunch. So, you okay after last night?"

"*Me?* How's Kody?" I might be on mental overload with everything they told me, but I wasn't in physical pain.

"Sore. Let's not talk about him. I want you to enjoy your special day. So what're you doing?"

"Um...taking a bubble bath." *Wishing you were here with me.*

Silence.

I checked the phone to see if he'd hung up or if we lost the connection. "Kade, are you still there?"

"Sorry, I had to run back into the house and jump under a cold shower for a minute."

"What would you do if you were here?" *Whoa! Did I just ask him that?* Heat stung my cheeks.

He growled. "Lace."

The way he said my name, husky and dark, made my nipples hard. "Tell me, Kade," I said in a low voice, which didn't sound like me. *Bold much?*

"God, baby. You're killing me here."

"Please," I said in a pouty voice. "I'm..." A throbbing began between my legs. I imagined him sitting behind me, my back to his front, flesh against flesh. His lips on my neck, tracing a sensuous path to my ear, nipping. I shivered. With his arms around me, one hand roamed intimately over my breast, teasing. My nipples firmed. The other disappeared below the bubbles. Anticipation made me squirm as I imagined his magical fingers blazing a lust-arousing path downward. "I need to feel you."

"Fuck," he groaned, breathing heavily. "I'll pick you up at seven. Then I'll show you." Pain saturated his tone.

"Promise?" The throbbing sensation pulsed out of control. Waiting was going to prove difficult today.

"More than promise. See you tonight." The phone went dead.

I giggled. *Where was Lacey Robinson?* I'd never acted like that before. I didn't feel embarrassed. If anything, I was enlivened. Like a cat waking from a yearlong slumber.

⚅⚅

I'D CALLED Becca on our way to lunch. She had to help her dad at the Cave that night, so I didn't feel bad about postponing our girls' night out. Lunch with Mary and Dad had been eye opening. We ate at a small restaurant in town, Wiley's Bar and Grill. I'd learned Mary had eaten lunch here a few times since she'd met Mr. Wiley at the farmer's market. I'd also come to the conclusion that Mr. Wiley—sharp angular jaw and piercing green eyes—was attracted to Mary. Maybe it was the soft peck on her cheek. Or the intimate embrace between them. I had never before seen her with a man. I was happy for her. I'd wanted to talk to her more about her new friend, but Dad had been with us.

When we returned from lunch, I lounged in my room, listening to music until it was time to get ready for my date with Kade.

"Sweet Pea, you look great." Dad lifted his gaze as I walked into his study. He sat on the couch reading through a file.

"Thanks." Kade liked the thigh-high boots, so I wore those with black skinny jeans and a pink blouse with a sweetheart neckline. "Kade should be here soon."

"Have a great time." The bruise under his left eye had turned a yellowish color.

"Thank you, Dad." I leaned down and kissed him on the head.

"Sweet Pea, I love you."

"I love you, too."

A horn blew outside.

Once I had everything, I flew out the door and hopped in Kade's truck. As soon as our eyes met, my heart jolted. His honey-brown hair curled around his ears, the glow of the dashboard lights highlighting his strong jaw, and his kiss-me lips were stretched into a grin, showing me those dimples I so loved.

"What's wrong?" Kade asked. "Did you forget something?"

"Nah. It's nothing."

He leaned over and captured my lips in his—warm, wet, and minty. When he had his fill, he backed out of the driveway with a smug grin on his face. "So, I thought we would stop and grab a bite to eat. Afterwards, do you want to go to the Cave?"

I shrugged a shoulder. I wasn't hungry, and I wanted to continue our conversation from earlier. "Weren't you going to show me something?" I asked coyly.

"You're going to kill me before I even get out of your driveway." He released a breath. "Let's eat first. I need some energy." His voice was gruff as he squirmed in his seat.

I smiled. We drove into town, and Kade parked in front of Wiley's Bar and Grill.

"We're eating here?" I raised my eyebrows.

"Yeah, why? You don't like this place?"

I laughed, wagging my head. "I ate lunch here today." Mr. Wiley might think it was odd I was back so soon.

"The food is good," he said as he got out of the truck.

When I opened the passenger door and jumped out, Kade's six-foot frame held me prisoner.

"Don't tease me in there. I'm barely hanging on as it is." A muscle ticked in his jaw.

"And if I do?" I challenged. This should be a blast. Besides, it was my birthday. Wasn't fun supposed to be part of the celebration?

"Lace," he said, yanking me flush to him. "Do you feel that?" he whispered. "It wouldn't be cool for me to walk in with a bulge in my jeans."

I giggled.

"You're enjoying this, aren't you?" he asked, still holding me close. "Please, ease up. Just looking at you is tearing me to pieces."

"Then let's get out of here," I suggested.

"I'm food-hungry, too." He let me go and walked down to a tailor shop right next door, groaning. After a minute or two, he trudged back. "Don't talk until we're seated. Okay?"

"Huh?" I had a permanent smile on my face as we entered Wiley's.

A blond-haired girl glanced up from her podium when Kade and I cut through the waiting patrons. "Hey, Kade," she said.

"You must come here a lot," I said. What was I saying? This was the second time within hours I'd been here.

"No talking," he reiterated.

I batted my eyes as I stuck out my tongue. *Okay. I was officially a mean person.* The guy was in pain. I shouldn't be torturing him, but I couldn't help it. It was entertaining.

We followed the hostess, walking past tables with families and couples at others. Some guy shouted from the bar in the far left corner. I glanced over to find a football game on the TV screen.

"Watch your step," she said over her shoulder, gesturing to the floor.

We climbed a set of stairs. Where was she taking us? We'd passed the main dining room. We banked left at the top of the landing.

The hostess kept going. Clearly, she was in no hurry. Finally, she stopped in front of a set of closed double doors. "In here." She nodded at Kade. Then she left.

"What's going on?" I peered up at the sexy beast, and shouldn't have.

Sparks of fire shot out of his eyes as though he wanted to burn me to the wall. Without a word, he opened the door.

"Surprise!" several people shouted.

I jerked my head toward the room. The triplets, Becca, and Hunt mingled around the brick fireplace. Coach Dean and Mary stood near a white linen-covered table that had a buffet of various finger foods. Shock and excitement surged through me. I'd suspected something, but this wasn't it. I considered Mary. She smiled and winked, her pink-blush cheeks sparkling in the dimly lit room.

I swung my gaze to Kade who was now showing me his dimples. *Thank God.* Heat pinched my cheeks as I thought of him in pain a minute ago.

"Happy Birthday!" He placed his hand at the small of my back as we walked in.

"Oh, my God. Coach Dean?" *Why was he here?* He stood tall and proud, wearing pressed khakis with a plaid oxford-cloth button-down shirt.

"Wait. Where's my dad?" I whispered.

"Behind you, Sweet Pea."

Spinning around, I ran into his arms. "Is this why you took the night off?"

"I wouldn't miss this for the world, Lacey," he said. "I just couldn't get here before you."

After Dad let me go, I mingled with everyone.

"I thought you had to help your dad," I said to Becca, who always looked like she stepped out of one of those expensive boutiques in Beverly Hills. She wore a cream-colored cami under a jade-colored lace top and a black miniskirt with knee-high black boots.

"I did. Now I'm here. Happy Birthday." She hugged me. "We're going to have a good time tonight at the Cave."

"You look great, by the way. I love the outfit," I said.

"We'll get you in a skirt yet," she said, her long lashes sweeping down then up as she skimmed her gaze over me. "Although you look great, too."

"Was Tyler invited?" I asked. "Have you talked to him?"

"I called him this morning. His shoulder is killing him."

Becca and I hung by a doorway that opened into a private dining room. Kade, Coach Dean, and Hunt huddled in front of the fire, talking as though they were discussing something top secret. Dad, Mary, Kross, and Kody chatted by the food table.

Kelton swaggered up with his bottom lip sucked into his mouth, his blue eyes appraising Becca and me. "Christ, girls. You two know how to make a guy squirm, don't you?" he drawled.

Becca and I exchanged looks, rolling our eyes at the same time.

He hugged me. "My brother is the luckiest fucking guy alive," he whispered in my ear. "Happy Birthday." He kissed me lightly on the lips.

"Kade is going to have a cow." I kept my hands at my sides.

"I think he is," Becca said, matter of fact.

I peered around Kelton and locked eyes with Kade. He had one of his blank expressions, although the area around his eyes twitched.

"Nah. I warned him," Kelton said.

He might have, but something told me Kade didn't like his brother kissing his girl.

Kross and Kody made their way over to us. Both wore faded jeans. Kross had on a white button-front shirt with the sleeves rolled up to his elbows. Kody had a plain, dark-blue cotton shirt that brought out his blue eyes even more. The major difference with Kody was that his nose was swollen, and he had the beginnings of black eyes, which seemed to be a theme among my close family and friends. First I'd given Kade one. Then Dad had one from his fight at the club. Now Kody.

"You're hogging her," Kross drawled.

"Happy Birthday," Kody said. "You're officially an adult."

I'd stopped being a kid the night the lights were off.

Mr. Wiley sauntered in. His green eyes stood out against his dark hair and his unshaven jaw. "Dinner will be served in a moment. Why don't you make your way into the dining room?" he said, waving his hand at the open doorway next to Becca and me.

I stole a glance at Mary. Her dark eyes were fixed on our host like she wanted to eat him for dinner. I almost giggled. I didn't want to embarrass her, though.

Becca and I went in first. "Lacey, please sit at the head of the table," Mr. Wiley said as I walked by him.

There was only one chair at the head at the far end of the elegant-looking table. Red linen covered it, with five chairs along each side. A small arrangement of carnations and lilies sat in the center, the fragrant smell permeating the room.

"I'll let Kade and your dad sit next to you," Becca said.

The group wandered in. Mary lingered at the door, talking to Mr. Wiley. Kade smiled as he sauntered over to sit down on my right. Dad followed with a glass of water in hand and sat on my left, and Coach took a seat next to Dad. Everyone else found seats. Mr. Wiley rattled off the menu selections, while three waiters entered and surrounded the table. One poured water. One placed breadbaskets on the table. The other took drink orders.

The conversations flowed. I bounced my knee under the table. While I enjoyed having everyone here celebrating my birthday, I really wanted to spend time getting to know Kade more. I moved my foot to the right until I found Kade's leg. He gave me a lopsided grin and snaked his hand under the table and onto my knee and squeezed.

"Lacey, have you been following my orders this weekend?" Coach asked.

Dad cocked his head as he glanced my way.

"Yes, sir. I'm resting and I haven't practiced. I go back to see the doctor on Monday." I met Dad's gaze as I replied to Coach.

The muscles around Dad's eyes loosened. He probably thought I had gotten into more trouble.

"Good. I want to see a note from the doctor saying you're clear to pitch on Friday," Coach added.

"So, Coach, did you find out who broke into Lacey's locker?" Dad asked.

All heads swung to Coach.

"No one is talking," Coach said as he patted his mouth with his napkin.

Kade and his brothers didn't look dismayed. Dad, on the other hand, pressed his lips into a thin line, shaking his head slightly. Maybe Coach would never find out who'd done it. Given what the guys had told me last night, I wasn't going to hold my breath waiting. I just had to make sure I was on guard during the second round of tryouts.

For the next hour, we ate a seven-course meal. Food hadn't been on my mind when I walked in, but when the aroma from the chicken and beef filtered into the room, my stomach perked up. I took small bites of my chicken parmesan, eating slowly, savoring the delicious taste. Although I had debated whether to devour my food like the boys were,

I didn't want to seem too anxious to get out of there. Becca moved the food around on her plate like she wasn't hungry. Mary kept making eye contact with Mr. Wiley every time he entered the room. When the plates were cleared, Mr. Wiley carted in a large rectangular cake with *Happy Birthday, Lacey* scripted in frosting.

After everyone sang Happy Birthday, we got up to stretch. Mary helped Mr. Wiley cut the cake on the cart. Kade went down to the end of the table to talk to Hunt.

I was about to use the little girls' room when Coach cornered me. "Lacey, I heard that the fight the boys got into revolved around you," Coach whispered. "I asked you the other day if anyone had confronted you about not playing ball. Do you want to change your answer?" His grimace had me cringing. *He knew I was lying, or at least not telling him everything.*

"Is that why you're here?" I asked. I wasn't ready to have this conversation. I wanted to enjoy my birthday. Fear and anger had no place in my world tonight. Plus Dad was here. I didn't want him to know anything about Greg or Aaron.

"Kade invited me. I thought it would be good to see how you were doing. And I want to make sure I don't have any trouble this year."

"Do you go out of your way to visit each of us?" I found it odd that he was there. Actually, extremely weird—Coaches didn't attend birthday dinners of students they hardly knew. Did they? And why had Kade invited him?

"I do what I think is best for the school's sports program. I want you in my office first thing Monday morning. Between now and then, I want you to think hard about your answer. Have a nice birthday," he said. Then he was off to mingle with the adults.

Jeepers. Thanks for spoiling a great day.

"We're all going over to the Cave, now," Becca said. "We'll see you over there. Okay?"

"Sure. I guess." My mind was stuck on the conversation with Coach and why Kade had invited him.

Kade touched the small of my back. "Are you ready?"

I was more than ready to blow this place. But the Cave had no appeal to me tonight. One person consumed my thoughts.

"Bye, Dad." I waved. "I'll call if I'm going to be late."

He nodded and Mary waved. Coach didn't say anything. As we

were walking out, I kept my fingers crossed that Coach wouldn't share any details about Greg or Aaron with Dad.

The scent of rain hit me as we made our way to the truck. I glanced up at the sky. A lone cloud passed in front of the full moon before several more drifted in. In a matter of seconds, the moon disappeared.

"Why did you invite Coach Dean?" I asked as we buckled in.

"He called the house today and talked with Kody and me. Kody explained the fight between him and Greg and Tyler. Then I got on the phone. He asked about you. He seemed worried, so I asked him if he wanted to join us for dinner. That way he could see you were fine. Mary and your dad said it was okay." He merged into traffic. "Why? What did he say to you?"

"Nothing much. I have to meet him on Monday morning. He wants to know if someone threatened me in so many words. I don't want to tell him. I'm not a snitch." Plus I didn't want to fuel the fire with Aaron and Greg. Not when I was trying to keep Kade away from them.

"You need to be honest with him. He won't run to Aaron and reprimand him. If he knows, he'll be watchful, that's all. He'll only step in if he has to."

"I don't like it."

"I know. Let's forget Coach. Remember, this is your day. I want you to focus on what I'm going to do to you tonight."

At that moment, everything I worried about fell away. My stomach flip-flopped and the ache I'd had earlier between my thighs came roaring back. "And that would be...?" I swallowed.

"Nope. I want you to use your imagination."

"So you're going to tease me all night in a club full of people?" I asked.

"Who said we were going to a club?"

I glanced out the side window. The two-story colonial homes lining the country road told me this wasn't the way to the Cave.

CHAPTER 19

Fifteen minutes later we were in Kade's kitchen. He grabbed a Coke out of the fridge, popped the top, and guzzled it as though he had just walked a mile in the hot desert.

"Is everything okay?" I asked.

After we established that the Cave wasn't on his agenda, Kross had called. Kade had been on the phone with him until we parked in the driveway.

His lips split into a devious smile as he threw the can into the sink. Stalking toward me, his eyes danced with desire and a warning.

My breath caught. My throat was bone dry. Now *I* needed a soda, or maybe a bucket of ice water. *Yeah, right.* No amount of liquid would cool the fire raging through me. Only one person could douse my flames right now.

Caging me with his arms, his muscles strained against the fabric of his shirt as he held onto the island for dear life. His chest rose and fell as he stared down at me. Pure, raw hunger lingered beneath his mile-long lashes.

Our bodies were so close. Yet not close enough. I closed my eyes and quietly inhaled, breathing him in. I quivered as his scent seeped into me.

"Open those beautiful green eyes," he whispered as one of his fingers rested under my chin. "I want to see every emotion."

I whimpered and shuddered at the same time.

"Shit," he choked out. "The way you react to me... I haven't even touched you yet."

His voice made my adrenaline climb, clouding my mind. Without thinking, I pressed my body to his. I sucked in a sharp breath when our hips collided. He was as hard as the granite countertop he had me trapped with.

He let out a low rumble just before he took my lips in his. He was greedy when his mouth crashed against mine. His tongue barreled in and tasted every crevice. It was as though he were punishing me for teasing him on the phone today. I matched him in intensity. My tongue roamed through the cavern of his mouth as he hauled me onto the countertop, lifting me by my waist. I'd fantasized about his kiss all day. *Well, more than just his kiss.*

All of a sudden, he broke away.

"What's...wrong?" I labored for air. *Was he having second thoughts?*

He held my face between his hands. "I have to know you're sure, baby. Tell me," he rasped. "I need to hear the words."

Reaching out, I fisted my hands in his shirt. "I want to feel you against me. Skin to skin."

Growling, he ripped open his shirt. Buttons flew in all directions before the cotton fabric floated to the floor.

I chewed my bottom lip. I'd seen his upper torso bare last night, but for some reason, it seemed like I was looking at him for the very first time. Every corded muscle was sculpted to perfection. His biceps, his abs, his chest bunched as I raked my gaze over him.

"How come there are only four hearts and not five?" My fingers traced over the tattoos above his left breast.

"The fifth one is the one beating inside me."

My head shot up. Right then, I wanted him more than I wanted a baseball scholarship.

His fingers circled my wrist, lifting my hand to his mouth. "You set my blood on fire, Lace. I want to be inside you. Feel you losing control around me." He sucked on one of my fingers, and a stream of fire wormed its way down to my core.

A strangled whimper barely fell from my lips as he whisked me away to his room. He kicked the door shut and somehow managed to lock it with me in his arms. After setting me on the bed, he flicked on the warm glow of the lamp on the nightstand.

"I want to memorize every inch of your body tonight. But first, last chance to tell me no, Lace."

"Yes," I said. My body pulsed with the need to feel his naked body against mine.

Suddenly, he became a madman. My blouse flew over my head. My bra followed. My boots ended up somewhere in the room. I was stripped down to my jeans.

"Lie back." The possessiveness in his tone shot arrows of heat through me, and I obeyed.

He kissed and licked his way up my body, the soft strands of his hair feathering over me, leaving tingles in its wake. His heated mouth was everywhere. My navel. My stomach. Yet nowhere. He tormented me until I was writhing under him, falling into a deep realm of pleasure. Looking down at me, his dimples emerged. He seemed to be enjoying my pleasurable pain.

My nipples swelled to painful peaks, and a slow, steady ache took root between my thighs. The sensations were too much and not enough.

Or at least I'd thought so, until he sucked in one swollen nipple, and I thrashed violently. He pressed his body to mine, licking his way over to the other breast.

"You're beautiful," he breathed as he inched his way off me until he was standing. Slowly, methodically his nimble fingers unbuttoned my jeans, peeling them down over my hips. "Fucking incredible," he murmured as his hand traced the outline of my black thong.

"K-k-ade?" The word *agony* flitted through my brain. He was going at a snail's pace. Patience wasn't one of my strongest virtues. *But—oh, my*. It was his. He'd told me so.

"Shhh." He peered down at me, his darkened eyes sparking with lust. Then he slipped off my thong. "Unconscious beauty," he whispered when I was completely naked.

A shiver washed over me as his eyes swallowed me, shattered me, loved me. I opened my arms. I needed him on me, around me, in me.

"Not yet." His tone was low.

I pouted.

"Baby, relax. You wanted to know what I would do to you. Right?"

I barely nodded, holding my breath.

"Well, I'm going to show you."

I swallowed. *Was he going to...?*

His callused hands slid up my thighs, the roughness abrading my skin. A wild tap dance suddenly beat inside me. Before I registered another sensation, he yanked me to the end of the bed. Nudging my legs apart, his fingers drifted down my inner thighs. He held my gaze as he knelt on the floor and lowered his head. Then his mouth closed over my bundle of nerves, and I practically flew off the bed. I wasn't a virgin, but Brad had never... *Oh... my... God...* My brain fogged.

His tongue teased, swirled, and circled my clit. He slowed. Sped up. Each time, the muscles in my stomach tightened. I was lost, drunk on him, his heady scent, his touch. A million bright stars flashed before the tightness in my belly exploded. I clutched the blanket as I arched my back. When I did, his tongue plunged into me.

"Kade!" I cried out as a thousand tingles cascaded over me. He continued to tease with his tongue until the last of the tremors left me.

"Sweet Jesus," Kade muttered as he crept up onto the bed, his forehead against mine. "I'm ruined."

I licked my dry lips, smiling. He wasn't the only one. Suddenly, I wanted more. *More of him.* "I want all of you, Kade," I whispered.

His eyes flashed with a *hell-yeah* look. In one fluid motion he stood and tore off the rest of his clothes. My heart went from fifty to a hundred beats per minute in an instant as I skimmed his naked, jaw-dropping, beautiful body. Every inch of him was ripped and toned—a work of art from head to toe.

My gaze traveled from him to his nightstand where he snatched a foil packet from the drawer. He rolled the condom onto his length. Excitement welled up. Fear pushed it down.

My cheeks burned as I thought about how he would fit. Plus it had been well over a year since I was with anyone.

"I'll go slow," he said, as though he knew what I was thinking.

He lowered himself over me, and I opened to him. We locked eyes as he eased inside.

I sucked in a breath.

"Breathe, Lace." He stilled, bracing his hands on each side of me, biceps straining.

It hurt, but it wasn't as bad as I'd anticipated. "I'm okay." I grasped his shoulders.

He pushed in a little at a time, and each time my body stretched, molding to him. When he was all the way in he stopped. "You sure you're okay?" he said, his lips brushing mine.

"Perfect." It was the only word to describe how I felt. My mind, body, and soul were his to take, to love.

With a roll of his hips, he pushed in, then pulled out slowly. I moved with him, flattening my hands on his back. *I was here with this man who made my stomach burn, roll, flip-flop, and tingle. His kiss. Oh, God.* His kiss shattered all the nightmares, made the bad stuff go away. I loved the way he looked at me, the sureness of what he wanted—*me.*

I dragged my nails along his back as we got into a rhythm. Grunting, he clenched his jaw as though he was trying to be gentle. I was past slow and easy. I wrapped my legs around him and pushed down onto him, hard.

"What the... I'm going to fucking lose it if you—"

Deviously, I smiled as I rocked into him again. Without blinking, he took possession of my body. His mouth closed over mine as he gripped my butt, pushing deeper.

I sucked on his tongue. He tasted like candy, sinful and sweet. A low rumble crawled up his chest. "Kade," I breathed. "I'm...in...love with you."

He stopped moving, his eyes searching mine.

No, please don't shut down.

"Don't mess with me, Lace."

"The heart knows." *And mine was all his.*

A long excruciating silence squeezed between us as he worked out whatever was going on in his head. Tears suddenly burned my eyes. Did I say the wrong thing? Oh, God. I shouldn't have brought up something his dead sister had said. My heart was trying to get out of my chest. *Say something.*

Finally, he brushed his lips along my jaw to my ear. "You're mine, Lace. My polar bear."

A jolt of electricity kick-started my heart. The sudden unease coiling in me untangled.

Then we got lost in each other, moving in perfect sync as that familiar sensation roared back to life in my stomach. I dug my nails into his back, rolling my hips forward, wanting everything he had to give me.

"You feel so fucking good," he whispered. "Perfect."

My body hummed, the pressure building. My core went liquid. Then he pressed his hips up, rubbing against my nerves. I screamed his name as spasm after spasm rocked my body in one glorious wave after another. I shuddered as he drove deeper once, then twice more before his body tensed.

"Lace," he groaned as he buried his lips against my ear, thrusting one last time as he came.

We stayed connected, trying to catch our breath.

"I love the crap out of you," he rasped, resting his forehead on mine.

"Best birthday present ever," I said. I'd never experienced passion, tenderness, and desire like this until Kade Maxwell.

◈◈◈

ON SUNDAY I didn't see Kade. His dad finally came home from a long business trip. He and his brothers were catching up with him. Kade and I talked via text messaging. Mostly "I miss you" and "I love you" messages, until he had a chance to call me before he went to bed. I daydreamed about him all of Sunday, replaying how he touched me, softly and tenderly. When I finally heard his voice, husky and smooth, a familiar ache took root inside me. After we talked about his day with his dad, he told me he wouldn't be in school on Monday. His dad wanted him and his brothers to accompany him to see their mother, who lived in a mental health facility in the Berkshires.

I'd had a follow-up doctor's appointment on Monday before school. The attending physician who'd examined me ran a few tests, then gave me a note clearing me to resume activity. When I got to school, I slipped my doctor's note under Coach Dean's door, then ran out of the sports complex. I was still reluctant to snitch on Aaron.

Becca bugged me all day to dish about my night with Kade. A girl shouldn't kiss and tell. At least, that was what my mom had said. I gave Becca a bland answer about having a good time.

After two days of not seeing Kade, I was having withdrawals. He'd texted me around nine the night before to let me know he was on his way back home. We agreed to meet before school where he normally parked his truck in the lot of the sports complex...only I forgot to set my phone alarm. I'd been up late studying trig and calculus. Mrs. Flowers had told me on Friday that my tests were scheduled for Wednesday the next week. If Kade hadn't called me, I'd probably have kept sleeping. Usually Mary would've woken me up, but she was missing in action when I ducked into the kitchen to grab a banana.

Later she'd explained she'd had a date with Mr. Wiley and didn't get in until midnight, so she slept in.

The cafeteria was bustling. Tuesdays were busier since pizza was on the menu. I sat at a table in the far corner, cramming more math. I would've gone to the library, but Kade had cornered me between classes and said we needed to talk at lunch. I'd tried to get him to tell me what it was about.

"I have an English test I'm late for," he'd said tersely.

What had I done? He'd been sweet on the phone that morning. I sifted through our conversations and text messages. Nothing jumped out waving a red flag. *Had I spilled my feelings too soon? Had I scared him all of a sudden?* An ugly thought sprang to mind. Maybe after seeing his mother, he'd decided he didn't want to handle my PTSD and all the craziness that came with my illness. No matter how strongly I felt about him, doubt still survived in me, and probably would for a long time. Nausea churned my stomach, and I kept trying to tell myself it wasn't about us.

"Hey, Lacey," a familiar male voice said.

I glanced up from my book.

Tyler stood over me, his arm in a sling. "You know Coach is looking for you."

"Yeah." I was surprised he hadn't tracked me down or summoned me to his office.

"Where's Becca today?" Tyler asked. "You two have been inseparable."

"She's out sick." Becca had sent me a text early this morning. *Got the flu. Take notes for me.*

He scanned my face. "I know this isn't the best time, but I'd like to talk. I got football all this week after school. Coach is making me take notes while my arm is in a sling. Can we meet for a shake on Thursday? I can let you know then what time I expect to be done with football practice." His free hand gripped the back of the metal chair as he studied me.

"Sure." It was time to clear the air about our friendship. I didn't want to lose him as a friend.

The conversations around me suddenly quieted. Then girls tittered and whispered.

"Hey, Kade." A girl's voice hitched.

Tyler moved aside just as I was leaning, not to see Kade, but to see the cheerleader who was gushing or foaming at the mouth. Every instinct in me wanted to shut her up or cut her eyes out. *Whoa!* I hadn't been jealous in the past. Even when girls had swooned over Brad, it never bothered me. This was a new feeling.

I almost sprang out of my seat like a jumping bean. The petite cheerleader drooled as she watched Kade swagger over to my table.

Kade appeared to have one thing on his mind—actually, one person. He homed in on me.

"He looks pissed," Tyler said. "The last time I saw that look on his face, he beat the crap out of Sullivan. Do you want me to stay, Lacey?"

"No. Let me know about Thursday." Kade wasn't going to hurt me.

Tyler hesitated for a minute before he nodded at Kade then faded from my vision.

Kade pulled out a chair beside me, twirled it, then straddled the seat with his arms on the back, facing me.

"Hi," I said hesitantly.

He glowered at me. The room fell eerily silent. I darted my gaze around. Yep, we definitely had an audience. They waited like vultures to see what happened between Kade and me. Did they expect him to wig out on me like he had with Greg?

"Are you going to talk or stare?" I asked in a low voice.

He still didn't say a word. He shot daggers at me as he glared. Even angry, the guy knew how to twist my insides in a delicious uproar. *Oh, heck.* I leaned over and smacked my lips to his. If he wasn't going to talk, then I'd at least get some reaction out of him. *Toad face.* My tongue traced the outline of his lips. The same ones that had been everywhere on my body just Saturday, and I wanted on me right now. Anger or no anger, I didn't care. *Didn't they say angry sex was hot?*

He kept his lips glued together, not moving. "People are watching, Lace," he finally said.

"So? It didn't stop you from making love to my ear at the football game in front of hundreds of people. Or what about the picture Greg took of us kissing? Remember?"

No reaction from him. A faint ringing hummed in my ears. The doubt had awakened. He usually growled or grunted at the mention of his enemy. I pushed my tongue through his lips—at least I tried. The guy still didn't budge.

What the heck? Now the ringing turned into a drone as crankiness took root.

He grinned.

I plunged my tongue into his mouth.

"Fuck, Lace. Are you trying to kill me here?" he said, his voice low.

"Kiss me. Maybe our audience will mind their own damn business."

"I'm mad at you," he said, taking the mechanical pencil out of my hand.

Did he think I was going to use it as a weapon? "Kiss me, then we can talk."

"Goddamn, woman. You know I can't just kiss you." He set the pencil down on my open trig book.

"Buck up, big guy. No one's going to see your hard-on."

"You're something else." He nipped my lips before his tongue plunged into my mouth.

Our tongues tangoed for a few minutes before he broke free. I whimpered. He laughed. *Good. At least he was laughing.* The buzzing in my head died.

Conversations around us had resumed.

"Why didn't you talk with Coach?" Kade asked.

"Is that why you're ornery?"

"Coach told you to be in his office on Monday to talk. So why weren't you?"

My stomach suddenly hurt, killing my mood. "Why are you so set on me talking with Coach? Wait. Did he run to you when I didn't show?"

I waited. No response. A completely blank face stared back at me.

I sighed. "I'm not a snitch. I told you that. And I'm not so sure Aaron isn't all talk."

The skin around his eyes tightened while his lips formed into a thin line. "Did you not hear what we told you the other night about Aaron? You need to tell Coach he threatened you."

"Why? Because you told me he's good at getting into people's heads, and baseball is his life? Newsflash—baseball is my life, too. Besides, what's Coach going to do? Yell at Aaron because he told me in so many words he doesn't want me on the team? He'll deny it. Then he'll only pick on me more."

"Coach can help. He knows what went down a couple of years ago. Hell, when we found out you enrolled..." He combed his fingers through his hair and looked past me.

A large ball of hysteria collected in my chest. "Finish that sentence." Tiny little pinpricks covered my body as numbness set in.

"Shit." His lids slid shut.

"Kade? Finish the fucking sentence." My voice rose.

A male voice from somewhere in the room said, "Oh, shit."

I didn't turn to look. Instead the blood drained from my body.

He opened his eyes and immediately looked away again. Not good.

"Talk," I demanded in a shaky voice, my hands clenching into fists.

The freaking bell rang, and I flinched. The crowd filed out. Dings, thuds and clangs sounded, I imagined from students dumping their trash and trays.

"We need to get to class," he said, about to stand.

"Oh, fuck no. You're talking." The devil invaded my body, or at least his voice did.

His eyebrows went up. I wasn't sure if he was shocked I had said the F-word, or the hardness in my tone. Either way, I didn't care. A fire could break out in the kitchen—Kade was still going to talk.

"They'll kick us out of here," he said.

The badass guy who'd been in jail was worried about us getting kicked out of the cafeteria. Really?

"So let them. Until they do, talk." No emotion in my voice.

"Fuck." He ran his hands through his hair again. "We found out"—he met my eyes—"you were coming to this school."

My mouth gaped open. "Excuse me? You knew about me before I got here?" The hairs on my arms stood up. I knew Coach had to have done his homework on me. Any coach would've. But Kade? Why would he have known who I was? I didn't want to panic, but the way he was acting scared me. I had the sudden feeling I'd been violated.

A few expletives spewed from his lips.

Silence dangled between us.

I slammed my book shut, the sound echoing over the two lunch ladies chatting behind the food line. "You going to talk? If not, I'm out of here." I couldn't breathe. I needed air.

He grasped my wrist. "Please. Don't go."

"Do I even want to hear this, Kade?" Tears welled up. My angry bee circled inside my head. My hands became clammy.

"I don't want anything to happen to you," he said.

"Wrong answer." I kicked back my chair, wrenching away my hand.

"Lace?" He said my name so low I wasn't sure I heard it.

"Why did you pursue me so hard?" All I could hear were Coach's words. *The Maxwell brothers protected Mandy.* "Did Coach put you up to it?" *If that were true, was our relationship a lie?*

He dropped his gaze. Pain shot through my chest as though someone stuck a knife in me. I threw my books in my backpack and stepped around the table. *Exit. I had to find the nearest one.*

"Coach came to me in July." His tone matched the regret in his eyes.

I stilled.

"He told me about a kick-ass female ball player who was enrolling for her senior year," Kade continued. "He knew Aaron might make waves. And he was worried about history repeating itself. He knew my brothers were going to spend their last year at Kensington and play baseball. He saw a perfect storm. He wanted my help."

Air. Need air. The buzzing in my head intensified, as did the pounding of my heart in my chest.

"That first night I met you. You weren't at the ball field looking for Kelton, were you?"

"Lace."

"Tell me!" I was on the verge of becoming a hysterical sociopath.

"Shit." He shook his head. "I didn't want a repeat of two years ago," he said softly.

"So you were only pursuing me because you were told to? Everything you said to me is a lie, then. You don't love me." My heart severed in two. "I was a job to you. Protect the girl so I don't end up like Mandy. Well, don't do me any favors. I can protect myself."

"Baby, it's not like that." He jumped out his chair and reached for me.

I backed away. "Isn't it?" I stormed out. The halls were empty. Once outside, I sprinted to my car. The fall air provided a welcome relief against my heated skin. *Why was I such a moron when it came to reading people? Brad had turned out to be gay. Now, Kade had only been babysitting me.*

"Lace!" Kade yelled behind me.

The wind whipped my hair in all directions. Holding onto what was left of my heart, I ran across campus and out into the lot. Tears spilled as I passed cars.

Boy, Tyler was right. "Trust me when I tell you: stay away from Kade." Kade showered me with words, and I fell for every freaking one of them. *God, how stupid was I?* With shaking hands, I rummaged through my bag for my car keys. My backpack fell, books spilling out, papers swirling in the wind. *Fucking great!* I dropped to the ground, propping back my head against my car door. *Idiot.*

"Lace," Kade's voice was strained, above me.

"Get out of here!" I screamed.

"Baby, please."

"I'm not your baby."

He sat on the ground opposite me with his back against someone else's car door. "My feelings for you are real."

"So tell me something. Are your brothers only friends with me because it's their job, too?"

"Hell, no. They adore you, Lace. You snared them, just like you got me."

I wasn't so sure I snared anyone. I wiped my nose with the back of my hand.

"Lace." His voice quivered. "Please, don't shut me out."

I desperately wanted to believe him. *I couldn't. Not right now.* I had to think. "I can't do this, Kade. Us. This isn't going to work. I came here to fix what was broken inside me, not to break it more. I gave you my heart." Tears streamed down my face.

Scooting closer, he reached out to wipe a tear away, and I flinched.

"Crap. Let me touch you. Don't do this," he pleaded.

I pushed to my feet. My papers blew away, but I didn't care. I picked up my books. He stood, helping me. I found my keys. My hands shook as I tried to unlock my door.

He grabbed the keys and unlocked it for me. He leaned in, kissed my neck softly, and then he left.

Blowing out all the air in my lungs, I opened my door and fell into my car. I sobbed against my steering wheel. After what seemed like hours, I wiped my face with my fingers, started the engine and took off. I had no idea where I was going. I couldn't stay here. Someone would see me. I couldn't go home. Dad and Mary would grill me, and I wasn't ready for their onslaught of questions.

I drove and before long, small quaint buildings lined the streets of Lancaster. I rolled into the small space outside of Dr. Davis's office. Throwing the car into park, I slumped over the steering wheel, contemplating whether or not to go in. My appointment with him wasn't until tomorrow. *Maybe he had time to see me today.*

A knock on the window snapped me back. I rolled down the window.

"Lacey?" Dr. Davis had his head tilted to one side. "Is everything okay?" He was holding a Wendy's bag. He must've been bringing lunch back to the office.

I shook my head.

"Follow me. I don't have another appointment for thirty minutes."

After locking my car, I followed him upstairs and into his office, where he set the Wendy's bag down on his desk.

"I'm sorry. I'm interrupting your lunch," I said.

"Sit." He motioned to his couch while he pushed a button on his desk phone.

I sat on the edge of the cushion, bouncing my knee.

"Tell me what happened." He eased down into a chair opposite me, crossing one leg over the other.

"Are you sure I'm not bothering you?" I twined a strand of my hair between my fingers.

"You're not." He crossed his hands in his lap.

Before I even said a word, I started crying as I thought about Kade. I grabbed the box of tissues off the end table and set it in my lap. In between sobbing and blowing my nose, I finally spilled my guts to him about what Kade had told me. Afterwards, I didn't feel any better. Just recounting the story made me feel worse.

"Let me get this straight." He rubbed his goatee. "You're upset because Coach is worried about your wellbeing and that he wanted Kade to watch out for you so you wouldn't be bullied."

I nodded, patting my nose with a Kleenex. He made it sound like I was off my rocker.

"Is Kade doing this for the other girls on the team?" With his elbow on the arm of the chair he held up his chin with his fingers.

"I don't know. I don't think so." Were the Maxwell brothers protecting Renee too? I filed the thought away. It wouldn't change how I felt at the moment. I made a mental note to ask Kade. Well, if I ever spoke to him again.

"What else, Lacey? It seems like you may be upset about more than you told me."

"You know how you asked me to play that get-to-know-you game?"

His chin dipped once.

"I did with Kade. Or at least I think I did. The more I hung out with Kade, the more we talked. He told me a few things about his past. I told him about my PTSD, my mom, and my sister. He told me he loved me. One thing led to another, and I shared my feelings with him." I left out the intimate details, of course. "But he lied to me. I was only a job to him."

"You think Kade told you how he felt to protect you? And his feelings aren't real?" He dropped his hand from his chin.

"It's all a lie." I didn't know what to believe anymore. The softness of his touch, the love in his eyes, the passion behind his kiss was real. *Wasn't it? Could someone turn feelings on and off in the blink of an eye?*

"Why, Lacey?" He tilted his head.

"Coach put him up to it."

"Did Coach Dean tell Kade to love you?"

"Well...no," I said in a small voice, dropping my gaze.

"People don't just tell others they love them because someone else put them up to it. Love is a strong emotion. In my personal experience, the majority of people in this world tread carefully when first using the word love. And I believe it's harder for men to express that emotion. Besides, how is the fact that Kade loves you going to protect you? Some would argue that if Kade had any enemies, you would be in more danger."

My lips parted slightly. I didn't mention anything about Greg Sullivan. Did he know about Greg and Kade's hatred for one another? I mean, Kody was a patient of his. Was Dr. Davis defending the Maxwells because he knew Kody?

A headache throbbed, and I rubbed my temples.

"Lacey, how's everything else?"

I lifted my head. I wasn't sure I had time to tell him about my latest trigger, Renee, and I didn't want to. I had too much swimming around in my head right now. "Okay. Can we reschedule tomorrow's appointment? I have a couple of tests after school."

"Sure. In the meantime, I want you to talk with Kade—when you're ready, of course. He deserves to understand how you feel. It's not healthy to shut down, not with your PTSD. This could slow your progress."

"I'll try." *Not anytime soon.* My heart hurt too much to even think about talking to him.

When I left his office, I called Dad. He didn't answer, so I left him a voice message in case the school informed him of my absence. I explained I needed a quiet place to study for my tests, and I would be at the town library.

The librarian nodded to me when I walked in. A few people sat at the tables, reading or typing on their laptops. I found a spot away from the front and did nothing more than stare off into space. I loved the solitude of a library. For me, the place gave me a chance to gather my thoughts. I drifted off, thinking of a thousand things. *What harm would there be in talking to Coach about Aaron?* I'd just ask him to keep our conversation confidential. He already knew Aaron had a history of bullying.

Then something Dr. Davis had said nagged at me. "Did Coach tell Kade to love you?"

Christ! Kade didn't strike me as the type of guy to tell any woman willy-nilly that he loved her. Plus Kody had said Kade was head over heels in love with me, and that he hadn't allowed anyone in since his sister's death. So why did my heart still feel like a steamroller kept running over it?

CHAPTER 20

After I got home from the library, I locked myself in my room. Mary had tried to get me to eat. Nausea percolated in my stomach at the mention of food. Then Dad knocked on my door. When he walked in rubbing his neck, the blood drained from me.

"So, do you want to tell me why you left school early?" he'd asked.

No. "I went to see Dr. Davis." I had to 'fess up. He'd see the doctor's bill. "I had too much going on in my head. I had to see him," I'd said.

"In the middle of a school day? Is this about the girl that looks like..."

I didn't remember if I'd told him about Renee, but I did tell Mary. Anger welled up in me.

"Say her name, Dad. Please?" I cried. I wanted to hear him say Julie or Mom. I was afraid if he couldn't, we'd grow farther apart.

"Lacey, we've had this conversation. Now, you're grounded for a week. No hanging out with friends or Kade. You're to go to school then come straight home, with the exception of tryouts on Friday. Is that understood?" he said in an unyielding tone.

I didn't bother to tell him I wasn't talking to Kade. I wasn't sure what good it would do, anyway. Sleep didn't come easily. I tried to study. I couldn't concentrate. So I pulled out the box in my closet with the scrapbook that Julie had given me for Christmas a couple of years ago. Various pictures of Mom, Dad, Rob, Julie and me covered the pages. I reminisced as I flipped through the book—a picture of Julie and me, sunbathing on the beach at Lake Tahoe—another with her and me dressed in gowns for one of Mom's charity balls. I trailed my finger over a picture of Mom and Dad. Rob had captured a shot of them in a quiet moment where Dad had his forehead against Mom's with his hand on her face. A tear dropped to my comforter. They looked like they'd carved their own private world. The last page had words, not pictures. *You have a pure heart and a beautiful soul. Always protect it. Love Ya, Julie*, written on the satiny paper. More tears streamed down my face. I'd forgotten she'd written this in the back. I read it again. More tears. More sniffles.

"I wish you were here, Sis," I said out loud. "I wish you could meet Kade. You'd like him. You'd probably beat him for making me cry, but I think he'd let you. He's not like Brad. Kade stirs feelings in me I never thought I had. I've been a mess since you've been gone. Dad has, too. If Mom is with you, say hi for me. We miss you guys so much."

Afterwards, I'd thrown my head into my pillow and cried myself to sleep.

I'd thought after all the crying I'd done, I'd feel better in the morning. But my heart still ached, my eyes were puffy, and I hated the world. I would've loved to stay home from school, but Dad would've grounded me for a year instead of a week, and I had to take my math tests.

The sun beat down as I got out of my car. I wasn't looking forward to seeing Kade. I had no idea yet how I'd react.

"Hey, girl," Becca said, walking up to me as I crossed the school lot. Red tinted the area around her nose, and her eyes were swollen like mine.

"Hi. Are you feeling better?" I asked.

"Are you coming down with something, too? You look like crap."

"Nah. Kade and I had a fight."

"Over...?" she asked as we stopped near the flagpole.

I told her what had happened between Kade and me yesterday in the hopes she'd have a different perspective than Dr. Davis.

"So you think Kade's feelings for you are a lie, and he's doing a job ordered by Coach Dean?" She pushed strands of her hair behind her ear.

"In a nutshell," I said. I adjusted my backpack on my shoulder.

She rapped her knuckles on my head. "Is there a brain inside your thick skull? For a smart girl, you're stupid. What guy in their right mind would ever tell a girl he loves her just to protect her? Are you serious?"

"Becca—"

"No. I know your past still haunts you. It would haunt me, too, if I lost my mom. Maybe someday you can explain the whole thing to me, but right now, learn to let go. Kade loves you. Everyone in this school can tell. Hell, everyone is shocked. Yes, you've pissed off a few girls around here, but my God, who the flip cares? Kade is yours. Take him. Love him. If you don't, I will stage an intervention, and you won't like it." She put her fists on her jeans-clad hips.

I berated myself as her voice rose and fell. She made me feel more like an idiot than Dr. Davis had. "I'm not ready to talk to him. And he should've told me."

"Fine, but you better talk to him eventually," she said. "Now, let's get to homeroom."

We walked in silence until we reached the door. "Wait." I grabbed her arm.

She lifted her perfectly manicured eyebrows.

"Thank you for being a friend. I didn't have any friends who were girls in California."

She threw her arms around me in a tight hug. "I got your back."

We split up when we entered the building since we didn't have homeroom together. No sooner had I sat down than Ms. Vander told me to go to Coach Dean's office. *Great! So much for avoiding Coach.*

As I approached Coach's office, the voices trickling out of it stopped me in my tracks. Familiar ones. I wasn't facing Kade for the first time since our argument in front of Coach. *What was he doing in there anyway?* Then one of the triplets laughed. Suddenly, Becca's idea of an intervention skittered through my brain. *Oh, no. Hell, no, actually.* They were not getting me into Coach's office to gang up on me. Pivoting, I started back the way I came. My nose itched. I squeezed it together. *Don't sneeze.* As soon as I let go, I sneezed. The sound reverberated off the walls.

Footsteps scuffed behind me.

Keep walking.

"Where're you going?" A large hand gripped my arm.

I muttered several swear words under my breath.

"We just want to talk." Kelton's blue eyes looked down at me. "It's just Coach, me and my brothers. This has to happen, Lacey. I know you're pissed at Kade. But don't be. Be pissed with me. I'm the one who is forcing this meeting between you and Coach. Kade has nothing to do with it."

"Mind your own business, Kelton. I don't need your protection or help."

"Is that what you think we're doing?" He chuckled. "We're not the secret service. We don't protect anyone but our family. You're family, Lacey, whether you want to believe that or not. My brother is so fucking sick over your fight yesterday. Wake up, girl. Stop being stupid."

"Fuck you, Kelton. I get why Coach did his homework on me. But Kade? He was at the ball field that first night to watch me. To me, that's stalking."

"So what? Didn't you have several people in the stands watching you practice? Were they all stalking you too?" Underneath his lashes, anger burned in his eyes.

"I haven't even made the team. I don't know what the big deal is. I may not even do well on Friday."

"I swear if you weren't a girl, I'd punch you. You're going to go tell Coach why you passed out. You're also going to tell him that Aaron has threatened you. Then you and my brother are going to be locked in a room, and you're not coming out until you both work out your differences."

"Who made you boss?" I yanked away my arm.

"Lacey, don't test me. I think the world of you, but I will not hesitate to carry you over my shoulder into the office if you decide to walk out of here."

I laughed.

He didn't. He bent over and wrapped his arms around my legs, throwing me over his shoulder. My backpack fell off my arm, thudding to the floor.

"Kelton, put me down." I was mortified, but I was even angrier at his arrogance.

"No, I like the view. You do have a nice ass."

"I swear I'm going to cut your balls off."

"Get in line. I know several girls who are ahead of you."

I beat on his back as I kicked his front, hoping I would hit his manly parts. I hit something hard.

"That was my hip. Try again." He laughed.

Asshat. I was on the verge of screaming.

"Kel, put her down," Kade barked.

He set me upright in Coach's office next to Kade, who reached out to steady me, but I lunged for Kelton. I was going to kill him. Kade grabbed my waist and gently held me as Kelton stepped away with his hands in the air.

"This isn't over with, Kelton," I snapped, storming toward the door.

"Lacey, where are you going?" Coach asked.

"I need to get my backpack." Then run like the wind. Who the hell did Kelton think he was? Once I had my backpack I shuffled grudgingly back into the office. Kade and Kelton stood to my right. Kross and Kody to the left.

"Have a seat, Lacey," Coach said in a calm tone as he propped his elbows up on top of his desk.

I huffed as I sat, not looking at Kade or the triplets.

"Close the door, Kross," Coach ordered.

The room fell silent as Kross nudged it shut. Well, except for Kelton, who was behind me, snickering. *Ass.*

"Lacey," Coach began. "The boys here are only trying to help. *I* want to help."

"Sorry, Coach, but how do you think you can help me? Aaron and I exchanged pleasantries. He hasn't bothered me since. End of story. I'm not on the team yet, so none of this should matter."

"Stubborn," Kade muttered.

I glared his way, and all I got was a crooked grin. *Ass number two.*

"If you don't clean up your attitude, there won't be a second tryout for you." Coach's eyes hardened.

Biting my tongue, I tensed every muscle. The man held my dream in his freaking hands.

"Now, can we talk?" he asked.

"Only, if these morons leave." I knew I was being a bitch, and I hadn't meant to be with Kody and Kross. They were being nice and quiet. Regardless, I wasn't going to talk about Julie in front of the triplets.

"Out, all of you."

"But, Coach," Kelton whined.

"Go," Coach barked.

Once Kade and his brothers closed the door, Coach said, "Tell me about Aaron." He leaned back in his chair.

"There's nothing to tell." I tucked my hair around my ear. "He doesn't want a girl showing him up on the field. I'm sure you knew that. He hasn't done anything to me, unless he's the one who broke into my locker."

"Well, that was the other reason I wanted to talk to you. We found the guilty party."

My eyes widened as I clutched the arm of the chair.

"A girl who had been in the locker room the day your gear was stolen came forward. She saw Tammy Reese prying open a locker with a screwdriver. At first she didn't think anything was suspicious. She pointed out that students forget their combinations occasionally, especially at the beginning of the school year. After questioning Tammy, she's now been suspended."

I wasn't surprised, and I should be relieved, but I wasn't. My gut told me Aaron still had something to do with this. Or did Tammy just decide to make my life hell since I was dating Kade? Regardless, they were both trouble.

"Who was the girl?" I didn't think he would tell me. I mean, I wouldn't want anyone to know if I came forward to rat on someone, but I wanted to thank her.

His brown eyes assessed me. "Details and witnesses are confidential. But I want you to tell me if Aaron bothers you. Or if there's any backlash from Tammy when she returns. Understood?"

"Yes." *No.* I had no intentions of running to Coach every time Aaron made idle threats. As far as Tammy was concerned, I would handle any crap she threw my way. *...Not sure how yet.*

"Anything else?" he asked as though he was waiting for me to tell him more.

Should I tell him why I passed out? Would it help my chances on Friday? He might give me a break. *No.* I didn't want help. I had to do this on my own. But if I didn't tell him and I passed out again, or worse, hurt someone, I might never have a chance at baseball. "Um..." I glanced at him. He leaned forward in his chair. "I didn't pass out from not eating or nerves."

"Lacey, I know you're still grieving. Principal Sanders and I are the only staff members who are aware. Remember, she talked to the principal at Crestview." He interlocked his fingers, prayer-like.

I did recall her mentioning something about talking to my last school when I'd gotten into a fight with Tammy. They did know Mom and Julie died. However, like everyone else, the details of their deaths were not revealed, since the police wanted to keep it quiet for their investigation.

"I am..." I started. "But because of their deaths, I developed PTSD. And certain triggers can cause me to black out. Renee was a trigger. She reminded me of my sister."

He had a blank expression on his face.

Dropping my gaze, I picked at nothing on my jeans. I didn't know if he was going to let me try out now. He'd said he was worried about the safety of his players. *What if he thought I was a risk?*

"Lacey, thank you for telling me. I know that had to be hard for you," he said softly.

I looked up. He'd taken off his hat, the fluorescent light above shining on his balding head.

"Are you still going to let me try out?" I asked, biting the inside of my lip.

He rubbed his jaw. "I believe in second chances. But if I see you wavering at all, I'll pull you out. You have to understand I need you at one hundred percent. If you can't show me that, then you won't be considered for a spot on the team. Clear?" he asked.

I nodded.

"You're free to go," he said as he tapped a few keys on his computer.

I didn't move. "One question. Why did you ask Kade to watch me?"

"I never asked Kade to watch you." He knitted his eyebrows together.

"But he said—"

"Lacey, no one who was around here two years ago wants a repeat performance. Sure, I would like to win state again, but not at the expense of fighting and bullying. When I found out the triplets were coming back to Kensington, you were enrolling specifically to try out for the team, and Renee expressed interest, I got concerned. I went to Kade and his father and shared those concerns."

"But why? What do the triplets have to do with me playing ball?"

"Nothing. You're not any different than Renee. Aaron has a few problems this year. He doesn't like girls on the team. He doesn't want anyone taking the spotlight away from him. And it's no secret, the rivalry between him and the Maxwell brothers. Frankly, out of everything I just said, my biggest concern is Kelton. He and Aaron have butted heads in the past. Kelton has a tendency to stir up trouble, too. When he does, the brothers stick together, and fists fly. So I needed the Maxwell family's guarantee they wouldn't be a problem. Nothing more. I don't want bad publicity this year."

"So why not ban Aaron from playing?"

"He hasn't done anything for me to sideline him. He's a good ballplayer. I already had a talk with him. He knows what's at stake. Now, you should get to class."

I pushed to my feet. I had one foot out the door then turned. "Coach, will I be facing Renee again on Friday?"

He looked up from his computer. "Sometimes, Lacey, facing your fears scares the demons away."

CHAPTER 21

After I left Coach's office, word about Tammy's suspension spread at lightning speed. Kids whispered in the halls and classes. I didn't pay attention to the gossip. A small part of me wished Coach hadn't found out. Sometimes people who got outed only returned with a vengeance. I prayed the name of the witness stayed hidden.

Kade and his brothers didn't bother me. I'd thought Kelton would've continually hounded me until Kade and I talked. Surprisingly, Kelton kept his distance in chemistry and throughout the entire day, as did Kross and Kody. Kody was my lab partner, but he didn't bring up Kade or Aaron. Even Kade didn't spare me a look in psychology. When I sneaked looks at him, he had his head buried in his book or looking at Mr. Dobson.

My trig and calculus tests were brutal. I didn't feel good when I handed them to Mrs. Flowers. It was hard to concentrate when all I kept thinking about was baseball, my conversation with Coach, Kade, Dad, my life, and the list went on. Would Coach have me facing Renee at tryouts? If so, could I face her again without having a panic attack? Now that Coach knew about my PTSD would he treat me any differently? Given that he'd said, "the way to get over your fears is to face your demons," I didn't think he would.

Then there was Kade. I loved him so much it hurt me to see him and infuriated me at the same time. Would I or could I get past the anger and the pain? Maybe Dad had it right all along when he hid behind his work to forget and to ease his pain. Maybe I needed to focus on school and baseball and forget about Kade.

The next day was much the same. Kross, Kelton, and Kody barely said anything to me. Kade gave me a passing glance in the hall. My heart exploded into a thousand pieces at the sadness in his eyes. I'd given him a second chance at my trust. He broke it. *How could I continue to trust him? How did anyone learn how to trust?*

I was on my way to meet Mark Wayland. I'd asked him at lunch if he would work with me on the ball field. Since he would be catching tomorrow during tryouts, I wanted us to get to know each other. A pitcher's success in part lay in the hands of the catcher. Catchers were more or less a pitcher's coach. Mark had agreed to practice, which surprised me since he knew Aaron.

Tyler was talking to Mark when I walked onto the field. "Hey, Lacey," Mark said, his red hair matted to his head. "Tyler was trying to give me advice on what pitches you need to practice."

I appreciated Tyler's interest in my success, and all the time he'd spent with me since I moved here, but he needed to cut the apron strings. I knew what to work on.

Tyler glanced at me, and shrugged the arm he had in a sling. "Are we still on for a shake tonight?"

I'd forgotten all about getting together with Tyler. "I'm sorry. I can't. My dad needs me home."

His smile faded. I didn't want to tell him I was grounded. I didn't know Mark that well. He hung out with Aaron. I didn't need any more rumors going around school about me.

"I gotta run," Tyler said abruptly. He tucked a hand in his pocket and started for the stairs.

I let out sigh. "Tyler, wait." I jogged up to him.

"I'm grounded," I said low. "Why don't you come by the house later?" Dad had work, and Mary was supposedly going out with Mr. Wiley again. Tyler wouldn't stay long, anyway.

"Great," Tyler said as his lips spread slowly.

Mark and I practiced. I worked on all three of my pitches and focused on the slider, which was getting better. Mark even complimented me on it. After about thirty minutes, it started to drizzle. I continued to throw. He continued to catch and coach me. We lasted an additional thirty minutes before the dark clouds really opened up. Large raindrops battered down on us, which was our cue to call it quits.

By the time I got home, I was a wet noodle. I kicked off my cleats in the laundry room between the garage and kitchen, then found Dad with his keys in hand, ready to leave for work.

"Don't forget tryouts are tomorrow," I said.

"I know." He kissed my hair. "Mary is out. She left dinner for you in the fridge." Then he was gone.

I made a beeline for the shower. After I peeled off my wet clothes, I stood in the middle of the tiled bathroom, contemplating if I wanted to take a bath or shower. The more I stared absently at the tub, the more my mind started to conjure up images of Kade, naked Kade. Kade and me naked, bodies twined together. Kade on top of me. Kade inside me. Kade's lips on me. Kade's sad eyes at school today. *Stop torturing yourself.*

My inner voice scolded me all through my shower and as I dressed. I had to keep the little devil talking in my head so I wouldn't break down and cry. Tyler texted me around six p.m. and said he was on his way. I loped down to the kitchen. Mary had made spaghetti. She'd packaged individual servings. I pulled out a container, popped the top and heated it up in the microwave. When it dinged, so did the door-bell. I went and opened the door.

The rain beat against the gutters, the sound dinging like a low note on a xylophone.

I waved Tyler in before pushing the door shut.

"I was just heating up dinner. Would you like a bowl of spaghetti?" I asked.

"Sure," he said as he followed me into the kitchen. He made himself comfortable on one of the barstools at the kitchen island and combed his fingers through his damp blond hair.

While I prepared a bowl for him, Tyler asked, "How did practice go?"

"Good. I think I have my slider tuned up. Mark was great in helping me. I should do well tomorrow." Aside from how depressed I felt over Kade, I did feel confident about my pitching—although if I thought about whether Coach was going to make me pitch to Renee, my nerves kicked in.

When the food was ready, I sat down next to Tyler.

An awkward silence grew as we ate. I struggled to find words. What could I say that I hadn't already said to him?

"Lacey." He set down his fork, his hand reaching out to touch mine. "I want to be more than friends."

Whoa! I hopped off the barstool, taking my plate of spaghetti with me. *How many times did I have to tell him I wasn't interested?* Not to mention, he knew Kade and I were an item.

He followed me. "Hey, let me finish."

"Look, Tyler." I turned midstride, colliding with him. As I did, my spaghetti ended up on my chest. *Crap*!

He grabbed a dishtowel that was sitting on the island behind him, then handed it to me. I needed more than a towel to clean myself as the spaghetti had slid down my legs to the floor.

"I need to change clothes," I said as I dumped the container in the sink. I also wanted a chance to clear my head for a moment so I could think of another way to let him down without being a bitch.

"Lacey, let me start over." He stood a few feet away near the fridge. "I came here to apologize. I shouldn't have been an ass to you. You've been clear with me. While I do want more with you, I won't risk our friendship."

I was officially an idiot for overreacting. Still, he should have started his speech like that in the first place. Could we even truly be friends if he wanted more? I thought about Becca. She was beautiful and a good person. Why didn't Tyler like her? I studied him as he stood beneath the recessed lights. Softness shone in his eyes, but a muscle ticked in his jaw. This had to be hard for him.

"I'm sorry, Tyler. I shouldn't have lost it. I've been a little on edge lately. Let me change, then we can finish talking." I hurried upstairs to my room. I shucked my sauce-ridden clothes for an old pair of worn-out jeans and a button-up blouse.

The doorbell rang.

"Tyler, can you get the door?" I shouted as I crossed the hall into the bathroom.

It was probably a door-to-door salesperson. We'd gotten a few solicitors since we moved here. I used the facilities then washed my hands. As I made my way downstairs, I noticed a couple of buttons weren't fastened on my blouse. I had my hand on a button when Kade's fiery voice made the hairs on my arm stand at attention.

"What are you doing here, Tyler?" Kade asked in a tone that could cut metal.

I ran down, jumping the steps two at a time. I flew around the bannister, down the hall and into the kitchen. A knot coiled tightly in my stomach.

"It's none of your business," Tyler said.

Oh, God. Kade and Tyler were nose to nose near the island.

"I think it is my business. You're trying to move in on my girl?" Kade said through clenched teeth.

"What are you doing here, Kade?" I asked as I grabbed hold of his flexing bicep.

He looked at me, his gaze traveling down my chest, where it lingered for a second before he narrowed his eyes at me.

I glanced down. *Crap!* My cleavage was on display. "You should leave, Kade." He needed to cool off.

"I should go," Tyler said, backing away from Kade.

"No," I blurted out. Tyler was my guest, and Kade wasn't going to bully him into leaving.

Kade glowered at me, his nostrils flaring. Then he stormed out of the kitchen.

I'll be right back, I mouthed to Tyler. I scurried to the front door. "Kade?"

I followed him onto the porch, closing the door behind me. "Kade," I called again. Maybe he shouldn't drive in the state of mind he was in. I remembered the ride to the hospital, when he almost hit a car.

He turned from the edge of the porch, hands in his torn jeans, hair wet, eyes appraising. He glanced at Tyler's SUV then back at me.

Leaves swirled and rustled in the yard. Water dripped from somewhere off the roof or the gutters.

"So you get mad at me then run to Tyler." His tone was colder than ice, if that were possible, but his eyes flashed with hurt.

I clenched my hands at my side so he wouldn't see them shaking. My emotions were on a death-defying rollercoaster ride—anger, love, disappointment, hurt, the cycle continually repeating.

"It's not what you think," I said quietly.

He glanced at my cleavage. "It isn't, huh?"

I was convinced that anything I said wouldn't help to soothe his anger or the pain.

Nature's sounds: twittering, rain, leaves scraping together, drips, dings, everything but his voice or mine. He studied me for what felt like forever. My body shivered and not from the brisk air. Then he closed the distance between us, his lips infinitesimally close to mine. I wanted to crawl up his beautiful, hard body and kiss him to death. But his rage only served to heighten mine.

The hurt in his eyes cleared. In its place was a blank mass of nothing. When he brushed his lips lightly over mine, I turned my head. I wasn't ready to kiss and make up, not in his state of emotional chaos, or mine.

He hit the door above my head with his hand.

I flinched.

He marched to his truck, taking long strides through the rain. I didn't move until the sound of his engine became a whisper in the night air. I dragged my back down the door until my butt hit the cold wet porch. I hugged my knees to my chest and shuddered. Tears pooled in my eyes. *Did I just lose Kade Maxwell?*

⚜

AFTER KADE LEFT me at my doorstep, I'd gone back inside to apologize to Tyler. When he looked at me with puppy dog eyes, the dam of water burst. I'd tried to stop the tears, but they only got worse when he hugged me. I hated for him to see me like that. But the gentleness of his touch calmed me, and I didn't want to be alone. We didn't talk about Kade or the almost-fight between them. He just held me. I appreciated the quiet between us. The last thing I wanted to hear was *I told you so*. But a good friend wouldn't say something like that.

Puddles of water dotted the road's edge in the morning. The rain had quit sometime during the night. I should have been excited that it wasn't raining because tryouts were that afternoon. I had one last chance at my baseball dream. But as I drove myself to school, all I had on my mind was Kade. The hurt in his eyes kept me awake for most of the night. I shook off the thought as I searched for a parking space in the school's lot. I could understand why Kade parked down at the sports complex. I'd just found a space at the end of an aisle when I spotted Kelton, Kross and Kody leaning against Kross's red Jeep Wrangler three spaces over from me.

I gathered my backpack, jumped out, and walked straight behind my car, between two parked cars to the next aisle. I wasn't trying to be rude. I didn't want to talk about Kade or hear what they had to say. Actually, given Kelton's arrogance and how he carried me into Coach's office, I didn't trust him, and I wanted to try and concentrate on baseball, not Kade.

"Lacey," one of the triplets shouted.

Grabbing the straps of my backpack, I walked at a brisk pace. I passed a boy with black-rimmed glasses.

"Kelton is calling you," the boy said.

I smiled and walked faster, hopping up onto the sidewalk in front of an oak tree. I'd just taken one step past the oak when voices behind me cut through the soft breeze.

"Lacey, we just want to talk," one of the triplets said.

Listen to them. Then maybe they'll leave you alone. I spun around. "What?"

"Whoa," Kelton said. "Who pissed in your cornflakes?"

The Maxwells. All three of them were a force to be reckoned with, standing together, their broad shoulders back, strong jaws jutting forward and eyes shining with confidence and determination.

I narrowed my eyes at the pompous idiot. "Kelton, don't start with me today. Now, say what's on your mind. I have to get to class."

"We have twenty minutes before the bell," Kody said as a matter of fact.

"I don't. So talk." I did, but I wasn't telling them that.

A short redheaded girl with streaks of white through her hair passed us. "Hi, Kody," she said.

Kody didn't look at or acknowledge the girl.

"Would you and Kade please talk?" Kross asked in a sweet tone.

"Have you ever tried to talk to someone when you're mad?" I asked as I pinned my gaze on each of them.

They held their backpacks on one shoulder, scrutinizing me like I was this weird chick who'd just dropped down from another planet.

"If you haven't, I'll tell you: the outcome is never good. You end up either getting angrier, or saying things you shouldn't have. So until I'm ready, I'm not talking to Kade." He probably didn't want to have anything to do with me after he saw Tyler at my house. "And while I appreciate your love for your brother, the tension between us is our business." I stormed away, leaving the triplets with their mouths hanging open.

The rest of the morning was quiet. I sat through my classes daydreaming about Kade or baseball. I'd wanted to tell Becca about what happened with Kade last night, but I couldn't risk crying again. For the past few days that was all I'd been doing.

At around lunchtime, the halls started to thin out. I'd seen Grace in English. I overheard her telling one of her friends the cheerleaders were leaving after lunch for an away football game tonight. Speaking of cheerleaders, Tammy was back from her three-day suspension. I'd seen her in the hall earlier. As usual, we both just snarled at one another.

Becca and I walked into the cafeteria. The room buzzed with chatter, kids setting plates and silverware on trays, the ding of the cash register, and the scrape of chairs along the floor. We scanned the room, searching for an empty spot. I guessed the halls were fairly empty since everyone was in here.

"Over there." Becca pointed a purple nail to an empty table halfway down along the window.

"I don't think so. Let's find another one." Kade and his brothers sat directly behind the table she chose. As though he knew I had walked in, he lifted his gaze. With no emotion on his face, he sized me up, head to toe, slow and leisurely. My pulse quickened.

"You're going to have to make nice. I don't see another place right at the moment," she said. "Just sit with your back to them."

Easier said than done. With my luck, Kelton would turn around and pester me. Then I would do something I would regret, like punch him and end up in the principal's office.

"Come on," Becca said as she hooked her fingers around my arm as though we were going for a stroll in the park.

I didn't have much of choice if I wanted to eat. Reluctantly, I trudged down the open aisle with Becca tethered to me. As we did, I spotted Renee, sitting with a girl at a table on our right. I froze.

Becca faltered. "What's wrong, Lacey? Hey, Renee. Hi, Glory." Becca let go of my arm. "Oh, can we sit with you?" she asked Renee.

"Sure, these two chairs aren't taken," Renee said.

I'd avoided Renee every chance I had this past week. Even in psych class. Lifting her amber gaze, she looked directly at me. All the blood in my veins thickened. Images of Julie surfaced. I squeezed my eyes shut. *She's not Julie. She's not my sister.*

My system came alive when I slowly opened my eyes and found a body, tall and muscular, shielding my view.

"Baby?" Kade's voice massaged my ears.

Blinking, I craned my neck upward. Worry lines etched his forehead.

"I'm not sure I can pitch to her today," I whispered.

"Maybe you should talk to her. It might help."

I swallowed. Would it? *Push forward. Face your demons.* Words of doctors scampered through my brain. Even Coach said something similar.

"Just try, Lace. I'm here if you need me." He crossed the floor to rejoin his brothers. As he turned to sit he inclined his head, urging me.

I centered on Kade like he was my lifeline. He knew some of my demons, and even though I was mad at him, he was the only one in this room I trusted to save me if I freaked. He dipped his head again. I steeled my shoulders, and swung my gaze to Renee, Becca, and a girl I hadn't met.

"Lacey, sit," Becca said.

I slid into a chair next to Renee and opposite Becca. I could do this. *Relax. Breathe.*

"What did he say?" Becca shot a quick glance over her shoulder at Kade.

"I'll tell you later."

"Lacey, this is Glory," Renee introduced us.

"Hey," Glory said. She had blond hair, big blue eyes, and the longest lashes I'd ever seen.

"Are you ready for today, Lacey?" Renee asked.

"I guess." Before Kade showed up at my house last night, I would've said yes. But when I left the house this morning, I had my doubts if I was ready for anything today. Now, sitting here with Renee, I wasn't anywhere near ready for tryouts.

"So, what happened to you on the mound last week, if you don't mind me asking?" Renee's voice was gentle.

Honesty is the best policy. Face your demons. "I got upset because you remind me of someone I once knew who passed away." I'd told Becca Mom died, but not Julie. I owed Becca the story before Renee. I'd hoped Becca didn't question why I thought Renee reminded me of my mom—at least, not here.

Becca's tiny warm hand covered mine.

"I'm so sorry," Renee said softly.

I had to get away before the emotion clogging my throat exploded, or worse—I'd flashback, then black out.

"Thank you. I better go." I jumped out of my seat, not looking at Renee or anyone at the table. I needed one person right now.

"Lacey." Becca trailed behind.

"I'm fine," I said as I practically ran to Kade.

He slipped into the empty chair between him and Kross before I reached the table. I needed his warmth, and for him to tell me I would be okay.

Leaning in, he draped an arm over the back of my chair. "She's not your sister," he whispered. "I'm right here." His voice, soft and silky, caressed my frazzled nerves.

Becca plopped down in the chair on the opposite side of the table, between Kelton and Kody.

"So, Lacey. You're not mad at Kade anymore?" Kelton's eyebrows rose.

"Shut it, Kel," Kade said. "Actually, Kross, Kody, and Kelton: leave. Becca, would you mind if I talk with Lacey?"

Grinning like a cat who just caught a mouse, Kelton pushed back his chair, picked up his tray, and blended into the crowd of students who were depositing their dirty trays at the opposite end of the lunch line. With no expression on his face, Kody followed Kelton.

Kross unfolded his bulk. "Becca, can I talk to you?" He lifted his tray.

She rose. "Lacey, are you going to be okay?" She eyed Kade then me.

"I'll be fine," I said. In that moment, I felt protected. Not that I was in any danger with Kade, but I hadn't had a girl friend who'd worried about me. Most of my friends were guys back at Crestview. The last girl I had as a best friend was in the eighth grade, and she moved away just before high school started.

Kross and Becca's voices waned, leaving Kade and me alone.

"Are you going to be okay at tryouts this afternoon?" he asked.

"Yeah." *I don't know.* At least no one was going to steal my sports bag unless they broke into my car. As soon as school ended I had to rush to my car, get my gear and change. "Thank you for helping me with Renee."

"I'd do anything for you, Lace."

"I know," I mumbled.

"Can we talk later?" he asked.

Someone in the cafeteria shouted Aaron's name. I looked up. Aaron strutted into the room, tall and slim, like he owned the school, with Tammy Reese on his arm. She wore her cheerleader uniform and had a blue and black painted bulldog on her left cheek.

They wandered toward us and stopped at our table. "Lacey? Kade?" Aaron said, smiling.

He oozed sleaze. I had a strong desire to run into the girls' bathroom and scrub my hands several times, even though I hadn't shaken his hand. Tammy glowered at me. At least she didn't come off as fake. I could handle honesty.

"So, Lacey. Did you bring your gear today? Or—"

Kade's chair flew backwards as he stood. "Get the fuck out of here," Kade barked as he got in Aaron's face.

Every conversation ceased in the room. All eyes focused on us.

"Or what, Maxwell? Go ahead. Touch me. I dare you." Aaron puffed out his chest.

I leapt to my feet and grabbed hold of Kade's fist. "He's not worth it," I said to Kade.

"Listen to your crazy girlfriend," Aaron said in a cloying, slimy tone.

"You know, Aaron, you should be afraid of a crazy girl like me." My tone was calm. Then I shifted my attention to Tammy. "Welcome back. Hopefully, you learned a lesson."

"Oh, I've learned quite a bit." She sneered.

"I hope you make the team, Lacey." Again, his words didn't match his tone or the threat in his eyes. "Good luck today. I'll see you on the field." Aaron brushed Kade's shoulder as he and Tammy strode to a table somewhere behind us.

۞

AFTER LUNCH I couldn't think straight. Not only because of Aaron and Tammy's little display of bravado, but because of how natural it was for me to seek out Kade in a state of near panic. I was shocked how his voice tamed my inner crisis. I mentally slapped myself a few times to stop thinking of him. I had to think about baseball and tryouts. Not the guy I wanted to curl up with and snuggle. Not the guy I wanted to feel against me. And certainly not the guy I wanted to do all kinds of

R-rated things with. Thankfully, when the bell rang at the end of the day, my concentration on Kade diminished. Well, almost—I'd been about to run out of psychology class when out of my peripheral vision I caught Kade looking at me. I stared back, trying to read through his clinical expression when a body passed in front of me. I blinked and found Renee walking by.

"See you on the field, Lacey," she said with her lips curved on one side.

Just like that, my world of Kade died and fear crawled through me. My pulse beat erratically as though I was riding shotgun in a NASCAR race. *She's not your sister.*

I'd bolted out of class, sidestepping the mass of students who wanted to get the heck out of school and start their weekend. I just wanted air. *Outside air.* Thankfully, on my way to my car, a hard wind blew, helping to cool the burn in my lungs. After I retrieved my gear, I changed in one of the girls' bathrooms in the sports complex. I wasn't going anywhere near the locker room for two reasons. One: I didn't know if Renee would be in there changing. I had to keep my nerves under control. The less I saw of her, the better. That way if I had to pitch to her again, I might not freak. The second reason was that I didn't trust Tammy. I didn't want anything to go wrong. My self-defense instructor had taught me to never take the same route home. Always spice up a routine with variety. It keeps the potential attackers off kilter.

Once I suited up, I headed down to the field. My route today wasn't through the tunnel. Instead I exited the sports complex and followed a path down to a small opening leading to the stairs. The field was designed somewhat like a fishbowl. On the left field side, a small grassy hill curved down from the parking lot to the bleachers. As I climbed down, a few kids were lounging on the hill, their voices a whisper on the steady wind. I tuned them out, going through my breathing exercises as I gave myself a pep talk. Then I visualized my pitches in my head. *Fastball. Curveball. Slider.*

Leaves kicked up around me, and so did the fragrance of freshly cut grass. Small, puffy clouds floated by, blocking out the sun every few seconds. I'd just planted a cleated foot on the field when I spotted Aaron walking out of the dugout, messing with his glove. I steeled my shoulders and tucked my glove under my arm. I glanced out into right field. I needed to get to the bullpen. I could breeze past him or I could walk out over the pitching mound then out to the bullpen. The problem was that Kelton was throwing to a boy at first base, so I had to walk by Aaron. Surely he wouldn't give me attitude with Coach Dean standing outside the right field dugout. I started to jog, but didn't get far. Aaron held up his gloved hand. I slowed my pace, but kept walking. He tagged alongside me.

"So, are you going to pass out today, Lacey?" he asked, his blond hair curling over the back of his ball cap.

Don't let him get to you. "You know, I'm sure at one point in your life you were a sweet boy. But I think one too many baseballs hit you in the head," I said calmly.

We approached Coach, who had a concerned look on his face. I smiled. The tightness around Coach's eyes relaxed.

"I see you didn't have any problems with losing your sports bag." He looked down at me with a cocksure smile on his face as we walked past Coach, his green eyes alight with pleasure. Then he glanced over his shoulder and back at me. "I was sad to hear that my plan got Tammy in trouble."

Keep it together. "Should we walk back to Coach and tell him your confession?"

"You can tell him. But it will be my word against yours."

I had to get through tryouts. "Hopefully, I'll get a chance to pitch to you today. Maybe then I can knock some respect into your thick skull."

He smirked. "I look forward to it. And if you do make the team, I'll make it so you never pitch again." He lost his smile as his eyes hardened. "Oh, and again, you can tattle all you want. Remember—my word against yours." Then he trotted off.

I stilled for a minute as the words *sleaze* and *asswipe* flittered through my mind. *Was he serious? Stay focused. He's only trying to scare you so you'll pass out again. He's messing with your mind.* The Maxwells had said Aaron would get into my head. That was it. Besides, I'd come too far to let a creep like him scare me out of my dream. *Never give up.* My mom's advice rang in my head. I took a breath then jogged out to the bullpen, repeating, *Fastball. Curveball. Slider.*

When I entered the bullpen a boy named Todd was warming up.

"Glad you could join us, Robinson," Coach Lee said. "You're two minutes late. Is this how you want to start?" He glanced at the watch on his right wrist.

Holy crap! I hadn't even made the team, and I was already getting my butt handed to me.

"No sir," I said as I glanced at Todd, who had fear stamped on his baby-face. Todd and three other boys cowered at the snap in Coach's voice.

"Todd, take a seat. Lacey, warm up," Coach Lee ordered.

I went through my normal routine. My pitches were all over the place. *What the heck was going on?* I'd practiced yesterday. My arm was loose. *Stop thinking about Aaron and pitch the damn ball, and find your flippin' zone.* I laughed.

"Something funny, Robinson? Because I don't think you should be laughing at the way you're pitching," Coach Lee said as he caught my last ball.

"No sir." I glanced at the boys sitting on the bench—their eyes downcast at their cleats or the ground.

"Mmmm," he said as he threw the ball back.

I continued to warm up, rotating among fastball, curveball, and slider. My arm got looser, my pitches better. I'd wanted to practice my slider a few more times, but Coach Dean called everyone in.

The five of us vying for a spot on the team trudged out. Coach Dean had three pitching spots available. I'd watched each of the boys pitch, and they were good. I especially worried about Todd. He had a wicked fastball. I couldn't say how fast his clocked, but his delivery was smooth, high cock of his leg, balance in his delivery, and a beautiful snap when the ball hit the catcher's glove. While his fastball was good, he had a perfect splitter pitch. I tried to throw a splitter, which was really a split-finger fastball, but my hands weren't big enough. In order to execute it flawlessly, the ball had to be choked deep into the hand, and Todd had big hands.

No sooner had we settled in the dugout than Coach Dean called my name. I grabbed my glove and headed out. The stands had several spectators, and I immediately homed in on Kade, who was sitting next to a man with honey-brown hair much like Kade's. Was that his dad? My gaze lingered for a second before I continued to scan the crowd to look for my own dad. He sat on Kade's right. Relief washed over me. I'd reminded him last night before he left for work, but I hadn't known for sure if some problem at the club would prevent him from being here again. He nodded and smiled. *The two men in my life were here to support me. I could do this.* I swept my gaze over the rest of the stands.

Becca sat next to my dad, and Kody sat next to his. The only other person I would've liked to be here was Tyler, even with the tension between him and Kade. Tyler had a doctor's appointment this morning to get his arm looked at, and then he was off to the away game. Three rows behind Kade sat Greg Sullivan and two guys who seemed too old to be on school grounds. Actually, the hairs on my neck rose when one of them pointed at me. I'd wondered if those were the men who Hunt had said worked for that Pitt guy.

"Lacey." Coach Dean's voice broke through my concentration. "Since you didn't get to finish pitching last week, you'll be facing two batters today. Aaron is up first."

My wish came true. Maybe I should try to ruin one of his arms so he couldn't throw. Then he might falter in tryouts and not make the team.

Mark Wayland ran out of the dugout in full catcher's gear. "Same setup as last week, Lacey. Remember your follow through like yesterday," he said as we walked out to home plate. "One for curveball, two for fastball, and three for slider." He handed me the ball.

"Got it." I walked out to the mound, turning the ball inside my glove. *Fastball. Curveball. Slider. Zone.* When I stepped onto the mound, I dug my heel in the dirt around the rubber.

Kelton and Kross were sitting in the dugout. Coach had other boys I didn't know playing the field.

I threw a few warm-up pitches to Mark. Aaron took a couple of practice swings before crowding the plate. As usual, I checked to ensure the field was ready. I wound up and released. Coach Lee, who'd resumed his umpire position, called it a strike. My shoulders relaxed. After two more pitches, the count was one ball and two strikes.

A few of the spectators screamed, "Strike him out!"

Inwardly, I smiled. Outwardly, Aaron didn't. He glowered at me. He was probably waiting for me to plant my face in the dirt like I did last week. *Not going to happen.* At least, not with him. If anything, he fueled my adrenaline, making me dip into my zone. *Maybe I should hold true to my threat to knock some respect into him.*

Aaron kicked one foot out of the box, a sign he needed a minute. He wiped his hands down his pants while he kept the bat between his legs. Then he rubbed both hands together before gripping the bat. He crouched into his stance and swung a few times.

Coach had said that Aaron was a good ballplayer. His batting average every season teetered on four hundred. I couldn't worry about his average. I only needed one more strike. I inhaled and watched Mark for the signs. I adjusted my ball cap, my gaze traveling from Mark to Aaron. He released one of his hands from the bat and pointed to the outfield. *Was he doing what I think he was doing?* I gripped the ball tightly. He was good, but he wasn't Babe Ruth. I had to take him down a notch. The crowd jumped to their feet.

Mark called time. "Lacey," Mark said, jogging up to me. The infield joined him, surrounding us. "Don't let him get to you. He's doing that to intimidate you."

"I know. He's being a dick."

"No. He's playing the game," one of the boys said. "I can tell you're in your zone, so don't break the momentum. You're doing great."

"One more strike is all you need. Get him out. It will boost your confidence to pitch to the next batter. *Capiche?*" Mark tapped me on my glove.

I didn't know he was suddenly my shrink. Regardless, I welcomed his encouragement. It was good to know he focused on the game, and not on threats or rivalries.

I nodded and covered my mouth with my glove. "Fastball?"

"Slider."

Worried, I raised my glove to shield my eyes. I didn't want anyone seeing my expression. My slider was weak. Sure, I practiced it, but it wasn't the pitch to use on Aaron if I wanted to strike him out.

"You have a great fastball. But that's what Aaron is expecting, or another curveball. He's good at reading pitches after he has a chance to see them. He won't be expecting a slider. Besides, it looked good yesterday when we practiced." Mark tapped my glove again then my shoulder.

My stomach clenched.

"Lacey, I've seen you pitch," the dark-haired boy at shortstop said. "Your slider is good. You're in your zone. Stay in it," he said, and he jogged back to his shortstop position.

You're in your zone. Don't blow it, I silently chanted.

I went through my breathing routine as I planted two feet on the mound. Then I got into position. The grip for the slider was similar to the fastball, but the placement of the fingers was different. I gripped the ball, making sure my thumb was holding it tight, along with my middle finger. I let out a breath and released the ball, following it all the way into Mark's glove where it made a resounding snap. In an instant, I tensed every muscle, waiting for Coach Lee's sign.

"Strike three," he called.

Aaron's head jerked toward Coach Lee. "Bullshit. That wasn't close to a strike," he yelled.

Coach Lee ignored him as Aaron slowly walked back to the dugout, tossing a death glare over his shoulder at me. *Sore loser* came to mind. But as fast as the term hit me, it was gone when Coach Dean called Renee to bat. *So much for rejoicing at my awesome feat.* I'd had a feeling Coach would make me pitch to Renee given his statement. I hadn't dwelled on the thought of me pitching to Renee again. Sometimes the anticipation leading up to an event could be scarier than the event itself, the way giving blood was, for me. I'd psych myself out every time. I hated needles. I hated to be poked. But the needle poking me wasn't as bad as I made it out to be.

Renee slipped on her helmet, grabbed her bat and swung it a few times before stepping into the batter's box.

Kelton ran out of the dugout, pointing to the boy who'd been playing shortstop. I guess they were exchanging places. While Kelton warmed up, Renee trotted out to the mound.

What was she doing?

"Hey," she said. "I wanted to make sure you were all right. You ran off at lunch and again after psychology. Then you didn't show up in the locker room. I wanted a chance to talk to you. Don't see me as someone you once knew. Try to see me as Aaron. You did so well pitching to him."

"Probably because I don't like him. And he's a far cry from resembling anyone I knew."

"Try anyway. I'm just another batter." She ran back to the batter's box.

I didn't know what to think of Renee's pep talk.

"Okay, people. Let's continue," Coach Dean shouted from the dugout.

Mark crouched down into his catcher's position, giving a signal for a fastball. Renee nodded, curling her lips higher on one side. *No. No. No. Why did she have to smile?* All of a sudden a bead of sweat trickled down my temple. My body heated. My fingers became icicles as they gripped the ball so tight I wasn't sure I could release it. *She's not your sister. Yeah. Tell that to my freaking brain.* My familiar bumblebee buzzed in my head. Without another thought, I threw the ball. It sailed down to home plate, narrowly missing Renee's head. She stumbled backwards out of the batter's box.

"Lacey, girl?" Kelton said, running up to me.

"I don't think I can do this, Kelton," I whispered.

A few of the infielders crowded us.

"Leave," Kelton bit out.

They went back to their positions.

Then Mark trotted up. "What the—"

"I got this, Mark," Kelton said. "Let me handle her."

My head shot up. *Handle me. How was he going to handle me?*

Mark shook his head and went back to home plate.

"Kade wanted me to give you a message. Are you listening to me, Lacey?" He shook me.

"Yeah." *No.* The buzzing in my head was loud, and I didn't warm to the idea of someone *handling* me. But I wasn't in any state to argue with him.

"God, forgive me for this. I promised myself these words would never leave my lips for any girl," Kelton said.

I rubbed my neck.

Coach Dean came out to the mound. "Lacey?"

"Coach, I got this," Kelton said. "I promise she'll pitch."

Coach raked his hand across his head. "Hurry it up. We don't have all day." Then he trotted away.

I wiped the sweat from my brow.

"Lacey, I...love the crap out of you," Kelton whispered.

"What!" My jaw hit the dirt.

"Kade's message. *Kade's*. Not mine. My brother is fucked up. How do you put 'crap' and 'love' in the same sentence?" His blue eyes swam with embarrassment.

A wave of warmth flowed over me. Even though Kelton's tone was a little rough, his voice sounded like Kade's. The word *family* whispered in the back of my head. *God, Kade continued to surprise me.* He knew this would be rough for me, and he took every measure to ensure I would be fine even when we were angry with each other. A smile split my lips more at the pain on Kelton's face.

"He knows you two haven't made up yet, but he said it might help," Kelton added.

"Do you have a problem with love?"

"Not the time, girl. You okay?"

I nodded once.

"Good. Now, get your ass in gear and pitch the fucking ball." He hit me on the ass and took his position at shortstop.

I wasn't sure Kade's message would help, but it was good to know he loved me, and for that, I pitched the ball.

This time the ball soared over the plate, and not Renee's head.

"Ball," Coach Lee called.

I inhaled the fresh air as I caught the ball from Mark. He flashed the curveball sign for the next pitch. This time, I concentrated on the grip of the ball, the plate, and Mark, making sure I didn't look at Renee. When I did, the ball hit Mark's glove dead-on, with a thud. The count was now two balls and one strike. *Same thing. Don't look at her.*

Mark sent the ball back to me. Then he gave me a signal for a slider. I readied the ball and my stance. As soon as I planted my foot on the ground, the ball left my glove and then...crack! The ball met the bat and flew into the outfield. *Damn slider.* I had to practice that pitch more.

Renee ran the bases, and I wanted to run with her to bask in my own joy. I hated that I didn't strike her out, but I didn't have a panic attack. Letting out all the air in my lungs, I relaxed every muscle in me as the boy in center field chased the ball. It rolled against the fence. When he picked it up Renee slid into second base easily.

Then Coach Dean called me in. As I jogged to the dugout, Todd ran out.

"You did well," he said. "Nice pitching to Aaron. Better you than me, though."

"Thanks. Good luck," I said.

I couldn't tell what Coach was thinking. Did he like how I pitched to Aaron and Renee? I gave it my best—at least with Aaron I had. With Renee, my performance was less than stellar, but I didn't quit and I didn't pass out, and that alone I had to celebrate.

CHAPTER 22

The headlights of my car bobbed along the dark country road as I drove out to Kade's house. He wanted to talk, and I'd never had a chance to answer him. I could've texted him, but I wanted to surprise him. When tryouts ended, I spent some time with Renee, apologizing to her for my behavior in the lunchroom, and I owed her a huge thank-you for the little pep talk we had at the mound. Becca had joined us in the girls' locker room, and the three of us sat and chatted for over an hour. I shared the story of Mom and Julie. I definitely owed it to Becca, but I'd hoped telling Renee would help me get past my issue with her. I couldn't say if it had or it hadn't yet. But as I examined her features, I felt the need to touch her to make sure she wasn't my sister. I didn't, though. She'd probably hit me. They were both sympathetic, and while I didn't want them to feel sorry for me, I did appreciate the tears they shed with me.

When we finally walked out to the parking lot, only a few cars remained, and Kade's wasn't one of them. I didn't expect to see Dad either, since I'd told him I wouldn't be home right away. I also asked if he would lift my punishment, if only for the night. I explained to him I needed to apologize to Kade, and I didn't want to do it over the phone. He studied me for the longest time before he obliged. Instead of one night, he lifted it permanently with one condition: if I stepped out of line again, he wouldn't hesitate to ground me for the rest of the school year. I assured him I would do my best to stay out of trouble, but I didn't make any promises. After I'd gotten home, showered, and changed my clothes, Dad gave me money to pay Kade for fixing my car.

I turned down the road with the tunnel of trees as I drew closer to Kade's house. I wiped a clammy hand on my black skinny jeans. Becca had said the man sitting next to Kade was his dad. *Maybe surprising Kade wasn't a good idea. What if they were having dinner? What if they weren't home? Had Kade told his dad about me? Would he like me?*

The landscape lighting gave the home a warm, inviting feel as I drove down the driveway to park behind Kade's truck. I sat in my car for a minute, trying to drum up enough nerve to get out. This was a bad idea. *You love the guy. Make nice. But what if he doesn't want to now?*

I glanced in my rearview mirror, and the lights were on in the kitchen. One of the triplets peered out from the sliding glass door. Then the door opened and he loped onto the deck. Blowing out a breath, I got out of my car. *Face your demons.* The Maxwells weren't my demons. Although Kelton might be able to pass for one. I giggled at that notion.

"Something funny?" Kelton asked as he swaggered down the steps of the deck, feet bare, chest bare, jeans sitting low on his hips, Calvin Kleins poking out of the waist of his jeans.

I looked away, embarrassed for checking him out. *Bad girl.*

"See something you like, Lacey?" he drawled.

Asshat.

"Is Kade home?" I asked, meeting his blue eyes.

"Maybe. You did well today. Coach should have the roster posted after school on Monday," he said.

Since I was on an apologizing-and-thanking tour, I owed Kelton a thank-you. "You helped me out on the field. If it weren't for you, I might have lost it," I said.

He shook his head. "Don't thank me. Thank my brother, girl. He owes me though." He sat down on the top step of the deck.

"Why? Because you said the word love? What's all that about anyway?" I leaned against the stair rail.

He rubbed two fingers over his chin. "I see how torn up Kody is over the loss of Mandy. He's been a wreck for the past couple of years. I see how my dad hurts because of my mom. I don't want to get like that." He dropped his gaze to his bare feet.

I had this itch to hug him and tell him that losing someone to God or a mental health facility wouldn't happen to him. But I'd be lying. I didn't know what the future held for me, let alone for him. I also understood his apprehension since I knew how it felt to get my heart broken. I looked down at my black flats.

The sound of the sliding door opening drew my gaze up. A tall man strode out, his shiny shoes clomping on the wood deck.

"Kelton, why are you out here with no shirt in front of this pretty girl?" He grinned and two dimples popped out on his cheeks. "I apologize for my son's rude display and lack of manners. You must be Lacey." He had the same copper eyes as Kade.

"Yes, sir," I said, not moving. I was mesmerized by how alike Kade and he looked.

He tapped Kelton on the head. "Go put a shirt on. And get Kade," he said. "Come, Lacey. You don't have to wait out here for Kade."

Kade didn't even know I was here. Or did he? I climbed the stairs, nerves poking my stomach. What had Kade told his dad about me? Kelton stood and disappeared into the house. When I reached the door, Dr. Maxwell waited for me to go in before him. Then he closed the door behind him.

"Please, have a seat." He waved a hand at the barstools at the kitchen island.

"No, thanks. I was just stopping by to give Kade money for fixing my car." *And to tell him I love him.*

"I see." He tucked his hands into his pants pockets. "I was impressed by your pitching today. I've never seen a girl pitch in boys' baseball before. My boys told me how good you were. Forgive me if I sound skeptical."

"That's okay, Dr. Maxwell. I'm used to it. But it really isn't any different than girl's fast pitch softball. Sure, the mechanics are different and the ball is bigger, but those girls throw just as fast and hard as I do, or most boys pitching." *God, I hope he didn't think I was being disrespectful.*

He grinned again. A door banged from somewhere in the house. Then footsteps grew louder.

"Ah, maybe that's Kade. The boys were down in the game room, getting ready to watch a movie."

"Hey," Kade said as he walked in. His dark Zeal T-shirt stretched across his chest, and my fingers itched to touch the bare skin underneath. His hair appeared damp as though he'd just gotten out of the shower, and yes, my fingers twitched with the urge to feel his soft hair.

I didn't bother sizing him up any farther, not with his father standing next to me. Prickly heat danced over my skin, and I prayed I didn't appear red.

"Son, I'm meeting Buster tonight for a late dinner. It was nice meeting you, Lacey. And, oh, please, call me Martin." At least his name didn't begin with a K. He grabbed his keys off the counter and left through the sliding glass door.

"So, that's your dad," I said, breaking the awkward moment. The last time we were really alone, he left me at my doorstep, wondering if we would be together again.

"Do you want to talk about my dad?" he asked as he crossed the kitchen floor. His tone was hard.

"Nah, I came to give you money for fixing my car." I pulled out a folded envelope from my back pocket, and set it on the gold-speckled granite surface. "And you said you wanted to talk."

Dragging his palm slowly along the smooth granite surface, Kade rounded the island. His eyes flashed with anger, hurt then lust. I swallowed. Was I ready to make nice? *Yeah.* Was I ready for him to devour me? *Hell, yeah.*

Before I opened my mouth, his hand gripped the granite edge on my right, and the other came up to settle on my face. His eyes skimmed over me. "I've missed you," he whispered.

"I'm still mad at you," I said, keeping my gaze on his full lips as I licked my own.

"The feeling is mutual." He lowered his mouth to mine.

"So is kissing me your way of talking?"

"They say make-up sex is the best," he said.

"Your dad might walk back in," I said.

He glanced over his shoulder as his hand coasted down from my face to the counter. Now I was barricaded between him and the granite surface, the same position he'd had me in on my birthday. I leaned to my left. A red glow illuminated the darkness in the driveway as the car backed out of the garage. The engine purred slowly. Then the lights dimmed, as did the sound of the engine.

He turned back around, eyes soft, his scent heady. "Let's go to my room." He grabbed my hand.

The hallway was dark ahead, and suddenly I stopped, wrenching my hand away. *It's not your old house. Breathe, girl.*

He turned, took one look at me and reached around my arm and switched on the hall light. "I'm so sorry. Breathe," he said.

"I am." I closed my eyes, taking in his silken tone. His voice was always a safe haven. Before I opened my eyes, I was airborne in his arms, my body bouncing with every footstep.

Once inside, he set me on his bed, shut and locked the door, then flipped on the bedside lamp. Then he sat down next to me. "I'm truly sorry." Our thighs were touching.

"Hey, I'm fine. You were there. I didn't black out."

"I know." He turned, facing me. "But I'm also apologizing for not telling you about Coach wanting me to watch out for you."

So we were on that topic. "Coach said he *didn't* ask you to watch me, though."

"Well, he asked us to watch Aaron. He wanted to make sure Aaron wasn't going to bother you or Renee."

Should I tell him about Aaron's recent threat? If I did, he'd probably make me tell Coach. Then I would start a shit storm when I didn't even know yet if I even made the team.

"I went down to the field that night to see who you were so I would know who I was supposed to keep Aaron away from. I already knew Renee from school. But after you pulled that gun on me, you showed me you could look after yourself." The backs of his fingers slid up my arm, leaving goosebumps in their wake, and Aaron vanished from my memory.

I didn't want to talk anymore. I'd been angry, sad, depressed. He and I had been apologizing to each other from the start of our relationship, it seemed. Now it was time to show him how much I loved him. I reached out, touching his face.

His fingers circled my wrists, guiding my hand down to my lap. "I need to know what Tyler was doing at your house the other night." His tone lowered.

"I told you, it's not what you think." I hopped off the bed.

"Then tell me what it was, Lace."

I walked over to his dresser. *If you're going to build a relationship, tell the truth.* Quarters, dimes, and nickels were strewn over the wood top. A photo of a little boy standing in front of a massive pool of water with a polar bear swimming in it sat on his dresser.

"Lace," he said. "I've never been the jealous type." His reflection grew larger in the glass-framed picture. "It makes me crazy when I see how guys look at you." Standing behind me, he swept my hair to one side. "And even crazier to think of another guy touching you." He licked a path along the column of my neck up to my ear. "Now tell me." He nipped at my ear. "What was Tyler doing at your house? And why was your blouse open?"

I'd probably be asking the same question, if the roles were reversed. I'd kill any girl who had the nerve to throw herself at Kade. "He wanted to make sure we were still friends. And I spilled spaghetti sauce all over me, so I went upstairs to change. When I heard your voice, I ran downstairs."

His hand came around and flattened against my stomach as he pressed into me. "What do you mean, he wanted to make sure you were friends?"

I couldn't concentrate with his tongue in my ear. "Kade, there's nothing going on with Tyler and me." I knew I should tell him Tyler wanted to be more than friends. But then he wouldn't trust Tyler around me. I didn't want to alienate Tyler and the Maxwells. Weren't they friends too? Well, maybe Kade wasn't going to be so kind to him now.

"I swear he'll never play football again if he tries anything with you." His hand tensed against my stomach. "You're mine, Lace. No one else can have you. I want to hear you say it."

I shuddered. *Why was his dominance such a damn turn-on?*

He slipped one hand into my jeans. I squirmed against him as his fingers dipped inside my panties. "Tell me you're mine, baby."

"Kade?" I panted out his name, opening my legs slightly.

"You want me to go lower?" His other hand trailed upward under my blouse.

"Yes," My body screamed for him to sate the need building inside me.

He teased, his fingers slipping between my folds. "I want to hear the words, Lace."

"I'm yours." I sank into him.

He removed his hand. Whimpering, I turned. He grabbed the edges of his Zeal T-shirt and pulled it up over his head, the muscles along his abs tightening. I traced a finger over one, then two, then three. Up and down, each one, until I mapped out all six. His hooded gaze was fixed on me, as though he didn't know what he wanted to do next. I smiled. As though that were his cue to take control, my clothes came off in a flash, and his were next. We stood naked as he bent down and sucked in one nipple. I arched into him as I rubbed along his length, so soft and so very hard. He groaned, husky and dark, sucked the nipple of my other breast into his mouth, and nipped lightly. Sparks of heat sped down through me. He clutched my hips in his hands, lifting his head. Gold and brown tones weaved through his copper eyes as they dilated.

"Legs around me," he said, picking me up.

I locked my ankles behind his waist, my hands behind his neck. He walked us over to his bed, where he gently eased us down. Untangling my body from his, I clenched my fingers in his hair, pulling him down and kissing him, thoroughly, sensually, and with everything I had. His lips were soft, wet, and tasted of sugar. I loved him and wanted to be loved by him. I wanted every ounce of what he had to offer, faults and all. As our tongues tangled, twisted, and tasted, our bodies molded to each other.

He broke the kiss, pinning my arms over my head. "Leave them there," he growled as he snatched a condom from his nightstand.

His dominant tone made me obey and quiver at the same time. A frisson of heat propelled itself south and kept going all the way to my toes. He tore through the wrapper, the sound an intimate whisper in the quiet room. The soft glow of the bedside lamp licked across his strong jaw. He glanced at me while he sheathed himself in the condom. His eyes flashed a warning—*last chance to run before I ravage your body*.

At least, those were the words screaming through my head. I licked my dry lips, and the copper in his eyes disintegrated, melting in a deep, dark brown. I barely moved my arm, and he secured my wrists with one hand while the other teased its way down over my breast, my waist, my hip, stimulating already heightened nerve endings. His knee eased my legs apart.

"I told you to leave your arms up," he growled.

"I'm not afraid of you," I countered. I wasn't sure why those words came out of me. Maybe it was the fire in his eyes or the bite in his tone.

"You should be." He pushed into me, hard.

I cried out, and his mouth covered mine, catching my gasp. A tingle took root just below my bellybutton, coursing through me. He paused, our bodies stuck in neutral as he held me captive.

"Do you still want me to tell you what I'm going to do to you?" he asked in challenge.

"Show. Tell. Do." I grasped his hips, trying to get him to move.

"Do what?" He lifted his head up slightly with a freaking impish grin on his face.

I wiggled under him, my efforts ineffective.

"No, Baby. I'm not moving until you tell me."

Asshat!

He stared down at me.

"I want you to love me. Touch me. Kiss me."

"Why?" His hips began to move.

I closed my eyes.

"Open those pretty peepers, Lace." *God, he was demanding.* In this instance his possessiveness only served to arouse me more.

"Please, Kade. I want you. I love you."

"Magical words," he breathed as he flipped us.

Now I was on top. *I was in control.* Or so I thought, until he sat up, shifting us so I was on my knees, feet behind me, straddling him. He took hold of my hips, guiding me up, then down as he thrust at a slow pace. I grasped his shoulders to anchor myself to him, smashing my mouth to his.

"You feel like heaven." His voice was thick with lust as his fingers weaved through the long strands of my hair, licking his way down my neck.

I tilted back my head as a pulsing sensation began between my legs. I arched slightly, and his strong hands anchored me. His mouth found my breasts, heavy and swollen. A bead of sweat trickled down my cleavage. I didn't know if it was from him or me. It didn't matter. I wanted to stay like this forever, to bask in the way our bodies fit perfectly together. To feel every inch of him on me and inside me. He shaped my hips, guiding me as we moved together. A whispered moan escaped my lips. He snaked a hand between us, his fingers settling on my bundle of nerves. One stroke and the fireworks in my belly exploded, shooting intense waves of glorious heat down my legs, making my body shudder around him. I'd barely caught my breath, and I was on my back. He began a frenzied pace, thrusting in and out as he buried his head in the crook of my neck, his breath pounding together with mine.

"Lace," he growled as he pushed deep one last time before his body quaked. He held onto me tightly as he kissed me gently on the lips. "I'm never letting you go." He peeled away my hair from my sweat-slicked forehead. "Unconscious beauty." His voice was soft and sensual as he dragged his lips along my jaw, down my neck.

I titled my head to give him better access. "Kade."

"Yeah, polar bear?" He supported himself on his elbows.

"What does *unconscious beauty* mean?" I lightly dragged my nails along his lower back. I had yet to ask him. I was more curious than anything.

He nipped my chin. "When you walk into a room, you turn heads without even knowing it. The way you carry yourself with confidence, poise, and beauty. And those damn green eyes of yours make every guy's dick hard instantly."

"Like yours is now." I giggled.

"Round two?" He combed over one of my eyebrows with the tip of his finger, grinning.

CHAPTER 23

The weekend came and went. I didn't see Kade at all. He and his family were spending the weekend in the Berkshires. His father was apartment hunting. He wanted to find a temporary place where he could stay to be closer to his wife on occasion. Becca, Mary, and I went shopping. Mary had wanted to get me something for my birthday, but she wanted me to choose the gift. We strolled through the mall, and Becca kept showing me clothes that would look good on me. After two hours of trying on different outfits, Mary and Becca coaxed me into buying two skirts. One was a black-layered lace miniskirt with a scalloped hem. The other was a floral printed mini with a crocheted lace overlay. *Now I just had to wear them.*

When Monday rolled in, the sun shone bright in the stark blue sky. After a tense day on Friday, I'd had a fun and relaxing weekend. I'd made amends with Kade, which afterwards I'd dreamed about, any chance I had to myself. I spent time with Becca, shopping, laughing, and bonding. She'd told me Kross had asked her out. She wasn't sure if she wanted to get involved, since she was in love with Tyler. She asked again about Kade, and how he kissed, and other private details. My response to her had been: he was terrible. Then we giggled until our stomachs hurt. Becca and I had probed Mary about Mr. Wiley. Like me, she wasn't kissing and telling.

I'd thought Friday was big with tryouts, but Monday was even more heart-palpitating as Coach announced in homeroom that morning that the roster selection would be posted outside his office sometime during the school day. Between English and chemistry, Mrs. Flowers informed me I scored high on both my trig and calculus exams. I was surprised, given I didn't have a warm and fuzzy feeling when I handed them in.

"Earth to Lacey," Becca said, snapping her fingers in my face.

"Sorry. Did you say something?"

Becca and I sat in our usual spot during our free period, in the school's courtyard, basking in the warm sun. Indian summer had been the weather theme for the past two days. I almost felt like I was back in LA with the sixty-degree temperatures.

"No. You were in a trance though," she said.

"So, have you decided if you're going to go out with Kross?" I asked.

She twisted her long black hair and pinned it up with a clip. "I might do a movie with him this weekend. I guess it wouldn't hurt to hang out with him. He is hot."

"Why don't you ask Tyler to a movie?" I plopped my legs onto the empty chair next to me. *What was wrong with a girl asking a guy out?*

"Are you kidding me?" She narrowed her eyes. "Tyler made it clear two years ago he wasn't interested when he broke it off."

"That was in the past, girl. Dip your toe in the water."

"And if it freezes?" She angled her face toward the sun.

"I'll be there to thaw you out."

A few other students had the same idea as Becca and me, soaking up the warm rays. Before long, the cold New England winter would be here. We had to take advantage of every ounce of natural vitamin D we could.

Deep familiar male voices resonated near the entrance to the school. I warmed as soon as I met Kade's eyes. He tapped Kelton on the arm. They strode over with a sense of purpose and confidence like they owned the school.

"Hey, baby," Kade rasped as he leaned down to kiss me, his lips warm and inviting.

When he broke the kiss, I straightened my spine, dropping my feet from the chair, and Kade slid into it. Kelton stole a chair from an empty table next to us.

"Aren't you guys supposed to be in class?" Becca asked.

"Maybe," Kelton said, biting his lower lip.

Kade and Kelton had those blank expressions I hated. Becca and I shared a perplexed look.

"Lace," Kade twined his fingers with mine. "Coach Dean will have the roster posted outside his office in fifteen minutes."

"How do you know?" I tilted my head, nerves suddenly biting my stomach.

"Kel and I just came from his office. I had to talk with him, and Kelton wanted to find out when the names for the team would be ready. Lace...you know I love you, and I can tolerate some pain...but I do need my fingers."

I looked down and my nails were embedded in his skin. "Sorry." I blew out a breath, removing my hand.

"I want to beat the rush before classes let out," Kelton said. "It will take us five minutes to get over there."

Kade snatched my bag. Becca jumped up. Kelton was already walking around tables toward the path that led from the courtyard to the sports complex. I needed a minute to take in a few quick calming breaths to ease the low whirring hum in my head.

"Good or bad, I'll be there to catch you," Kade said. He knew me too well already. Whether I did or didn't make the team, I'd probably collapse from the built-up anticipation.

He splayed a hand on my lower back as we headed in the same direction as Kelton. On our way to the sports complex, Kelton and Becca chatted. I tuned them out. If I didn't make it, I would be devastated. I kept trying to tell myself I wouldn't be, but I'd been kidding myself. I wanted this dream, this opportunity, no matter the consequences. Dad and I moved here to help me realize my dream. I couldn't disappoint him or my brother, Rob. I was counting on the baseball scholarship from ASU. I'd live through the bullying and any obstacles that would be thrown my way. I replayed Mom's speech, the one she'd given me when I was waiting to see if I'd made the team at Crestview.

Lacey, my beautiful girl. You're feisty, stubborn, sweet, determined, and tough. Those are the ingredients to fulfill your dream of baseball. Never give up.

"Lace." A callused hand stroked my cheek. "Why are you crying?" Kade said.

"Oh." I wiped tears from my eyes. "I was just thinking of my mom. Why are we standing here?" *Wow*! I didn't even remember the walk from the courtyard to the back entrance of the sports complex. Coach's office was just inside the brick building and down the main hall.

"Kelton and Becca ran in to read the roster. I thought with you crying you might want a minute. This way if your name isn't on the list, we can sneak out to my truck. Well, even if you did make it, we might want to skip the rest of the day and celebrate." He lowered his head and rubbed my nose with his. "And we could find something to do in my room."

God, he smelled like sugar and rain, sweet and inviting. A tingly tap dance began in my belly, marching lower. *I so wanted to leave right this minute.*

A door opened, the handlebar snapping up.

"Kade. Lacey." Kelton's voice stopped Kade from slipping his tongue in my mouth. "Get in here."

"You ready?" Kade asked before he let go of me.

"Now or never. The reason I moved here." I grasped his hand.

Kelton pressed his back against the inside of the door as he held it open. I didn't look at his face as I walked in. Taking a deep breath, I let it out. The hall straight ahead appeared ominous. Doors dotted both sides. I homed in on the one at the very end of the hall, where a boy who looked like Todd stood reading the wall. The whirring noise in my head slowly ramped up.

Kade had no problem keeping up with his brother. I did, though. I had to walk faster to keep up with them. I almost asked Kade for a piggyback ride. I quickly shelved the idea and froze midway down. Sweat coated my palms. I wiped them on my jeans.

Todd turned to face us and fist-pumped the air. I guessed he made the team.

"Congrats, man." Kelton slapped him on the back.

"You, too," Todd said.

"Are you going to stand there?" Kade asked. "Don't be afraid. You look like you're about to pass out."

More like black out.

Kelton whispered in Todd's ear. Then Todd breezed past me. The boy didn't even give me the time of day. *What did Kelton say to him? Did he not want Todd to speak? Was he afraid Todd would tell me the bad news? Or say, "Sorry, Lacey. You deserved it over..."*

My heart raced like a sprinter in the Olympics. My mind wreaked havoc on my emotions. *Just go up to the board and freaking read it.* My legs began to quake as I inched over to Kelton, who was blocking the bulletin board.

"Now, Lace. I want you to know that I'm proud of you no matter—"

"Get the fuck out of the way, Kel, before I push you through the wall," Kade growled, yanking Kelton by the arm, then pushing him into Coach's office. "Stay," Kade said, blocking the doorway next to me.

The white sheet seemed to blind me as I scanned the list. My vision blurred in and out. I rubbed my palms on my jeans again, then again. I licked my dry lips, blinked a few times. I stepped closer, then ran a shaky finger down the list of names. I didn't see mine. I started at the top again. A warm, strong finger looped around my left pinky finger. I swallowed as I landed on Kross's name. *Where the hell was Robinson?* Coach had the last names listed first. *Maxwell, Pritchard, Ravine, Robinson, Stanley, Switzer. Wait. Back up.* My name, *Robinson, Lacey*. I read it again. Tears streamed down. The buzzing in my head began to clear. I dropped my head in my hands and dropped to my knees. *Thank you, God.*

"Can I come out now?" Kelton's voice echoed in the hall.

"Touch her, I'll cut off your balls," Kade said.

"Hey, you let me kiss her at her birthday dinner."

"One time. No more." Kade's voice was steadfast.

I had no idea what was going on above me. I didn't want to look either. I wanted to keep my face hidden, until the tears dried up, and savor the moment.

A delicate hand touched my back. "Lacey," Becca said. "Congratulations, girl."

I didn't mind if Becca saw my tears, but I wanted to be strong for Coach. I didn't know if he was in his office or in the hall now.

"It's okay. No one is going to laugh at your tears. If they do, I'll kick their ass. You should cry tears of joy. Those are the best kind," she said, as though she knew what I'd been thinking.

I sucked in a breath, dashed away any remaining tears, and pushed to my feet. Before I had a chance to balance myself or register where everyone was, Kelton's arms snaked around, sucking me into one of his strong bear hugs.

"Welcome to the team, Lacey Robinson," he cheered. "You fucking made it."

"I...can't...breathe, Kel." I really needed to teach him how to hug a person.

He kissed me on the lips. In a blur, Kelton was pulled away from me. Keys fell next to Kelton. Grunts and more grunts ensued.

"What's going on out here?" Coach Dean ran out of his office.

Becca rolled her eyes. Kade had Kelton pinned to the floor. "I'm the only one who puts lips on her," Kade snapped.

"Congratulations, Lacey," Coach said, ignoring Kelton, who now had Kade immobilized. "Hard work is what I expect from you."

"Yes, sir. Thank you for the opportunity. I won't let you down." I'd walk on hot coals before I did anything to screw up my chances.

He nodded. "Now, all of you get out of here," Coach ordered.

Kade and Kelton brushed off their jeans and raked their hands through their hair.

"I'm so excited for you," Becca said, sidling up to me.

"Thanks." Now that my head was clear, I read through the roster.

Renee had made it too. Not surprisingly, Kross, Kelton, and Aaron had been selected. After all, they were great ballplayers. I might not like Aaron, but I wouldn't fault him for his talent.

Kade draped an arm around me. "I'm so proud of you. We do need to celebrate."

I warmed to the fact that he knew not to pick me up like Kelton. A simple touch meant more to me than anything.

"I can't skip school. Maybe tonight." Part of being on the team meant toeing the line, on and off the field. Which meant no ditching school—at least not today.

◌⚜◌

FOR THE REST of the school day, I'd carried a bittersweet feeling with me from class to class. So many emotions coursed through me. A few times I spaced out, smiling at nothing. Becca caught me once and had to bring me back to reality. I pouted. I'd wanted to continue to enjoy the surreal moment. I'd worked so hard over the past few months to focus on baseball, overcoming my PTSD, new friends, new school, new home. While euphoria felt wonderful, fear carved out a space inside me. What did Aaron have in store for me now that I'd made the team? Would he follow through on his threat? Fortunately for me, I didn't run into Aaron at all, not even in the halls. Becca heard Aaron was absent today. I'd always believed that things happen in threes. Today proved to me how true that theory was: I found out I passed my math tests. I made the team, and I didn't have Aaron to bother me.

During the last class, psychology, the news was all over school of who made the team. Renee had found out she'd made it. So when she came into psych, she had a smile from ear to ear. Thankfully, she didn't have that half smile like Julie. We fist bumped and congratulated each other. I would've hugged her, but I didn't want to come off as sappy. Not that I would've cared. I just had to keep rumors to a minimum, so I wouldn't be tempted to lash out. Principal Sanders already gave me one strike. I couldn't get any more. I had to be the perfect student and perfect daughter, at least through the end of the school year.

I'd bounced my knee all through psych. I wanted to get home and share the great news with Dad. He had texted me around lunchtime telling me to come straight home and not to go to Dr. Davis's office this afternoon. I asked if my appointment was cancelled. But all he said was "just come home." I was also excited to share the news with Tyler. I'd seen him this morning before I'd found out, but hadn't since. Actually, I didn't expect to. We didn't have any afternoon classes together. He'd been instrumental in pushing me to practice. His skills had been invaluable in showing me how to grip the ball, my stance, my follow through. We hadn't talked since he held me the other night. I left that part out when I told Kade we were just friends, especially after Kade said he'd make it so Tyler never played football again.

Kade and I had just walked out of the school on the way to my car when Tyler strutted up from the parking lot. His SUV was parked in the loading zone along the curb. His arm wasn't in a sling anymore, and his grin stretched wide. Kade's hand tensed in mine.

"Now, be nice," I whispered. "He's my friend and yours, too."

"He touches you, I swear..." he muttered.

"You made it," Tyler said, excitement all over his face.

"I know, right?" I pulled my hand from Kade's. Or at least I tried. He had a death grip around my fingers. It was a good thing it was my left hand and not my pitching hand. I tugged again, glaring up at the love of my life.

Lines formed around Kade's eyes as he glued a death stare on Tyler.

"Kade, baby. I need my hand."

Reluctantly, he let go, his gaze never wavering.

Tyler glanced from me to Kade. "Hey, man. Your girl made it. You should be happy."

I almost laughed. Kade's grimace looked as though he were pushing all his brain waves into Tyler to mind-speak to him.

Students passed by on their way to the parking lot. Some waved at us. Others kept their heads down.

"Anyway, I saw you walking out," Tyler said as he gave me his full attention. "I wanted to congratulate you. Which means I'm going to hug you. I'm giving fair warning, man." He eyed Kade again. Then he swooped down and wrapped his good arm around me. I guessed the other one was still tender.

I hugged him back. I couldn't see Kade from my peripheral vision, but I didn't have to. He muttered something under his breath. Tyler didn't linger long. He knew Kade wasn't thrilled with the idea.

"Hey, man," Tyler said to Kade. "Are you calm so we can talk?"

Oh, no. What did Tyler have up his sleeve? Was he going to tell Kade how he comforted me when Kade left the other night?

"What is it?" A muscle ticked in Kade's jaw.

"I heard Sullivan is hanging with a couple of guys who work for Jeremy Pitt."

"Yeah, we knew that," Kade said.

"Were those the two guys with him at tryouts on Friday?" I'd seen Greg and two men sitting in the stands.

"Probably. So what's your point, Tyler?" Kade asked.

"When I had dinner at Wiley's over the weekend, Aaron, Greg, and these two guys were there. I didn't hear the whole conversation, but they're scheming up something if Lacey made the team. Now that she has, I thought I'd warn you."

Kade ran a hand through his hair. "Fuck."

"Look, Kade. I got your back. I know you're pissed at me. Frankly, I probably would be too if I walked into my girlfriend's house and there was a guy there. Either way, I'm not going to let anything happen to Lacey." Tyler swung his gaze between us. "But you need to watch your back too, dude. Greg is gunning for you. Look, I gotta run. I'll keep my ears open. You guys do the same." Then Tyler jogged back to his SUV.

Despite the tension between Tyler and Kade, I wasn't too surprised at Tyler for siding with Kade. Tyler didn't care for Greg or Aaron. I didn't see a need to bring up what Aaron had said to me on the field.

I'd only add fuel to Kade's ire, at the moment. While all the threats bothered me, I couldn't do much about them except watch my back. Plus I had the Maxwells behind me, and Tyler as well.

When I grasped Kade's hand he instead wrapped his arms around me. "Are you okay?" he asked.

"Me? What about you? You look like you're about to tear someone's skull off." I wasn't sure who he would start with—Tyler, Aaron, or Greg.

He searched my face before letting go of me. Then we continued our walk to my car in silence.

When we reached my Mustang, he asked, "I know baseball is important to you. I would never get in the way of your dreams. But I have to ask, Lace. Are you—?"

"I'm not giving up everything I've worked hard for because some asshole is intimidated by me. Besides, you said Aaron plays mind games. So, let him play." I gave Kade a weak smile. "I've got to get home. My dad is waiting for me." This day was turning into a downer.

"Hey." He framed my face with his hands. "I had to ask."

I blew out a breath. "I know. Can we not talk about Tyler or Aaron or Greg?" I didn't want to go home in a bad mood. I wanted to be excited when I told my dad. "I love you." I tucked my fingers in the waist of his jeans.

His eyebrows rose as he sucked in air, and he grinned. I reached up and traced one of his dimples.

"Put your fingers back where they were," he protested.

"Later." I lifted up on my tiptoes and brushed my lips over his. "I'll show you how magical my hands can be."

He growled as he bit my lower lip. "You're mine. You know that." Then he threaded his fingers through my hair, kissed me hard, wet, and fast, leaving me breathless before he stalked away. I rubbed my lips as I jumped into my car and headed home. I felt his anger and jealousy in that kiss, but I didn't have time to soothe his doubts. I was going to see him tonight anyway. We'd planned to meet for dinner to celebrate. Actually, Becca, the triplets, Kade, and I were supposed to go to Wiley's Bar and Grill.

When I got home, I shoved aside any lingering signs of bad mojo before I walked into the house.

"Dad? Dad? Where are you?" I headed straight to his office first.

"I gotta run." His voice spilled out into the hall.

I poked my head around his office door, smiling.

"Sweet Pea, you look happy. Did you make the team?" He circled around to the front of his desk. His eyes were wide, his smile wider.

I ran in and jumped in his arms like I was six years old again. "I can't believe it," I said, locking my hands around his neck.

"I'm so proud of you, Sweet Pea. So, so proud." He hugged me back.

Tears flowed. I didn't care either. We'd been through so much, and the tightness of his hug told me he was just as relieved as I was. I never wanted to disappoint my father. He was a great man and a great father.

"I have some news for you." He set me down, searching my face with his watery eyes. "You and I have an appointment with Dr. Davis this afternoon."

My mouth opened.

"I want us to work together to heal, Lacey. I love you, and I don't want my pain to hurt you. I'm not promising this will be easy for you or me. But we have to move on with our lives. And we're stuck in a place that isn't healthy for us."

I threw my arms around him again. This time I cried harder than I had a few minutes ago.

"We'll leave in ten minutes," he said.

I peeled away my wet face, kissed him on the cheek, and went up to my room. This day had been filled with so much emotion, and while making the baseball team was one of the best things to happen to me, my dad getting help bested that.

I freshened up and changed into one of my new miniskirts. I chose the black-layered lace one with black tights and my simple black flats. For a top I went with a soft pink fitted knit one with a shirred bodice. If my dad could seek help, then I could wear a skirt. He'd wanted me to dress up like a girl once in a while. What better day than today to show him?

When I met him at the car he smiled again. I loved to see him happy.

"My beautiful Lacey," he said as we got into the car. "It's been years since I've seen you in a skirt."

The last time anyone had addressed me like that was Mom. I'd been "Sweet Pea" to Dad. Maybe he was opening his heart to heal.

"You've seen me in ball gowns, Dad," I reminded him.

"Not the same. Julie would fall off her chair too."

I swallowed, putting my fingers over my mouth. Did he just say my sister's name?

"You can breathe, Sweet Pea."

Every ounce of adrenaline drained from me as we drove to Dr. Davis' office. I thought about where I started, close to a year ago. Actually, the funeral had been in early January. Immediately afterward, the nightmares began along with anxiety attacks, panic attacks, and blackouts. Now nine months later I still had all those symptoms of PTSD, but I knew with Dad getting help, my new friends, and Kade, I could handle life a little better. Would I ever overcome PTSD? Maybe with time. Maybe if I had closure with Julie and Mom's deaths.

For now, I had a guy who loved me and opened my heart to love again. I was going to play baseball again, and Dad was on the road to recovery. I couldn't ask for much more out of life.

DEAR READER

I hope you enjoyed the first book in the Maxwell Series. It's story that is near and dear to my heart since I'd always wanted to play boys' baseball. If you would like to continue to read more about Kade and Lacey or any of the other Maxwell men, then check out the rest of the books in the series.

Dare to Dream - Kade and Lacey
Dare to Love - Kelton Maxwell
Dare to Dance - Kross Maxwell
Dare to Live - Kody Maxwell
Dare to Breathe - Final book on Kade and Lacey.

Dare to Kiss and Dare to Dream should be read in order.

However, Dare to Love, Dare to Dance, and Dare to Live can all be read as a stand alone.

Dare to Breathe should be read after reading Dare to Kiss and Dare to Dream.

Also, if you have moment to spare, I would super appreciate a short review. Your help in sharing your excitement and spreading the word about the Maxwell brothers would be greatly appreciated.

TITLES BY S.B. ALEXANDER

To read samples and find out where to purchase all books visit:
http://sbalexander.com/books

The Maxwell Series:
Dare to Kiss - Book 1
Dare to Dream – Book 2
Dare to Love – Book 3
Dare to Dance - Book 4
Dare to Live - Book 5
Dare to Breathe - Book 6
The Maxwell Series Boxed Set – Books 1-3
Dare to Kiss Coloring Book Companion

The Vampire SEAL Series:
On the Edge of Humanity – Book 1
On the Edge of Eternity – Book 2
On the Edge of Destiny – Book 3
On the Edge of Misery - Book 4
On the Edge of Infinity - Book 5
The Vampire SEAL Collection - Boxed Set

ACKNOWLEDGMENTS

I want to thank my fans, readers and bloggers. Without you guys I wouldn't be writing. You motivate me, you support me, and you encourage me. I'm humbled by all the reviews and messages I've received along the way. Hugs and kisses to each and every one of you for taking the time to take this journey with me and sharing your excitement.

To everyone in Maxwell Mania, I love the crap out of you. Thank you for loving the series, and the Maxwell boys. Most of all, thank you for spreading the word, your excitement means more than you know.

The team at Red Adept Editing is without a doubt the best editing team in the industry.

An enormous thank you to the talented Hang Le for her creativity and book cover design. You're absolutely amazing.

Marketing a book is one of the hardest aspects for an author, and I'm so lucky and overjoyed that I'd met Marissa at JKS Communications. She had a vision for Dare to Kiss, and she has an even bigger vision for the future of my books. To Marissa, Angelle and the entire team at JKS, thank you.

The publishing industry changes constantly, and without Katey Coffing's inspiration and coaching I wouldn't have come this far without her. Love you, girl.

Wendy Kupinewicz, you are a superb lady, a great friend, and poet. The poem you've written is perfect. Much love and thanks.

Kylie Sharp, thank you for all your support, feedback and advice. Love you.

Tracy Hope, you are my super fan. You've read my drafts and every line I've ever written, even when it was rewritten fifteen times. You're honest in your feedback when something isn't working. You kick me in the butt when I need it. And you've brought my books to life with your creative vision and superb producing skills of my book trailers. Love and hugs!

Finally, to the man who stole my heart. I love you more than you know.

WHO ARE YOU?

BY WENDY KUPINEWICZ

Who are you? Wait, do you know?
Are you defined by where you go?
Or what you say, or wear, or be?
Or where you live or what you see?
Or what you drive or what you need?
Or what you want or what you read?
If you changed what's at your core,
Would those who love you, love you more?
Would you love you differently?
Would you see the you they see?
Maybe not and maybe so.
Perhaps less is more, you know?
So...
Love those we love for love alone.
Increase our kindness, soften tone.
Be ourselves, and soldier on.
Keep living 'til the life is gone.
Be proud of all you are and do.
I love you all for being YOU!

Wendy, thank you for allowing me to use this poem. There's so much meaning to every word and every line. You're an inspiration, a poet and a great friend.

CPSIA information can be obtained
at www.ICGtesting.com
Printed in the USA
BVHW03s0007280918
528541BV00057B/122/P